NightHawk Crossing

By

C. Edgar North

Nighthawk Crossing

Copyright November 2010
By G. Witter writing as C. Edgar North

Third printing (June 2017)

ISBN 9780987678041

Printed in China

Contact: cedgarnorth@gmail.com

Chapter 1

In her brief 16 years, Su Kim had never experienced terrain like this. The mountain trail was narrow and steep. So far, after two hours, it wound through one deep dry gully, up across the scree at the bottom of a cliff face and down through another gully. The guide said it was a deer trail. He had instructed the group to hold hands and walk carefully in single file following him. No lights were used. Su Kim felt the motions of the girl in front of her more than she saw the path. It took a while for the followers to get their little bit of night vision as the moon was in its last quarter and many sections of the trail had been shadowed. As it was, they could barely see. The guide was wearing a hat with large goggles, which he said were night vision goggles.

He had assured them he had made the trek many times. They were in a desert, he told them, even though they were in the North West of America on the border between British Columbia, Canada and Washington, USA. He had lectured them on the night creatures, not to sit down or rest on rocks as rattlesnakes were both nocturnal and poisonous and there was also the possibility of poisonous black widow spiders that would be seeking their body heat. Cactus could also be a problem if stepped on or brushed with their legs as they walked past.

They were told not to make any noise even if bitten or punctured and to use hand signals if they have a problem or wanted to stop by squeezing the hands of the persons in front and behind who would relay this to the guide at the head of the line and to the "snake head" leader bringing up the rear of the line. They would pause to rest for five minutes every thirty minutes and only when he signaled it. These would be times when he would go ahead to scout out the path. At the rest stops they could sip – only sip – from the two 500 ml bottles of water each carried in their backpacks. They must not leave any refuse.

Su Kim reflected on the journey so far. With the exception of the guide, the little group had been together since the "snake head" in

Seoul, Korea assembled them. Su Kim was the third daughter of a poor family living in the slums near the East Gate market in Seoul. She had come to realize she had no future there as she had little schooling and felt she was a burden to her parents. She could remain and help her family or she could seek greater opportunity. Although she missed her mother and father, she knew if she remained, she would see no better future than sewing garments at home on a piece rate basis that hardly bought food basics and paid the rent. No, the sewing contractors made sure they kept the profits and the individual contractors were pitted against each other, keeping piece rates low in order to be competitive.

She could get married but with such a low education and poor family, she would only expect to marry someone of similar background to her laborer father. She had willingly accepted the idea of going to America to become a "hostess" for a Korean restaurant. She was proud that the snakehead thought so highly of her beauty that he paid her father ten million Won for her. The snakehead had said it was the equivalent of about nine thousand U.S. dollars.

She had marveled at the new casual clothes, toiletries and backpack he brought her for the journey and was excited to meet the nineteen other young women who were also going to America. Dressed in the same style and color sweatshirts and sweat pants with "made in Korea" athletic walking shoes, the group looked like a girls' athletic team. She was pleased with the picture in her passport and had been impressed that the passport was made right in front of her at the print shop in one of the many streets of small print shops in the warren of East Gate. It had been most exciting learning how to behave like a tourist, what to expect on her first airplane ride and how to behave as the leader cleared them as a group through Customs and Immigration at YVR, Vancouver airport, claiming their baggage and moving as a group following the leader holding his tour flag toward their waiting tour bus.

She and the others had watched a video of girls playing volleyball and had been coached how to answer questions which immigration personnel might ask concerning their team, the game and their abilities. The snakehead said he did not expect questions, as he would be handling everything, explaining that they were all from the

4

same school and really on a sightseeing holiday to explore the mountains of British Columbia and Alberta.

It was exciting to see such a clean and spacious city as the tour bus wound its way through Vancouver's suburbs to the highway, which took them east on Highway One through rich farmland into the mountains. The tour bus climbed through rain forest which changed to high alpine forest with snow-capped mountain peaks and eventually descended into a desert valley that the snakehead said was called the Similkameen which was a native Indian name.

On the other side of the first set of mountains, the tour bus had stopped for dinner in Princeton. It was a small town at the bottom of a valley surrounded by hills with dry grasslands and pine trees. Su Kim saw her first real cowboys in Western hats and cowboy boots. The bus pulled into a large parking lot adjacent to a path with signage in English and Korean welcoming visitors to the Castle, a large building which seemed to be a hotel, with beautifully landscaped gardens fronting a small river.

Two Korean women met the group on the steps of the entrance, welcomed them in Korean and escorted them to a private dining room where a large buffet of Korean foods was waiting. After dinner, the snakehead thanked them for making the journey so well so far and cautioned them that, although they were tired from the long flight and the bus ride, the most difficult part was now to come. They were going to enter America by crossing the border illegally and on foot. From now on, they could never tell anyone where they were from or how they had gotten into America. They were going to become aliens living in the United States and must always hide from the authorities.

After the snakehead had checked everyone's health and footwear, he escorted them back to the bus. Twilight was falling. Su Kim marveled at the surrounding high mountains outlined by the last rays of the sun.

Their bus journey continued east following Highway 3 along the valley of the Similkameen for another couple of hours. Then they left the highway and headed south across flat farmland beside the river, giving way to scrubby hills and then they began climbing, on a steep and rugged gravel road, into a barren mountain pass. Turning

5

and twisting. Climbing with the bus in low gear. The headlights of the bus reflected a narrow rough road. Eventually, the road ended at a rock face.

In darkness, at the end of the road, the bus dropped off its passengers, managed to see-saw a turnaround with the help of the snakehead, then headed back the way it came. Waiting for the group was a young Asian man who spoke fluent Korean. He told them he was their crossing guide. He then lectured them on what to expect and how to behave. With luck, he told them, they would hike for five to six hours, then board another bus waiting for them in America.

Yes, Su Kim thought, it had been a long journey. So far. So fast. So much new to see for someone who had spent her entire life in a Seoul slum.

Thankfully, the night was warm. It was mid-summer and although temperatures during the day had migrated from about 70 degrees Fahrenheit on the Lower Mainland near Vancouver to 97 degrees in Princeton, the evening was cooler now at about 70.

Single file, holding hands, the group had been walking now for a couple of hours. They had stopped a number of times for quick rests while the guide scouted ahead. So far, the journey had been uneventful. Although she found herself breathing hard at times, the path had been easy enough that no one had lost their footing and no one had signaled to stop for anything. Her legs were getting tired, she was thirsty and her feet were a bit sore but she recognized she was on the downward slope, perhaps nearing their destination. She had noticed red flashing lights high up on the mountains both left and right of her, but these they had left behind some time ago.

Now, her partner in front squeezed her hand twice, signaling a rest stop and Su Kim passed the signal to the person behind her. They had come into a little gully with a sand and gravel bottom – probably a dry creek bed. In the faint moonlight, she could see the sides were close and the walls didn't go much higher than a few feet over her head. She crouched on her haunches, sipped a little water, relaxed and waited.

Suddenly from the rear, a bright white light was focused on them. Just as the guide sprang ahead in reaction to the light, another bright light was brought to bear on them from directly in front and another from above, on Su Kim's right.

"Hold it!" Came a voice from the front of the gully. The guide froze and slowly raised his hands.

Another voice from behind said, "Hands on your head" and the snakehead slowly raised his hands to the top of his head.

This was followed a minute later by the "whump whump whump" of a helicopter as it came from behind Kruger Mountain and lit up the scene with its "night sun."

Someone spoke into a radio. "Oroville Base, this is Border Patrol 5-6. We have located the aliens and are taking them into custody. I am transponding our location. We are about a quarter mile north of the Loomis-Oroville road in table canyon wash."

"5-6 this is base, we copy, out."

At each end of the gully, two officers dressed in camouflage, wearing bulletproof vests and helmets with lanterns, appeared in the light. Officers with large police dogs took up positions blocking the exits at each end of the gully. The first officers worked their way along the line of aliens, handcuffing each with plastic restraints after a quick pat-down for weapons. Finally, a rope was looped through the handcuffs, linking the aliens together. The backpacks were searched.

"Base, this 5-6. We have 2-2 in custody. I say again two-two in custody."

"5-6 this is base. We copy 2-2 in custody. Do you need extra transport?"

"Base, this is 5-6. Affirmative. We will meet you at the road. We will leave 2-7, 4-5 and K-9-3 to follow the trail back to the border just in case others are around, but this looks like the batch. We have two zero females, all Asian, and two Asian males. No identifications."

"Roger that. See you soon. Base out."

A small group of three uniformed officers, two male and one female stood beside the dispatcher along the north wall of the open office which served as the radio room at Border Patrol base in Oroville, six miles south of the Oroville border crossing. Division Chief Roger

Sanchez of the Border Patrol, with a huge smile showing under his jet-black mustache, turned to Field Operations Supervisor Ken O'Brien.

"Well, Ken, looks as if our tipster earned herself $10,000 tonight."

"I'll say! Nice to see a tip work out. Most of the group is females, so I'll take Maryanne with me and we'll take the larger passenger van to pick them up. Too many people for the Sheriff's jail, so I better tell the guys up at the border crossing we'll be bringing some guests. Wonder what nationality they are or if we can communicate much with English."

"Good idea taking them out to the crossing, maybe one of the crew there can help determine their nationality."

Border Patrol Agent Maryanne MacDonald spoke up. "By the sound of it, I doubt if my Spanish or your French will help much. If they follow form, likely the men speak English but will keep silent. Any betting on what nationality?"

"Well, the flavors of the day are Korean, Sri Lankan and Chinese," responded O'Brien. "Maybe East Indian. Anybody's guess. We'll soon see."

"I had better alert the ops desk in Seattle and start making arrangements to transport them there after preliminary screening," said Sanchez. They'll probably send a bus and maybe fly up a couple of interrogators."

Sanchez turned back to Mary West, the dispatcher. "Mary, It's probably too much to expect we can apprehend their reception party. It's likely they saw our activity on the road and took off. However, let's alert the Oroville Sheriff, County and State police, also the Canadians at their border crossings and our own border crossing personnel to be on the lookout for busses and panel trucks – especially with Asian drivers. Request their patrols as far as 30 miles out to stop anything suspicious which might hold 20-plus people. There's little we can do to the drivers and we can't seize the vehicles but we could get some license plates and names to trace."

Roger Sanchez, a thirty-year veteran of the Border Patrol, had spent most of his time, twenty-three years, along the USA-Mexican border. He' been posted to Oroville seven years ago and had

8

been thoroughly enjoying it. An outdoors person with a family, he owned a one hundred and fifty-acre farm with fifty arable acres and lots of arid and rocky foothill on the east side of town. He claimed working the land kept his squat five foot eight-inch, one hundred eighty-pound weight lifter's frame in great shape.

His land, on a hillside along the Chesaw Road, afforded a sweeping view from his front window across to the town of Oroville nestled below tall foothills, and up Osoyoos Lake to Osoyoos and its western ridge of mountains on the Canadian side of the border. From his master bedroom window, which faced north, he had a postcard view of Oroville's Dorothy Scott airport, Eastlake Road and the housing nestled on the American side of the 49th parallel, the east side of Osoyoos with the Indian vineyards and Anarchist Mountain with Highway 3 see-sawing its way up the southern face of it. Too bad the border wasn't a touch south of the 49th parallel here, and then the Canadians would have been able to run their highway through the gentler slope at the base of the mountain and would have avoided all those hairpin curves.

The southern view from his kitchen was equally grand, showcasing the Okanagan Valley's southern side with the dry bare mountains contrasting with the occasional plateaus bearing large orchards irrigated from the Okanagan River. Closer in on the left side of the valley, one could barely make out the confluence where the Similkameen River merged with the Okanagan flowing out of Osoyoos Lake.

Roger Sanchez and his wife Maria were looking forward to retiring on that property. His sector of the border was not a busy one. He felt he had a great staff and good relationships with the parallel agencies. He and his wife were well entrenched and thriving in the town. Their three children were now adults and college graduates making their own careers, one as a marine officer, one a dentist, and one a chiropractor. Life was good and retirement was only a few years away.

Border Patrol base Oroville was housed in a crowded wooden-framed building fronted by Highway 97 and adjoining 11th Avenue on its south side in the center of the little village of Oroville, just off the terminus of the rail yards and at the end of the main industrial section. The building consisted mainly of an open office layout with twelve desks in three rows, plus the communications center in one corner. Along one wall was a series of four enclosed offices with windows facing into the open office. The Division Chief and the patrol agent in charge of the shift use two of them and the others are a small interview room and a coffee room. Washrooms were near the rear door, and there were no cells as the patrol had an arrangement with the local sheriff to house prisoners or, if there is an overload, there were cells for thirty people at the border crossing, six miles away.

This night, O'Brien was the duty officer of the Alpha Team, the first of four shift rosters comprising eighteen officers. The station ran on a "48 in 8" basis with each team logging four twelve-hour shifts in the span of eight days. The shifts rotated, with each officer taking turns between day and night shifts on a monthly basis.

Sanchez, as officer in charge of the detachment, "floated" as he saw fit between the shifts and depending on activities. The Division had one sub-detachment with twenty personnel on the east side of his district, at the Frontier-Paterson crossing (seventy-five miles east), which was also a border crossing open twenty-four hours. Six crossings east of Oroville – up to the Idaho border –comprised his Eastern district. Past Frontier-Paterson crossing, his district also included Boundary-Waneta crossing and Mataline Falls-Nelway crossing, both daytime crossings with opening hours varying with the seasons. To the west, his territory was mountainous, in the Coast-Cascade range beginning at Ross Lake, just south of the Canadian city of Hope. Due to the rugged mountains, there was only one other crossing, NightHawk-Chopaka, about ten miles east of Oroville in the Similkameen valley where the Similkameen River enters the USA.

Passing his right hand through his crew cut gray hair (a familiar habit), Sanchez turned to Mary West. "Mary, call the patrols we have at each end of the Loomis-Oroville road between NightHawk and Oroville and get them to stop and check anyone coming or going. We're probably looking for an Asian or a couple of Asians in a van – but not necessarily. Anyway, they know the drill. Tell them to keep that up for the next few hours. Also, get some of the guys coming out of the gulch to interview the people in the nearby properties to see if they saw anything.

"There aren't many properties along that canyon road. Maybe the caretaker at the golf course noticed something – I gather they had a party going on there this evening. Maybe someone noticed a vehicle or something turning up that old forestry fire access road. Then, send AirCon 17 south toward Loomis. They can work across to Riverside, then come back checking Highway 97 and the parallel roads from Tonasket into Oroville."

"Will do. Should we divert AirCon 405 to check for movement on the roads to the east?" asked Mary.

AirCon 405, a fixed wing Cessna T182 Turbo Skylane equipped with night vision called forward looking infrared radar (FLIR), was currently in the air with a two-person crew on patrol along the Eastern range of the border.

"Where is it?"

"They checked in five minutes ago. They were passing Boundary-Wanela crossing and will turn around at the Idaho border."

"That puts them, what, one hundred miles plus?"

"Radar shows them one hundred twenty-three miles away right now."

"That's at least forty-five minutes away."

"Too far away to do any good for this situation. No, keep them on patrol. Also, keep the drone on its patrol, it should be just about at the west end of our region, right?"

"Let's see." Mary looked up as a relay monitor from the drone control base traced the path of the drone over a topographical map. "Yep, just coming up to its turnaround point at Ross Lake."

"It would probably be back overhead in four hours. Drone Control was going to do a bit of a run down the Cascade trail tonight and meander over some of the valleys. On the other hand, AirCon 17 is closer and still has lots of fuel and there are not many roads to worry about. They can easily follow the southern road out of there out NightHawk way for about twenty to thirty miles, maybe pull east checking the roads as far as Riverside. Also, no sense pulling in the patrols along the border east of here. I think we have enough

resources on the west side to handle things. We can alert the local and
state police about the activity to look for unusual traffic."

"OK."

Su Kim, escorted as a prisoner with the others down to the
road and into the waiting border patrol bus, began to cry quietly. She
felt she had disgraced her family and disappointed the snakehead. She
gazed out the window through the heavy wire mesh of the prisoner
transport van. What next? she wondered. She glanced across to the
snakehead. He appeared calm and sullen. When he saw her looking
toward him, he checked to make sure no guard was watching and
motioned with his index finger to his lips reminding her to keep silent.

Chapter 2

As he picked up the microphone of one of the tactical radios mounted under the center of the dashboard of the patrol truck, Harry Forsythe reflected on his good luck. He had joined the Border Patrol three years ago, just after graduating from college in Kentucky with a degree in Criminal Justice. He had been assigned to Oroville directly after training. Here he was, at age twenty-six, on a road running almost parallel to the USA/Canada border on a beautiful summer evening.

At about thirty-nine hundred feet, the elevation was a good three thousand feet above that of home base in Oroville, down in the Okanagan Valley. Approaching midnight, the thermometer in the SUV registered an outside temperature of sixty-five degrees. The stars were out in their grandeur with just a sliver of remaining moon and no light reflecting off a city to interfere. With his side window down, he could smell the pine, spruce and fir trees. Beautiful. Nice to be up here in the alpine forest cruising along a good road with no traffic.

Harry was of sturdy build, suggesting his love for weight lifting and swimming which had earned him letters and a scholarship to college. He was a natural blonde, reflecting his mother's Dutch heritage. He was six foot tall, one hundred eighty pounds and all muscle. He and his wife, Jenny, and little Sammy, age two, had taken to the relaxed country life. Marveling at the low property prices, with the help of his parents contributing toward the down payment, they had bought a small acreage along O'Neil Road just south of Oroville, parallel to Highway 97. The ten acres boasted a mid-seventies three-bedroom rancher, a barn and horse paddock and eight acres of Fuji apples. They leased the orchard to a local farmer and this revenue paid the taxes and a fair bit toward the mortgage payments.

Thank God he hadn't been posted to the Mexican border! This was paradise! Where else could you enjoy bountiful sunshine, the variety of activities afforded by four full seasons – from swimming and boating on the very warm Lake Osoyoos to fly fishing and camping in the many lakes and streams, hunting, snowmobiling and cross-country skiing. If they wanted to shop in a bigger town, Omak was just 45 minutes away and Wenatchee was farther down the Okanagan Valley on the Columbia River two hours away. Or, they can always go a few hours' drive east to the big city of Spokane.

If they wanted a fancy dinner, there was Osoyoos, just across the border, much larger, crowded with tourists in summer, stronger beer and far more expensive everything than little Oroville.

Tonight, Harry was partnered with John Russel, a long-time hand in the Border Patrol boasting twenty-nine years' service during which he had served in postings in San Diego, Brownsville, Yuma and Skagway. With a little paunch beginning to show on his sturdy fifty-three-year-old, five foot eleven inch, one hundred seventy pound frame and with swept-back stringy white hair reflecting the need for a long overdue haircut, Harry had the weathered look of a man who had been in too much cold weather and smoked too much. Under pressure from his fellow officers, he had stopped smoking when he was transferred to Oroville five years ago. Interesting, he had noted, how people smoked more in some parts of the country. Here though, it was fast becoming unpopular. Even the teens shunned it – except for smoking joints.

John was happily married to Alison, whom he had met and wed during his first posting in San Diego. She was an all-California girl who had borne him three wonderful children: Max, age twenty; Cindy, age eighteen; and Harry Junior, age fifteen. Like John, Alison considered this posting paradise. They were well imbedded in the social life of Oroville as members of the Lutheran congregation, the golf club, Kiwanis, and one of the fraternal orders. Like Harry and Jenny, they had a hobby farm of twenty-one acres and a soft spot for horses which had resulted in the farm planted in grass to supply feed to four cast-away horses: a mare and three geldings; and they earned rent from keeping eight mounts of the border patrol. Horses and trail riding were their passion.

Harry and John were riding in the standard issue four-door, four-wheel-drive SUV. It was well equipped for their purposes with a police computer for license checks, automatic license plate reader, five radios enabling contact with base, air patrol and their Canadian counterparts, and a satellite transponder/phone which was constantly tracking the vehicle and showing on the GPS monitor at home base. Standard equipment included hiking and mountaineering gear, a winter survival kit with emergency blankets, water and rations, bolt cutters, a tool kit, fire extinguisher, flares, tow rope, "come-along" hand winch, Level III first aid kit (for first responders), a seven-shot, twelve-gauge shotgun, an M16 combat rifle with night scope, a sledge hammer, a battering ram and night vision goggles.

As well, they wore personal gear which included, in addition to upper body bullet-proof vest, a 9-millimeter Glock pistol, two-way

14

radio with base and six tactical frequencies, a cell phone, flashlight, snake bite kit, emergency first aid kit, pepper spray, a tazer, one pair of metal police handcuffs and a half dozen plastic handcuff ties. Both had tossed their Kevlar helmets equipped with LED headlamps into the back seat.

Their assignment was to be the first of a series of four patrols that shift beginning with separate teams three hours apart to cover a seventy-mile section of the border. They would patrol a stretch of roads running up to and parallel to the border beginning at Lake Osoyoos on the west side to the Ferry-Midway border crossing at their eastern turnaround point seventy odd miles to the east. The area varied in terrain from sharp, craggy mountains to rolling grassland foothills. The sector had been uneventful for months. Occasionally deer, coyotes, wild dogs, stray cattle or bear crossed the border, setting off sensors and necessitating a team being dispatched to investigate.

Harry pushed the talk button on the mike. "Oroville Base, this is Patrol Alpha East Zone One over."

"Patrol Alpha East Zone One, go ahead. Over."

"Oroville base, Patrol Alpha East Zone One on Chesaw Road eastbound passing Fields Road junction. S.Q. Out."

"Alpha East Zone. Base copy S.Q. Out."

Mary West duly noted the radio contact with Patrol Alpha East Zone One in her hard copy logbook. She recorded the time and "S.Q." meaning all quiet in that sector. The logbook was a throwback to days before the automated recording of the transmission and continuous broadcasting of their GPS position but it came in handy when one wanted a quick glance at the status of the patrols and a quick reminder when patrols were due to check in. Every twenty minutes was the norm.

"Looks as if all the activity is on the West side of the lake tonight," Harry commented, hanging up the mike.

"Harry, my friend, when was the last time there was some action in this sector?"

"I guess it had to be, what, about three months ago when that drunk got pissed off that the Ferry-Midway crossing was closed and he ran through the barrier?"

"Yeah. Big deal," said John. "The County Sheriff's officer caught him after he had pulled off at that Mile 320 lookout about 7 miles south of Ferry – you know, just before Curlew. He was sleeping like a baby."

"That's what I like about this posting. Mainly quiet."

"Right, real quiet but the occasional thing to justify our existence. Thinking of that, did you hear the scuttlebutt that there may be a reduction of personnel in this sector?"

"What?"

"Yeah. I was talking to Marjorie Pearson who's on agricultural inspection at Osoyoos crossing."

"I know Marjorie," said Harry. "Good golfer. What'd she say?"

"Just that there's a rumor that twenty of the crossing crew will be reassigned to the Mexican border."

"I guess I can see that. Oroville was supplemented with thirty people two years ago yet traffic at the crossing hasn't really increased. We may get a reduction too."

"Yeah, I gather there's a lot of "make-work" going on at the Oroville crossing. Marjorie was telling me about one of her new guys getting over zealous. He inspected a fifth wheel trailer of a retired Canadian couple – you know, snowbirds – on their way to Arizona for the winter. He found a bit if a rotten old potato, a potato peel actually, in the back under the sink in the trailer beside the garbage can. He fined them $160. It turns out the husband is a retired Royal Canadian Mounted Police officer – you know, RCMP. Anyway, he complained to the superintendent but got nowhere. Yet the superintendent – George – took Marjorie's guy aside for a little talk telling him how lucky he should be to be posted to this paradise and all that."

"Who was it?"

"Doesn't matter. He was so gung-ho, he wanted to be where the action is and George gladly transferred him to Detroit."

"Ha! Transferred either to the Ambassador Bridge or the Detroit-Windsor tunnel crossing no doubt? Serves the asshole right! Both the Tunnel and the Bridge are probably the most hectic on this border. And what about the living conditions? It can be dangerous just getting to and from work."

Since they left base in Oroville, their path began easterly with the Chesaw Road, ascending from the desert floor of the Okanagan Valley into foothills where the irrigated orchards yielded to sparse pine trees and grassland too high and arid to cultivate, and transitioning at even higher elevations into steeper, mountainous terrain and dense fir and spruce forest. They had deviated off the Chesaw Road onto Nine Mile Road which ran close to the border, then through the old mining town and former rail stop of Molson, where they stopped for coffee, resuming their patrol along and

16

backtracking on lanes and byways that led north toward the border, then returning eastward along the Chesaw Road. Currently, they were eight miles below the border on the Chesaw Road weaving their way around Strawberry Mountain, descending toward Chesaw about five miles away. In Chesaw, they planned to follow the valley north toward the border again.

John, driving the SUV, had slowed to make a 20 mph curve where the road clung to the steep hillside. He knew the metal and concrete barrier was an attempt to prevent cars from a sharp drop about three hundred feet to a streambed that was probably dried up to a mere trickle at this time of year. The protective barrier showed many scrapes and colors of paint scrapings from vehicles that had failed to heed the posted "reduce speed" sign. As they pulled out of the curve, the SUV's headlights panned across a lane and to the dense forest bracketing it.

Just then Harry barked, "Hold it! I just caught glint of something down that lane we went by. Maybe we should check it out."

"OK."

John slowed the SUV, made a U-turn, turning off the lights in the process, and then crept back to the lane. Braking with the emergency foot brake so as not to show taillights, he turned slowly into the lane. He then switched on the headlights which illuminated the rear of a trailer about two hundred feet ahead parked in a pull-off at the side of the road.

"What's that up ahead?"

John switched on the six auxiliary off-road lights that were lined up on the front bar of the roof rack. With over six million combined candlepower, the road ahead and the trees beside were illuminated as bright as day.

"Looks like a toy hauler-type fifth wheel trailer with its garage ramp down. You know, like Bob Sweeny has? The type, so big, you can store a couple of quads or motorcycles in their own garage? He's got his loading ramp to the "toy box" down."

"Yeah. Is that a guy standing beside the ramp?"

"I'll flick on our emergency lights. We can stop for a little chat. Do you see the license plate?"

"Barely. Oh yeah, I see it to the left of the ramp. A Utah plate? He's quite a ways from home. I'll run a make." While John kept an eye on the man, the trailer, and the bush beside it, he also took quick glances to the left and right sides of their vehicle and into the rear view mirrors but saw no movement. Harry quickly typed the

17

plate number into the computer. It came back with ownership to a Mr. Westley Miller, Provost, Utah.

"Westley Miller, Provost Utah. No wants or warrants. Let's call it in and check him out."

Harry reached for and keyed the mike. "Oroville base this is Patrol Alpha East Zone One. Over."

"Alpha East Zone One. Base. Go ahead."

"Base, Alpha East Zone One. We are exiting to check out a recreational trailer parked in Theo Lane. Out."

"Alpha East Zone One. Base. Roger that, Theo Lane. Out." Mary dutifully recorded the transmission into the log at 11:33 p.m.

Donning their helmets as they got out of the SUV, John put his right hand on his pistol butt and veered slightly left, as trained, knowing that Harry had his six (backside) covered and had similarly veered right which gave him more of a sightline down the right side of the trailer. Harry had his hand on his gun butt still in its holster but had unsnapped the restraining strap on it. John approached the man who was standing by the trailer ramp on the roadside.

"Evening sir. Why are you stopped on this road? Do you have a problem?"

"Hello officer. Way out here, I didn't expect to run into the police at this time of night. I've run out of diesel fuel. I under-estimated the fuel consumption in these hills. Thought I could squeeze another fifteen miles out of it to get me to the next station."

"Is this your vehicle? May I see your driver's license please?"

"Yes. Sure." Westley Miller slowly reached into his right side back pocket, pulled out his wallet, produced his driver's license and handed it to John.

"Westley Miller, Provost Utah?"

"Yes sir."

John handed back the license and asked, "Mr. Miller, are you alone?"

"I have my son with me but he's taken the quad to get fuel."

"Which way did he head?"

"Toward Chesaw. We passed a station that was closed down in Chesaw about five miles back. He felt maybe he could wake someone and get some fuel. Otherwise, he'll come back here to bed down for the night then try again in the morning."

"OK. Mr. Miller, just as a precaution, my partner is going to go to the front of your rig and check out your vehicle. Now, you assure me there is no one else around or in it?"

"Correct, sir."

As John nodded to Harry, Harry proceeded down the right side of the trailer checking to see the trailer door was locked and then, using his flashlight extended arm length out to his left side, moved forward to the rear right side, shining his light through the back window of the truck. He noted the truck was a fairly recent Dodge Ram four-door, four-wheel drive 3500 HD with "duals" – double rear wheels. He also noted the trailer hitch sitting square over the rear axle. He saw nothing unusual in the back or front seats or cargo bed of the truck –pretty neat actually, he thought. He then walked back to assume his position beside the SUV.

"Clean."

"OK Mr. Miller, we can put you in touch with a tow company than can bring some fuel out if you want but it would be about an hour's run for them."

"No, that would likely cost a fortune and I don't know if my son has had any luck. Thanks anyway, though. We can just bed down in the rig and wait for morning if we need to."

"OK. We'll advise base to have the following patrols aware of your situation. This is a quiet lane with room to pass you and not much traffic. The nearest house is about two miles further over the hill. I doubt if there will be any traffic overnight. I see no problem with you spending the night camped here if you have to. We'll be on our way."

"Thanks, officer."

As John was walking back to the SUV, Harry remained in his position watching Mr. Miller. Just as John was opening his driver's door, the "whump whump whump" of a helicopter's rotors could be heard. Both men paused to listen. It was coming closer and in low. John looked up searching for navigation lights of the helicopter but could see none.

"Harry, that can't be ours. When we were briefed, the chopper was supposed to be working West Zone One tonight. Didn't the scanner pick up Dispatch assigning AirCon 17 to search south of NightHawk crossing to look for a possible transport for the aliens?"

"Yeah. And we're too far across the border for a Canadian helicopter. We're about eight miles south of it. No lights. It's coming closer and lower."

"I smell a rat. Let's talk to Mr. Miller again. Call it in."

Harry was reaching toward his left lapel for the mike on his portable radio when he suddenly lurched forward and to his left. He let out a gasp as he hit the side of the SUV and crumpled to the ground.

John's reaction was slowed for a second watching Harry's movement but his training kicked in and he crouched while turning left to face the trailer and drawing his Glock pistol. He was a little slow drawing his gun as the tie down strap was still in place – unlike Harry who had undone the strap while guarding John's six. Halfway into the crouch, John was hit in the chest with a force so powerful as to knock him backward and take his breath away. His gun was half out of the holster but flung out of his hand as the momentum of the force sent him sprawling backwards.

John lay on the ground thinking, "I'm hit! I'm hit in the chest. It hurts like hell but I must still be alive. I'm conscious. I can hear footsteps."

A man appeared out of the shadows on the right side of the road walking toward the SUV. He was carrying a pistol with a silencer and a rifle. He shouldered the rifle on its sling and kept the handgun pointed at John as he could see his labored breathing and could hear his moaning. He veered to his left to the right side of the SUV and quickly put two fingers of his free hand on Harry's carotid artery. With a thin smile on his face, he then went around the back of the SUV and approached John. He kicked John's Glock farther out of his reach then moved closer and looked down at John's face.

John opened his eyes when he heard the footsteps stop near his left ear and looked up. In the glowing yellow and blue lights of the emergency beacons, all John could make out through his eyes half closed in pain was a tall dark person dressed all in black. He didn't have time to register more as the man pointed the pistol at John's face and put two silenced rounds into his left eye.

For a few seconds, the man stood over John. He slowly made a thin lipless smile. Then he turned around and headed toward the trailer. The man known as "Mr. Miller" came out from under the arch of the 5th wheel between the rig and the truck and said, "Now what? They would have reported the position and the vehicle stop."

As the dark man looked back over the scene he said, "The chopper's about a minute away now. Switching the cargos shouldn't take more than three or four minutes, then you can be underway as soon as we load you up and the guys we sent out as sentries return with the quads. We can upset this scene in such a way as to delay their reaction. I doubt if they'll be missed for at least twenty minutes and it will be at least half an hour after that before they can have resources organized. Their patrol plane for this sector is well east of us - a good twenty minutes away and heading further east yet. We've got time. But you need to change your identity. They'll have recorded your license plate in their computer so we'd better switch that and you can assume an alternate identity, "Mr. Miller."

"Sorry Chief, I didn't get the truck's dome light off fast enough."

"O.K. No problem. Shit happens."

About twenty minutes later, Mary began a routine transmission. Although their personal radios were still on, her call fell on dead ears. "Alpha East Zone One. Base. Over."

"Alpha East Zone One. Base. Over."

"Alpha East Zone One. This is Oroville Base. Over."

"Alpha East Zone One. This is Oroville Base. Over."

"Alpha East Zone One. This is Oroville Base. Over."

Chapter 3

Janet moaned a little as her cell phone, buzzing and bouncing around on the bedside table, awakened her from her sleep. After rubbing her throbbing head, she slowly turned and reached over to her right toward the table and began groping for the phone. She moaned a bit as her sore eyes focused on the big numbers of the alarm clock/radio. 5:27. Fuzzily, she thought it was just a few minutes before the alarm was set to ring at 6 a.m. Finally, she caught the phone and answered. "Uh, hah?"

"Janet, it's me, Richard, on the duty desk."

Starting to focus now, Janet mumbled, "OK, Richard. What have you got?"

"We've got a crime scene out in the woods up by Oroville. Two border patrol agents killed during a patrol along the border. Bob wants you to lead the investigation."

"Oroville? Oroville…Isn't that on the Canadian border 'bout halfway between here and Spokane?"

"Ah, you are starting to wake up! I hear you tied one on last night at Kelsey's. You were celebrating the Aurora Swindle convictions, so they say."

"Yeah. It hurts now."

"Well, you had good cause to celebrate. Your team put in a lot of time on that. Also hear that your testimony helped get their leader 15-20 years. Good going!"

"Thanks. Sorry to be a little slow right now," she mumbled, rubbing her hair and stifling a yawn. "Should Spokane office be handling this one? What about Homeland Security?"

"No, this has already bounced to headquarters in D.C. and around the many agencies that can be involved. The powers that be feel we in Seattle are better positioned for liaison with local Homeland Security and all their agencies that will have to be involved. The Homeland Security regional office for the sector of the crime scene is in Bellingham. Just in case the trail leads cross the border, we're the ones with liaison to the senior levels of the Canadian counterparts in the region – although we overlap with some of the Homeland Security initiatives. All parties in D.C. have agreed. FBI takes the lead on this case and, because federal agents were the victims, the local police agree it's an FBI case. I see no problems working with the local police as we've always had a great working relationship and some of their personnel are top notch."

"Good thinking. What are my resources? What's happened to date?"

"One thing at a time, please, for someone thinking so slow right now. OK, first the border patrol had two of their finest missing since about midnight. Even though they had GPS transponding, they weren't found until around 3:30. They were found in their vehicle at the bottom of a cliff in dense brush about three hundred feet below the road. There's a bad curve there and, at first it was assumed they had lost control and plunged over. Anyway, the patrol sent out to trace them couldn't find them for a while – there was no obvious sign of the vehicle going over the safety barrier on the curve and the vehicle was way down under dense brush in heavy forest."

"Did you say assumed?"

"Yeah, when one of the first officers on scene climbed down to the wreck he found both victims dead. One had been shot in the head – through an eye. At that point, he cleared out and they secured the scene."

"OK. What about resources? Is there a forensics team there? En route? What about coroner?"

"State police have a forensics team on way from Spokane by chopper. The closest coroner is in Omak. Apparently, he's a civilian on retainer for the County Sheriff and who also serves Oroville town Sheriff's office. As it is border patrol officers involved, you may want to supplement with someone more professionals and with better lab resources."

"Good thinking. Maybe I should take someone from here. We'll worry later about the logistics of getting the bodies back to Seattle."

"Thought you'd get around to that. I've called out Dr. Herman. I've also organized a flight on our own wonderful FBI airline. Your flight departs from Boeing field at 8:00 a.m. It should take less than 40 minutes flying time. You can have the aircraft and crew standing by for up to six hours. That should be enough time to examine and remove the bodies from the scene. They can airlift Doc Herman and the bodies back. You'll be met in Oroville by a border patrol representative and then choppered to the scene. Doc Herman and your number two will fly in with you."

"Yeah. Yeah. Thanks. OK, I'm still thinking slow, who'd the boss assign to my team?"

"You've got Fred Mayfield going with you as your number two. Spokane will send you two or four people if you need them, same

----

with Wenatchee office and Bellingham. You can have up to four more from here if you want. That should give you a good base of manpower. And you have Dr. Herman and his staff. State police and the county sheriff's people are also available. The forensics crew the state police are sending from Spokane is top notch. There are also the border patrol people in the district and the border crossing staff at Oroville and the other agencies and programs of Homeland Security to be coordinated by you. Lots of diplomacy needed. You've got the border patrol chopper at your disposal. Spokane state police will also assign their chopper to you for the day, if you need it."

Janet felt relieved that she and Fred Mayfield would be teamed together again. Fred Mayfield was African-American, six foot two, one ninety pounds, thirty-three years old and had been with the agency for six years after a stint in Naval Intelligence. He had a law degree from the University of Michigan but had never sought to be called to the bar. Janet had frequently been a teammate with him since coming to the Seattle posting and always found him thoughtful, unflappable, organized, detailed and not a backbiter. She often spent time with him and his family: wife Lucy; Nicole, age five; and Robert, age three.

"Good," she replied. "Best not to call in anyone other than those called now until I get there and scope the scene. I'm sure Homeland Security – border patrol and quite a few of their other departments at both regional and national levels, maybe even DEA and ATF – will also be in the loop and that the executives at our headquarters in D.C., in additional to regional supervisors, will want frequent updates."

"Right! Good to see you're waking up!"

"Who do we have involved at the local level?" Janet went on. "County Sheriff? State Police?"

"You've got it. They understand you are in charge and they have pledged their full assistance."

"Thanks," Janet replied. "Glad you got that clear. You're always a jump ahead."

"Your fifteen years of experience in our wonderful paramilitary agency is starting to surface. And you live so close to Boeing Field, you have plenty of time to wake up by your usual jog around Lake Union and get a bite to eat. The flight can't leave any earlier than 8 a.m. as we're waiting on Fred to get in from Marysville, for Doc Herman to get in from Redmond and for flight crew and clearance."

"A jog and a shower it will be. Thanks Richard, it's always good to have someone like you putting things together. Say hi to Susan for me. Bye."

As she closed the phone, Janet was cognizant of the bright sunlight creeping around the closed window curtains. Although she knew it was getting light around 5 a.m. this time of the year, a sunny summer day in rainy Seattle was always a bonus and should not be wasted – even with a monster hangover. She slowly uncoiled her slim five foot ten inch one hundred fifty-five pound frame out of bed, stretched, went over to the window, pulled the curtain aside slightly and peeked out to Lake Union's south end overlooking a shipyard, a waterfront seafood restaurant, the wooden boat club and the Naval Reserve facility. Already, there were a number of joggers out and about.

"Time to get going, kid,' she said to herself. Aspirin time." At least, she thought, there is no cat or dog to look after or significant other to notify at the moment. She was still on the rebound from a less than amicable divorce, content in her third floor one-bedroom apartment in a hillside condo overlooking Lake Union and only steps to Salty's, her favorite lakeshore restaurant.

She stumbled into the bathroom and forced a peek at herself in the mirror. Her green eyes looked back at her, showing some red blood vessels. Without makeup, she still looked pretty and youthful despite her forty years. There was only the odd gray hair showing in her now messy pageboy-cut auburn hair. She opened the medicine cabinet and found the aspirin bottle, shook out a couple and downed them with the help of a glass of water. After the toilet, she got into her jogging outfit and headed out the door.

Looking out the window as the aircraft descended between the mountains delineating the Okanagan Valley, Janet thought, "This is a first for me, why have I never thought of visiting? It's beautiful!" As the aircraft banked, descending toward the landing field, she viewed a city straddling the lake and glistening in the bright sunlight. A causeway and a bridge linked two sides of the lake in the middle of the business section of the city; motels flanked both the causeway road and the lakeshore.

The lake looked as if it extended about 15 miles and it seemed full of water skiers. Mountains lined both sides of the lake. From the lakeshore, they began with shallow slopes mainly planted in orchards and vineyards or dotted with houses, then rose steep and craggy. They were nearly barren on the mid slopes, with only a few clusters of pine trees scattered among rock faces, gullies and ancient landslides until much higher up, where a tree line began. The forefront mountains yielded to even taller mountains and green forest higher up and beyond the valley.

She had never really been in the central interior of Washington State. A couple of years ago, she had worked on a case involving a right-wing militia and murder which put her on the Idaho-Washington border in the Spokane-Lake Coeur d'Alene area. That was another beautiful spot but not as arid. However, then she had flown via Spokane and had never crossed the state by road. For holiday time, she gravitated to the Pacific Ocean along the Oregon and Washington coasts for diving and surfing or home to Boston to see her parents and old friends.

As the aircraft taxied to a halt and shut down in front of a small hut with a "Border Patrol" sign on it, a uniformed border patrol officer approached. Janet was the first to descend from the aircraft and was taken aback by the intense heat.

"Agent Murphy? I'm Roger Sanchez, Chief Patrol Agent in command of this border patrol district. Welcome to Oroville."

As they shook hands, Janet said, "Agent Sanchez, thank you. I'm sorry about your loss. I guess you knew the men well?"

"Yes, this is a small town and we are closely knit. Yes, I knew them both professionally and socially."

Trying to change the subject, Janet said, "This is my first time to Oroville. We got a great view from the plane as we were approaching. You have a beautiful city."

Smiling, Agent Sanchez said, "I think you're referring to Osoyoos – that's on the Canadian side. It is beautiful. It's quite a summer tourist area for the Canadians as it boasts some of the hottest temperatures, very little rain and the warmest lake in Canada. A lot of people make that mistake as the border is not that visible unless you're looking for it and this airfield is almost right on the border. No, Oroville is just a hot, dusty little farm town at the south end of the lake. On the desert floor here, we can expect the temperature to reach 105 degrees today. It's great for crops and summer vacationers but a little warm for our type of work. Anyway, the crime scene is up in the mountains where it's a good bit cooler."

"Oh. Well, Osoyoos looks inviting. Maybe someday I'll visit. Permit me to introduce Doctor Herman, our pathologist, and Agent

Fred Mayfield. Agent Mayfield is my number two. We haven't organized any others yet until we get an idea of the situation."

"Good. Our chopper is waiting over there to take us out to the scene. I can fill you in on the way."

They proceeded to the helicopter idling about three hundred feet away. After buckling in and donning headsets for communication, they began to ascend up the hillside on the east side of the valley.

Agent Sanchez, sitting opposite the three FBI agents, raised his right hand and pointed out the window to the road below. His voice came over the headsets. "We're following the Chesaw Road up into the mountains east of Oroville. We found the SUV just off the road, about three hundred feet down the mountainside about five miles before Chesaw. That's about thirty-five miles from here. The first assumption was that they may have gone out of control on the sharp curve there as their GPS positioned them there.

"When the first searchers arrived, they could find no new sign on the guardrail of anyone going over. No paint scrapes. No damage to the guardrail. No skid marks. Nothing. They couldn't see anything below as the forest is very dense there. They tracked a short distance back and forth along the road a few times and verified the GPS coordinates with base. Nothing showing. Finally, they got out their climbing gear and one worked his way down into the floor of the ravine. He found the SUV upside down in the dry creek bed well under the canopy of brush. A close look found both officers dead. The airbags had deployed. Both are in their seat belts. On the driver's side, the officer's head – that's Sergeant John Russel – is partly resting out the open window. It looks as if he took a bullet in his left eye."

"When do you think this happened?" asked Fred Mayfield.

Agent Sanchez looked out the window, rubbed his mustache and said, "Last we heard from them was about 11:49, just before midnight. They had called in a traffic stop. They were going to check out a vehicle parked in Theo Lane."

Fred said, "Theo Lane?"

"Yes. It's a road branching off from Chesaw Road just at the northwest end of the sharp curve and gully where they were found. It runs around the mountain for about two miles to a ranch. When they didn't come on the air again after twenty minutes, our dispatcher began calling. She also checked the GPS, which showed the SUV on Chesaw Road by Theo Lane. We diverted our fixed wing patrol aircraft – it was over the border westbound coming toward Chesaw

Valley. It came on scene about fifteen minutes later but they couldn't spot anything – even though they have FLIR, the infrared couldn't spot any heat signature.

"The ground patrol arrived in the area around one o'clock and it was a good half hour before they found the wreck. They secured the scene and when the County Sheriff's deputies arrived, the Chesaw Road was blocked off at Chesaw and about half a mile past Theo Lane. They also checked out Theo Lane then positioned a man to block it off about a half mile up, as they feel it may be part of the scene. When it started to get daylight, one of the deputies walking the guardrail for a second time found fresh paint scrapings the color of our vehicles. That's at the very end of the guardrail, just near Theo Lane. He also found broken branches indicating the vehicle may have slipped over the edge between the end of the guardrail and the bank."

"Why were your people first on the scene?" Fred asked. "Isn't this area handled by the county sheriff's people?"

"It is. But you also have to appreciate the territory. This is a remote area with a small population and very little trouble. The sheriff's closest people were over sixty minutes away. We patrol the roads frequently and communicate with them if there's something in their area of responsibility and we back each other up from time to time. We also work closely with the park rangers and the conservation officers. The crime scene is only about eight miles from the border."

Fred glanced out the window at the increasingly dense forest and noted the helicopter was roughly following a road winding through rolling hills toward a mountain. "You mentioned the Sheriff's deputies feel Theo Lane may be part of the scene?"

"Yes, their K-9 and handler arrived shortly after 4:45 and began a search along the curve. Although they didn't go down to the wreck to get a scent or scents to work with, they picked up a scent where the SUV went over and followed it just inside Theo Lane about one hundred yards. Looks like they found some blood. And, no, they didn't contaminate the scene too much. They assure me they backed out and didn't go deeper into the lane in case there may be something more for the forensics team. When we sent the deputy in to secure the other end of the road, we took him over by chopper."

"What about the forensics team?" Fred probed. "Have they arrived?"

"They're from the State Police Spokane lab. Came in by helicopter about 6:00 and are hard at it."

The helicopter began a descent and Agent Sanchez said, "We're coming in. The pilot will take us over the scene first so I can point out some things."

Janet looked out the window on her side of the cabin. She saw they were over a heavily forested ravine or gully with fir trees and brush so dense she could not see the bottom. She could see a winding paved road with double white center line and a hairpin curve with a metal safety barrier. The road looked as if it was clinging to the mountain. Parked on the road in the middle of the curve and also at one end just before a lane were seven emergency vehicles: two sheriff's sedans, a sheriff's K-9 SUV, three border patrol SUVs, and a very large tow truck.

Farther up and down the road, she could see police vehicles and emergency barriers blocking the road. Midway in the curve, she could make out two officers talking, one with a foot resting on the top of the guardrail beside two orange ropes that descended into the canopy of the forest below. Past the curve, parked on a flat area of the downward slope of the road, well out of the taped-off crime scene, was a state police helicopter with its two crew members sitting in the rear doorway.

"I don't see the wreck," Janet said. "Is anything visible?"

"No," replied Agent Sanchez. "You really can't see anything from up here, let alone right from the road. It's no wonder it was so hard to find. We'll go over the Theo Lane entrance and work in a bit, and then we'll land. We'll have to keep a fair height so no prop wash hits the scene."

At over two thousand feet, the chopper positioned so that Theo Lane was off the right side, then slowly advanced up the road and turned back when they reached the sheriff's deputy guarding the top end of the road. They landed on Chesaw Road just behind the other helicopter. At the junction of Theo Lane and Chesaw Road, they could see two people in white suits bent over, looking down at the road, slowly walking.

As everyone was getting out and the helicopter was winding down, Doc Herman, Janet and Fred were introduced to Sergeant Dave Fox, the sheriff's deputy in charge of the crime scene. He was in uniform, fitting it well with his forty-five-year-old trim six-foot frame and one hundred eighty-five pounds of what seemed all muscle. He wore a peaked baseball cap bearing the decal of the Sheriff's office, hiding his short-cropped black and graying "salt and pepper" hair. His freckled face reflected his Scottish ancestry. His nose reflected combat as it had been broken and poorly mended.

Sergeant Fox turned to Doctor Herman and said, "It's good to see you. We split the forensics team into two groups. One group is down at the wreck and the other is working the roads. The forensics crew at the wreck have finished with photos and all else they can do with the SUV until you have done your thing and cleared the bodies. Right now, they're fanning out around the vehicle searching for details. They've still got to come up the path the vehicle descended checking to see if anything fell out or off."

Doc Herman said, "OK. I've worked with the Spokane forensic people before. They'll be thorough."

"Great," replied Sergeant Fox. "I guess they'll be with you photographing everything when you examine and move the bodies. I see you've hiking boots and jeans on. Looks as if you came prepared for the terrain. The slope is steep but we have ropes you can hold on to as you climb down. I wouldn't put your anti-contamination gear on until you get down there though."

Doc Herman looked down the slope by the ropes and winced. "Can't see a thing from here. That's real dense bush. What are your thought on getting the bodies up to the road?"

"Well," said Sergeant Fox, "we could cut some trees down to give enough space in the forest canopy for a helicopter to lower stretcher baskets. We might upset the Fisheries people by disturbing the "riparian way" of the creek, though. Or, we could hump the stretcher baskets up with ropes. Maybe use the tow truck's winch. Your call once you see the scene down there. There are some anti-contamination coveralls and booties over there in the first vehicle if you need them."

Janet said, "OK Doc, while you're doing that, Ken and I will learn more from Agent Sanchez and Sergeant Fox and see how the forensics people on the road scene are making out."

As they walked toward Theo Lane, carefully skirting the opposite side of the road and the trail of evidence, Janet could see a number of yellow plastic tent-type evidence markers, each bearing a different black number. From the sequence of numbers, she could see that the technicians had started at the end of the guard rail, likely where the vehicle went over the bank, and were now up to number 17 where they were crouching to take a photograph, about one hundred yards in on Theo Lane from the junction.

"We'd better not get much closer to where they're working for fear of contaminating something," Advised Sergeant Fox. "Cindy! Ed!" he called. "I'd like you to meet the FBI folk."

Straightening up and turning, both looking at the ground, Cindy and Ed made their way over to where the group was standing.

After introductions were made all round, Janet said, "What have you found?"

Cindy looked at Janet and said, "Didn't we meet at a murder scene in Coeur d'Alene? Weren't you tracking a militant cult?"

"Yes! Now I remember!" exclaimed Janet. "We were introduced at the murder scene and you made a great presentation at the trial. Good to see you again."

"Well, Janet, this scene is quite a bit different. We found where the SUV left the road and back from that spot to here, there's very little. But where we're working now, which was originally found by the K-9, we have two likely pools of blood spaced as if a vehicle was in between them. We've also found two casings from a .22 caliber gun – probably a pistol. There is a scrape mark on the pavement a little further up that runs perpendicular to the road, sort of like a loading ramp scrape where the ramp met the road. It looks fresh. We're still working our way up the lane. But, as it's paved, there's little hope for vehicle evidence. When we finish with the road, we'll get the K-9 back to search the bush on each side of the road."

"Looks as if they were killed here," Ken said, "and put in their vehicle and then the vehicle dumped into the gully."

"Sort of looks that way to us at the moment," agreed Ed, the other forensics technician. "But we always keep an open mind at this stage of the investigation."

Janet turned to Agent Sanchez. "Agent, any idea what type of vehicle your men were approaching?"

"No, all the dispatcher recorded was 'recreational trailer' and when we played back the audio file, our recording also said only 'recreational trailer.'"

"Isn't it protocol to check the license plate of the vehicle before they approach it?" suggested Sergeant Fox.

Agent Sanchez slapped his forehead. "Yi! You're right. They would have entered a vehicle search on their computer. But it's probably in the wreck of the SUV. Hold on, I'll get my dispatcher to access the vehicle search files in the database. Sorry. Slow thinking by me – lack of sleep I guess."

He reached for the microphone of his personal radio on his lapel and called dispatch. "Oroville base, this is Agent Sanchez, over."

"Agent Sanchez. Oroville base. Over"

"Robbie, check to see if Alpha One checked out a vehicle last night just before they lost contact. Over."

"Roger that. Stand by."

Two minutes lapse before Roberta came back on the air. "Agent Sanchez. Base. We confirm a vehicle search at 11:43 p.m. Over"

"Oroville base, this is Agent Sanchez. Read it off please. Over."

"Agent Sanchez. Oroville base. The plate is a Utah plate for a recreational trailer. Plate number 47365 registered to a Mr. Westley Miller of Provost, Utah. The search came up negative, no record of being stolen. Over."

"Base, Roger that. Sanchez out."

Agent Sanchez looked up at Janet. "Not much to go on."

"We can get our people in Provost to follow this up," said Fred. "They can look up Mr. Miller and see if he still has the trailer."

"Right," replied Janet. "Now, we should canvass the neighbors around here. Agent Sanchez, Sergeant Fox, you know the area. What do you think?"

Sergeant Fox spoke first. "Well, there's the farm house up Theo Lane here. It's about two miles in. The road winds around the mountain into a valley and the ranch takes up the entire valley, about three thousand acres. Not much else around on the Chesaw Road. First homes to the east are about four miles away as you begin to descend into Chesaw. Probably about five of them. West of here, the first house is about three miles away, then, maybe five or six spotted along the next two-mile stretch. It won't be too hard to canvass the occupants to learn if they saw or heard anything unusual."

"Right," said Agent Sanchez. "It may be best if the Sheriff's personnel and maybe some from the border patrol did this, rather than bringing in FBI personnel."

Janet was a bit surprised. "Why?"

"Well," responded Sergeant Fox, "This is a remote area and it draws people seeking solitude. Frontier folk? An independent bunch overall. Many are very right wing and many very left wing. Some are Vietnam and Gulf War combat vets who would not fit into urban society. Some are hard workers scratching a living from the land and some are on remittance like disability pensions, welfare, etc. Some are what once were called hippies or flower children who went back to the land – may even be growing pot or making moonshine, something illegal. It's a pretty closed society in a way. They don't take to outsiders and the FBI is not popular after that Waco, Texas massacre. I suspect many won't give you the time of day."

"Oh," sighed Janet. "Best you handle it then. However, can we get on to this quickly?"

"Sergeant Fox and I will organize a canvass of Chesaw Road right now," replied Agent Sanchez. "I think we have enough resources between us, either here or soon to arrive in the vicinity. However, I suggest we airlift someone in to the farmhouse up Theo Lane right now. We have two choppers; we can spare one for that for a few minutes."

"Good idea," said Janet.

"I'll switch Deputy Rosemary Carlson off from blocking the east side of the road below the choppers and send her in. She knows the family that lives up there," said Sergeant Fox as he keyed his radio microphone.

"Good. I guess we should check in on Doc Herman and see how he's progressing." Janice and Ken left the two officers to organize the house-by-house canvassing and walked back to the scene of the wreck.

When they got back to the curve in the road, Janet saw that the large tow truck had been maneuvered to the middle of the curve and backed up with its crane hanging over the guardrail and a steel cable being played out down toward the wreck. A sheriff's deputy was at the rear of the truck with one foot up on the guardrail beside the two climbing ropes that had been used by the crew to get down to the wreck. He had just finished talking into a walkie-talkie. "They've decided to winch the bodies up by the tow truck," he said when Janet and Ken arrived. "We're sending down two basket stretchers."

As the retrieval got under way, a woman in deputy sheriff's uniform boarded the helicopter and it took off.

Janet and Ken could overhear the radio conversations between the crew at the wreck site and the deputy at the tow truck. Soon the winch began slowly winding the cargo up the steep slope of the ravine. Eventually, the top edge of one stretcher could be seen through the underbrush with a man climbing beside it holding on to the stretcher for upwards momentum and sometimes guiding it around obstacles. Next, came the second stretcher, which was linked to the first by a short stretch of rope, similarly accompanied by a man on either side guiding it. Doc Herman was one of them.

Once the stretchers were laid on the road, Doc Herman turned to Janet and Ken. "Definitely murder, folks. One was shot through the eye, as the first officer on scene determined, but the other was shot high up his right side at the armpit. Of course, that's the obvious. I'll tell you much more after the autopsy and forensic examination of their clothing, bullets if recoverable, and so on."

"Great, Doc," said Janet. "Our aircraft is standing by in Oroville. Why don't you take the bodies there by the chopper and then fly with them back to your lab in Seattle? "

"Right. I'll get going then. Ken, will you set up liaison/coordination with the on-scene forensics people? No doubt they're more comfortable working in their Spokane lab but we'll need to centralize all info."

Ken nodded. "Consider it done Doc. See you back in Seattle."

Agent Sanchez and Sergeant Fox had arrived during that conversation. "I'll tell our pilot to take you to Oroville and then return for us," said Agent Sanchez to Doc Herman. The he turned to Janet and Ken. "We've got the house-to-house canvassing under way on Chesaw Road. We've also got people going into Molson and Chesaw to ask around."

Sergeant Fox said, "The forensics team working the wreck have cleared it for retrieval. They want to take it to their Spokane lab for examination. Is that OK with everyone?"

Janet and Ken nodded their approval. "Mind if we set up in your headquarters?" Janet asked Agent Sanchez. "Can we coordinate everything from there?"

"No problem. I guess that includes Sergeant Fox for a while as well."

"Good."

They heard a helicopter approaching and watched it land on the road. The sheriff's deputy emerged and came over to them. "Hi, I'm Deputy Rosemary Carlson, the one you sent over to the farmhouse back on Theo Lane."

After introductions all round, Deputy Rosemary Carlson made her report. "The family is Larry and Donna Milton. They live there alone as their kids are grown and moved on. I've known them for at least a dozen years. For around here, they have a fairly

----

prosperous farm. They run two hundred cattle and sell some surplus hay."

Ken spoke up. "Were they able to shed any light on the mystery?"

"Well, they both go to bed early but they sleep with a screened window open. Donna was awakened around midnight by the sound of a helicopter approaching down their valley from the north. It passed them flying low between the mountains, or so it seemed to her, then it went around the mountain south of them and the sound faded out. She got up for a bathroom break and was just settling back to sleep about twenty minutes later when she heard it flying the same route but going north. She got out of bed and went to the window but she could see no aircraft lights. She mentioned it to her husband in the morning but they really thought nothing of it."

"You say they didn't think anything of it. Why is that?" asked Ken.

"I asked the same question," replied Deputy Carlson. "Donna said this is a frequent occurrence, maybe six or seven times a year. They assumed it was the border patrol searching as they're fairly close to the border."

"It wasn't us last night," replied Agent Sanchez. "Our chopper was working one of our Western zones on the Korean aliens incident. Our fixed wing aircraft was east of here. If they mistook the time, it still wouldn't be the fixed wing as it was well above the mountains during the search for the vehicle."

"Maybe there was a little smuggling going on," said Ken. "Could they get across the border undetected?"

"This part of the border is mountainous with lots of creeks and streams crossing that have carved canyons and ravines. Land-based radar has problems with that. We have the "eyes-in-the-sky" in the form of patrolling aircraft both manned and drones but they can't be everywhere at once. We're not considered a very active zone so we don't qualify for radar blimps or tightly spaced mountaintop radars or motion sensors in the canyons. Yes, it's quite possible to fly low and get in undetected, especially by following a ravine or canyon. It would take some good flying and night vision to do so, though," said Agent Sanchez.

"Rosemary, were you able to pin down some of the other times the Miltons heard the helicopter, say, over the past six months?"

"Not really. The last one they think was about six or eight weeks ago. They did mention it was always on a night with little or no moon and never in bad weather."

Ken asked the question that was on Janet's mind. "Agent, what types of smuggling are common in this sector?"

"Drugs mostly. Mainly marijuana and meth, sometimes heroin, coming down from Canada. Cocaine and guns going north. Also prescription drugs from Canada – but that tends to be at the ports of entry border crossings. We do get some smuggling of people – usually blatantly trying to enter at a port of entry border crossing but sometimes, like last night, organized groups hiking in. We've caught about one hundred and fifty total in the past twelve months. That's up about fifteen percent from last year.

"We divide the drug smuggling into two different groups, organized crime and free lancers. Needless to say, we have more luck catching the free lancers. We can also separate between those trying to get through a border crossing port and those going cross-country. Our biggest hits have been at the border crossing ports with vehicles loaded with large quantities."

"How's your success rate on cross-country type of smugglers?" Janet asked.

"We're never sure what we miss, of course. We have our patrols and we have sensors but most of the time we wind up chasing animals that have tripped the sensors. And we are spread pretty thin. I have seventy-two officers to cover three hundred miles of mountains 24/7. Our patrols do get lucky from time to time. For example, last month we had a mounted patrol working with park rangers patrolling the hiking trail, called the Pacific Crest Trail, along the top of the Cascades. It's about one hundred twenty miles west of here. We picked up eight backpackers bringing in two hundred twenty pounds of marijuana. Street value of drugs seized the past twelve months exceeded twenty five million dollars. Most often, the success is from intelligence supplied by the Canadian police or DEA tracking dealers or from tips."

"Tips?"

"Yes. We pay up to $10,000 for big successes. For example, that led us to intercept the Koreans last night. A woman on the NightHawk Indian reserve on the Canadian side of the border called in the tip."

"Sensors?"

"Mainly infrared, like trip wires. But some pick up ground vibrations. The border is too long and mountainous to cover everything. We tend to set them along streambeds and animal trails plus roads and pathways. We also have sonar and acoustical sensors for Osoyoos Lake and others."

Janet and Ken watched the tow truck bring the wrecked SUV up the steep side of the ravine. There was a little difficulty clearing the guardrail with it but the operator managed to do it without adding any damage to the wreck. In the meantime, a flat deck tow truck arrived and the wreck was loaded onto it, wrapped in a tarp and tied down after additional photos were taken. It was agreed, in order to keep the chain of evidence secure, that one of the forensics technicians would ride with the driver until the wreck was delivered to the forensics lab in Spokane. As well, they would be escorted by a sheriff's car with two officers as far as Grand Coulee Dam where a state police highway patrol team would relieve them.

The helicopter, which had taken the bodies to Oroville airport, returned for Janet, Ken and Agent Sanchez. They left Sergeant Fox to wrap up and close out the crime scenes as they returned to Oroville to set up their temporary command center. A conference call was scheduled for 3 p.m. to provide a status report to the "powers that be" in D.C

Chapter 4

Kelowna, B.C., Canada, next day

At 8:07 a.m., in Studio A of the Canadian National Broadcasting Regional Center in Kelowna, British Columbia, Canada – sixty miles north of the Oroville-Osoyoos border crossing – a man and a woman sat awaiting their cue to begin broadcasting.

The woman was about 50, plump, short, with a peasant's face, grey hair swept back in a ponytail, no makeup. She was under-dressed with a short-sleeved white blouse, a small, thin gold necklace with a single imitation sapphire pendant in a gold setting, blue jeans and sandals.

The man, about mid-40s, at a slim, trim six foot two, was very handsome, with jet-black crew cut hair. He was dressed semi-casually with brown Gucci loafers and no socks, navy blue slacks with razor's edge crease, brown alligator skin belt with a large buckle in the shape of a gold feather, and an open-necked white short-sleeve shirt with a monogrammed "J.B." on the breast pocket. Around his neck was a gold necklace with a two inch gold pendant in the shape of a feather. On his left wrist, he wore a Rolex Mariner watch with a stainless steel and gold-filled wristband. He had a large gold chain bracelet on his right wrist. In a holster on his belt was an i-Phone.

At her cue from the control room, the woman spoke into the microphone. "Hello, my friends in radioland. This is national radio – Kelowna – serving the Okanagan, Shuswap, Similkameen and West Kootenays. And… this is The Morning Talk Show. I am your host, Tina Linkoff. Today, I have a very special guest, Chief Joseph Branson, Chief of the Midlake Indian Band and former Grand Chief of the Federation of Okanagan, Shuswap and Similkameen Tribal Aboriginal People. Chief, welcome again to The Morning Talk Show."

"Thank you Tina, it is a great pleasure to be here again."

"Chief, today you are going to update us all about the Aboriginal Fisheries Enhancement Initiative – the AFEI. I understand you have some very pleasant news."

"Tina, as you and many listeners may recall, the AFEI was founded five years ago as a joint initiative of the various departments of fisheries and water management, and aboriginal tribal federations on both sides of the border. The objective we shared was to bring natural runs of wild sockeye salmon back to the Okanagan. As you know, even Okanagan Lake, before it was dammed, had sockeye salmon making the journey to the Columbia River, out to sea and returning in four to five year cycles to spawn. We still have the trapped sockeye salmon in Lake Okanagan but, as they are landlocked, they are called Kokanee. They still spawn in four to five year cycles but they do not grow as large as if they were ocean raised."

"Yes, I understand the kokanee have been endangered but now they are making a comeback."

"Correct, Tina. That has been a little success story in its own right! Now, we have something bigger. The AFEI began a sockeye hatchery program releasing sockeye fingerlings into the Okanagan River just below the dam at Okanagan Falls. As well, the streambeds here in Canada were enhanced for over fifteen miles to provide excellent spawning grounds for the returning mature fish. Concurrently, tribes along the Okanagan and Columbia Rivers on the U.S. side of the border also enhanced spawning grounds. Four years ago, our first sockeye fingerlings were released to make their way down rivers to the open ocean."

"Excellent."

"Yes, the fish have to migrate down and back following the Okanagan River to its confluence with the Columbia and then down the Columbia to the Pacific Ocean. It's a journey of over eight hundred miles or thirteen hundred kilometers during which they have to pass through fish channels on over ten dams on the Columbia. It is indeed an arduous journey – it's amazing."

"Truly amazing."

"Tina, I'm here to share a little premature celebration with you. According to the fisheries people on the lower Columbia River, the first of the salmon released at Okanagan Falls are on their way home to spawn. The numbers look very good! We should expect to see the spawners in the Okanagan River by the end of September."

"Wonderful! Will there be places to observe them spawning?"

"Yes, Tina. The bike path along the river below Okanagan Falls, the wildlife viewing path at Vaseaux Lake, and also the one at the head of Osoyoos Lake should provide plenty of opportunity."

"Chief, it is excellent to see the fruits of labor like this. But, from another point of view, this must have taken extreme diplomacy and coordination to get all the various parties who are partnering in the initiative to cooperate. My goodness, you must have three or four bureaucracies, like fisheries, environment, water management, and, oh yes, the hydroelectricity management people who had to have their say. On top of that, it is not an easy thing to organize and train the many volunteers from the tribes to enhance the channels – plus organize financing for the hatchery."

"You're right, Tina. But when one feels strongly enough about an issue, it is amazing what can happen. The greatest asset was the cooperation of all the aboriginal tribes along the waterway – they all have a vested interest in seeing traditional fishing rights enhanced. Along with this, we recruited farmers and fishing sports clubs and local politicians."

"I understand, if there are surplus fish, the Aboriginal Peoples will have first claim on a quota."

"Right. We deserve the fruit of our labor and it is the recognition of historic food fishing rights. There'll be a restriction on sport fishing for the public until we're sure the fishery is entrenched but we expect there will be a short opening "season" for them. After all, sport fishing is a major revenue producer in our local tourist industry and we want to support it."

"Chief, I understand there is still a lot of work to do?"

"You're right there, Tina. We're trying to get the Canada Fisheries and Oceans people and others involved to allow a fish ladder at the Okanagan Falls dams and the Okanagan Lake dam to allow fish to enter Okanagan Lake. It's turning out to be a hard battle but our argument is that the sockeye once came to Okanagan Lake, as is evidenced by the fish – the kokanee – landlocked there. I feel we have the argument of "nature's heritage" on our side. We'll win eventually."

"We're also protesting the idea of a dam in the Similkameen canyon – that's just west of Oroville on the American side of the border. It will back up into Canada and flood part of the NightHawk tribal reservation. On the American side, just at the border, the Similkameen meanders through a marsh, Chopaka Marshlands, which is an excellent wildlife habitat – especially for migrating birds. Flooding from the dam would destroy this. AFEI has purchased all the marshland for a wildlife preserve. This gives us a clear voice in discussions on the impact of the dam. We don't seem to be getting anywhere with that and that is starting to alarm the aboriginal tribes. And, of course, on the Canadian side, we have not settled our land

----

claims with the Province of British Columbia and we're agitating strongly to get our lands back."

"Well, Chief, in addition to managing your own aboriginal reservation of Midlake, you certainly sound as if you are busy!"

"You're right. It is very rewarding to see some good things happening, though."

"As always, Chief, it has been a great pleasure to have you on the show and to learn more about the returning sockeye. Will you come back on air with us when the run materializes?"

"Of course, Tina. Thank you for having me."

"OK, let's go to a commercial and station identification."

The Chief shook hands with Tina and the producer, gave bear hugs all around and left. Outside, in front of the broadcast offices he walked over to a parked SUV, a black two-year-old GMC Yukon, where his son, David, was waiting, leaning on the front curbside fender. David, age twenty-eight, was similar in appearance to his dad with jet black hair, handsome face with a strong jaw, sharp nose and a six foot three inch solid athlete's frame. Both got in and they took off with David driving. The Chief was all smiles when David said, "Dad, you look as if everything went well?"

"Son, it always pays to make good PR. It is always good to nurture the image that we're champions of nature and protectors of natural resources. Yes, it went well."

"Where to now, the lab?"

"Yeah. But after a quick stop at the tribal office to see if anything's urgent. It's on the way anyway. At the lab, we need to see how soon we can get the next order shipped out. We also have to coordinate getting the next load of B.C. Bud together from the other producers and see if Ken's getting settled in. How did your little debt collection exercise go?"

"Well, let's just say the guy won't be skiing again. After breaking the first kneecap, the boys managed to get him to fork over $6,000 cash and we got him to sign over his car – there's probably $15,000 equity in it at wholesale – so he made good."

"Good son. Did the coke get delivered to the bikers? Are they happy?"

"Yeah, I was talking to Donny Fortunato. He's moved it out already to Edmonton, Calgary and Vancouver. He wants a load of meth next Tuesday. Are you going to tell him about being jumped by the border patrol the other night?"

"Nah, he doesn't need to know. We picked up and delivered his goods as promised. Not his concern how we get his stuff moved, as long as it gets delivered."

"Mona from the NightHawk band called to thank you. Looks as if she'll get the maximum $10,000 reward from the U.S. Border Agency for giving them that tip on the Koreans crossing the border. Apparently, they'll pay her within the month. She says call her anytime you want something like that again."

"Good. Good," Joseph replied. "She deserves the money. Not bad for a few seconds work on her part to report seeing them hiking toward the border. I hope she doesn't brag it around though. Those Koreans might like revenge."

"Yeah. I suspect they'll have tumbled to the fact they were set up. It serves them right for trying to cut us out. Do you think Mr. Lee will come after you?"

"Yeah. They'd be pretty dumb if they didn't think we set them up. It serves that bastard Lee right for cutting us out. We helped him cross, what, eight times? At ten grand a crossing for us, it was fair change but he got greedy and cut us out. That type will have lost face with his superiors in Korea. He might be able to save face by gunning for us or his superiors might just have him eliminated for making a mistake. After all, things were going good before he got greedy. We'll have to take care of him."

"When?"

"Let's leave it for a couple of weeks to see if his superiors take him out. In the meantime, I doubt if they would be stupid enough to target us on the reserve but we should have two of the boys cover each of our backs when off the reserve. Same for all wives, kids and Hazel. Also, give Mona a call and tell her she's also won an all-expense paid trip for a month to the Northwest Territories. She's got close relatives up there in Yellowknife. It'll get her out of the way as I'm sure the Koreans will be able to trace who reported them. Get one of the boys to move her out tonight. Fly her out of Kelowna to Edmonton then on to Yellowknife from there. She can collect the reward later."

"We should keep an eye on Mr. Lee. Didn't Donny once say he had a contact in Vancouver who did surveillance?"

"Yeah, Dad. I think the guy went by the nickname "Little Spook." Do you want me to talk to Donny and get something set up?"

"Yes. Wiretaps would be no good, as they would be speaking Korean. Maybe he can put bugs on their vehicles and keep track of their movements. He could alert us if any head this way. I doubt if they're into contracting a hit. Mr. Lee will need to do it himself or use his own people."

"You may be right, Dad. Consider it done. I'll see Donny and I'll get Mona moved. What about Ken's stuff? Are you going to involve Donny?"

"Nope! That project is ours and ours alone. It means I'll have to travel offshore again and you'll be left minding the store while I'm away."

"No problem. Are you taking Mom this time?"

"I think she'll enjoy a vacation in the Maldives, don't you?"

"I'll say! Great scuba diving, exotic islands and five to seven star resorts? I'll kill for that! Where will you stay? Are you going to try that resort with the underwater restaurant that you were talking about? When can I go?"

"I guess we could try the resort with the underwater restaurant but there's a new one advertising only Nordic blonds on the serving staff – that's more your style. But then, we could always charter a yacht."

"That's an idea too. I'd love to try a scuba dive live aboard."

"We can work that out later. Right now, depending on negotiations, I may have to leave your mom there for a few days by herself. So, the resort is best – she loves the sun and sand and pampering."

"Right on!"

After a brief stop in the Midlake Indian band's office, they drove through the reserve on a winding road that entered a canyon and followed a stream upward. At the nineteen-mile point, they crossed a cattle guard where a sign on the fence signified they had exited the tribal reserve. After about forty-five minutes and many switchbacks on the road, they were well up in elevation, at about five thousand feet and still climbing. The road was good gravel, well graded, and wide to accommodate two passing logging trucks as the area was densely forested with mature fir and spruce trees.

Along the main road, there were occasional branch roads, some flagged and labeled with caution signs warning drivers the area was actively logged and to expect logging trucks, which had the right of way, and to tune their CB radios to specific frequencies for the operation. Other branch roads showed disuse with significant erosion due to the long winters and heavy rains common in the mountains.

Some signs pointed to provincial parks and lakes which the government stocked annually with trout. Eventually, the road leveled out at an elevation of about seven thousand feet. They were riding the ridge of the mountain that stretched for twenty miles. Shortly afterward, they crossed another cattle guard, passing a fence bearing a large sign stating they were entering the Midlake Indian Reserve #2 and that the road was private. A larger sign declared:

NO TRESPASSING
WITHOUT PERMISSION
OF THE MIDLAKE BAND OFFICE.

They proceeded for ten miles until they reached another fence and a large gate, which they unlocked and drove through. Another sign declared:

GREAT SIMILKAMEEN MINE
HISTORIC GHOST TOWN
This project funded by the Province of British Columbia.
Managed by the Midlake Indian Band.
Tours from Smelter Village Daily 9 – 5
May 15 – September 15
SERVICE ENTRANCE ONLY

A short distance down the road, now one lane of gravel, they pulled to the left into a parking lot for the old mining town – an assortment of wooden clapboard buildings, all labeled, which included a dining hall, wash house, dormitory, first aid house, tool sheds and an office. Off to the right was a mineshaft entrance. Farther to the right, another mineshaft entrance.

They walked to the right following a path, which took them past the second shaft to another fenced area with a gate and the sign:

DANGER
UNSAFE AREA
KEEP OUT

They unlocked the gate, entered and relocked the gate, then proceeded down the path until they reached a mineshaft entrance that was boarded up with a locked door in the middle of the wall. After unlocking the door, they entered, closed and locked the door and

----

turned on a light switch which revealed another, similar door in the boarded up shaft, which they opened. They entered a fully lit passageway which they followed about one hundred feet to a side tunnel which opened into a large brightly lit chamber, about one hundred fifty feet width by eighty feet long.

It was a chemical lab. Modern, well ventilated, the best of equipment. They could feel a draft on their backs from air entering the lab. *"Good cross-ventilation – the fans are working very well,"* thought Joseph. In the lab paraphernalia, things were bubbling away. There were three people in the room, all in white lab coats, two wearing respirator masks and busy pouring and testing chemicals and adjusting Bunsen burners. The third person was sitting at a desk making some notes. He looked up, then came to greet the new arrivals. "Hi Chief, David. Good to see ya!"

This was Ross Emory, lead chemist, twenty-nine years old, a chemistry graduate from an Iowa university. He had a dark complexion, brown eyes and dark hair, of slight build. Ross had a lengthy criminal record for manufacturing illegal chemicals in California and Colorado. Joseph had "rescued" him when he was paroled after serving two years of a nine-year sentence for running a meth lab in Eureka, California. Once he agreed to work for Joseph, he had been quickly whisked across the border to set up this meth lab for Joseph.

That had been three years ago. Ross was his new identity and he was now a full-blooded registered First Nations Indian living openly in a four-bedroom log chalet he built on a one hundred acre piece of land deeded to him as a "locatee" on the Midlake tribal reserve. He had full band rights and even voted in elections – of course, always voting for Joseph's slate of elders. He could develop his piece of land as he wished, even leasing it or starting a commercial enterprise, but he could never sell it. He had married one of the Midlake tribal beauties and they were expecting their first child.

"Hey Ross. How's the wife coming along? Isn't she about three months from due?"

"Yeah, we saw the doctor the other day. He says it should be an easy delivery. We're just about through the order. Should be finished in an hour or so distilling then just a matter of pressing out the capsules."

"Excellent. Well ahead of schedule. You've earned a couple of weeks off."

"Thanks Chief, nice to have a little free time in the summertime. I've got to get some time in with the wife for pre-natal classes."

After saying good-by, Joseph and David turned back out of the chamber, then proceeded further down the main tunnel to another side tunnel and walked a couple of hundred feet down it to a door that took them into a large, brightly illuminated cave-like room with many tunnels branching off it. Both temperature and humidity were high. The "cave" contained row upon row of marijuana plants that were growing in hydroponic solution in long, narrow and shallow vats. They were strung to overhead wires running the length of each vat. Also suspended over each vat was a string of "grow lights" – intense high wattage lights designed to replicate sunshine.

As in the previous room, only much hotter, Joseph could feel the air flow on his back coming from the main shaft and flowing out to a ventilation shaft about a mile away in the dense forest. The side rooms radiating from the main "cave" also contained hydroponic gardens with marijuana plants in various stages of growth. "Looks O.K. here," said Joseph. "I guess John Jumping Elk is down in the generator room. Let's go down there. We can check in on Ken on the way."

They exited the "cave" and followed the main tunnel a few hundred yards, past other side tunnels. Turning left, they entered another tunnel ending at a white door set in the wall. Once through it, they were in another large room. Again, there was good cross-ventilation. Five men were in the room assembling tables and machinery. At one end, close to a large exit ventilation fan and electrical panel, was a massive kiln. One of the men broke away from the others and exchanged bear hugs with Joseph. He looked about sixty years old. He had balding red hair, green eyes, and a light complexion. He was about two hundred pounds on a five foot eleven inch frame.

Joseph said, "Ken, great to see you! I see you're making some good progress. How soon can we start production?"

Ken responded, "Hi. Thanks for dropping in. Yeah, we'll probably be ready to start production tomorrow. The material has arrived. We just have to finish some wiring for the machine tools and kiln. The molds are all here. I like the ventilation and the space. We should be comfortable."

"Speaking of comfortable," said David, "how's the cabin on the lake? Have you tried fishing yet?"

"Yep, caught a one and a half pound rainbow trout early this morning before breakfast. Saw a couple of elk this morning too. They were down by the dam spillway. The cabin's great, reminds me of my place. With three bedrooms and twenty-five hundred square feet, there's plenty of room. It's got a great kitchen too. I walked over from the lake; there's a good trail that'll help get me back in shape for hunting."

"And how's Patsy, your new housekeeper making out?"

"We are. Thank you. You made a great choice there. She keeps me warm. She's also not too bad of a cook."

After leaving Ken, they went back to the main shaft to another door marked "STAIRS TO HISTORICAL POWERHOUSE." They entered onto a platform, and before them was a vertical shaft with stairs leading downward. Many sets of stairs later, they reached bottom, about three hundred feet down, a door opened onto another tunnel. It had another entrance from the left. The tunnel was well lit and had signage directing one to the historical powerhouse – this part of the tunnel was used by the tour groups. They followed the arrows a couple of hundred feet, then through another door, which opened to a large, white and noisy room brightly lit. The room contained both a large Pelton Wheel and a massive Doebel Waterwheel generator, which were both humming. On a panel between them, voltage meters showed the amounts of electricity each was producing.

The generators were powered by water flowing through a pipeline running three miles from a lake at a higher level on the reservation. The pipeline was an extraordinary bit of engineering as it flowed through three tunnels that had been bored in various rock outcrops by the original owners of the mine who had introduced hydroelectric power in 1902. The Pelton Wheel dated back to 1902 and the Doebel to 1934. Both waterwheels were hooked to 1930s Westinghouse generators. The drop, or "head" of the water descending to the turbines was about four hundred twenty feet, which provided significant pressure to spin the turbines with a small volume of water.

The waterwheels were enclosed with the water exhausting down a shaft another six hundred feet to be once again diverted into two new Pelton Wheels that produced electricity for Smelter Village at the base of the mountain. Eventually the water came out in a creek a half mile distant, near the ruins of a smelter that had, from 1902 to 1955, refined gold, zinc and copper from the rich ore of the

NightHawk Crossing By C. Edgar North

Similkameen Mountain. From there, the water flowed into the Similkameen River, about a half-mile away.

Both pieces of historical machinery had been carefully restored and were a major feature in the mining tour, which was open to the public. Together the generators produced over three thousand horsepower generating over two hundred eighty kilowatts of electricity. Tourists were told that the electricity was used to supply the village and the restored heritage tourism project and that the surplus was sold into the local electrical grid. In reality, little made it to the local electrical grid as the grow op in the mine, and others nearby, took most of the electricity.

The top of the mountain had become a major gold find in the late 1890s during the gold rush that swept through on its way from California to Alaska and the Yukon. Over its mining life span, the mountain had yielded three hundred forty-six tons of gold. Well over one hundred of those early prospectors had claimed every square foot of the surface of the mountain. Over the next fifty years, many had succeeded in developing mines, plunging their shafts into the bowels of the mountain following various veins of gold-bearing rock.

Eventually, there was some consolidation in ownership of two smelters at the base of the mountain, over two thousand feet below, where the ore was brought by cable car. For a period of thirty years, two rival mining operations dominated the top of the mountain, which resulted in two separate mining towns for the workers.

One, which now drew all the attention, was perched on a cliff face, quite visible from Smelter Village over two thousand feet below. It looked as if it was barely clinging to the rock of the mountain as it stretched over three hundred feet down a cliff to a mine portal on the cliff face. It was this village that the Midlake Indian Band restored as a tourist attraction, thanks to a grant from the Provincial Ministry of Tourism. The attraction included visiting a restored section of one of the mineshafts to see examples of machines at work, a tour of the historic powerhouse and a tour of the town clinging to the side of the cliff. Tourists were bussed by road up to the top of the mountain, past the abandoned open pit mine that was operating in the 1980s and then bussed back down to the base at the mining museum below at the smelter. One of the thrills of the trip was walking along seemingly flimsy boardwalks clinging to the cliff with a sheer drop of over two thousand feet, protected by only a fragile wooden railing for safety. It was not for those with a fear of heights.

The Midlake Indian Band had been allocated the land of the mountain and most of the valley below in 1867, but had lost the mining area due to a corrupt provincial government officer who yielded to claims by prospectors. After a bitter political battle involving both federal and provincial governments from 1979 to 1994, the land was returned to the Midlake Band.

The mountain was a rabbit warren of vertical and horizontal shafts totaling over twenty two miles of tunneling – of which only a small portion of fifteen hundred feet, which terminated at the historical power house, was open to the public during guided tours.

Joseph and David found John Jumping Elk sitting at a desk, reading a hunting magazine. He had long black hair swept back with two braids, a hawk-like nose, black eyes, and an acne-pocked complexion. He was six foot two, and a large frame held his two hundred sixty pounds. He had big calloused hands, and sizeable wrists with a stainless steel diver's watch on his left wrist. He was wearing a blue polo shirt, blue jeans held up with a silver Western style belt buckle inlaid with turquoise, brown penny loafers and brown socks.

At thirty-five, he was a business administration graduate from a Manitoba university. He was listening to an iPod, but jumped up when he saw them and they all exchanged bear hugs. After John took the earphones off, Joseph said, "Hey, John, how's it going?"

"Great, Chief. We're actually sending a little surplus electricity into the grid, so some revenue there. I don't want to do too much as we need to maintain a good level in the reservoir for the fall and, besides, too much production may raise suspicions. The grow op is doing well, so far no problems, the next round of harvesting will be in two weeks, which should produce over a ton of bud.

"Tourism has been steady but revenues are down a bit in the souvenir shops both at the museum down below and at the shop on top. We're getting an average of three busloads of tourists daily plus an average of two hundred daily car and RV walk-ins. We still have capacity for more tourists though. Our café at the museum has done OK, so has the one on top here and so has the historical restaurant on Main Street in Smelter Village. The RV resort isn't doing too well though. I think we need to do some major renovations there this winter. Overall, we can't complain."

"Good going John," said Joseph. "We'll do a bud shipment then in three weeks. We'll combine our production with what the bikers are assembling. The order is for five tons this time."

"Same route as last with the helicopter? That's a few trips."

"No," said Joseph. "That route is burned for now. We'll use another route. Make sure your packaging is really watertight. Your vacuum packing is great. Pack the one-kilo bags in plastic barrels. The bud's going swimming. David, make sure you tell Donny to do the same with his stuff."

"No problem," replied John. Can you stay for lunch?"

"Just a quick bite at the café up here, though. I've got to get back to the tribal office for a two p.m. meeting, then get organized for the tribal council meeting at five. On top of that, we have a sweetgrass ceremony at sunset."

Chapter 5

Day 2 of Investigation

Janet and Ken were settled in an office of the Border Patrol in Oroville where they had set up a command center to coordinate the investigation. Janet had arranged to report, daily at 1:00 p.m. Pacific Time, to her superiors at FBI Seattle and Washington D.C. offices and to coordinates at FBI Spokane, Washington State Police in Spokane and Olympia, Washington, the county deputy sheriff's office in Omak, Alcohol, Tobacco and Firearms (ATF) in Seattle and Washington, D.C., and to Border Patrol and Homeland Security in Bellingham, Seattle, Spokane Washington and to Washington D.C. So far, there had been little to report.

Today's teleconference began with all stations checking in and Hector Skog, the case officer of FBI Washington, D.C., speaking for everyone when he asked, "Well, Janet, are you making any progress?"

"Yes, I think so," Janice began. "The local police did an exhaustive door-to-door canvass of the residents up to twenty miles around the crime scene. No one took any notice of traffic, although it's a remote area with little traffic during the night of the crime. No one took notice of an RV, as they're common in the area this time of the year. However, a number of people commented on low flying helicopters from time to time but all assumed it was the border patrol doing their job.

"We did make some progress on the RV license plate that the deceased officers recorded in their license check. It belongs to a Westley Miller of Provost, Utah. Our FBI Office there managed to contact Mr. Miller, who is a college professor teaching Economics. He has evening classes and was at one the night of the crime. We also checked his wife and she also is a college professor and accounted for. Mr. Miller took our agents to the storage facility where he keeps his RV, a 5th wheel "toy box." The facility is very secure, with sign in and out requirements and TV monitors – and, no, the rig had not moved from the storage facility for five weeks. However, the license plate had been stolen and that was only noticed when our people visited. No telling how long it has been missing but our people are checking the security tapes of the storage facility.

"Doctor Herman, our pathologist who did the autopsies, made an unusual discovery. One officer was killed by two shots from a low caliber weapon, a .22 most likely as two .22 caliber casings were found at the death scene. Bullet fragments were hard to identify although the weight of the bullet fragments recovered point to a .22 caliber. He also found a significant bruise over the heart, which corresponded to a fabric indentation on the victim's bulletproof vest. Looks as if he could have been shot at the chest first, which stunned him, then killed at close range by the .22 caliber weapon. Yet, the forensics crew at the scene found nothing that may have done it.

"More significant was the way the other victim died. He received a shot through the right armpit – he must have had his arm raised exposing a part of his body the vest did not protect. That shot turned out to be a projectile in the form of an arrow, such as from a cross bow. The arrow did not exit the body but was fully buried in the chest cavity of the victim."

Someone on the conference call interrupted: "A cross bow?"

"Well, that is what Doctor Herman thought but he passed it among his forensics people for review. The arrow is a bit unusual as it's made from carbon fiber and shorter than a typical crossbow arrow. One of the forensics people got curious about the shaft and its composition. Upon checking around with crossbow experts, this is not your ordinary arrow – in fact, it's most unusual. We sent it to Quantico for analysis."

"Janet, this is Max Lee, of Homeland Security and Border Patrol Bellingham. Did you manage to make some sense of the comments about low flying helicopters?'

"Hello Max. Not really. We tried to pinpoint times and dates but people have been hearing this over the past few years and not much attention has been paid. We did manage to get some dates and times, about six were quite clear, but when correlated to border patrol flight logs, there were no flights in the areas at the time. All were at periods of little or no moon."

"So, there may be a smuggling operation utilizing helicopters?"

"Yes. But they have managed to be where your people are not at the time. Captain Sanchez is working on reviewing this. Maybe there is some awareness of your patrol patterns or diversion or both. For example, the night of the murders and, nearly coincident, there was a major capture of twenty-two aliens crossing at another sector."

"Thanks Janet. That makes sense. It also suggests a very well organized smuggling operation. Possibly some inside knowledge. Ouch!"

D.C. FBI Case Officer Skog joined the conversation. "Thanks Janet. What happens now?"

"Well, sir, I suggest Agent Fred Mayfield and I return to Seattle and operate out of there as we've exhausted the local scene. I've also requested our Provost, Utah agents to dig deeper into the backgrounds of the couple owning the RV. Also, if the officers were caught unawares, maybe the perpetrator or perpetrators had identification to match the trailer license. So, we will see if we can find a trail using that I.D. As mentioned, we await more analysis on the arrow.

"Also, Hector, is it possible for you to check with the Canadians to see if they're aware of any smuggling activity, or rumored activity on their side? Max? In your discussions with the Canadians, are your people aware of anything?"

"Max here. Nothing unusual. Certainly no mention of helicopters. There have been a few tips about individuals attempting to drive across at the border crossing with marijuana and some people smuggling stuff down the Cascade Trail but nothing as far east as you."

"I'll check with the Canadians and get back to you," Hector responded.

"Janet, this is Richard Rollings from ATF. I checked with our people and they have nothing solid. There have been some rumors of activity in that area but nothing specific. Their main thread is that marijuana grown in British Columbia – known as "B.C. Bud" – is very much in demand in California, Nevada and the Pacific Northwest. It sells for a premium, as it is highly potent. They grow it by hydroponics and have managed to up the potency considerably. It is also showing up "on the street" in good quantity – so, it's getting across the border somehow. There are also complaints from the Canadians that cocaine and guns are getting across to their side of the border. They've caught nothing in the area but there are rumors of two-way smuggling with marijuana being exchanged for guns and coke."

"Thanks for that," replied Janet. We also hear rumors to that extent. I guess we await more analysis on the arrow and more probing on the identification of Mr. Westley Miller. We have a couple of

----

undercover agents roaming the Chesaw area listening to local gossip but nothing new there. Hope we get a break soon.

Chapter 6

After an overnight flight from Gatwick, England, British Airways Flight BA2043 was on its final approach to Male' International Airport, the Maldives, for on-time arrival at 09:20 local time. Hazel Branson marveled at the pristine view from the window of the aircraft. The sun was intense. The sky was clear and she could see the bright, calm sapphire-blue ocean which was dotted with small, flat, sandy islands barely above the level of the ocean, many with barrier reefs and clear lagoons speckled with low-rise resorts – most had thatched huts on stilts which were linked by boardwalks. Just as the plane was landing, she could see an island about half a mile away filled with high-rise buildings which seemed to take up every inch of the land. That island seemed no greater than a mile long and half as wide.

The aircraft touched down on a landing strip built on the lagoon and, as the aircraft slowed, she could see the airfield was very narrow. The plane went to the end of the runway where the apron was wide enough for it to turn around and then doubled back along the runway to a taxi-way leading to the terminal's small parking apron, just off the middle of the runway, with barely enough space for six large aircraft. Hazel noted aircraft from Sri Lanka, Japan, Thailand, Russia and Germany at the terminal.

The purser's voice came on the speakers announcing their arrival, welcoming them to Male' airport and advising the local time and temperature. He noted the airfield was on its own separate island but linked by road to a new suburban island of Male', called Hulhumale, which had been dredged out of the ocean. For those traveling to downtown Male', there was a pedestrian ferry service available for the seven-minute ride. Those going to resorts would be met as they exited Customs and Immigration and taken to their waiting boats or seaplanes.

The purser cautioned all passengers that this was a Muslim country where importation of non-Muslim religious materials was banned, as was the importation of liquor or drugs. For those going to tourist resort islands, liquor was available at the resort. Male' city proper and its suburban islands of Hulhumale' and Viligil, however, were dry areas although the airport hotel on this island served liquor. He also cautioned that Muslims found nudity and public displays of affection offensive, prompting resorts to respond with rules against full nudity. He also advised ladies to cover up if going to a native populated island, as shorts, short sleeves and bare heads were frowned upon.

Directly after that announcement, one of the pilots welcomed everyone and advised there would be a short wait for a parking spot as space was very limited.

Hazel sat beside Joseph in First Class. Both had managed to take advantage of the full beds and get a refreshing night's sleep. Holding her hand, he gave it a little squeeze and said, "Not like our place in the Florida Keys but pretty nice, just the same."

"Well, darling, life is not dull! You've managed to take me to many lovely spots for second honeymoons over our twenty-nine years of marriage. I'm looking forward to this romantic getaway where we can play newlyweds."

"Yes, dear. But remember, I do have to get a little business done too. However, it looks as if I'll always be back in plenty of time for dinner. My contacts tend to go to prayers in the early evening."

"Not too much time on business, please. Let's take a little time for ourselves too."

He patted her hand. "Yes, dear, I promise."

Hazel reflected back on her twenty-nine years of marriage, which had produced three handsome sons and a daughter whom Joseph called the "spitting image of her mom." They had met when Joseph had come to visit her father, then the Chief of the Midlake Band. Life had begun at that point when he swept her off her feet in a fast romance. Luckily, the romance had never faded and they made a strong partnership, both in bed, as a family and in business.

Hazel was, in the opinion of all who met her, a native beauty with fine features, long jet black hair, the long fingers of a pianist, and a slim, leggy frame. She had excellent bearing, cultured manners and a pleasant personality that had been perfected at an exclusive women's college in Ontario. On top of that, Joseph had told her many times that he loved her brains, perception and business sense, assets that had made her his most trusted partner.

Deplaning and processing through Customs and Immigration was quick as no visa was required. Upon exiting the restricted area with a porter bringing their luggage, they spotted a man holding a sign with their names. He greeted them and escorted them a short distance out of the airport to a dock and a waiting boat. They began to feel the heat and the hot sun on the way to the boat. It was about 95 degrees Fahrenheit and near 100% humidity. The boat was locally made, a sleek forty-six feet of fiberglass with a covered passenger lounge and cockpit, powered with twin 250-horsepower outboards – similar in appearance to many others loading passengers at the docks. They waited for three more couples to join them, then cast off.

The ride, at about thirty miles an hour, took them an hour and fifteen minutes away from the airport and the island city of Male'. The boat brought them to a resort on its own small island. The resort blended in to its physical surroundings. It was a jumble of thatched huts, many on stilts over the water that were joined by boardwalks and others nestled on shore along the beaches. The main beach, sparkling white sand dotted with small sailing craft, jet-skis and kayaks pulled up on shore or tethered to mooring buoys, was inside a protective jetty. A concrete pier came out from the right side of the beach extending for about three hundred feet. At the end of it was a large building with roofs overhanging and shading outdoor patios that housed a bar and restaurant. On the lea side of the island, vacationers with surfboards and parachutes were harnessing the wind for some great surfing. At the end of the jetty, on the windward side, about half a dozen surfers were enjoying six-foot curlers.

The guests were welcomed and escorted to the reception building in the center of the island where they were met with welcome drinks and cold perfumed hand towels, then given a lecture on the amenities of the all-inclusive seven star resort. They were told the resort was the only facility on the island and that behind the scenes, the resort strove to be environmentally correct, making fresh water from the sea, utilizing a state of the art sewage treatment plant which recycled water for toilets and gardens, generating some of their electricity from solar panels and wind turbines to supplement the diesel power plant, and recycling. They had a hydroponics garden for growing their own vegetables, herbs and fruits, such as melons, lettuce, basil, mint and tomatoes.

Amenities included a full-function scuba diving facility with dive boats, guides and instructors and a master underwater photographer. There were also kayaks, sailboats, surfboards and equipment for wind and parachute surfing and jet skis with instructors for all equipment and sports. The resort boasted the first full-view underwater restaurant, made entirely of Plexiglas. As well, the resort had a beauty salon, oriental massage parlor, five restaurants, seven bars and room service. Access to the resort was by boat or seaplane. The concierge could arrange excursions to other islands, deep-sea fishing or aerial sightseeing and photography. Communications were excellent with cell phone service, internet by wi-fi, satellite HDTV, and excellent local cell phone service.

Joseph had selected a cottage on stilts over a lagoon. Once they had been escorted to it and shown the features, such as the privacy patio with hot tub, their own two-person kayak which was tethered to their own private dock, TV, Wii and gaming console, four-poster bed with mosquito netting, a ceiling fan, and air conditioning, Hazel hugged and kissed Joseph, saying, "It's beautiful! Let's go for a swim, maybe also a little kayak ride. Let's enjoy the day!"

Joseph, fiddling in one of his suitcases, found his satellite phone, inserted the batteries and turned it on. It worked. Full charge. "Fine darling, but first, let me make a call to arrange my meeting for tomorrow. I'll have to get the concierge to charter a fast boat or seaplane for me for tomorrow to take me to Igor's yacht. It's sitting offshore from Bandos Island Resort where our clients are staying. I won't be long. Go get changed and freshen up. I'll be right with you."

When Hazel emerged from the bathroom in her gold string bikini which accentuated her light caramel skin, Joseph had completed arrangements and was changing into swim trunks. He looked up when she entered. "Wow! Gorgeous as ever! Come here love. The swim can wait."

Their first kiss led to a tight hug and a deeper longer kiss, then falling on the bed in a writhing embrace, quick removal of bikini and trunks and very passionate sex. After a little rest and cuddle, they spent the rest of the day sunbathing, kayaking, snorkeling and walking the beach. They had drinks and dinner at the lounge/restaurant on the pier where they watched the sunset with other patrons and enjoyed a gourmet seafood dinner.

The next day, Joseph was up with the dawn for a twenty-minute jog barefoot on the white sand beach. Then a shower and breakfast by room service for him and Hazel. At the patio table where they had breakfast, Joseph looked at his watch. "Well, it's about time I wandered down to the pier and met the plane."

"When do you expect to be back? What time should I book dinner?"

"I'll be back before six o'clock. The planes don't fly at night and the pilot will want to be back at base by nightfall. I gather sunset is around six thirty. Let's have dinner about nine, if that suits you. What are your plans for the day?"

"Well, I booked a three-tank dive around some outer islands which probably will return around 4 p.m.. Apparently, the manta rays have migrated in and there's a cleaning station nearby where they come in to scrape off parasites and have little wrasse fish nibble at the parasites. There's a great chance we'll get to photograph some. Then, perhaps I'll indulge in a massage. We can visit the bar before dinner and catch the sunset, I guess."

"Sounds good. Shall we try dinner in the underwater restaurant? Don't different fish come out at night? Up to you though. Remember to be careful of the sun on your first full day in it! Bye love!" They hugged and kissed.

About 7:30 a twin engine de Havilland Twin Otter aircraft rigged with seaplane pontoons landed, taxied into the lagoon and, with engines cut at the last moment, drifted nose first up to a low portion of the dock where a waiting resort worker secured it. Joseph was to be the only passenger. Upon boarding, he gave instructions to the pilots as the plane was pushed off. The pilots started its engines, taxied out of the harbor and took off. Fifteen minutes later, the plane flew over Bandos Island, providing Joseph a great aerial view of the resort, which seemed almost deserted, then circled around a large white yacht, about three hundred fifty feet long, anchored two miles off the south side of the island opposite the harbor. Joseph knew about Bandos Island. It was one of the first resorts in the Maldives. It encompassed the whole island with sprawling cottages but also boasted conference facilities with a large capacity.

The plane landed and taxied up to the yacht where part of the stern had been lowered to water level, making a dock. The yacht was huge, with five decks above the waterline. The roof of the top deck and the mast behind it sprouted a vast array of communications aerials and dishes. One deck above the waterline, on the stern flagstaff, where customarily a flag is flown identifying the country of registry of the ship, a flag of the small island tax haven of Mauritius was waving gently in the offshore breeze. Upon the landing approach, which circled the yacht, Joseph noted the name *Blue Northern II* on one side and the same, but in Cyrillic letters, on the other side. He also noted a blue polar bear logo on the front of the wheelhouse below the panoramic windows.

He had also seen four small Zodiac boats, equipped with large outboard motors, lazily circling the ship, keeping about a half-mile distance. He knew this was added security to keep the uninvited away from the ship. Below and behind the wheelhouse were a hangar

59

and a landing deck for a helicopter. There was a second helicopter deck on the bow. The hangar door was open, revealing a small helicopter and two men in white jumpsuits working on its engine.

Joseph stepped down the plane's short ladder to the right side pontoon then off its tip onto the waterline dock of the yacht. The stern had been folded down to make a flat deck at the waterline as a dock for the small craft. This left a gaping hole in the stern revealing a storage room for the watercraft. He noticed racks of jet skis, surfboards, kayaks and diving tanks, underwater sleds, outboard motors, and an empty rack, which must have housed the inshore boats that were out doing picket duty.

As he set foot on the deck he was met by a slim, tall, handsome, blond haired, blue eyed and well sun-tanned man. He was barefoot, wearing white slacks and a soft blue polo shirt with a gold and silver monogram of a polar bear on the left breast pocket. This was Igor Romanoff, a notorious Russian entrepreneur and known arms dealer. He didn't look his sixty-three years.

Joseph well knew his history of ruthlessness honed in the bureaucratic in-fighting of the KGB and Kremlin of the former Soviet Union. When the new Russia was formed, Igor had managed to grab significant corporate assets at fire sale prices, often simply taking over by rule of force. He had been careful to play the diplomatic game with the emerging and aspiring leaders in the political turmoil of the new Russia, assisting all parties financially and with his large and growing network of contacts at home and abroad. He made it clear he never wanted a role in politics and this had enabled him to develop his empire without interference.

It was rumored that his major partner was the Russian government. In the new Russian order, he also played a role in intelligence gathering. The yacht was one of two he currently owned. Both had cost upwards of US$400 million. There were rumors to the effect that military analysts classified the vessels as auxiliary Russian navy vessels (Intelligence Gathering) but the paper trail of ownership on the *Blue Northern II* rested entirely with one of Igor's companies registered in the tax haven of Mauritius.

The plane was pushed off by two deckhands in white uniforms. It quickly turned away, taxied and took off. After a strong handshake and bear hug, Joseph said, "Igor! It's great to see you again!"

"Same here, my friend! Come, no talk until we are in the secure room. There are too many trying to observe and listen in." He

----

led Joseph into the interior of the ship, down one flight of stairs and forward past four doors on the left (port) side which Joseph knew to be crew state rooms, then opened an unlocked door on the right side and entered. Joseph followed. The interior room was a communications center of some kind, spacious with a round "lazy Susan" board table that could double as a dinner table and plush chairs for eight. It was windowless, as Joseph knew he was in the center of the ship.

At one end of the room there was an array of radios, computers, flat screen TVs and other electronics with two people working at computers – a man and a woman of obvious Russian-Nordic appearance, casually uniformed in white pants and polo shirts. Igor pushed a button that brought down a partition from the ceiling separating the boardroom from the communications area. The wall of the partition contained an illuminated map of the world. Then he turned to Joseph. "Now we can talk."

"Things have been a bit hectic here since the "clients" arrived," Igor began. Both the Taliban and Al Qaeda have sent people. They have been in discussion among themselves for the past three weeks – trying to come up with a common position and exploring contingencies. Next week, emissaries from the Afghan government will arrive to begin peace and power-sharing discussions. I doubt if it will lead to anything for a while as both sides are poles apart but the one thing they agree on is that they want to see NATO troops out of the country. I suspect they will be here for months, as most seem to be enjoying the warm ocean and the beaches. They've rented the whole resort and had the management cut back on workforce, laying off all the foreign workers and retaining only enough local Maldivians for their needs.

"The Maldives is a perfect neutral ground for all sides. First, there is no visa requirement and all are welcome. It is, after all, a Muslim country so there is added tolerance. Bandos Island is remote enough to be fairly secure – save for the electronic snooping. I understand there are at least six governments engaged in electronic eavesdropping. Some of it we have intercepted. Some of it is so obvious that even the Taliban have resorted to putting things in writing and passing notes among themselves. I have made some secure rooms aboard available to them for private discussions, which they have made good use of. We, of course, listen in. I made up a prayer room for them in a stateroom, and one of my cooks can do Afghan, Pakistani and Saudi meals, so they are happy.

"Today, our Taliban clients came aboard from Bandos Island before dawn as we did not want prying eyes. But before we greet them, let me fill you in on progress for our venture. We have secured an option on Minora Fushi Island in Baa Atoll under the guise of it becoming a research station to develop cultured blue pearls and research the pharmacological potential of some sea life. It will be a good location for distribution to Africa, the Middle East and Asia. We can have the island on a thirty-year lease as part of the Maldivian government's economic stimulus.

"The island is only fifteen hectares and, although a bit remote – away from others on the outer edge of the atoll, it is fairly close by water to an airfield that has seen little use but will soon be extended by the Maldivian government. It's called Hanimaadhoo – has the IATA code HAQ and is on Haa Dhaalu atoll. The government has recently declared it an international airport and established a small Customs and Immigration office. Right now the airfield is a bit short, but you can get a 727 or Russian equivalent, even a stretched 737 in with a full cargo load if the plane is equipped for short airfield landings. You know, all that means is that the aircraft have brakes on the front landing wheels in addition to the standard brakes on the main landing gear."

"Igor, I'm impressed how quickly you have things coming together. Let's discuss this further after we deal with our Taliban friends. Shall we meet them?"

"Of course. I presume we remain agreed on the terms and conditions? Shall I do the talking? Better to have just one talking or they will try to divide and conquer."

"Agreed. I'll stick to product demonstration. You handle pricing and delivery terms."

Igor pressed a button on the table and a man, dressed in white uniform, entered the room. Igor told him, "Stephan, you may bring our clients." Stephan exited and soon returned with four bearded men, all similarly dressed in brown and tan shades of their traditional Afghan salwar kameez pants and tops plus vests. Each had different head coverings – two in turbans (lungee), and two more in kufi hats with no brims. All bowed individually when introduced and each said *Salamat* or *May Allah be with you.* It was soon obvious that all were fluent in English and that all had been educated outside of their native country or countries.

Once they were seated around the board table, tea had been served, pleasantries exchanged and the servants excused, Igor said,

"Gentlemen. It is a great pleasure to welcome Joseph again. As you know, he promised to bring something of interest for your cause. Joseph, perhaps you will demonstrate?"

"Thank you Igor." As he began to speak, he reached under the table by his seat and produced a box. He stood and ceremoniously placed it on the table. All eyes were riveted on the box. "Gentlemen, before you is a secret weapon that has been deployed to some NATO forces special commando-type troops. It has been a secret since it was introduced in its basic format in the 1980s. Since then, it has been refined, capacity and accuracy upgraded. It is silent, compact, not bulky or awkward to handle, easy to conceal, non-metallic and deadly. Like the AK 47, it is rugged. It has been designed and proven to work perfectly under extreme abusive conditions from hot, sandy deserts to muddy paddy fields and the very cold arctic. It still works well even when impeded by foreign substances, such as sand, mud or snow. In fact, it also fires accurately under water – but with a shorter range.

"Out of the water, it packs a significant punch. It's accurate at 300 meters, or 330 yards, and remains deadly at 1000 meters, or 1100 yards. It has a muzzle velocity of 710 meters per second, or 2,300 feet per second, if you like. That's similar to an AK 47. However, it has far more muzzle energy, or mass, due to the size of the projectile.

"It's made completely from carbon fiber. Thus, it can pass through metal detectors. When broken down, the largest component is 60 centimeters, that's two feet, long. Total weight varies between 1.5 kilos for the basic version without projectiles, to 3.5 kilos with infrared optics and laser sights and a full magazine of projectiles. The version I am about to show you has a magazine of 10 projectiles."

One of the Taliban, who had been introduced earlier as Mohammed Adul, spoke up. "You keep saying projectile. What type of projectile?"

"I'll get to that. First, let's take a look at the weapon." At that point, Joseph lifted the lid of the box, took out the weapon and gently laid it on the table in front of the men. It looked similar to a rifle with a 24-inch barrel, a receiver housing the trigger and the firing mechanism and a stock. Nestled onto the stock was a handle that was part of the trigger guard, reminiscent of a lever action rifle like the Winchester 73 or a Daisy air rifle. At the bottom of the receiver was a chamber about 30 centimeters, or 12 inches, long, which seemed to be where the magazine would feed projectiles into the breech. On top

----

of the receiver was a series of screw holes. "You see these screw holes on the receiver? They are for night vision and laser scopes." Along the right side of the stock and the barrel housing were two clips for a carrying strap. At the base of the stock, there was a circular cap, which unscrewed to reveal a chamber containing cleaning and adjustment tools.

Laying a scope and laser sight on the table, Joseph said, "Various scopes fit but we suggest this one. It has variable magnification from 1.5X to 5X and is a dual day/night scope. It weighs just less than a kilo and is very rugged. It uses two lithium-ion batteries of a very common size. The small laser sight mounts on the stock under the barrel. It's very compact and weighs little. We recommend the green, rather than the red laser."

"Now, Mohammed, to answer your question." Joseph reached beneath the table again and produced two items and laid them slowly on the table. The larger object was about a foot long by an inch and a half wide and 5 inches deep. Looking down into it from the top, one could make out a number of arrow-like shafts clipped in. Joseph pointed to the single shaft that was beside the magazine. "This is the projectile. It's just like a crossbow arrow but a bit smaller. The shaft is carbon fiber. It has tail feathers, just like an arrow, that pop up when fired. The shaft has a removable tip that can be changed to a variety of delivery ordinance ranging from carbon tip – as you see now – to full metal jackets, dum-dums, explosive and poison tips." He pointed to the larger object and said, "This is the magazine. It holds ten arrows."

"Explosive tips?" asked another Taliban, who had been introduced as Saqulain Hassan.

"Yes, in case you want to go shark hunting. Underwater."

This met with a roar of laughter and the comment from Saqulain, "We have some land based "sharks" too!" and more laughter.

"You said accurate. How accurate?" Mohammed asked. "And silent, how does that work?" The others nodded.

"It's silent because the firing mechanism is a coiled carbon fiber spring which is recharged by lever action. Depending on the gunner, it can fire at a rate of one shot every two seconds. Let me show you a video of the weapon in use. I am sure you will enjoy the part where the shooter splits his first projectile with a second from 100 yards. The video will also take you through loading, choice of sights etc., use in various conditions, stripping and maintenance – by the way, there is very little maintenance."

After the video and follow-up questions, Joseph turned the meeting over to Igor who said, "Now gentlemen, I am sure you will want to test this yourselves. We will up anchor and move to a spot where we have less chance of being observed. We will set up a target for you. In the meantime, let's have morning tea, then give you time to discuss this and other matters."

Once anchored in a more secluded spot, the crew set out targets on inner tubes. The target practice went well with three of the four Taliban scoring bulls eyes on their second and third tries at 100 yards when the weapon was rigged out with a scope and laser. One of the men, Abdul Kosair, was chided by his companions for missing the bull's eye but blamed his inaccuracy on having to wear trifocal glasses.

"Now, my sons," he retaliated, "do not speak ill of your elder like that. I learned to shoot a moving target from a galloping horse in the best Afghan fashion but not with trifocal glasses! Let me remove the scope and laser. Then I'll show you." He removed the scope and turned off the laser, stood up, quickly aimed and got a bulls eye at one hundred yards on the first shot. "There, the old war horse can still shoot!" His companions laughed and clapped him on the back.

After lunch and noon prayers during the trip back to the anchorage, the meeting resumed around the board table. Igor started off. "Well gentlemen, now that you have had time to test the weapon, what do you say?"

Mohammed responded, taking the lead. "We have tried your marvelous weapon. We have discussed it. Yes, we can see where it would be a beneficial addition to our arsenal. But you have not told us the price or delivery conditions. We must now begin serious negotiations."

"Well stated, Mohammed," Igor responded. "I am pleased you like the weapon. It has remained an important and secret NATO covert weapon but now, with some difficulty, we are able to obtain some for you. If the price was right, how many would you want in the first order and where and when would you want delivery? As you know, delivery location and speed of delivery has to be factored into the price and can be a significant cost."

"We feel we would like to begin with a thousand weapons, five hundred arrows for each, and ten percent spare parts. As for arrows, to begin with, we will take forty percent in carbon fiber, twenty percent in dum-dum, ten percent in explosive and the rest in full metal jacket. We also want the full rig on sights, all to have the dual day/night vision with variable magnification scopes and green laser sighting. Each weapon to be individually packed in its own box with 100 arrows equal assortment then packed in an outer box of ten. Additional arrows to be packed in cases of 100 equal assortments. As far as delivery F.O.B. point, how about Osh, in the Fergana valley of Kyrgyzstan? We use that airport a lot and probably would not attract suspicion. We can transfer to our aircraft there."

"Well, gentlemen, give me a few moments to calculate this out. Do you want to see this broken out on a per unit basis as well as total?"

"Yes. Then we can refine this if need be. It is also dependent on the form of payment you wish."

"Our price will vary with the terms of payment, of course, depending if you pay in gold, a hard currency, such as Euros, Yen or U.S. Dollars, or if you wish to pay in a commodity like opium or refined heroin or a combination of this."

After a few minutes, Igor came up with a price and explained it. The Taliban then recessed to discuss it and returned about twenty minutes later. Negotiations then began in earnest. After two hours hard bargaining a deal was struck: $5 million in round figures based on delivery to Osh airport, Kyrgyzstan within 120 days in exchange for a deposit of $1 million in gold held in trust at a Swiss bank to be turned over on delivery, another $1 million US Dollars upon delivery wired to a bank in Belize and the balance in raw opium.

Considerable time was devoted to settling on the weight of opium for the US$3 million value. They reviewed the average value others were paying for shipments crossing the Afghanistan border in the current harvest period. This was also compared to the average prices for getting raw opium out of the next nearest large producer area, the so-called Golden Triangle of South East Asia, which included Hanan province of China, Northern Thailand, Laos, Viet Nam and Miramar. They settled on US$500 a kilo, which meant 6,000 kilos would have to be transported, refined and marketed without upsetting the current prices in the distribution system.

Upon handshakes to seal the deal all round, Igor turned to Joseph and said, "Well, my friend, a good day's work! Let's call in your plane and get you back to your wonderful wife. Shall we meet again tomorrow, same time, same place?"

"Absolutely. We have much to discuss. Now, let's join our guests for tea before the plane arrives."

During the tea break, in a ceremonial fashion Joseph presented the box containing the weapon, sights and ten arrows to Abdul Kosair, leader of the Taliban group. "Abdul, gentlemen, in honor of our deal, please permit Igor and me to present you with this sample of the weapon. I have included some carbon fiber tips for the arrows, rather than metal ones, so that you can easily get this through security screening devices. I am sure you will want to demonstrate it to your comrades at home. I suggest you put the components in separate pieces of baggage. The sights have some metal in them and the shape of the scope may draw some attention at screening."

Abdul said, "Thank you Joseph and Igor. You are most considerate. We welcome the sample weapon and, indeed, will quickly put it to trial use. As far as security screening, there will be none as we have a charter flight arranged to travel home. May Allah be with you!"

The seaplane picked Joseph up and returned him to his resort by 5:30. Time for a swim with Hazel and lingering on the beach to watch the sunset. Time to help Hazel remove her bikini and play on the bed when they got back to their lodgings. And time for a couple of leisurely drinks on a lagoon side patio bar with other guests before descending the ramp through the Plexiglas tube into the underwater restaurant. At night, the restaurant offered a spectacular 180 x 360 degree view of the ocean. The light of the restaurant diffused and seemed to magnify under water, attracting curious fish and allowing a great glimpse of the night marine life. Bliss.

Next day, Joseph was back on board the *Blue Northern II* with Igor to work out the logistical details of the deal.

"It was great thinking on your part to take the opium instead of refined heroin," Joseph commented.

"Yes, my friend. I wouldn't trust them for quality control when refining. Besides, it gives us an option to produce either heroin or morphine base depending on the market opportunities. Right now, I tend to favor the majority of it in morphine base or even fully refined into morphine, as many of my arms clients want it. It's the major reason for setting up the facility on Minora Fushi Island. I appreciate you providing the expertise to set up and run the lab. It was convenient that the archery weapon deal came along. I could have brought in people from Russia or the Golden Triangle to do it but I think your people will work out better. After all, the lab will only run periodically when shipments come in and your people can easily handle the jobs by flying in for the occasions."

"My people will think of it as a perk, a chance to get some vacation time in a tropical paradise after each job is done."

"The island will also serve as a quiet place to assemble weapons and serve as a logistics center for transshipments."

"Good point. However, it's harder for me to distribute my share as morphine base or morphine. It's easier to trickle heroin into the organized crime system where I'm from."

"Be careful, my friend. Those entrenched in the traditional distribution systems do not like interlopers. I'll be pleased to sell it for you into the international arms deals."

"I'll see. My biker friends have a national distribution system. If they cooperate, I'll have no problem. Besides, I can get a much higher profit margin. In the meantime, now that we need to start a pharmaceutical company, I guess we can call that option on the island and get a lab organized. I presume we're still in agreement that we are equal partners on the lab."

"Yes. Of course, in consideration that you supervise and provide the lead chemist and experts to refine the opium, run the meth and hydroponics operations and supply technicians to manufacture the archery weapons."

"Agreed. But in consideration, except for the marijuana hydroponics, the other operations will be periodic, "when needed" so that I can continue operations in Canada."

"Agreed. Also, I will be supplying opium from other deals you will not be participating in, but you will run the refining operations on that for ten percent of the production."

"Agreed."

"The bud and meth production and sales is strictly a fifty-fifty proposition but distribution will not be into North America as I am already there."

"Agreed. From this location, I am looking at East Africa and the Middle East as the main opportunities for the meth, and bud. Most of the customers will be the ones purchasing arms as well."

Igor was making a list of things to do, checking each off as they discussed it. "You have given me an extensive list of equipment for the lab and grow op," he said. "I have the construction in hand. I have secured a prefabricated cookhouse, dining room, recreation quarters and machine shop from a construction auction in Turkey. They are being loaded on a ship as we speak along with all other construction materials and equipment. The living quarters will be individual cottages of concrete block and metal roofs. We'll also make the lab and a warehouse out of concrete block. I have a construction crew on the way from Bangladesh and an engineering firm from New Delhi contracted to do the construction. They shall be arriving on the site within ten days. Next is transport of the opium and the weapons."

"Time is a factor. It would take at least six weeks for a container to travel by sea to a port, then be transshipped overland to Osh. Best ports of entry may be Istanbul, St. Petersburg or Vladivostok. What about by air either all the way or from a seaport?"

"For control, a charter air freighter all the way would be best. We can easily disguise the weapons as aircraft or machine parts as far as customs clearance is concerned. Wherever they land for refueling, there's no need for customs inspection. As long as the papers and onward flight clearance is in order, they travel "in bond." The same aircraft, if it is a tramp, can easily load up in Osh and bring the opium down to the Maldives. Only problem is ensuring the tramp charter operator assures discretion and their aircraft has a clean reputation and the required airworthiness certification to land in Canada and such. We need someone who has done this before and will not draw attention of the authorities."

"I know of a small charter company based in London, England, which has an office in Toronto, said Joseph. They have a retrofitted 727 with short runway capability plus other aircraft. I've used them before."

"I bet that's the Gopal brothers, those crazy Punjabis. Right?"

"Yes, I've used them occasionally. A few months ago, I had them move hemp fabric from Manitoba to France. How do you know them?"

"Guns and medicine to Africa. Clothing from China, the 'Stans and India to Western Russia, France and Africa. Whatever. I've used them a number of times. They are reliable and discrete."

"OK. Shall I make the arrangements with them? I'll set one condition that they don't let their father near the deal or fly the aircraft. He's a crazy lunatic since he screwed up that deal with the Georgian mafia to set up an airline to run between India and London."

"Good, if you're going to do that, why don't you handle the arrangements for a safe and secure reception in Osh. We must budget for that."

"Will do," agreed Joseph. "But first, I'll have to get back to Canada to push production of the weapons. We'll easily be able to cover the deadline. I have all the carbon fiber I need but getting that quantity of sights will be a problem."

Igor shrugged, spread his arms wide in an expansive manner, smiled and said, "You have a partner, remember? My business is arms, remember? I'll ship the sights to you from my Miami warehouse – it's a legitimate sporting goods wholesaler/retailer and we even sell to Homeland Security agents. Price will be the normal wholesale for that volume. Only hitch is the goods are under Government Export Restriction but your specialty is border crossing, so I think no problem. I can make a paper trail of legitimate sales for the scopes to cover any governmental audit at my company. Where do you want to take delivery?"

"I always like delivery close to the border. I have a warehouse near Omak, Washington. That's about fifty miles from the border. It's staffed during working hours. It would be a good spot. You could even ship overland with one of the major parcel services."

After a few more hours of planning and an elegant lunch, Igor said, "My friend, I think we have covered most of the considerations. I just received an e-mail that the down payment of gold has been placed in trust for us at our Swiss bank, so we are moving right along. I will set up the lab. You will set up transport and you have weapons production well in hand. It is up to you to decide if you wish to take a share in heroin or let me distribute it as morphine base. We can decide that later. Anyway, we base our partnership for this sale of the archery weapons on splitting the gold, dollars and raw opium equally after all expenses including manufacturing the weapons and producing the pharmaceuticals. We will ensure fairness on the deal. After all, this is just one of many."

One of the crew knocked and entered to advise that Joseph's plane had arrived. Igor and Joseph walked back to the stern to the waiting floatplane. The two shook hands, exchanged a strong bear hug and Joseph said, "Thank you, Igor. We have always worked well together and we go back a long way. I look forward to this deal."

Joseph climbed over to the plane's right float and clambered up the short ladder into the fuselage. One of the pilots closed the door. The plane was pushed off from the stern of the ship by two of the ship's crew. The pilot started its engines, drifted away from the ship, turned, taxied and took off.

Back at his resort, Joseph and Hazel exchanged reviews of their day, found time to swim, laze on the beach and watch the sunset. After they made plans for dinner, he helped Hazel with her bikini, which ended in a shared shower. Joseph decided he deserved a few days of scuba diving with Hazel and, for a final day, a tour of Male'.

Chapter 7

After a week, Janet was at her desk in Seattle. Frustratingly, there had been nothing developing on the case and she was working other cases as well. She answered her telephone on the first ring. The caller said, "Hi Janet, it's Hector from D.C. Anything new since our conference call last week?"

"Hi Hector. Not much. The agents in Provost, Utah managed to track down a driver's license renewal for Mr. Westley Miller. The real Mr. Westley Miller was not aware of it. The head shot photo is not very helpful. It doesn't look like the real Mr. Westley Miller though. They're trying to trace through facial recognition but it's been a slow process. The license was mailed out to the address of the real Mr. Westley Miller. It must have been intercepted and that looks easy enough as he's away at work during the day when the mail is delivered to mail boxes in the foyer of his condo building. They're also trying to see if any new credit cards have been issued to Mr. Westley Miller that he's not aware of."

"Slow going. Nothing new in the area of the crime scene?"

"No, I'm sorry to say. We still have a couple of operatives undercover roaming the area as tourists looking to buy some land but they haven't picked up any leads. Nothing surfacing from all the agencies of Homeland Security, the DEA or ATF either."

"Well, I have something for you. How about a trip to D.C.? Can you make it by tomorrow early afternoon?"

"Sure, Hector, I'll make arrangements and let you know my ETA. But why so mysterious?"

"Sensitive stuff, Janet. I want you with me when we meet a few of the players. Bye."

Next day, when Janet arrived at FBI Headquarters in Washington, D.C., she showed her identification, hung it around her neck, signed in, and was escorted to Hector Skog's office. He jumped up from behind his desk and came toward the door to shake her hand. He ushered her to sit on a plush chair facing a coffee table, then he went and sat in an equally plush chair opposite to her. He poured coffee for the two of them from the carafe on the table, then sat back, looked her in her eyes and said, "It's great to see you! I'm sorry to have been a bit mysterious but you will understand soon enough."

"No problem. But I must admit to being curious. Is it something to do with the Border Patrol case? Has Quantico made any progress on that arrow?"

"You're in the ball park, Janet. Quantico has made great progress on the arrow. It turns out to have a military connection. They took it over to military intelligence and things have ping-ponged around the Pentagon. We have an appointment in a few minutes at the Pentagon with a colonel in the procurement section. It's a bit strange. Normally each branch of the military handles their own procurement but his section handles procurement of some items for various branches of the military and other government agencies. It's taken a while to arrange the meeting as we had to get security clearance and they took some time after being contacted with the problem. As it is, the level of security clearance still restricts what they feel able to tell us. Shall we go?"

After finally finding a visitor's parking space somewhere reasonably near the Pentagon entrance they had been told to enter, and after having their credentials verified, they were issued visitor's passes and then escorted through the labyrinth of halls, finally entering the waiting room of a Colonel Malcolm Drake. A young woman in Navy uniform bearing the rank of lieutenant shook hands with both and greeted them. "Hello, welcome. I'm Lieutenant Diane Prescott. I'm one of Colonel Drake's aides. Follow me, please. The others are waiting in conference room C-9W."

She led them a short way down the hall and into the conference room. Seated at the table were four men and two women. One man, who was in the uniform of a naval Chief Petty Officer, had a steno machine for taking notes.

The Colonel stood up along with the others and welcomed Hector and Janet. "Hi, I'm Colonel Malcolm Drake, welcome to this little portion of the Pentagon. Permit me to introduce the others: Mr. Martin LeRoy, from the Canadian Embassy; Dr. Lorraine Willows, from your Quantico forensics lab; Ms. Ruth Dempsey from Homeland Security. I am sure you know; Mr. Roger Pearson from the Canadian Embassy; and Chief Petty Officer Bob McIvar, our recording secretary."

After all were seated, Colonel Drake took the lead. "I have to caution you that this matter touches on some classified information but I am confident you will learn all you need to know. As well, let me remind you, although we are taking formal minutes of this meeting, some information you may learn is classified and may not be revealed in a court of law. Am I clear? The presence of Mr. Pearson and Mr. LeRoy will be understood later.

"O.K. Let's talk about your arrow. Dr. Willows has maintained your chain of evidence. The arrow, or projectile as we often call it, has not left her custody. She has been present at all times when our people examined it. She and her lab staff must be complimented for their thoroughness and ability to identify the projectile as a military weapon and in contacting military intelligence about it. Eventually, our intelligence people passed this matter on to my department, which is responsible for procurement of, ah, let's say clandestine tools for all branches of the military and some, ah, agencies. In short, the projectile fits a weapon we have purchased.

"This prompted a physical inventory of all armories storing the weapon, verifying our inventories of both weapons and projectiles. That is why we were a little slow in responding. Dr. Willows was sworn to secrecy on this and could not reveal the nature of the exercise to her superiors or counterparts. I am happy to report all our weapons and projectiles have been fully accounted for.

"We also did a spectrographic analysis of the carbon in the projectile looking for "telltales" – chemical additives we require incorporated in the material that will identify it as a U.S.A weapon. There were none. No markers were present for any of the NATO countries that also use the weapon. That led us on a trail back to the manufacturer. That involves the Canadian Embassy here in D.C. and the presence today of Messers Pearson and LeRoy. You see, the weapon and projectiles are made in Canada. Mr. Pearson, would you like to explain, please."

"Thank you Colonel. Canada and the USA have a mutual defense treaty, as you know. We also are both members of the NATO pact – The North Atlantic Treaty Organization. The significance of this is an agreement enabling weapons manufacturers to sell their wares to all member countries once they have been proven and adopted in their home country.

That is the case with this weapon and projectile it fires. In this instance, the manufacturer is a corporation, Belanger Arms, owned by the Government of Canada. The weapon and projectiles are manufactured at one of its plants in Ajax Ontario. As the projectile did not contain the trace elements of any of the member countries, this has us worried. Could there be a leakage from our plant? This prompted us to contact the Auditor General's Office in Ottawa and they responded immediately with a "flying audit" – that is an intense unannounced audit of the plant.

The audit did not find anything and that has us worried, of course. Perhaps an employee or employees or ex-employees are freelancing or others have copied the product. We are tracing that, but so far nothing has come to light. We have interviewed all employees and subjected them to polygraph but nothing. We have wiretaps in place at the plant and employee and ex-employee's phones and cell phones, but nothing. We are doing new background profiles of all employees and ex-employees but nothing has surfaced to date. At this point, let me turn this over to Monsieur Le Roy."

"Thank you, Roger. We have our "feelers" out in the criminal scene of Canada but little has surfaced. We also traced back the origins of the weapon. It was invented about 1986 by a Metis in Vancouver, British Columbia, by the name of Kenneth Davidson."

Janet interrupted. "Excuse me, but what is this Metis?"

Martin Le Roy said, "Sorry. That's a Canadian term for a person of half aboriginal blood. Usually the product of a marriage between an aboriginal and another race – more often French Canadian. In this case, Kenneth Davidson had an aboriginal mother, full blooded, from the Iroquois tribe and a Scottish-French father. Both deceased. The parents produced two sons, Robert, now age fifty-five and Kenneth, now age sixty-one. Both sons have much of the father in them with flaming red hair and green eyes. The mother was a high school teacher of physics and the father was a mechanical engineer. The sons were raised as a prosperous middle class family in a good neighborhood in Winnipeg, Manitoba.

"Both graduated with honors degrees in mechanical engineering. One, Kenneth, started a firm building and installing heating and air conditioning systems in Vancouver. He later got into heat pumps at an early stage and made some technological advances. Robert is a bit of an opposite to Kenneth. He's a follower and detail oriented, a great administrator. He partnered with Kenneth in the Vancouver business as the number two in charge of operations – in charge of the details. This left Kenneth to handle marketing and to experiment and invent – which he was good at.

"Anyway, Kenneth invented the weapon as a better way to pursue his passion of hunting with a bow and arrow – but he replaced the bow with the "archery weapon" that he invented. He presented it to the Canadian military and they bought into it. In fact, they took it over, restricting sale to others in an exclusive arrangement. This frustrated Kenneth as he saw potential for greater sales volume and the Canadian Government assisted him by opening up sales to other NATO countries – but through their control. They reached an agreement to buy him out – worth millions. He sold exclusive rights of manufacture to the Canadian government – and he went away satisfied, with a pocket full of money, but restricted from free-lancing. They also tied him up under an ongoing contract for developmental research on advancements to the weapon and this has paid off handsomely for both with many innovations and bucks in his pocket."

"And where are Kenneth and Robert now?" Janet asked. "Have they been checked out?"

"Robert is no problem. He accepted the position of President of the division of Belanger Arms that is producing the weapon. He is comfortably settled in Ajax, Ontario with his family – wife and four children. We checked him and them out most thoroughly and have him and his family under surveillance. They seem clean."

"What about the other brother, the inventor, Kenneth?"

"Well, Kenneth is another story. He had a messy divorce two years ago and seems to be reeling from that. When he took the buy-out, he retreated to the Shuswap Lake country in British Columbia. His hobbies are hunting and fishing and he's a passionate conservationist. He's a renowned fly and fishing lure expert, making his own.

"He bought into a mechanical engineering firm installing geothermal heating systems in that area but has not been too active in the business other than inventing a new system – which, apparently has not worked very well. He settled on an Indian reservation on twenty acres with waterfront along Shuswap Lake and built a five thousand square foot log home. The closest town is Salmon Arm twenty miles away around the lake.

"We sent officers in to interview him but he was not home. Apparently, he's gone on holiday for a few months. His neighbors say he travels a lot to Eastern Canada and out of the country. We have his recent travel records but nothing significant except he seems to go to Colorado for skiing and Rotan for scuba diving. His trips within Canada are all to Ajax, Ontario which coincides with his visits to the factory and its research department or to Whitehorse, in the Yukon where he hunts. We found no local love interest but we are still researching that angle. He gave no forwarding address or e-mail contact to his neighbors but we got his e-mail address from his brother. He isn't answering his e-mail. His ex-wife is mad at him and has no idea of his whereabouts. A review of her telephone records and a peek into her computer confirms no contact. I feel he bears further follow-up and that is underway. We're still tracing his acquaintances, financial transactions and business dealings."

"That is very thorough and much appreciated information," Janet said. "Thank you. What department are you in?"

"Let's just appreciate the information and not delve too deeply into the Canadian bureaucracy, shall we?"

"But how may we reach you if we have follow-up questions?"

"I am resident liaison at the Canadian Embassy here in D.C. No problem to reach me 24 / 7/365. I'm at your service." He passed business cards across the table to Janet and Hector.

Janet asked another question, this time directed to Colonel Drake. "Colonel Drake, can you describe this "archery weapon"?"

"No. I am sorry, Janet, but that is classified beyond your level of clearance. You need to focus on the projectile, arrow as you call it, and we have given you our full input there. Everybody, I think we have exhausted the topic of discussion. Hector, I presume you will liaise with our Canadian friends and allies on further developments. I call this meeting adjourned. Thank you all for attending and, Janet, I hope you resolve this little mystery."

"Colonel, you're not helping us if you're unwilling to reveal the weapon," Janet replied. "How can we have our agents searching for it if we're not allowed to know what it looks like?"

"I am sorry, but right now, that is all I can reveal."

Ms. Ruth Dempsey from Homeland Security spoke up. "I have been brought up to speed on this issue by our ICE and CBP people. They've been active in following up the murders and trying to trace the smuggling that probably caused it. The regional IBETs team, which involves agencies on both sides of the border, has been searching for indications of drug or firearm smuggling and following up on the people-smuggling apprehension that was concurrent to the murders. The VTF, BVIC and border liaison officers have also been involved and we have been coordinating with ATF and DEA. Unfortunately, so far, nothing has surfaced."

Colonel Drake rubbed his temples with both hands and said, "Ruth, you guys are as bad as the military! You just ran off a list of codes or alphabet soup an outsider like me finds hard to follow. What is VTF, BVIC et al?"

Ruth blushed a bit and said, "Sorry Colonel, each organization likes to hide behind acronyms as a shorthand – possibly as a way to speed things up or create exclusivity. Let me explain them: ICE, you know is Immigration and Customs Enforcement; CBP is the newer label on Customs and Border Protection; IBETs stands for the Integrated Border Enforcement Teams composed of ICE, CBP, the US Coast Guard, the Royal Canadian Mounted Police – i.e. the RCMP and the Canada Border Services Agency – CBSA. You know ATF for Alcohol Tobacco, Firearms and Explosives and you know the DEA as Drug Enforcement Agency. WVTF is our Weapons Virtual Task Force and BVIC is our Border Violence Intelligence Cell. I'm afraid we have many more acronyms in our lexicon."

"Thank you Ruth. It's all Greek to some of us without a list of acronyms. That helps. And now, may we adjourn?"

"Where do we go from here on this one?" Janet asked Hector on the short drive to the Ronald Regan airport. "Wait it out until the Canadians find and interview Kenneth Davidson? I'm at a loss for other leads. We possibly wouldn't know the weapon if we saw it and I guess we're not allowed to pass what we learned today down to our investigators. We might get a break on the Mr. Westley Martin identity theft and we'll pursue that but what else?"

"Very little else, so far," commented Hector. "You're doing everything I would do. Maybe the undercover team will unearth something. Perhaps the Canadians will make some progress. Perhaps the Provost, Utah office might pick up on something. I do think the killer brought the weapon across the border and went back with it. Guess we have to be patient."

Chapter 8

British Airways Flight 84 from Vancouver, Canada, touched down at London's Heathrow Airport on time at 1:30 p.m. local time. He traveled light with only a carry-on bag, made good time through the immigration line and was waved through customs. It was a short walk across the lobby to the taxi stand where he queued up for his turn for a taxi. He directed the driver to take him to an address in Hemel Hempstead, about an 80-pound ($150) fare, which pleased the driver.

The taxi eventually pulled into a country lane, through a gate and up a long gravel driveway to a large, Victorian-style manor house. He paid the driver and got out of the spacious back door of the traditional British taxi. The door of the house opened and a tall, slim and white turbaned East Indian came down the stairs to greet him. He was about age forty-five, sporting a trim black beard. He was impeccably dressed in a very expensive and perfectly tailored tan Seville Row suit, with light blue silk tie, matching handkerchief in his breast pocket, and brown Gucci loafers. They shook hands and exchanged bear hugs.

This was Rishi Gopal, younger, by two years, of the two Gopal brothers, Rishi and Paul, who owned and operated Cashmere Air Cargo. They had taken over the business from their father, now an elderly seventy-eight year old beset with Alzheimer's. The boys, like their father, were "old money" and were part of an extended family of seven cousins, an aunt and an uncle, benefiting from a family trust which now amounted to billions of dollars.

Ancestors had earned the original wealth over centuries operating a trading business and, since the 1800s, an influential chain of one hundred twenty newspapers based in New Delhi, India. Although financially well off, the boys sought adventure. This had included stunt flying, base-jumping, paragliding and mountaineering in their youth. The family compound of rolling farmland was large enough to have its own grass airfield which their grandfather had put in for Ashok, their father. Their father learned to fly and had over one thousand hours logged before he could legally drive a car. He attended Royal Air Force College Cranwell and became a transport pilot in the RAF.

He left the service as soon as possible and started his own air cargo service, beginning with an old Douglas DC6. The boys had

NightHawk Crossing By C. Edgar North

followed in their dad's footsteps and were accomplished stunt flyers before they entered university. Upon graduation from Cranwell each had short, but distinguished, military careers in the RAF as fighter pilots. They were quickly absorbed as pilots in the family charter air cargo business, thriving on the variety and risks.

Rishi spoke first. "I say, Joseph, so good to see you again! It's been about eight months, what?"

"Right, Rishi! It was at the Winnipeg Airport when you picked up my cargo of hemp cloth for Marseilles, France. That was my trial shipment. The cloth now goes by container ship. I vividly remember having a time convincing a Canada Customs officer that hemp cloth is a real product and currently high value enough for airfreight. They went over the cargo with a finetooth comb – sniffer dogs and all. Anyway, the cloth went into designer jeans."

"I bought a pair the other day, supposed to wear like iron. Talk about pricey though, three hundred euros for the pair. How did you get into that venture, if you don't mind me asking?"

"No problem. I'm a major investor in a three thousand hectare farm and cloth factory on an Indian reservation near Winnipeg. Turns out the land is great for a hemp crop. It took quite a few years to convince the government bureaucrats that we had bred a quantity of hemp seeds with very low Cannabis THC and high CBD to win approval and certification as industrial hemp. We're under strict and constant government supervision but the project has turned out to be a success story as the cloth is far stronger than cotton. Currently, the military is testing it for clothing and canvas and we're anxiously awaiting the results."

"Sounds as if you know a bit about the subject."

"Yeah. Well, look at it this way. If you can modify the plant to increase potency of cannabis, you can also reverse it."

"That's why B.C. Bud earned its reputation for high potency, I guess. Now, Joseph, you will be my honored guest for the night. What time is your flight tomorrow? I can drive you to the airport."

"Thanks Rishi. I very much enjoy your hospitality. The flight is 3 p.m. tomorrow. I'll be going to Istanbul then on to Bishkek. We'll need some time to discuss business. As I mentioned on the phone, I have a charter for you."

"I know, your partner Igor called. It's great to see the two of you working together again. Now, let's get you settled. I had the upstairs maid prepare the blue room in the West Wing, the one you had last time. Tea is at four p.m. and dinner will be formal at eleven o'clock – there's a tuxedo your size in your closet. We'll have drinks and family time before, in the library beginning at nine. Did you get some rest on the flight over or do you want to rest and freshen up now?"

"I got the bed service in First Class, so managed to get a great sleep. No, I'm ready to discuss business now, if you are."

"Righto then. Let's adjourn to my study. Igor filled me in a bit but the devil is in the details."

"How is your dad doing?" Joseph asked. "I hear he hasn't been too well. Also, I gather your brother, Paul, is flying right now. I'm sorry I'll miss him."

"Yes, Paul's making a few round trips between Galveston, Texas and Port Harcourt, Nigeria right now moving some oil and gas processing equipment. He's flying our AN 124. It's our largest craft – good for 150 tons of cargo. As for dad, sad to say, Alzheimer's has taken over. We had to put him into a care home a few weeks ago. You know about his fiasco trying to set up that air service from Delhi to London with that airline in Uzbekistan? It took its toll on his health. He was never right after that."

Over several hours the details and costs began to take shape. They took one break to have tea with Rishi's family where Joseph became reacquainted with Rishi's wife, Mindy, her mother and father, Rishi's mother and Karpeet, the youngest daughter, who was home from boarding school on a break.

About 7:30, Rishi said, "O.K. Let's sum up what we have agreed on so far – at least as far as my notes go. We pick up your cargo in Kelowna B.C. – no problem there with runway length, refueling etc. and it's a cargo hub with export customs. We still have to determine your description of the cargo and the name of the recipient for the manifest, bill of lading and such. All refueling and airport fees are at my expense, included in the cost of the charter.

"The flight plan will be a great circle Arctic route, refueling in Anchorage – no problem about being inspected as the cargo will not be offloaded and we will be considered "in-bond." We will have obtained pre-clearance to over fly Russia and Kazakhstan on a common flyway so we will not be off the beaten track. I will arrange landing at Osh in the normal way – I doubt any problems as we have been there before. You will arrange for security at Osh at your cost. I will arrange for refueling at Osh and for cargo handling equipment and cover landing fees. As mentioned, all fueling and landing fees are paid by me as part of the total charter price. We estimate ground time in Osh, including cargo handling, refueling and filing the onward flight plan, to be two hours and I would like to shorten that somehow.

"We need a "cover" manifest, bill of lading, clearance papers stamped etc. for landing and departure cargos to pass approval of the authorities at Osh and you will attend to that as part of arranging security. I do not want to over fly Afghanistan or Pakistan on the way down to the Maldives so we will file a route over Tibet, Bangladesh, Eastern India and Sri Lanka where there is reasonable air traffic control. I need to learn more about the airfield at our Maldives destination. Haamaadho? It's easier to call it by the IATA designation of HAQ. I gather it once was a British field during and after WWII and you say the government is upgrading it. As they have already declared it an international airport, the navigation aids must be up to par. What are they flying into there now?"

"They're running domestic flights between there and Male' with Bombardier Q400's. There's also a Russian four-engine turboprop freighter running from Male' up to there on occasion and some private jets of holiday-goers and investors. There are also a few seaplanes based there serving the outer islands."

"The Q400 is a nice aircraft – a little hot rod. However, we've got a 727 that can go where they go. I'll check this out though. We won't be too heavy landing and we'll depart empty. Our 727, although it's a retrofit with modern engines, is a thirsty bird. I'll have to ensure they have sufficient fuel for me. As HAQ seems pretty remote, they may not get fuel delivery too often and probably budget it for their normal flights. If we can't book ahead to reserve some fuel, we can pack a bladder of fuel, enough to get us out to Colombo, Sri Lanka."

"Excellent!" said Joseph.

"Now, I presume you'll be riding with us all the way?"

"No, I'll meet you at Osh. I want to be sure of the security there. I'll ride with you from there. David, my son, will accompany the cargo all the way from Kelowna. He'll handle the loading in Kelowna."

"OK. Now to my price. It's take it or leave it and, of course, it has the risk factor built in."

After a few minutes, they settled on a price, which included costs to deadhead the aircraft from Toronto to Kelowna and from the Maldives back to London, and landing fees and accommodation for the crew for one night each in Kelowna and Colombo.

Joseph asked, "Rishi, can't you pick up cargo for the empty legs from Toronto to Kelowna and Colombo to London? This should be applied to my costs if you do."

"Consider it part of the risk factor fee, my friend. Yes, I'll list the availability of the aircraft on the Baltic Exchange for both those legs. I'll probably be able to pick up cargo from Toronto to Calgary, Vancouver or Edmonton and probably from Colombo to London. But, consider it gravy if it works out. It's also dependent on fixing the travel dates. If we do that, the dates cannot be altered. As it is, you're getting a deal because the aircraft will come from Toronto and not London or, if you look at it in reverse, you are not being charged to return the aircraft to Toronto. Tell you what I'll do though, if we pick up a charter on both or either of the dead head legs, I'll refund half the fuel cost for that leg."

"OK, OK. You have a deal."

They shook on it and Rishi said, "I'll have my secretary draw up the contract. It will be ready for signing tomorrow before you leave. Your flight is at three p.m.? That gives us some time in the morning to play. I have a new aerobatic plane I made from a kit. I'll take you up in the morning."

"You made it?"

"Well, I and some of our mechanics did. Don't worry. It's been certified airworthy. It's quite safe. I won't pull too many G's on you but let's go up before breakfast anyway. I don't want you messing up my new plane. We have a very low mechanical default rate on our aircraft. I have a little trick I learned from an ex-WWII B29 pilot – you know, they were the first pressurized aircraft and very unreliable. Anyway, after every major repair, we always take the bird up for a test flight."

"So, doesn't everyone do that?"

"Yes, but we take the mechanics who worked on the bird up on the test flight. That seems to keep them on their toes."

Feeling snookered into a crazy flight, Joseph said, "All right. Let's go flying in the morning. But do you have any suggestions for labeling the goods out of Canada? I need to have covering papers. You know the Osh region, what do you suggest?"

"Well, the most common thing is materials sent to Afghanistan or Uzbekistan from some charitable organization, like the Red Crescent, Islamic Relief Fund, or some other type of non-governmental organization or charity. I wouldn't use the Islamic Relief fund as that may draw attention in non-Muslim countries we pass through but it would probably work well going into the Maldives. Perhaps you change the paper work at Osh. One set for the goods being dropped off there and another set entirely for onward to the Maldives? Maybe Igor can help. He's very good at it.

"In the meantime, we've got just three-quarters of an hour to get dressed for drinks and dinner. Shall we adjourn? By the way, I have a new young chambermaid, Sargeet, who is very accommodating. I've asked her to help you with your bow tie. She'll also draw your bath for you but don't take too long. Mindy doesn't drink and frowns on me drinking alone. Sargeet will also warm your bed for you."

Pre-dinner drinks were a family affair with all members of the family present. Each was expected to describe their day, beginning with Karpeet, the youngest, and Mindy's father last. Everybody was expected to comment on each other's day. Promptly, at eleven o'clock, a maid whispered in Mindy's ear and she announced that dinner was ready. They proceeded to the dining room, which held a long table capable of accommodating forty guests. Places were set at one end of the table with Rishi taking the seat of honor at the end. After a lovely five-course dinner of French cuisine and great Bordeaux wine, all retired for the night.

When Joseph entered his bedroom, a soft light on the nightstand illuminated it. As well, there was a nightlight throwing a soft light from the bathroom. Sarjeet had prepared Joseph's bed and was lying in it, smelling of rose water perfume and wearing a very slim black negligee.

Joseph sat down on the bed and Sarjeet reached her warm hand up his leg and started to message his manhood. Joseph, after a few moments, turned and kissed her gently on the lips. Once, twice, pushing his tongue in deeper, while she slowly moved her hand up and down till he felt he could no longer wait. He suddenly pulled back and said, "Let me freshen up." Gently, he moved her hand onto the bed, then went into the bathroom.

When he returned, Sarjeet seductively got out of bed and helped him undress. She knelt in front of him as she pulled down his pants and jockey shorts exposing his very solid manhood. Joseph stood for a few moments while Sarjeet caressed and tongued him. After a moment, she looked up at his face and said, "Would you be more comfortable in bed?" Gripping his erection, she backed onto the bed pulling him with her.

After ensuring Joseph was content, a very satisfied Sarjeet

slipped out of the bed shortly after two a.m. She was glowing. She was fulfilled and Joseph was sound asleep. She blessed the old woman in her native village in Gujerat, India, who had trained her to a master's level in the art of *Kamma Sutra* – how to give and enjoy sensuous sex in multiple forms. Joseph, with a little gentle guidance into various positions and stimulation techniques, gave as much pleasure as he got, enabling her to experience three orgasms. She was sure he enjoyed it and that he was also exhausted.

Joseph was up early, in time to get in a little jog around one of the paths on the front of the property. He was showered and waiting in the foyer when Rishi joined him. A servant had brought a Land Rover SUV to the front door and they took it a short distance behind the manor to Rishi's private airfield. It was a grass strip about half a mile long. Mid-way, about one hundred feet off to one side was a large shed, which Joseph discovered to be a hangar with a small office on one side. On the roof was a pole with a bright orange windsock. At either end of the hangar on the roof were flagpoles, one flying the Union Jack and the other flying the flag of India. The hangar door was open and two mechanics were pushing out a small airplane. It resembled a low-wing crop duster but it was far sleeker. It reminded him of a Spitfire from WWII but it had a raked tail and rested on tricycle gear, rather than the two-wheeled Spitfire, which dragged its tail. Joseph remarked to Rishi, "It's beautiful! Does it fly as well as it looks?"

"Indeed it does. It's a kit plane from Novus Nomad. It has a modified fuel injected Lycoming IO-360 producing over 250 horsepower. Top speed is past 150 miles per hour. It's got four stage electronic flaps, disk brakes, 100-yard takeoff, 130 yard landing roll and will climb at over 1500 feet per minute. It's got twin seats and controls. It even has an emergency parachute. In aerobatics, it will pull up to +7G to –3.5G. It gives a good ride!"

Joseph groaned inwardly but put on a brave face. "Rishi, how many hours have you got on this?"

"I've logged about seven so far. I'm still learning its capabilities. But don't worry. I won't push it with you aboard. In fact, you can even take the controls for a barrel roll and back loop or two! Let's mount up."

It turned out the ride was not as bad as Joseph had feared. Rishi took the craft through a series of climbs, dives, rolls and loops and Joseph managed to hold it all in. Joseph took the controls for five minutes where Rishi assisted him through a barrel roll and a back loop. They landed safely, with Rishi at the controls, taxied up to the hangar, shut down and got out. Rishi said, "Hey man, that wasn't so bad. You didn't bring anything up. Did you enjoy it?"

"Rishi, it was excellent! That is one fine aircraft. You've got it mastered. But I still prefer helicopters."

They returned to the manor for breakfast with the family, then retreated to Rishi's office where they reviewed the contract the secretary had drafted. After a couple of minor changes, a final version was produced and jointly signed. The deal was sealed by Joseph transferring, by his laptop computer, a down payment of $250,000 to Rishi's corporate account in Guernsey, the Channel Islands. After lunch, Rishi deposited Joseph at the airport, where Joseph quickly made it through ticketing and security to relaxation in the first class lounge, then on to the aircraft, which departed three minutes late.

Joseph spent the night in Istanbul at the Sheraton Hotel near the airport. After a leisurely breakfast, he chartered a taxi with a driver fluent in English who was willing to give him a personal tour of the city. For lunch, his guide took him to an excellent restaurant along the waterfront on the Arab side of the city. He boarded the Turkish Airways 5:50 p.m. flight to Bishkek and managed to get a little sleep before landing at 3 in the morning.

He was greeted at the airport by a travel service, which had a car waiting to take him to the Hyatt Regency, in the center of the business district. He got into his hotel room by 4:30 and promptly went to bed. His meeting was not until late afternoon.

Joseph woke to his bedside alarm at 2 p.m. He opened the blinds in his room and was greeted by a bright, sunny day. In the distance, about fifteen miles away, he could see majestic mountains, part of the Himalayas, with the peaks of the higher ones covered in snow.

After a shower, he went to the coffee shop in the lobby for a sandwich and espresso. He next found the business office for hotel guests and had a copy made of the photo page of his passport and the page bearing his visa. He put most of his money and all his credit cards and his passport in a safe deposit box at the front desk. He kept the photocopied papers in his pocket, in case he was stopped by the police and had to produce identification. Bishkek had been the scene of political upheaval recently and the police were not very well paid. One had to be prepared for robbery or, as was very common, ransom by police officers who had a habit of stopping foreign-looking people, asking for identification and refusing to return their passports until "lunch money" was handed over.

Planning to catch a taxi, he walked out of the lobby to the street. He walked up to the row of waiting taxis and the cluster of drivers who were chatting, some smoking. He selected one of obvious Russian lineage named Serge, who was most fluent in English.

From his previous visit in 1999, Joseph knew the Russians who remained after the country broke away in the collapse of the old Soviet Union were discriminated against. They had dominated during the Soviet era, discriminating against the native Kyrgyz. Now the Kyrgyz were getting payback. Tens of thousands of Russians had migrated to Russia and those remaining tended to be confined to menial jobs.

They agreed on the taxi fare – U.S. dollars were preferred. The taxi ride was a short seven minutes but Serge apologized for having to take a slight detour due to crowds demonstrating in front of the government buildings on Fruenze Boulevard. Eventually, the taxi pulled up to a corner with a six-story Soviet-era building housing *The All Texan Bar and Grill*. Joseph paid Serge and exited the cab on the curbside.

He looked at the front of the bar and grill, noting that not much had changed. They still had their outdoor patio with multi-colored sun umbrellas advertising various international cigarette brands and beers and the waitresses were a very pretty selection of young Russian girls who all had the same costumes – blue denim short shorts, spike high heels accentuating smoothly tanned legs and white short-sleeved blouses with plunging necklines revealing major cleavage.

Joseph walked through the patio and into the main dining room. This was a large room fronted by a bar running the full length of one wall. The bar was complete with a brass foot rail, high stools with wrought iron captain chair-style seats, hammered copper counter top and a counter top to ceiling ornate beveled mirror behind shelves of bottles and glasses. Centered on the top of the mirror was a set of long horns bearing a brass nameplate: *Texas Long Horns*. On the wall opposite the bar hung a State of Texas flag. The back wall had a curved arch leading to a foyer with an elevator and a stairwell. Along that wall were blown up photos of a cattle roundup, cattle branding and an assortment of photos of cowboy stars. Behind the bar was a dark-haired crew-cut Russian-looking man, about age 50, sporting a black handlebar mustache. The bartender. His costume was a long-sleeved red and white vertically striped shirt with a red bow tie and a waist-high apron wrapped around his blue jeans.

A very lovely blonde waitress, tall in her high heels, approached Joseph and he asked for a table. He was escorted to a corner away from the entrance, to a picnic-style table for four, and presented with a menu. He ordered a beer and a Texas Longhorn Burger with fries. Sipping his beer and awaiting his food, he had opportunity to survey the room. There were about a dozen patrons, mainly Caucasian men, inside. Outside, the patio bustled with about thirty more. There was one beautiful, long-legged, raven-haired waitress in costume, sitting on a stool at the cash register end of the bar. She was sipping a beer and talking to a blonde man, about 35 years old, slim, six foot two, dressed in blue jeans, and cowboy shirt, snake skin cowboy boots. He looked up, saw Joseph, then excused himself from the woman and sauntered over.

"My gawd, Joseph! It's been a while! How are you? Did you come by motorcycle again?"

Joseph stood to exchange handshakes and a bear hug. The man called for a beer for himself and another for Joseph, then sat at the table while Joseph's dinner was served. "Well, Steve," said Joseph, "you're looking good, a little bit older but good just the same! Long time? Yes it has been. I was last here in '99. No, I flew in. Tell me, how's your dad? How's your brother Jed? What about that gorgeous Natasha, is she still hanging around your dad?"

"Dad's fine. Business has been great! Even with the changes in government, he still has his contacts. Jed married one of our waitresses a few years ago and they have twin girls, now age two. Me, I'm fine. I'm still single but, you know, being in charge of hiring for the bar and grill gives me lots to choose from. I don't think I'm ready for one woman yet. Natasha finally cornered dad in a weak moment. Although he swore never to get married again after that messy divorce in San Francisco, they were married nine years ago and are loving it. Jed and I now have two new brothers and a sister. They've been busy – you know how it is with long winters. Did you come here to see Dad?"

"Yes, Steve. Maybe we can do a little business."

"Great! Finish up and I'll take you upstairs."

On their way, as they passed a waitress carrying drinks, Joseph said, "I see you still have a sharp eye for Russian young ladies. They seem as young as ever."

"We have a high turnover, Joseph. The girls earn good wages and great tips but they're very anxious to get a leg up, so to speak. Our clientele is mainly male ex-pats: foreigners stationed here and single. There's a lot of attraction. I lost three last month alone to guys from that big gold mine that's an international joint venture. Most of the internationals that work in the country have been selected because they speak Russian, or they have to learn it. Best way to learn a language is in bed. Right? Anyway, there's no shortage of young lovelies wanting a chance to meet a dream ticket. We always have a waiting list of applicants. Many have been learning English and Turkish."

They went into the back room and walked up one flight of stairs to Arnold's office. Steve used a key to open the hand-carved solid wood door, which opened onto a reception room. Behind the reception counter along one wall were a few offices with glass partitions looking out into the reception area. As they walked into Arnold's large corner office, he got up from behind his desk, where he had been working at a computer, and hurried across the room. "Joseph! I saw you on the security monitor. It's great to see you again. Did you come by motorcycle again?" Arnold was sixty-three, with wavy blond hair, cornflower blue eyes, thin at one hundred eighty pounds and six feet tall.

In 1999, Joseph and three friends had bought Russian motorcycles in Vladivostok then traveled across the southern portion of the former Soviet through Russia, Mongolia, Kazakhstan, Kyrgyzstan, and Uzbekistan to Istanbul, Turkey. They had driven into Bishkek, discovered the *All Texan Bar and Grill*, and stayed for a month enjoying the company of Arnold, the boys and the waitresses. After a very messy divorce in San Francisco, Arnold had landed in Bishkek in 1989, just after the country had separated from the Soviets. He established the bar and grill, appealing to the swelling numbers of foreigners coming in to establish diplomatic ties, assist the new government, establish donor projects, and open up business.

He had become highly successful in the turmoil of a collapsed economy by nurturing impeccable relations with the new governing elite, those approaching it, emerging entrepreneurs and by co-opting impoverished bureaucrats. Shades of the old Bogart movie Casablanca, which was his favorite, he earned the reputation as "the fixer." If a foreign mining company wanted exploration rights, they saw him to make it happen. If you wanted to buy a fleet of MIG 21's from the government, you saw him first and last. If you wanted to

89

establish a car dealership for imported autos, you saw him. He'd become wealthy from his commissions and investments.

His sons, Jed and Steve, joined him in 1991. They took over management of the bar and grill and ran errands for their dad while they learned the business.

"Great to see you too, Arne," Joseph responded. "It looks as if life has been treating you well! No, I'm afraid no motorcycle this time. That was the trip of a lifetime! I came by air – to see you actually. I have something going that would benefit from your assistance."

"Well then, pull a chair up to the desk and tell us all about it." The desk was Russian style with an extension in front of it, forming a "tee" where it is customary for the visitors to sit and have their own desk space. Steve sat on one side of the "tee" and Joseph took the other side.

Joseph explained the situation. He had an air cargo going into Osh which would be exchanged for another cargo also being brought in by air and he needed Arne's assistance to ensure security on the ground and clearance by the authorities.

Arne said, "I presume you don't want the authorities questioning the true nature of the cargo? And I assume you want me to make sure the proper documents are on hand and cleared/certified by the right authorities?"

"Right on both counts. It's the sort of thing you're very good at."

"OK, so you're flying cargo in from Canada. And the cargo is going onward after the exchange to where? Afghanistan, Turkmenistan or Northern Pakistan maybe? This may be best under the guise of a donor agency. I can give you documentation for a legitimate donor involved in that region in agriculture development. That should cover any type of tools, seeds and farm implements so it may fit your, uh, products. Any thoughts on labeling the goods you get in exchange?"

Joseph said, "Well, they're going to a new research lab in the Maldives. That leaves room for a lot of creativity. I was thinking of chemicals, perhaps construction materials. Any suggestions?"

"Yeah. That's wide open. High value construction chemicals, such as concrete hardeners, epoxies, mix additives for self-sealing cracks – good for building water tanks. Same high value stuff one flies in when building concrete bridges in remote areas. I can give you a reasonable list of items and documentation that would pass muster and bore the hell out of inspectors."

"Great," said Joseph. "Can you provide a high level of security for me and my pilots when we are on the ground?"

"Of course. Don't trust your customers?"

"You know the old adage: "Respect them and suspect them." I always want my back covered."

"OK. I'll have a crew of my people watching out for you. Steve will lead it on the ground. I'll grease all the government people, including the mayor and the police chief, the local police and soldiers, customs inspectors, airport personnel, etc. My people will unload and load the cargo for you. The papers will be in order – signed and stamped by all the right people. No one will inspect the cargos. You will have no problems that way. You're dealing with the Taliban? I have worked with them through Osh before on 'cargo transfers.' I haven't encountered a problem. With them, they honor their agreements at least."

"Yes, the Taliban. And now for your fee?" Asked Joseph.

"Normally, I take a percentage of the full value of the deal, like five to fifteen percent. For you though, my old friend, I'll give you a flat fee: $200,000 U.S. dollars of which fifty percent is paid in advance to my bank in Cyprus and the balance by electronic transfer prior to your departure from Osh. But that discount fee is dependent on one thing: You must join Natasha, Steve, Jed and me for dinner tomorrow. I'd like you to meet the youngsters, then we'll leave them with their governess and have drinks and a quiet dinner and exchange updates. Natasha and Jed would love to see you!"

"That would be great! Let's arrange the wire transfer now. Can we work on the paperwork tomorrow?"

Joseph was not surprised to find his taxi driver, Serge, waiting for him when he left the bar and grill. Serge said, "I work for Arnold as well as drive taxi. Steve asked me to look after you while you are in Bishkek. Where can I take you now? If you have time, I can get you a ticket to the opera. *Aida* is playing tonight. The orchestra conductor is very good! He's Mongolian but trained in Kiev."

Joseph wound up spending the evening at the opera, which was very close to his hotel. He bought a ticket for Serge and they were tenth row front and center. The orchestra conductor, a native Mongolian-looking Kyrgyz, was excellent. The music was profound and the singers were in top form. Not bad for the equivalent of five dollars each for tickets, plus the four-dollar bottle of champagne they consumed at intermission. He got a good night's sleep.

Serge arrived next morning at ten o'clock and they took a long walk through parks, past the circus building and the casino and then had a leisurely lunch at one o'clock on the patio of a restaurant on Fruenze Street. Serge got him to his meeting with Arnold and Steve at the appointed hour of three. The paperwork brought them to seven p.m. when Arnold called it quits and took Joseph up by modern elevator to the sixth floor where the elevator opened to a massive marble-floored and walled vestibule. Centered in the wall opposite to the elevator doors was a large, solid rosewood door set in an over-large, carved rosewood frame. Arnold used a key to turn three deadbolts and opened the door to reveal a long hallway, also in marble flooring and walls. They walked along it to a large living room, which held a grand piano, and a couple of conversation areas with tan leather sofas and chairs.

Arnold said, "I own the building. I took the top floor for our residence. It's just about 10,000 square feet. The boys each have apartments on the floor below. Plus I put in a gym on the fourth floor, mainly for the kids but it has a workout area we share. On the third floor we have a steam bath, hot tub and sauna and a lap pool. It helps keep us busy through the long winters. Ah, here's Natasha!"

Natasha made her entrance from the arched dining room with arms widely outstretched. She was blond, with a duck cut curly perm, a slim, busty five foot six. A pair of black designer slacks complemented her long legs and her white open-necked short-sleeved blouse accentuated her ample bosom. She was wearing delicate gold sandals showing hot pink painted toenails matching her fingernails and lipstick. She wore a large diamond wedding ring with gold band and a large gold pendant and chain. The pendant was of an ornate design holding three large, oval brilliant cut blue sapphires that were balanced by three round brilliant cut diamonds. She ran up to Joseph, hugged and kissed him on the cheeks. "Joseph! So great to see you! I still have fond memories of your visit when we went with you and your friends on the motorcycles for a picnic in the mountains. Remember, we visited Adul Buriev, Arnold's friend who ran the agriculture college?"

"Natasha, you are as beautiful as ever! Yes, I remember. Lunch was an eight-course marathon of a meal laced with too many vodka, beer and wine toasts and I had to eat the sheep's eyeballs! We couldn't really leave until our host passed out and fell backward into the stream – and it wasn't before four o'clock that he did that. Thank goodness, half way through we got up and walked around the compound for a few minutes between each course while our host continued to drink with the other guests. And then, you taught me how to discreetly spill my drinks to cut back. I still don't know how we all made it back here safely!"

"Those were the days. Footloose and fancy free! Well, as you can see, things have changed here. Come and meet the children. Jed and Tina are with them."

Natasha led him by his left arm down the hall to a room where there was a fifty-two inch flat screen TV on which five children and a man and woman were intensely watching the English version of Mary Poppins. All were towhead blonds with blue eyes. Jed jumped up and greeted Joseph, exchanging bear hugs. "Joseph, great to see you again! It's been a long time man! Here, this is Tina, my wife, and those twin girls over there are Judy and Sue. They're two years old next October."

"And the rest belong to Arnold and me," chimed in Natasha. "There's George, Mike and Lisa. Oh, and here's Anna, our nanny, she will take over. We can adjourn to the front room for drinks."

After the maid served drinks, Arnold made a toast: "To a great old friend. Welcome back."

"Thank you," Joseph responded. "Great to see you all prospering and such a great family. I vividly remember my first visit. The country was so poor that the government employees hadn't been paid for six months and people were stealing anything from the collapsed businesses and even public fixtures that they could convert into cash. It was dangerous to drive or walk down the streets or sidewalks for fear of falling in an open manhole because someone had stolen the lid to sell as scrap metal to China."

Arnold replied, "In the years since you have been here, the country has had its ups and downs. There has always been a lot of corruption. Now, we are again in a down period with government workers unpaid for the past four months, the President and his family thrown out of office, riots and much uncertainty. Mind you, that makes government workers very interested in cold hard cash, which is helpful for me."

After a few drinks, the maid entered and signaled discreetly. Natasha clapped her hands and announced: "Dinner is served, everyone. Joseph, I had cook prepare mutton, just in your honor!"

"But I don't have to eat an eyeball this time, do I?" All laughed as they proceeded into the dining room.

The next day, Serge took Joseph to the airport. On the way, they were pulled over by a police officer with a radar gun. Serge pulled a few dollars out of his pocket, counted some out, and then left the car to talk to the officer. When he returned, he had no ticket. Joseph asked, "How much did that cost?"

"Five US bucks for the bribe. I don't mind. He caught me legitimately. I was over the speed limit. He's not been paid wages for months. He has to eat."

Joseph had an uneventful trip home broken with an overnight in a five-star hotel at Schiphol, Amsterdam's airport.

Chapter 9

Janet answered the phone on the second ring. It was Hector Skog. "Hi Janet, it's been about two weeks since you were out here in D.C. Time for another visit."

"What do you mean? Has something come up at your end on the Border Patrol murders?"

"There you go, clairvoyant as ever. Yes. Can you make it here by tomorrow afternoon?"

"Still playing with classified stuff, are we? I'll send you my ETA in a few minutes."

"Yep, classified again. See you tomorrow."

Next day, after they had settled in comfortable chairs around the coffee table, Hector said, "The Pentagon people have a flap on that involves the archery weapon. One assassinated an Afghan tribal leader in the town of Kheyrabad in the North of Afghanistan. Problem is, he was loyal to us and the arrow doesn't have any military telltales. We have a meeting with the powers that be in the Pentagon in forty-five minutes. It's with higher-ups this time. Let's get going."

After the usual parking traumas and check-in at the Pentagon, Janet and Hector were escorted into a meeting room in a different area than their last visit. They were greeted by an officer who introduced himself as General Keith Baker in military intelligence. Present at the meeting were: Martin Le Roy and Roger Pearson from the Canadian Embassy; an army sergeant by the name of Sue Ann Martin, who was the recording secretary; a Mr. Sanford Crosley, representing the C.I.A; a Ms Caroline Weston, representing the State Department; Ms Ruth Dempsey from Homeland Security (DHS); and an army captain, Adam Chavez, who was the General's aide.

After introductions and the opportunity to get self-serve coffee from a carafe on a credenza along the far wall, General Baker opened the discussion. "Thank you for coming. Colonel Drake filled me in on your visit and the murders related to the projectile sample you presented. I have also reviewed the minutes of your meeting with him. I am afraid the situation has progressed from your two murders in Washington State. The same type of projectile was used to assassinate an Afghan tribal leader in Northern Afghanistan – a leader loyal to us. The assassin got away cleanly. It's troubling to us to link two crimes, literally halfway around the world, to the same projectile.

95

"Our tests on the second projectile reveal no telltale markers and spectrographic analysis reveals the same composition as the first projectile, so we can assume this killing was not the work of us or any of our NATO members. What is troubling is the fear that someone is manufacturing one of our classified weapons and it is getting into the hands of the enemy. We must put a stop to this."

Roger Pearson spoke up. "General, on behalf of the Government of Canada, we pledge all our resources and cooperation to help resolve this issue."

"Thank you." The general directed a question to Mr. Sanford Crosley of the C.I.A. "Mr. Crosley, can we call on your people to assist us and to fully share information they gather on the matter?"

Sanford Crosley replied, "General, we share the great concern you have and will do everything possible to help resolve the situation. Yes, you have our full cooperation and yes, we will share all information in a timely manner."

Janet muttered, "When pigs fly!" under her breath, then said, "Mr. Crosely and Mr. Pearson, I'm still focusing on the murders in the Oroville area of Washington state. I'm sure there's some connection to smuggling from Canada. Can you give me some cooperation, some assistance, to trace smuggling activities in that area of Canada? Maybe it will lead us to the murderer."

Martin LeRoy spoke up. "As far as the border patrol officer killings, Janet, I'll introduce you to the judicial structure in British Columbia, the Attorney General's office and the Regional RCMP, as soon as you wish. Your own people stationed in British Columbia have good relations with them but it may be helpful to you to establish contact personally. I don't know how helpful that may be, but you never know. At least you may get a better perspective."

"Thank you Martin. Let's follow up with arrangements right after this meeting."

General Baker regained control of the meeting by saying, "Mr. Pearson, in reviewing Colonel Drake's minutes, I note you had lost contact with this inventor, Kenneth Davidson. Is there an update?"

"No, General. He seems to have vanished. We found no recent air, train or bus ticket records, rental car registrations, or charges to his credit cards. He has not left Canada – at least not under his own passport. His e-mail account and cell phone have been silent. We are now into in-depth background checking but nothing significant has surfaced. We found a current love interest but she has not seen him for a while and we continue to have her under surveillance. We've put more resources into this and consider it a high priority."

"What about the factory in Ajax, Ontario?" General Baker inquired. "Anything new there?"

"The flying audit found nothing. Our surveillance of employees and former employees continues but nothing has shown up. We are now tracing the materials suppliers and will do flying audits on them."

"Thank you," said the general. "As the problem transgresses across so many jurisdictions – including international – we need an apex coordinator with appropriate jurisdiction. This is not just a military matter as we have the murders of federal officers of the border patrol and the possibility that the, let's say, leakage of the weapons may be from Canada or another country. On top of that, we have a diplomatic issue with one of our allies in Afghanistan eliminated with the weapon. Due to the mix of relationships, the State Department feels it should be the coordinating agency and Ms Weston, with this problem, you are welcome to it."

Carole Weston spoke up. "Thank you, General. I hope that was a compliment. Anyway, I'm here to coordinate, open some doors and to ensure information exchange in a full and timely fashion. I know the history of animosity between you in the FBI and those in the CIA and now Department of Homeland Security and its many divisions. I'll strive to prevent that in this case. That goes for the various military intelligence and criminal investigation branches as well.

"Let's put it another way: if I need too, I'll kick some ass! Just try me! Anyway, we all want to get this resolved as quickly as possible and all your special talents can breed synergy with the whole much greater than the sum of its parts. Here's my card and 24/7 contact numbers." She paused to deal out her business cards to the other participants. "I want a conference call every Monday, noon, Eastern Standard time. OK?"

Janet spoke up. "General, without us knowing what this archery weapon is or looks like, we're a bit handicapped. We should be able to alert our agents what to look for, especially those in the region of the murders. Even the Homeland Security and border services people, including the field officers of border patrol should be included."

"I am sorry, but that information remains classified."

Carole Weston frowned, rolled her eyes to the ceiling, took a deep breath and said, "General, that is pure absolute horseshit! The weapon is not that high on the restricted information list. What is probably more a worry is the knowledge that our forces and NATO use the weapon – as if most of the military intelligence departments of half the world don't know this already. I'm sure we can alert the agencies in a discreet way – perhaps to look for components of a crossbow? I am quite sure a phone call or two from my superiors will ensure your utmost cooperation."

The General turned to Captain Chavez and said, "Adam, bring out the photos and specifications." He turned back to face Carol Weston, frowned, and said, "I was afraid of this. Our people and our Canadian friends discussed the matter before the meeting and agreed if you were content with the "classified argument" nothing would be revealed. But, we always prepare for contingencies. We have permission, reluctantly given, to reveal photos of the weapon – but still at a classified level not for public consumption. Adam is passing out information we feel will be sufficient. I agree with Ms Weston's point: it would be appropriate if we did not draw attention to the fact the weapon has been used for clandestine military purposes."

As the paper was being passed out and people were looking at it, Carole Weston said, "Thank you, General. We're making some progress. Yes, let's keep military reference out of this. Is everyone in agreement?"

All voiced agreement.

The paper each received contained color photos of the weapon, both assembled and disassembled. There was a brief description including dimensions and stating it was a spring-loaded archery weapon firing a crossbow arrow. It had the power of a good hunting crossbow, but without the bulky bow. It was emphasized that all parts were made of carbon fiber, which easily evaded metal detectors and was compact to be easily hidden in luggage. It would show up in x-ray scans but, because it could be disassembled and the components spread over various pieces of luggage, it may be hard to recognize. The most recognizable features were the stock and the arrows.

Ruth Dempsey, of Homeland Security, muttered "Oh, shit" under her breath, then spoke up. "It's not an easy one to find, is it? This is good, it's enough for us to alert our forces and train them what to look for."

Janet agreed. "We'll inform our people immediately. This also gives rise to the possibility that someone is making these illegally in America. Perhaps we can trace carbon fiber suppliers and see if it leads somewhere. We have the resources for that."

"We'll begin the same in Canada," said Roger Pearson. "Shouldn't be too hard – we have fewer suppliers than you."

General Baker then adjourned the meeting saying, "Thank you all. It's over to you to work on the matter from the North American end. Of course, our intel people and the CIA are working on the death in Afghanistan. We'll inform you of significant developments there and I trust we'll be informed of significant developments on your ends. May we adjourn?"

As people were leaving the meeting, Janet and Hector were approached by Sanford Crosley who introduced himself, shook Janet's hand, then leaned forward to whisper in her right ear. "Janet, Carole and I want a quick word after the meeting. Can you and Hector stay for a moment?"

After the others had left and they were once again seated around the table, Carole started the conversation. "Hector and Janet, we're taking this very seriously now that it looks as if someone is leaking clandestine weapons to the Taliban, probably to Al Qaeda too. You in the FBI can only do so much as far as investigation goes. You can go through formal channels with counterparts in Canada and it looks as if they are co-operating fully and have significant resources. But, let's say they have their own problems both of bureaucracies and their judicial structure – even the political climate – that may be limiting. We want this matter resolved fast – expeditiously and cleanly. We do not want mention of the weapon coming out at trial, in the press or whatever, but we'll have to address that if the time comes.

"Hector, I suggest you formally arrange through the Canadian Embassy for Janet and her number two to meet the regional RCMP and the right people in the British Columbia Attorney General's office. They might be able to give you some assistance, or at least a better perspective. Your FBI officer at the American Consulate in Vancouver will be able to introduce you. Also, Homeland Security people are there with good relations with the Canadians. You must not be seen as conducting your own investigation on Canadian soil without the Canadians' help so all proper protocols and limitations they may present must be adhered to. Also, Homeland Security people have to be in the loop. You don't want to embarrass the State Department. Clear?"

Janet and Hector nodded. Hector spoke. "In other words, you don't want bulls in the china shop upsetting carefully developed relationships or the status quo. In addition to FBI liaison and Homeland Security, I presume we have other agencies, such as our drug people liaising with the Canadians? The DEA also shares a responsibility for drugs and there's Alcohol, Tobacco and Firearms. Will they be able to help?"

As Carole was about to speak, Sanford Crosley interrupted. "You have a good point. Our agency has a pretty good relationship with them too. We've worked well in that region. We also have a liaison person at our consulate in Vancouver who is a must see. I'll handle introductions for you. We also have resources in place there – some in the Canadian Okanagan near your scene of the crime but they're in pretty deep cover. Our resources are managed out of our Bellingham, Washington office, close to the border. We're willing to help. Janet, how about I meet you at our Bellingham office the day after you return from meeting the RCMP and Attorney General people? I'll introduce you to our person who handles that region and we'll compare notes."

"That would be most welcome, Sanford. Thank you. Would 10 a.m. be good for you?"

"Sure. See you then."

After the meeting, while Hector drove her to the airport, Janet said, "I don't know what we'll be able turn up in Canada that the others haven't."

Hector looked a bit thoughtful, responding, "You never know. At least, you'll get a good perspective of law enforcement and the key players in the region. You never can tell, something may pop up. But please remember, from the FBI point of view, investigation in Canada has to be by the Canadians. You cannot and must not go chasing something by yourself even though they may view things differently."

"Understood.

Chapter 10

Janet and Fred flew from Seattle to Vancouver, B.C. on Horizon Air, arriving at YVR at 7:50 a.m. They had easily pre-cleared customs and immigration as they were not armed and Canadian Immigration had been advised of the pending visit. As instructed, they caught the light rapid transit *Canada Line* that quickly whisked them to downtown Vancouver. From their exit at Waterfront Station they caught a taxi for the short trip to the U.S. Consulate on Pender Street.

It was a clear day. From the taxi, they could see the North Shore mountains and inner harbor. They saw the North Shore had an industrial waterfront with many docks at which ocean going freighters were moored. Beyond that, climbing the hillside, was a dense array of apartments and office buildings which gave way to single family housing ending a third of the way up the string of mountains. At the top of one mountain – the taxi driver called it Grouse Mountain – at what seemed to be about four thousand feet of elevation, was a large windmill with an enclosed observation platform overlooking a series of winter ski hills. The taxi driver pointed out the twin peaks of an old volcano called The Lions that soared majestically behind Grouse Mountain.

At the consulate, they placed their passports and FBI credentials in a tray on the reception counter and pushed the tray into a trough under the bulletproof glass. A uniformed U.S. Marine on the other side of the partition took them and checked their names off on a list, picked up a telephone and placed a call. Shortly, a woman in a blue suit with white blouse and a U.S. Consulate identification tag hung around her neck came to the partition. Her badge identified her as Maggie Rushton. She held down a button on the wall and motioned for Janet and Fred to open the bulletproof stainless steel and glass door of a small vestibule that had a similar door on the other end of it. A sign on the first door read: *One person at a time. You will submit to a full body scan.*

Janet entered and closed the door. A voice from an overhead speaker said, "Hands over your head. Please don't move until the green light comes on." When the green light came on, the far door opened and Janet exited where she shook hands and introduced herself to the waiting woman. After Fred made his way through the chamber and introductions were made, Maggie escorted them to a meeting room where two men and a woman were waiting.

They introduced themselves as Warren Wong, the FBI liaison office; Jake Toppam, second in command of the Consulate; and Cybil Henderson, the Homeland Security liaison officer. Warren was of Chinese extraction and Janet had learned he was selected for the liaison job because he was fluent in Mandarin and Cantonese and because of the large Chinese population in the area. Cybil was East Indian, conversant in seven languages of India and fit in well with the large East Indian population in the area. After a chance to get self-serve coffee from a carafe on the credenza, the meeting began.

"Welcome to Vancouver!" John began. "You're very fortunate to arrive on a sunny day. The city is gorgeous and at its finest when the sun shines. We get more rain, a lot more, than Seattle. I hope you'll get some time to enjoy this city. We've arranged for you to meet key people in the RCMP and CSIS in Vancouver. They'll come here. And we have an appointment for you with the Attorney General's office in Victoria. We have a little time to chat about the situation before your first meeting.

"We're well aware of your murder case with the possibility of cross-border connections and the problem of a restricted military weapon invented in Canada. You are well aware of our efforts with the Canadian police forces, Customs and such and that nothing has surfaced to date."

Cybil spoke up. "As you know, we have excellent relations with the Canadians and we have a number of joint task forces addressing smuggling, criminal syndicates, etc. We've had some great successes from time to time. Just the other day, this region's Homeland Security's Integrated Border Enforcement Team, or IBET for short, along with some FBI, ATF and DEA assistance, helped the Canadian border services and RCMP nail a container with 3,000 kilos of heroin on the docks here. That resulted in arrests in San Francisco, Los Angeles, and here, in Vancouver – a total of 32 indictments. We even involved the Canadian Security and Intelligence Service, CISIS for short, but, you know, they like to keep a very low profile and refuse to take credit for anything.

"Well done!" said Janet. "When we were in telephone conference, you mentioned rumors of smuggling in the vicinity of our murder case. Is there anything new there?"

"Not really," replied Wong. "We're aware a lot of guns originating from America are showing up in the hands of the local criminals and that there's a flow of cocaine north across the border, but the Canadians have had seizure successes only at the border crossing points and with some amateur open country crossing attempts that are mainly on the Lower Mainland where 90% of the population of the province resides. They've had pretty good luck catching stuff in cars and transport trucks. So much so, that it seems to have gone quiet in this sector right now. However, stuff is still getting through. The local police have a good handle on this as they keep track of the street level price of drugs and guns and the availability of supply. Recently, prices have been stable and no shortage.

Cybil said, "There's a gang war going on in this area, the Lower Mainland. Lots of murders using guns. Most of the weapons have been traced back to America. The local gangs are warring over various components of the drug trade. They're getting pretty brazen, hurting some innocent bystanders. But it's nothing at all like the Mexican cartel wars."

"Yeah," said Warren. "You may have noticed the Asian mix of people as you made your way in from the airport. You've got to appreciate that the ethnic mix in this city has given rise to a lot of gangs. The metro area has 25% Chinese, of which 5% are old established from the days of railroad building, maybe 8% are from Taiwan and the majority are New Canadians from Hong Kong who moved in when the British handed Hong Kong back to China. And now, we seem to be an "in" destination for the newly rich from China.

"Another 12-14% of the population is Punjabi East Indian, mainly New Canadians. Plus, we have large numbers of South Koreans, Persians from Iran, Vietnamese boat people and so on. There's now an influx of Cambodians, Sudanese and Russians. Many of the parents work day and night to make a better life for their family and the kids are unsupervised. In some societies, the boys are pampered and can do no wrong. The worst gangs they have right now are Punjabis from Northern India, Chinese, Vietnamese, Russian, Iranian and Cambodian. And these guys play rough. There are even a few Columbians, Somalis, Jamaicans, Hondurans and Mexicans. Add in the old established gangs like the biker gangs and the Chinese triads, plus the Italians and the Portuguese, and we have an interesting mix."

"Does this Asian mixture go all across Canada or it local?" asked Janet.

"It's mainly local. Each of the big cities in Canada has a different ethnic profile. For example, Montreal has attracted a large number of Haitians and Senegalese. Toronto has a lot of Jamaicans and Sri Lankans plus Chinese and East Indian.

"In Vancouver, the large numbers that came over from Hong Kong to Vancouver, especially to Richmond near the airport, pushed property prices out of sight. The old timers, mainly Caucasians, bailed out to other parts of the province where land was relatively cheap. That caused some desired destinations to have land booms and exponential growth. It's the case in the Okanagan, the region of your crime scene, with a number of the cities growing rapidly. Lately, Punjabis have been picking up farmland there but they are still a very small number and they don't seem to be into the crime scene."

"John, what can you tell us about the Okanagan?"

"Well, it's a place I'd like to retire to! It has a long summer with great golf, water sports and fishing. It's cold and dry in the winter with great skiing and winter sports. Modern. Clean. Low crime rate. An international airport in Kelowna, the largest city. It's lake country with a series of lakes stretching roughly one hundred twenty miles down the Okanagan rift valley. The largest lake is Lake Okanagan along which are fairly good-sized cities, Vernon in the north, Penticton at the south lakehead of Okanagan Lake with Kelowna about in the middle. The far south has Lake Osoyoos straddling the border and the valley stretches down into Washington State a hundred or so miles as far as Wenatchee.

"Both Kelowna and Vernon have grown fast with the influx of people. The area attracts a lot of retirees from across Canada and Europe. It also has attracted a lot of dotcom millionaires who seem to love to establish boutique wineries. They've created a whole new industry in boutique wines and another reason for tourists to come and play. Most cities have significant seniors' populations. Kelowna is reputed to have the largest per capita portion of millionaires and billionaires in all of Canada and there is a fair bit of high tech industry in the region, albeit no individual firm has significant numbers of employees.

"Education is great. They have recently opened a university for the region and it's already generating a good reputation for quality and research. Oliver and Osoyoos are closer to the border. Osoyoos is right at the border. It's also growing but not as fast as the North Okanagan – probably because there's no international airport, and skiing is better up north."

Fred jokingly said, "My god! You could be a tourism booster for them!" All laughed.

John went on. "From an organized crime point of view, it's an interesting area. It's dominated by one national – no, international - biker gang, the Devil's Brew, and very little is seen of the Vancouver gangs except as well-behaved visitors. The biker gang has an accord with all other biker gangs that the Okanagan is neutral ground when they are wearing their colors and as long as they behave. There seems to be agreement with the Asian gangs, Russians etc. as well. The Devil's Brew has been in place there for decades and is well entrenched. They own a lot of legitimate businesses from girlie bars to funeral parlors, car and motorcycle dealerships, wineries and motels. On the criminal side, they're involved in drug dealing, prostitution, marijuana cultivation, debt collection, fencing, stolen autos, guns, and chop shops, and maybe hijacking. Few of their senior people have been arrested. From one point of view, they keep things quiet over there."

"What about smuggling?" Janet asked. "Are they involved?"

"That's the funny thing. No one has been able to link them to cross-border smuggling. At least, it doesn't seem they do it themselves. There's been linkage to them supplying marijuana for non-members to take across the border at their own peril. From one point of view, the area has been pretty quiet with little or no major organized crime activity surfacing. The crime rate is low. The big thing for the police in the whole province is busting marijuana grow ops as they have a new law on the books that allows the courts to seize property and dwellings as proceeds of crime – regardless of who is the owner. Conversely, those caught running a grow op only get their wrists slapped. Sort of like California but even lighter treatment. Probably the biggest industry in the Okanagan is marijuana. One economist estimates it at 40 – 60 percent of the local economy."

Fred said, "Yeah, I've heard about B.C. Bud. It's pretty potent stuff."

"Yes," replied Cybil. "It's in high demand and our DEA friends say it's showing up in great quantity as far as California and Nevada. It apparently is better than the Mexican stuff and that has the Mexican cartel annoyed. It has to be going south in large quantities. We keep intercepting some of it, large quantities actually, that people are trying to take across in trailer trucks, even by sea or rail containers. We get a lot of so-called amateurs trying to make their fortunes by bringing it across. However, there hasn't been all that much activity like that at the Oroville border crossing recently.

Maybe we're getting good at interception or they've found other ways."

"Other ways, probably," said Warren. "One thing you have to appreciate is that our Canadian friends in law enforcement are spread a little thin and they're concentrating their resources in responding to the gang wars and hard drug smuggling in Greater Vancouver. It's the major seaport, after all, and a lot comes in by ship. The gang wars are keeping them busy. In a way, marijuana is ignored."

There was a knock on the door and Maggie Rushton brought in a man in RCMP senior rank uniform. John said, "Ah, our first visitor has arrived: Chief Inspector Jack McGuire, with the RCMP." Introductions were made all around with business cards exchanged. Jack McGuire seemed about 55 years of age. He was about five foot ten, one seventy pounds. He had short, crew cut gray hair, and when he sat down, his back was ramrod straight. Jack McGuire basically went over the same ground they had already covered and left within an hour after complementing the great cooperation the force had with the FBI and Homeland Security and pledging continuing assistance in Janet's problem.

After Chief Inspector McGuire left, Warren said, "Well, you got the PR department BS there. The RCMP is run in a quasi-military fashion and is a typical large bureaucracy. They're also at the mercy of the Canadian justice system, which doesn't always work too well. For example: Just the other day they had a case go to court where they had raided a warehouse in Richmond, a suburb of Vancouver here, and found meth lab equipment."

"A meth lab?" Asked Janet.

"No. It was a factory making meth lab kits so that others could set up their own meth labs. They even were supplying cooking instructions and a starter set of key ingredients. Some two hundred finished kits were seized, some already packaged and addressed to the purchasers. They were shipping across North America, even to Australia. Thankfully the RCMP shared the customer list with other police agencies, DEA etc."

"Wow."

"The RCMP thought they had an ironclad case. So did the prosecutor. But the whole thing was thrown out when they went to trial."

"Why?"

106

"The RCMP had obtained a search warrant from a judge in another jurisdiction and that was ruled invalid."

"Uh, oh. Is there a hint of corruption here or just bureaucratic bungling?"

"I had a beer with a couple of the officers involved in the case. They inferred they were afraid the local judge was corrupt and that he would warn the ones running the factory if he was approached for a search warrant. That's why they went to a judge in another jurisdiction for the search warrant."

"So, more than one layer of corruption?"

"Possibly."

The second visitor was Marie LeFrance, a senior agent in CSIS, the Canadian Security and Intelligence Service. While waiting for Marie, John mentioned to Janet and Fred that CSIS was a relatively new service, having been spun off from the RCMP after a scandal caused by ineptitude of the RCMP intelligence services branch that had embarrassed the government. There was significant animosity between the two services which had contributed to a number of bungled cases. CSIS chose a role of intelligence gathering, remaining silent eavesdroppers refusing to appear as witnesses at trials, to reveal sources of information, or to have media public relations. Their specialty was eaves dropping – and they were good at it in a great variety of languages.

As Marie LeFrance entered, she said, "Bonjour. Welcome to Vancouver. This the first trip for both of you. No? Let me remind you that this meeting is confidential and off the record for background information only."

Janet and Fred both admitted it was their first trip and agreed to confidentiality.

'Well, how can our service be of help? We have been closely monitoring the gangs here on the Lower Mainland but little has surfaced. The only link we have picked up, just overnight so we haven't yet pushed it along, is that a South Korean gang leader who has been involved in people smuggling is most upset. He seems to have been the one locally behind the attempt to cross the border with twenty-two aliens near Osoyoos-Oroville the night your people were killed. He's running scared. Two of his superiors are arriving today from Korea. No doubt they will take him to task. We monitored him talking to one of his trusted lieutenants. Apparently, he will bear the blame because he had elected not to pay protection to someone. Regrettably, no names were mentioned or inferences given. I doubt if we will have to worry about that leader. His superiors do not like mistakes."

Janet and Fred glanced at each other with small grins. "Thank you for sharing that with us," Janet said. "It's a bit of a break. At least we know someone is offering protection to cross the border there. Would you have any idea who that could be?"

"No. Smuggling is not too high on our list of priorities unless it is terrorist related. And we've all been unable to pin the murders of the two border officers on smuggling or a connection to Canada, so we haven't done much about it. However, if your ongoing investigation targets some people on this side of the border, we will be happy to assist."

The group thanked Marie for her help and she left. John looked at his watch, turned to Warren and said, "Now, Warren, I gather you're going to escort our guests to Victoria to meet the folk at the AG's office. You probably have time to grab a quick bite to eat on your way to the plane. Janet and Fred, I'm sure you'll enjoy the trip. Victoria is a beautiful city. It's at the bottom tip of Vancouver Island and has a bit of a British affectation. We've arranged tickets for the floatplane service close to us here in the harbor. It takes you right to the inner harbor of Victoria – right where the government offices and Empress Hotel are located. With such a great day, you shouldn't have a bumpy ride and you'll get to see some spectacular scenery – especially when you fly over the Gulf Islands."

Warren turned to Janet and Fred. "You may not want to eat too much for lunch. We'll be meeting two of the AG's senior staff for "high tea" at the Empress Hotel. It's a quaint Victoria custom and a big tourist attraction."

After grabbing a leftover cinnamon bun and a Coke each from the credenza, they left the building, caught a taxi to the seaplane wharf and soon were in the aircraft, a de Havilland Twin Otter on floats, taxiing into the middle of the harbor and taking off. The plane took off toward the east of the harbor, then made a climbing circle north toward the North Shore mountains, then headed south west, passing directly over a suspension bridge which Warren identified as the Lions Gate bridge. On the left side of the aircraft, the bridge led to a large park, which Warren said was Stanley Park, providing one thousand acres of recreation right in the heart of the city.

As they headed toward Victoria in a southwesterly direction, they passed over the outer harbor, where over two dozen ocean going freighters were anchored, then across another expanse of woodland,

Endowment Lands of the University of British Columbia. They then flew over YVR, the major airport they had arrived at from Seattle, then over open water and across a number of large islands with inlets and channels dotted with all sorts of marine craft. They made a right turn across a golf course, Oak Bay Golf and Country Club, which was on a point of land, then descended with another right turn to a smooth landing on the water in Victoria's inner harbor.

The plane taxied to a dock in front of the Parliament buildings and a large stately, ivy-covered hotel sitting back from the road on a manicured lawn. A rooftop sign bore the name of the hotel: *Empress*. Once a thriving industrial port, Victoria's inner harbor had been gentrified and was now the "in" place to be, with a variety of hotels, townhouses, marinas, beachfront promenade and high-rise apartment blocks. It was all anchored in one corner by the Parliament buildings, a large museum, the dowager Empress Hotel and a downtown shopping area.

They deplaned, climbed the ramp from the landing dock to a street end that was a major tourist destination densely occupied by tourists loading and unloading on tour buses. They walked the short distance to the main entrance of the Empress where Warren was greeted by two men who were introduced to Janet and Fred as Peter Berubé' and Mark Emanuel.

Peter was the older of the two, about sixty. He was squat five foot eight, Caucasian of possibly Portuguese or Mediterranean complexion and extraction, about two hundred forty pounds with a pot belly. He was bald shaven with gray bushy eyebrows. Mark was about fifty years old, tall and heavyset. Peter was introduced by Warren as the leader. He was an Assistant Deputy Minister in the Attorney General's Ministry. Mark was his number two.

Peter spoke up. "Janet and Fred, welcome to Victoria. Warren told me it's your first time to Canada. We in Victoria like to think of our city as an outpost of England – those are our roots. Victoria was established by Britain first as a trading post. So, we keep a lot of the English traditions, like high tea, cricket, grass hockey and the queen's birthday. In honor of your visit, we can have our discussion over high tea here, at the Empress. The old Empress is famous for its high tea. I hope you brought your appetites. Shall we go in? I'll lead the way."

They were led to a sunny series of rooms with windows facing the waterfront. Wing-backed stuffed chairs and small tables peppered the rooms. Many tables had privacy screens of tropical

109

plants. When they were seated, Peter led Janet and Fred through the menu recommending crumpets, scones and a variety of tarts and demi-cakes. Janet, who originated in New England, was used to hot tea and willingly accepted Peter's suggestion of a rare Sri Lankan blend. Fred demurred, seeking black coffee. After being served, Peter got down to business. "We're aware of the two murders just south of our border in the Okanagan area and that there has not been much to go on to date. How can we help?"

"We're not even sure if the murders were related to a smuggling incident but one of the weapons used may be of Canadian origin," said Fred. "The inventor lives in your province and seems to have dropped out of sight. But then, we're not sure if he has anything to do with it. We've been led to believe there's organized smuggling in that area – at least of humans. There was the incident of twenty-two Koreans caught crossing the border just about the time of our murders and some inference that the leaders of it had been guided by locals in the past. How can we learn more about smuggling in that area and who are the key players on your side of the border?"

"I understand you met Jack McGuire of the RCMP?" remarked Peter. "Bet you didn't learn too much."

"You're perceptive," said Janet.

"Perhaps a little background of the police system here may help a bit," said Peter. "In some ways, the RCMP looks all-encompassing. It has a national mandate to combat organized and economic crime, terrorism and drug trafficking. They also handled espionage/domestic intelligence gathering but much of that has been passed off to CSIS – the Canadian Intelligence and Security Service – and relations are strained between the two with minimal co-operation and intelligence sharing.

"The RCMP also provides policing under contract to eight of the ten provinces of Canada and three territories. Only Ontario and Quebec each have their own provincial police forces. The main thing though, is they police over two hundred cities on local contracts. They also have the mandate to police the Great Lakes, St. Lawrence River and coastal waterways, as our Coast Guard is only for search and rescue.

"They're caught financially with funding from local governments and provinces for the local policing, which is their biggest role. The federal government provides funding for the national matters. Federal funding has been tightened and the force is complaining of not enough personnel – 30% less than they need.

Morale has been poor with a pay raise cut by 50% six months after it had been announced. Both their morale and public relations are at a low ebb. There have been a number of incidents of excessive force used by officers that have the public outraged and the same of sex discrimination. This has blackened the public image to the point they are not too popular in some circles.

"Generally, the RCMP is very good at local level policing, where they have been contracted to provide it. The funding structure is such that emphasis is on local policing of the villages and cities, rather than rural areas which does present gaps or delays in policing coverage."

"You infer that rural coverage is not good?" Asked Fred.

"You could say that, but it depends on the area. For example, it's common for a small town to have contracted for police coverage that forbids their officers from handling incidents beyond the boundaries of the town. The rural coverage around the town may be handled by a regional branch of the RCMP that is quite distant. It gets ridiculous when there is a rural incident, which the town's officers could reach in two minutes, but the rural patrol can't be there for an hour or so.

"On top of this, some cities have their own police forces, rather than contract for police services with the RCMP. That leads to jurisdictional conflicts, lack of communication, resentment and lack of coordination. However, there has been some progress with integrating major crime task forces.

"You would think, because the RCMP is so pervasive, there would be good data bases stretching nationwide but that isn't evident. For example, trying to recognize the trail of a serial killer who bounces across the country hasn't been in the books.

"Another thing: our judiciary is a bit different to yours. You incarcerate far more people on a per capita basis that do we. You jail in a ratio of eight people to our one. You'll see some of our sentences are far lighter, as for marijuana cultivation and possession."

"So, you're inferring that not much attention is paid to smuggling or marijuana cultivation in rural areas?" asked Janet.

"We would be more worried about smuggling into Canada. Let's put it this way, policing is pretty thin on the ground on the Canadian side of the border near your crime scene. It's rural, mountainous, with a sparse population that seems law abiding. Nothing has come to our attention. We, the Attorney General's Office, have other resources, such as a few armed conservation and fisheries officers that are active in that area from time to time but they haven't encountered anything either. Mind you, the conservation officers are more active in the fall during hunting season.

"I don't know what else we can do right now. I'm sorry if we seem unhelpful."

Janet said, "Peter, the background you've given us is helpful. As you know, we're making little progress ourselves. The one possible link here is the inventor of the archery weapon. Is it possible to put more resources on tracing his disappearance?"

"Roger Pearson and Martin Le Roy have also expressed the same to the Prime Minister's Office in Ottawa and they, in turn, have asked us to do so. RCMP are supposed to be on to it. We'll keep you in the loop in case anything develops. CSIS is now taking an interest," said Peter.

Warren looked at his watch. "Thank you both, Peter and Mark, for the meeting. I see the time has flown. Janet and Fred have to catch the seaplane to Seattle."

The meeting ended with all shaking hands at the hotel entrance. Peter said to Janet, "By the way, we have excellent liaison from one of your other agencies. I think you would find their knowledge and expertise quite helpful. We sometimes have mutual interests and work together. Do you know Shirley Bains in their Bellingham office?"

"No. What agency?"

"Oh, my dear, CIA of course!"

Chapter 11

Just after noon at Vancouver's YVR airport, Suk Kwan Lee was nervous. Cranky. Scared. The Korean Airlines flight had arrived on time. His superiors from South Korea were due to exit the YVR airport doors from Customs and Immigration any second now. He and his number two, Liu Wan, were among the crowd lining the red velvet rope barrier that separated the greeting crowd from an exit path for the deplaning passengers. It was his obligation to greet them. He could be dead soon.

Born in the ghetto of East Gate, Seoul Korea, Suk Kwan Lee was forty-two years old. He was short at five feet two, a stocky one hundred forty-five pounds. He had grown up on the mean streets East Gate, surviving by his wits until, at age ten, he had befriended a Triad executive who recognized his street smarts and potential. The Triad sent him to school, where he excelled, and then to business school. He minored in both English and Japanese languages.

He had climbed the ladder of the secret, criminal organization, from running errands to enforcing collections, to murder, and to establishing and managing the Vancouver operations. He had landed in Vancouver fifteen years ago as an immigrant entrepreneur with funds provided by the triad to establish some business ventures, such as a restaurant and a travel tour agency in Vancouver and the hotel in Princeton, B.C. He also ran the human smuggling, a prostitution ring, a loan shark operation serving fellow Korean immigrants and had a street level drug network. He now had dual Canadian and South Korean citizenships. Ten years ago, he had been recognized as *Young Entrepreneur of the Year* by a major Vancouver business magazine.

Liu Wan was thirty-one years old with a similar heritage. He, too, had started in Seoul's East Gate ghetto, had been recognized by the triad and sponsored through a good education. He was slighter in build, and taller at five foot eight. Both were wearing blue suits with tan ties, white monogrammed shirts and black shoes and socks.

The doors opened and his two superiors emerged. He and Liu Wan jumped over the barrier, bowed formally, very deeply, to greet them, took their luggage and led the way out of the reception hall to an awaiting black limousine. Suk Kwan Lee was more worried now. They had said nothing and their return bows were not as deep as normal. Their body language said he was in deep trouble.

113

Lee held the rear door open for his superiors then got in the back with them, taking a jump seat facing them. Liu Wan closed the rear door and got in the front seat with the driver. Suk Kwan said, in Korean, "I have arranged for your usual suite at the Four Seasons. Do you wish to go there first? Or do you wish to go to our restaurant where I have a private room waiting?"

Mr. Kim Seung answered for his leader, Mr. Yong Jong. Another signal of formality, of disrespect. "We will go to the hotel first. You may bring the car for us at eight p.m." Another signal. The ride to the hotel was silent. Eye contact avoided. Another signal. Executive check-in at the hotel went smoothly and his superiors refused his offer to accompany them to their suite. Another signal. After bowing very low in farewell and backing away, he and Liu Wan returned to the limo and ordered the driver to take them to the restaurant. They had about seven very nervous hours to kill.

At eight p.m., precisely, Suk Kwan Lee had the concierge call up to the suite and announce their presence. After ten minutes, Messers Seung and Jong came down and, after formal greeting bows again signaling discontent, were silently escorted to the limo. At the restaurant, which was bustling with patrons, they were ushered into a private room where a buffet banquet had been prepared and a table for four – an unlucky number in Asian cultures – had been set. Mr. Seung turned to Suk Kwan Lee and Liu Wan and said, "You will wait outside. We will summon you when we have eaten. But first, have your waiter remove two place settings, you know that four is unlucky. You are becoming too Westernized!"

At nine-thirty, after standing obediently outside the room on either side of the doorway, they were summoned by a single loud handclap. They entered, Suk Kwan Lee first, with Liu Wan one pace behind and to the right. Both bowed low then kept their heads down, shoulders hunched. Mr. Yong Jong said, "You have cost us over a million dollars and the loss of a route into America. Explain."

"I am so sorry, sir," replied Suk Kwan Lee. "It was all my fault. We were betrayed."

"How so?" asked Yong Jong.

"Previously, we employed the services of a local criminal boss, an aboriginal Indian chieftain, in the area of the crossings to guide us and ensure each crossing would be safe. We used the same route many times and felt we no longer needed the chieftain's services. It looks as if one of his people informed the Americans of the last crossing. This was possibly at his encouragement."

"Why? Had you not had good relations with this criminal boss?"

"We employed his services for eight crossings. Each of those crossings went as planned. As our own escorts learned the route well, I decided we no longer needed the services of the chieftain. He charged US $10,000 each crossing."

"You were trying to save some money. Is that it?"

"Yes, sir."

"And now, Suk Kwan Lee, your attempt to economize has cost us dearly. We have lost two good escorts as it looks as if they will be jailed for a couple of years before they are deported. Plus, our customers do not pay for failure. We have to recruit another twenty women. We are out the costs of the operation and we must find another safe route into America. Although you profess to know it, I think you do not understand the local culture. You underestimated this chieftain."

"I have been organizing another safe route. It is farther east. They would cross near Trail, B.C. and come out near Spokane, Washington. I have found people who assure safe passage."

"That is considerably farther east. Is it not at least four or five additional hours by highway? Wouldn't we have to wait a day for another night to cross?"

"Yes. Some costs would go up."

"I do not like it. The risk increases the more the cargo is on this side of the border and once they cross the border, the more distance they have to cover to a place where they can be absorbed in the mix of legitimate Asian tourists. Spokane is not really on the tourist track for Asians. I am more comfortable if you can make your peace with the chieftain. Obviously he has the resources to monitor and evade border patrols in that area. Your new source is uncertain. There is much risk."

"Yes sir, I will try to make my peace with the chieftain."

"You have a month. If you fail, you will be replaced. Now, take us back to the hotel."

Suk Kwon Lee knew that replacement meant his death. He shuddered. He was also angry with Chief Joseph.

The next day, Suk Kwan Lee and Liu Wan escorted their superiors to the airport and saw them off. In the limo returning them to the restaurant, Liu Wan spoke. "What are your plans now?"

Suk Kwan Lee looked out of the side window of the limo, thought for a while then spoke. "I will teach our chieftain a lesson, I will humble him. Then he will work for us!"

Lieu Wan closed his eyes and said, "Are you sure? In this strange culture, you may only anger the chieftain."

"Then I will kill him."

Chapter 12

True to his word, Sanford Crosley arranged a meeting in Bellingham, Washington for Janet and Fred to meet the regional CIA. officer. They met at the CIA's Bellingham office at ten a.m. and were introduced to two people: Richard Adair, the station manager and Shirley Bains, the control agent for British Columbia.

Richard was fifty-nine years old, five foot ten, bald, gray side hair, with a reddish complexion, thin lips, angular nose and weighed about one hundred ninety pounds. He had blue piercing eyes and a habit of looking people in the eye most of the time.

Shirley Bains was an attractive, sun-tanned bottle blond somewhere around fifty years old with brown eyes and a thin smile. Her five-foot four-inch frame held a trim one hundred thirty pounds.

After introductions and help-yourself coffee and buns from the credenza along one side of the room, Sandford opened the conversation. "Janet and Fred, both Richard and Shirley have been briefed. As we have a matter that seems to link with terrorists, you have our undivided attention and assistance. We have some assets in place in British Columbia, and even some in the Okanagan, who may be helpful. But, and this is a big but, we cannot allow information you glean from us or our assets to see the light of day in a courtroom in the form of testimony. There must not be any disclosure of sources or inference that we played a part.

"You must also accept to ignore other, peripheral crimes, in pursuit of the archery weapon source and the murderer or murderers, if indeed, they are in Canada. Above all, we do not wish to compromise any of our assets in place in Canada or bring to light any of our activities there. Is that clear?"

"I think so," said Janet. "But I'm not quite sure what you mean."

"In the new spirit of co-operation," continued Richard, "and because this is, to us, a terrorism link, we will introduce you to some of our assets in British Columbia, but you cannot and will not be introduced as a "cop" seeking to make a bust on anything and everything illegal you encounter. You have to have blinders on to some of the things you will see. You may only participate in information gathering directed at finding the source of the weapons and the murderers. You, the FBI, cannot do anything on Canadian soil except help the Canadians build a case for the Canadian justice

----

system – if they are interested – or help build your own murder case for extradition to bring the murderer(s) back to America for trial."

"What do you mean, if they are interested?" asked Janet.

"The Canadian system is different. You'll learn this when we introduce you to some of our assets."

Shirley pitched in. "From another point of view, we often operate in the muddy waters – dealing with criminal elements. In fact, we occasionally exchange services and make things happen when needed, and we do not want our carefully developed network of relationships compromised. They can be quite helpful at times."

"I still am not fully clear on this," said Janet. "But I'll go along with it. Are you saying there could be difficulties bringing this criminal element to justice in Canada?"

"In some situations, yes. You'll see. I understand from Peter Berubé and Jay Topham that you met a representative of the RCMP and that was not enlightening. I was also talking with Marie LeFrance of CSIS and am aware that Peter gave you a background of the policing in the country."

"Yes," said Janet. "Looks as if you folk are well connected and informed."

"Mmm. Yes," said Shirley. "If you agree to our requirements, we may be able to show you a more realistic perspective. I'll take you into British Columbia and we'll meet with some of our assets in place. Some may be full-time CIA, others on part-time payroll and others are just paid informers or associates with whom we occasionally do some business. Some will be the criminal element. However, I insist only you, Janet, enter Canada. With all due respect, Fred, you stand out a bit – you look and act like a cop – and two people plus me would arouse suspicions much faster than one of you alone. Janet, you will travel un-armed and without your credentials – we will be posing as innocent holidaying civilians not throwing any "I'm a cop" weight around. Is that O.K.?"

"Sure. O.K. If you think it will help, I'm all for it. Fred will have to mind the store in Seattle. When can we go?"

"That's up to you. We should plan to be away for about a week, though. You should pack and dress down for a summer vacation at the beach. Ditch your FBI uniform."

"I need to clear my desk. How about two days after tomorrow?"

"O.K. Now, let me show you something." Shirley reached into her briefcase, produced a small laptop computer and plugged it

118

into the desktop projector. After it was booted up, she found the site she wanted and projected it onto the large screen at the far end of the room. Displayed was a map of Greater Vancouver with opaque orange points with number codes flashing in various spots, mainly in the core of Vancouver. Shirley explained. "The orange flags identify various vehicles being tracked. What you see is just part of a computer program that tracks and identifies movement patterns of the vehicles, where they stop, for how long, etc. Also, when one deviates out of its "normal" or routine pattern, an alert shows on the screens of those monitoring the case. We can even send alerts to cell phones."

"In this case, who are you monitoring?" asked Fred.

"Remember Marie LaFrance mentioned that Korean? The one likely linked to the human smuggling interception at the time of your killings? We have a part-time operative who runs a surveillance company. You know, security checks, divorce stuff, warehouse pilferage investigations and such. He has a few employees and a good reputation. He's ex-army intelligence and pretty well all his employees in operations are ex-British SAS – good people. They are very much into electronics and computers and developed the program you see. Well, he was commissioned by a biker gang based in the Okanagan, the Devil's Brew, to keep track of the movements of these Koreans. He bugged the Korean's vehicles, had them followed for a while to establish normal patterns: what they did, where they stopped, etc. When he set the biker gang up with this software, he also sold it to us. The bugs are extremely small and their batteries last for months. In the spirit of co-operation, CSIS is also monitoring this and will provide translation transcripts of the conversations in Korean."

"Do you think this may lead to something?" Fred asked.

"Well, the leader, one Suk Kwan Lee, is into a lot of things, not only people smuggling. He's also running street level drug dealing and loan sharking. That's quite visible when following the vehicles, which our operative did. We're monitoring it to see where things lead. If anything develops out of the ordinary that may relate to America, we'll let you and Homeland Security know."

Three days later, Janet met Shirley in the CIA office parking garage in Bellingham where they transferred her luggage to a rental vehicle, a nondescript Ford Taurus, then set off for the Huntington-Abbotsford border crossing at Sumas, Washington. They only had to stop at the Canadian side where they presented their passports and, when asked, stated they were going to Kelowna on vacation. The border guard welcomed them to Canada then said, "Ms. Murphy, my computer says you are with the FBI. Are you bringing any firearms with you?"

"No sir, I'm strictly on holiday."

"Well then, have a great time. On your way."

Puzzled, Janet asked Shirley, "How come they were alerted to me and not you?"

Shirley smiled and handed her passport to Janet, who looked carefully at the information page then said, "Oh, how do you do, Ms. Shirley Woodward. I see. Under cover."

"We tend to keep our real names away from business in the field."

"Thanks. So I should avoid mentioning my last name?"

"That will do."

Once across the border it was only a few stoplights before they headed east on Trans Canada Highway One. A full hour later, they passed the mountain-ringed town of Hope, then branched off to Highway 5 taking them up into mountains and over the Coquihalla Pass. Forty-five minutes later they bypassed the town of Merritt switching southeast to Highway 97C along the high alpine road called the Coquihalla Connector. In less than an hour and a half, they descended into the large Okanagan rift valley.

Before them, in the bright sun, was a clear picture postcard perfect vista of the valley with its mountainous east side and a large lake that stretched southward around a bend between two steep mountains. Northward, the lake continued out of sight. A road sign welcomed them to West Kelowna, formerly called Westbank. Shirley mentioned that West Kelowna was one of the fastest growing towns in Canada and much of the land was on Indian reservation, which could only be leased. That Indian band was considered very prosperous with excellent business sense and a great welfare program for their people stemming from the development and leasing of land for sub-divisions and shopping centers

They continued northeast along the highway through West Kelowna and crossed the lake on a new-looking floating bridge into the downtown of Kelowna. Shirley turned left just after the bridge along a road paralleling a large lakeside park. A couple of blocks later, they stopped at the entrance to the Marquis Hotel, a luxury property boasting a casino, waterfront marina and rooms with water and mountain views.

They left the car with the valet, rolled their own bags in and registered. They had reserved two rooms overlooking the lakeside boardwalk and marina. They took half an hour to get settled, then met at an outdoor patio of one of the bars on the lakeside. Outdoors, away from the air-conditioned comfort of the hotel, it was hot. A dual Fahrenheit and Celsius thermometer in the shade on the wall of the bar registered a hundred and two degrees Fahrenheit. Janet was grateful for Shirley's suggestion to wear shorts, sandals and a light halter-top. After ordering white wine with a side of bottled cold water and snacks, Shirley said, "In Kelowna here, we'll meet one person late this afternoon and another tomorrow. I want you to meet The Deacon and Donny. I called The Deacon and he'll see us in an hour. He's a bit mysterious. He'll meet us here, then we can go for a walk. We meet Donny tomorrow afternoon."

Janet said, "The Deacon?"

"Yes. It's a nickname he got long ago. His dad was a deacon in a large religious cult that is still active in both Canada and America. Our Deacon followed in his dad's footsteps for a while, helping his dad to manage the cult's affairs in a region of Western Ontario. He became very good at money management. He did some preaching and was good at it. He's your classic sociopath – very charming, little conscience. A borderline psychopath. He went to the cult's theology college in the American Midwest, got a Master's degree in sociology but also mastered Spanish, French and Russian and did some missionary work in France, Italy and Finland. He started on a doctorate degree but got disillusioned.

"That was in the time of the Viet Nam war. He wound up running an underground railroad bringing draft dodgers to Canada and getting them citizenship papers – even doing lifestyle, identity and clothing makeovers. A great number of them settled just a little north of here in another lake area called the Shuswap – there's a large lake there by that name. The by-product, with so many bright people settling there, was a large number of high tech firms sprouting up.

"Anyway, the Deacon got bored with that and was recruited by us. He wound up as a diplomatic courier with the Canadian Prime Minister's Office, known as the PMO. His job was useful for covert operations and he was trained in espionage by both the Canadians and us. The PMO. is a "catch-all" department of the government hosting various branches the Prime Minister wants to keep under his or her control. The Deacon's branch handled the most delicate international relations – including covert operations. Some of the covert ops were joint actions with us, France and the U.K. – so he's well connected in intelligence circles.

"His field of operations was Europe, South and Central America. He retired at the end of the cold war and got into some deal making promoting start-up businesses and moving money around the world. He also got back into religion, studying some Asian ones. He was keen on American aboriginal religions for a while, then New Age variants. He's got his own little cult now with a number of followers – mainly older women who entrust him with their money.

"He's still dabbling in promoting start-up high tech companies. His past with the PMO. has made him very secretive, though. His phones, car, apartment etc. are in other people's names and he goes by an alias. He's been in some pretty slippery financial deals, one phony bond deal with gold bearing certificates from a South American country in particular that got the attention of the IRS, but he's managed to evade authorities. He's got U.S., British and Canadian citizenship under a couple of aliases. He also has a large network of contacts both here and abroad ranging from billionaires to mafia dons and mercenaries. You have to be warned, he's a smoothie and a real con artist when he wants to be. You have to lock up your checkbook, wallet and credit cards when he's talking and he'll manoeuver you into paying the bill every time."

"Interesting," said Janet.

They were just starting on coffee when a man wearing silvered sunglasses approached their table from the boardwalk. He was tall, about six feet, heavy set with a pot belly, thin gray hair combed with a part on the left side, oval face, medium lips and common nose. He was wearing brown, summer-weight dress slacks with a tan webbed belt and gold buckle, light brown polo shirt, brown loafers, brown socks. His wrists and hands were large. He wore a stainless steel Citizen solar watch on his right wrist.

"Shirley! So good to see you!" He greeted Shirley by picking up both her hands, helping her to stand. Then, they hugged and The Deacon kissed her on both cheeks. Still holding her hands, he stepped back a bit, looked her in the face, smiled and said, "Lord, you are even more gorgeous than the last time!" He then looked at Janet. "And who's this lovely lady?"

Shirley hastened with introductions. "Janet, meet Brian West. Brian, we're having coffee, please join us."

Brian West (The Deacon) pulled a chair over from an adjoining empty table and sat down. He caught the waiter's eye and

----

ordered a coffee and a blueberry muffin. They engaged in small talk, mostly about the weather and the beauty of the Okanagan until coffee was finished and Shirley paid the bill. They exited onto the boardwalk with Brian taking the waterside. As they walked, Brian offered a running commentary on the hotel, boardwalk, marina, and the current beautification project of the city until they entered a large park with a well-occupied children's water park and wall-to-wall sun worshipers tanning on the beach and grass. They walked over to an unoccupied picnic table shaded by a large chestnut tree that was remote from the crowd and boardwalk. After they were seated, Shirley said, "Brian, we have a little problem with a terrorism thing and a couple of federal officers murdered that may have some relationship to this area. I wondered if you might help."

"Certainly. Always for you. What are you looking for?"

Shirley pulled an envelope from her purse and brought out a photo of the archery weapon. She asked, "Ever seen one of these?"

Brian looked at the page, after a few seconds. "Yes. Similar, but not with the magazine. I saw it in the late 1980s or early nineties. The one I saw was single shot. May I know why?"

"In this case, I'm not going to say no, that it's need to know. You've been around and you know the drill. I am sure you will promise confidentiality. Right?"

"Of course. Why the worries with this weapon?"

"The weapon has been produced exclusively for Canadian military and some NATO services for clandestine purposes. It was invented in Canada," said Janet.

"I know. I helped set up the deal. You're looking for Ken Davidson, the inventor? Why?"

"You're a bit ahead of us, but yes, we would love to find and talk to the inventor. He seems to have disappeared. The reason for all this is that un-military copies of the weapon were used in Afghanistan to kill an Afghan leader loyal to us and to kill a border patrol agent along the border just south of here."

"I see. Interesting that it got into the hands of the Taliban. Let me explain how I know Ken. He's an avid hunter and fisherman. He's also a gifted tinkerer, always inventing things of some sort. He developed the original archery weapon to hunt elk, moose and deer as the crossbow he had been using was awkward to carry in dense brush. As a registered native Indian, he could hunt starting the season a month early if he used bow and arrow. He'd been experimenting with carbon fiber and found that a coiled spring made of it could be both powerful and durable. He made one, tried it. Got a moose on the first hunt and was pretty happy.

"At the time, I was living in the Shuswap where he had a vacation cabin and, somehow, we got introduced as I have a reputation for helping to finance start-up companies. Back then, he wanted to make the weapon for hunting but one of my old cold war colleagues saw it and introduced him to someone in military procurement. The government bought him up. They made him comfortably rich.

"His brother had been involved in production and he was hired to set up and manage the government-owned factory. Ken was put on retainer as a research consultant, paid to improve the weapon and develop new things for the military. For a while things went well, then he got bored and faded away. He's been up in Salmon Arm on Shuswap Lake ever since. I've seen him from time to time. He's got a heat pump business and has been playing with innovations in geothermal heating systems. He's not popular right now in some circles, as his new geothermal installations aren't working too well.

"He may be laying low because I hear the bikers are mad at him for messing up two of their high-end resort condo projects with the geothermal system. But then, he may be hiding from his ex-wife. I hear he had a pretty messy divorce recently. His typical way of disappearing is to go on a hunting or fishing trip far into the backcountry. I know he loves Alaska and the Yukon."

"Yet, there's no credit card trail or anything." Said Janet.

"Mmm. How else can I help?" asked Brian. "Other than keep my eyes and ears open?"

"I don't know what else, Brian. Did many of the weapons get produced before the government took over? Who may have gotten them?" asked Shirley.

"And who might be using one around here? Well, as I recall, Ken was pretty careful for whom he made a weapon. He would only sell to native Indians. I think only a few got made and sold, possibly half a dozen. He was getting a good dollar for them because carbon fiber was a new complex high technology – as simple as it now seems – and the weapons then were all handmade "one off" things that were time consuming to make. I think he was selling them for upwards of $6,000 apiece – the price of an expensive bicycle now – and that had a limited market at the time."

"Do you remember any of the buyers?" asked Janet.

"Not really. A couple went to guys on the reservations around Vancouver. One or two up here, but I don't know which bands they were associated with. Maybe one or two on the Prairies – I think Manitoba and Northern Saskatchewan. Maybe one in the Yukon."

After they said their goodbyes and Brian faded away in the direction of the boardwalk, Janet said, "An interesting man. But didn't you notice one thing? He never took off his sunglasses. We never got to look in his eyes."

"Yes," said Shirley. "That's because he has one weakness. His eyes flutter when he's lying. I'll bet he could remember the names of some of the buyers if he wanted."

They walked along the boardwalk, then into the restored old shopping district and eventually wound up back at the hotel by five-thirty. They agreed to meet at six-thirty in another outdoor restaurant/bar they had spotted near the marina. Janet arrived first, requested a table and was told there would be a half hour wait but she could wait at the bar, if she wanted. She settled at the bar on a stool near the cash register and ordered a Kokanee, a local beer, which the bartender recommended.

The bar wasn't too busy and she soon found herself engaged in conversation with the young, dark bushy-haired, brown-eyed bar tender who answered to "Nick." He was a tall six foot six on a lanky, all muscle frame and was dressed in black pants and belt, and a white short-sleeved shirt with black bow tie. She learned the young man was a black-diamond level daredevil ski bum who lived for the winter and deep powder snow. He was very talkative, trying to impress. A few innocent questions by Janet and he was soon volunteering information about the crime level and hierarchy of the valley.

"We don't have too much trouble from the bikers as one gang controls the whole valley," he said. "They allow visitors from other gangs as long as they behave. No, our crime is from the unorganized, like random robberies, B & Es for drug money, a spouse kills a spouse – that sort of thing. It's pretty quiet compared to the gang wars in Vancouver."

Janet asked innocently, "What about smuggling? Someone said there was pot going across the border?"

"Growing pot's the major industry here. As far as smuggling, I understand it's not the bikers – that it's more the Indians. Most of the Indian bands are very much business but there's one that seems less interested in legitimate business development and more in moving pot across in return for cocaine and guns. They're a bit odd that way. They don't like the public on their reservation. They've even blockaded the road going through their land to one of our best ski mountains from time to time demanding ransom. They're really big on claiming more land from the government."

"Oh, which band is that?"

He leaned across the bar and whispered into Janet's ear: "Midlake."

While this exchange was going on, two large, dark-haired men in designer jeans and polo shirts were sitting at a table in close proximity. One looked over his sunglasses to the other and muttered, "Oh Christ! A blabbermouth – anything to impress the women! He needs a lesson." They finished their drinks, settled the bill and left.

Shirley arrived just as the hostess announced their table was ready. They had a pleasant dinner – white wine, bottled cold water, seafood salad and yogurt ice cream for Janet, white wine, bottled cold water, king crab salad and decadent chocolate cheese cake for Shirley. As they took a walk along the boardwalk, enjoying the summer evening's sights, Janet recounted the conversation she had with Nick, the bartender.

"We know a good bit about the marijuana industry and drug distribution here," Shirley said. "It seems to be mainly under the control of the bikers. But the Indian band involvement is a new idea. It might make a bit of sense, as there are some reservations that run right up to the border. Midlake band has a few large pieces of land for reservations but none along the border. Mind you, they've gone into partnership on some ventures with the NightHawk band that has reservation land running along the border. Tell you what, if you want, we can drive down to the Midlake reservations and innocently look around a bit. There's only one road we're allowed on. That's a provincial road running through the band's land. How about tomorrow morning? We don't meet with Donny until two."

Janet agreed. "Good. You can fill me in on your Mr. Donny Fortunato on the way."

They returned to the hotel about ten-thirty, had a drink in an outdoor bar, and then turned in for the night.

The next day was a carbon copy of the past: clear, smog-free bright sun and soaring temperature. After a leisurely continental-style breakfast in the patio restaurant, they retrieved the car and headed south along Highway 97, retracing their path through West Kelowna then following the lake through Peachland. Eventually they found a crossroad with a sign pointing to a ski mountain some twenty miles distant and took it. They soon crossed a cattle guard and fencing with a large sign declaring:

MIDWAY INDIAN RESERVATION
PRIVATE ROADS
NO TRESSPASING
EXCEPT ON BUSINESS
STAY ON HIGHWAY ONLY

Janet said, "That sign is a bit confusing. I gather that the road is a provincial highway but we are not supposed to branch off it while on Indian land?"

"Yeah. Looks as if they don't like strangers. Other Indian bands often are more welcoming. But these guys are big on asserting their land claims."

The road meandered through a flat area interspersed with old housing, unkept, junky yards, a few industrial buildings including a small-scale sawmill in rickety condition, a log home manufacturing area and a gravel pit. The road took a path ascending from the flat land into a canyon following a river. On one side was a hill dotted with better quality homes and a large concrete building that Shirley identified as the tribal affairs office. Eventually, they crossed over another cattle guard with signage announcing the end of the reservation. They continued to follow the road as it climbed a mountain, passing through the large ski village of Sasquatch Mountain and continuing their climb along a wide gravel road passing numerous loaded logging trucks. They eventually came to another cattle guard and fence with signage again declaring:

MIDWAY INDIAN RESERVATION #2
PRIVATE ROADS
NO TRESSPASING
EXCEPT ON BUSINESS
STAY ON HIGHWAY ONLY

They followed the road until it ended at the locked gate for the Great Similkameen Mine tourist attraction. They turned around to retrace their trip planning on returning to Kelowna by noon. Just as their car passed over the cattle guard where #2 reservation started,

Janet noticed a vehicle, a brown minivan about ten years old, parked at the side of the road. A man, about six feet, one hundred eighty pounds, fair curly hair, fairly young, mid-thirties maybe, dressed in jeans, runners and brown tee shirt was taking photographs of wildflowers with an expensive-looking reflex camera. For a fleeting second Janet thought, "I've seen that guy before."

During the drive, Shirley filled Janet in on Mr. Donny Fortunato." I've known him for a long time. He was very helpful to us during both Gulf Wars when we were keeping tabs on some people in the region. We do other business as well. We exchange favors. Donny is capo of the Devil's Brew bikers who control the Okanagan. They're affiliated with others right across North America.

"Donny is pushing sixty now. He's Portuguese. He has a bachelor's degree in business administration and a keen business sense. He's been married to Cindy for thirty years and they have three children, all grown and out of the house. Cindy's from Sicily, is a charmer, a great cook and very family oriented. Donny comes across as a jovial, loud kind of guy but he has a mean streak when it comes to business. Rumor has it that he used to be top dog in knife and chain fights and has killed six people or more. Now, he's projecting the aura of a successful businessman.

"The bikers are big in drugs. They grow a lot of marijuana and finance a lot of free-lancers to grow it as well. They distribute all the other drugs, pretty much have control of it in the whole valley. They're also into hijacking, chop shops, loan sharking, prostitution and fencing stolen goods. Their profits have been put into legitimate business ventures to the point they own an awful lot of businesses in the valley like motels, night clubs, restaurants, RV, motorcycle, car and boat dealers, vineyards, orchards, mortgage brokers and condos – you name it, they'll be in it."

When they returned to their hotel, they had a lunch on the patio near the boardwalk. After signing the check, Shirley said, "Let's get ready. Better bring your swimsuit and sun tan oil. They have a pool. Oh, and I hope you know how to play bridge and lose gracefully."

"I gather we'll be visiting their residence. Yes, I play bridge."

The Fortunato residence turned out to be nestled lakeside on Kalamalka Lake on a thirty-acre estate, about a twenty-minute drive in traffic north on Highway 97 toward Vernon. The home was an architecturally designed rancher of about eight thousand square feet.

Picture windows presented a great view of the lake, their pier with a thirty-foot speedboat suspended out of the water on an elevating mechanism and the sixty-foot kidney shaped pool with adjoining hot tub. Near the hot tub end of the pool was a shade gazebo containing a round table with four chairs and a man seated at a white leather love seat reading a novel.

Cindy greeted them at the front door and, after Shirley and Cindy exchanged "long-time-no-see-don't-you-look-wonderful" greetings and Janet was properly introduced, she led them through the house and the pool deck to the gazebo. Donny jumped up and quickly walked toward Shirley with arms spread ready to hug. He was about five foot eleven, heavily built, two hundred forty pounds with potbelly, swarthy complexion, large hands and wrists, ample black curly hair, very hairy chest, arms and legs. He was barefoot, and shirtless, wearing blue boxer swim trunks.

After exchanging hugs and kisses on both cheeks, Shirley introduced Janet simply as "my friend."

Cindy took drink orders and disappeared into the kitchen. Donny sat them down around the table in the gazebo. After doing a little more "long-time-no-see" conversation, Donny turned to Janet and said, "Janet, are you in the same line of work?"

Shirley replied for her. "Similar."

"Well then, not just a social call today? You must stay for bridge and dinner of course. But let's get the business out of the way."

Shirley took the lead and explained their reason for the visit. "We've got a problem linked to Taliban terrorists and possibly Al Qaeda that has a link to the Okanagan on both sides of the border." She asked Janet to produce the picture of the archery weapon, which Donny carefully looked at after donning reading glasses. "Arrows from a non-military version of this," she continued, "killed a border patrol officer just east of Oroville and an Afghan warlord loyal to us in Northern Afghanistan.

Donny said, "That's not good. We've got a nephew serving with the forces in Kandahar. I've seen something similar, but single shot. It was many years ago."

"Years ago?"

"Yeah, late eighties, early nineties, something like that. It was a son-of-a-bitch named Ken Davidson, out of the Shuswap. He's a bit of an inventor – not always a good one. He was trying to get me to invest. Then, I heard he sold it to the Canadian military and wasn't allowed to produce any without their permission. That SOB isn't popular with me right now. He sold us on the idea of installing a new type of geothermal heat and aircon system in a couple of our condo projects. They cost over two million each and they don't work. We're stuck for millions to tear them out and replace with something effective. We're facing lawsuits from the strata councils of the buildings and we've sued his company. It's messy."

Shirley said, "We've been trying to locate Ken but he seems to have dropped out of sight."

"Well, he may be lying low over the geothermal problems, but I don't think anybody was out to hurt him – if you get my drift? We'll be tied up in the court case for years. He's also had a nasty divorce."

"Right!" said Shirley.

"I'll see if we can find him for you if you'd like. Can I reach you the same old way? When was that killing of the border patrol agents?"

"Thanks Donny, the agents were killed about six weeks ago."

"Mmm. Smugglers?"

"We really don't know. Maybe."

Cindy arrived with the drinks. Janet, Cindy and Shirley had white wine and Donny had a beer. Donny picked up a deck of cards that were on the table and said, "I have two new decks. Cindy and I would love a game of bridge. How about five dollars a point?"

After two hours, having finished the last hand with a flourish, Cindy called a halt to the game. Donny totaled up the score and said, "Not bad. A couple of times I thought you were going to be in the big money! Looks as if we win though, with 280 points over you. That's, let's see, fourteen hundred bucks you owe."

Shirley reached into her purse, brought out her wallet and counted out fourteen one hundred dollar bills, then, with both hands, presented them to Donny. Donny was all grins. Cindy was smiling. Donny said, "Thank you ladies. Now, how about a swim and another drink before dinner? Cindy's prepared veal, homemade pasta and one of her favorite sauces."

They had a leisurely candlelit dinner in the dining room, enjoying reminiscing and discussing the economy of the Okanagan. Red wine was served this time – an award-winning Shiraz from a vineyard in West Kelowna that Donny said he had an interest in.

It soon became evident that Donny was an expert on hydroponics and grow ops. At one point, when Cindy was out of the room, he said to Janet, "Lots of grow ops here. The income probably is half the economic base for the Okanagan. The quality is renowned and, in Canada, it's not too illegal. If someone gets busted for running an op, they seldom do time. The judges are very lenient. They're far harder on sex crimes and discrimination."

Shirley asked, "Are you still, ah, dabbling in politics?"

"Oh yeah. I guess we've got most of the judges and senators that have been appointed recently. Our contributions, above and under the table, to the political party in power and the one approaching it are pretty big and we earmark our contributions for very specific purposes. In the good old days, we used to be able to provide call girls and boys, coke and booze for the politicals but now, everybody just wants money."

The conversation abruptly changed when Cindy came back into the room.

Shirley and Janet bid their hosts good night about eleven o clock and made their way back to the hotel. In the car Janet said, "You know, we could have won the bridge game but you seemed to throw away some hands and how come you kicked me under the table on a couple of bids?"

Shirley smiles and said, "The bridge game is a nice way to pay him for his assistance. We were lucky at five bucks a point. He often wants ten or fifteen. Besides, he's very proud. Cindy is a Masters level player. And, on top of that, he doesn't like to lose. He gets very cranky when he loses. We did all right. We gave them enough challenge to keep them happy."

"Do you think he'll be helpful?" Janet asked.

"I'm not sure, but one thing I know, he's patriotic. He served four years in the military as a paratrooper."

"You're right about one thing. I'm getting a far better view of the real picture! Looks as if organized crime is very well organized."

The next day they checked out of their hotel and headed North on Highway 97, ending up in Salmon Arm, on Shuswap Lake. They got hotel rooms at a lakeside resort and settled in. Meeting at the patio restaurant a half hour later, they had lunch outdoors and surveyed the scenery. Unlike Okanagan Lake, Shuswap Lake branched into a number of inlets, some with mountainous fjords that tended to provide shelter for the myriad of boaters. The patio was surrounded with electronic bug "zappers" crackling periodically when a marauding mosquito landed on one. This was a contrast to Okanagan Lake where no bugs were present due to the orchard spraying.

The lake seemed full of houseboats. There were six charter houseboats, all luxurious, about fifty feet long, all by the same local maker, tied up at the resort's dock. All sprouted slides from the top deck to the water and all had hot tubs on the top deck. Four rental ski boats were moored in front of the houseboats. Tall mountains surrounded the lake. There were many white sandy beaches visible across the lake on the nearest shoreline. On some of the beaches, houseboats were nose in with their bows resting on the sand and an anchor line running off their sterns to hold them perpendicular the beach. It was hot. The area seemed to be a vacation mecca. The parking lot was filled with vehicles bearing license plates from other provinces and many American states.

After scanning the scenery, Janet said, "Don't be obvious when you look, but we may have been followed. There's a man over to your left, by the beach entrance. He's wearing silvered sunglasses, brown polo shirt, tan shorts and tan sandals and he's reading the menu now. We passed him yesterday on that gravel road just as we were exiting the number two reservation."

"Mmm. You're observant. There's hope for you yet," said Shirley as she turned toward the man, made a "come-here" motion with her left arm and hand and said, "Bob, over here!"

Grinning, the man named Bob joined them at their table. Shirley said, "You've been made, Bob. Took a little while though. Janet, this is Bob LeMay. He's been covering our backs."

"Hi Janet! Glad to meet you!" Said Bob as he reached to shake Janet's hand.

Shirley said, "Bob's full time with us. We've assigned him to this area for a while."

"I've had your backs since you came off the Coquihalla Connector the other day. You only seemed to draw attention once. Janet, when you were talking to that bartender the other night while waiting for Shirley, two guys at a table close to you took some interest. I think they overheard your conversation. Anyway, they left before Shirley arrived. After you two went in for the night, I kept an eye on the bartender and followed him to the parking lot after he got off shift. They jumped him. Gave him a good beating. Looks like they broke his kneecaps. Up here, that's the treatment you can expect for talking too much."

132

Janet said, "You didn't intervene?"

"Not in my job description on this assignment. Sorry."

"Oh."

"Anyway, I followed them. The trail led onto the Midlake reservation. Looks as if they both have homes there."

"That might be a lead," Shirley speculated. "Either that or the locals just plain don't like blabbermouths."

Janet said, "We'll do some research?"

Bob said, "It's under way. The Deacon's looking into it."

"Now, Shirley, what are your plans for this area?" asked Bob.

"The main thing was to meet up with you outside Kelowna. But, I'd like to take a look at Kenneth Davidson's place. I gather you've spent some time up here looking around."

"Yeah. We followed up on what the RCMP and CSIS did. CSIS bugged his house but there hasn't been anything. RCMP interviewed the neighbors but they don't know where he went. Ditto for his church group and his business partners and employees. Most think he's trying to lay low because of the problems with his geothermal systems. His place is a bit isolated with lots of property and dense forest from the road in to the house. Not much to see. Best view is from the lake. If you want, we can rent a ski boat for the afternoon and go take a look. We might be able to get some skiing in, too."

"Sounds good!" said Shirley. "Let's make arrangements for the boat, then we'll get changed."

"We'll need some mosquito repellent and I've got some suntan oil. Let's go."

Shirley signed the bill. Then they went to the boat rental office on the pier and arranged for a twenty-foot ski boat, skis and wake boards. After returning to their rooms and changing, they met back at the boat rental office for a safety lecture, temporary boat operator's licenses, and were then shown the safety, operation and recreation features of the boat. With Bob driving, they taxied, with no wake, out past the breakwater sheltering the pier, then took off across the lake.

After about half an hour at high speed, Bob throttled back the boat and it settled in the water. He pointed out Ken's house, a massive log structure. It was separated from its nearest neighbor by one thousand feet of beach and dense trees. At water's edge was a pier with a white ski boat elevated out of the water, its topside covered in canvas. Beside the house was a large 30 x 60 foot shed matching the architecture of the house with false log siding. It looked as if it could hold at least four vehicles. It had one double garage door off to the right on the side facing the water and a metal chimney was visible just below the peak of the roof. Bob said, "The shed looks like his workshop. Note, he has a basement below the house"

Shirley said, "Did you do your research?"

"Yeah, he has a pretty simple alarm system for both the house and the shed."

"Let's land on the beach in front and take a look." Shirley said.

"What? We're not going to break in are we?" asked a worried Janet. "I'm an officer of the law – albeit not in Canada. I can't do that!"

"You're not," Shirley said. "You haven't been trained for it. You can land us at the pier, then take the boat offshore, say a quarter of a mile, and do some sun bathing. You don't need to anchor, there's no wind. Don't be alarmed if you see people walking on the beach. In Canada, all beaches up to the highest water line are public. I doubt if any of the neighbors will come by. We can bring the boat up to the pier at an angle not visible to the neighbors."

After checking for people walking on the beach, Bob brought the boat in to the pier and Janet changed places with him. He took a small leather pouch out of the packsack he had brought and put it in his waistband at the back of his swim trunks. He was wearing black rubber beach shoes, tan swim trunks and a light tan tee shirt. Shirley, dressed in a white bikini and white tee shirt, had white canvas rubber soled beach shoes. Both had sunglasses.

Shirley and Bob clambered out of the boat onto the pier and calmly walked up toward the house. Janet backed the boat off, turned it around and backtracked out farther into the lake. Once she got a quarter mile offshore, she turned off the engine, removed the tan tee shirt she had over her red bikini, settled on a towel she placed on the stern over the engine compartment, and began lathering on sunscreen. All the while, she kept a wary eye on the shore.

It seemed like a half-hour before she saw Shirley wave from the beach about a hundred feet down from the pier. Janet started the boat and headed in. As she reached the pier, Bob and Shirley casually walked out and boarded the boat. Janet then backed out. They took the boat about a quarter mile offshore, slowed, and with the engine idling, Shirley put on a ski life jacket, sat on the stern of the boat and began adjusting a slalom ski to fit her foot. Bob fitted a ski rope to the tow mast.

While they were getting ready to ski, Shirley filled Janet in on what they saw. "I did the shed. It's got another three garage doors on the other side. It has a wood-fired stove and a kiln. There are some woodworking tools: table saw, planer, large lathe, large band saw, and a big workbench. He's got an arc welder, metal machinist's lathe, power hacksaw, metal bending press, a gas-fired forge and a small CAD-CAM boring mill. He's well equipped for tinkering. Parked at one end are a quad, a skidoo, a jet ski, a snow blower and a small utility trailer for hauling the quad and skidoo. There's also a jeep CJ equipped for off road. He has lots of toys."

Bob said, "The house is clean, no indication of where he's gone. The basement is another workshop. He's got an arsenal of hunting equipment down there, rifles, shotguns, a couple of bows and one single-shot archery weapon. He also has about a dozen fishing rods of every description from fly rods to trolling rods. Looks as if he's into fly tying, even making his own trolling lures. He has a computer hooked up to a small boring mill and plastic laser printer. That's the kind used to design and produce prototypes. I fired the computer up and copied his files. Our people can look at them later. There were some photos on the wall in the library. Many were hunting photos, some with other people with him. I took photos of them. Maybe we might identify some of his associates."

"Great," Said Janet.

Shirley, now with her left foot in the ski, swung over the side and eased into the water. Bob threw her the handles for the tow rope. With Janet driving, Shirley pulled out of the water with ease and quickly got into the rhythm of jumping the wake. In calm water they went down the lake about two miles before Shirley dropped the towline and settled gracefully in the water. Bob helped her out then got ready for his run. They spent the rest of the afternoon taking turns on the skis. Bob tried wakeboarding as well. They returned to the hotel about seven p.m., changed and met for dinner at the hotel's restaurant patio at eight.

After dinner, they met in Janet's room and held a strategy session. The information from the computer would be processed by Shirley's office. The photos Bob took would be run through both CIA and FBI databases and passed on to CSIS to see what they could come up with. They agreed the members of the Midlake band who beat up the bartender should get close attention. Bob would return to

Kelowna to work with The Deacon to help glean some information on Midlake band members while both Shirley and Janet's people conducted secondary information reviews. Shirley would also ask CSIS what they could provide. Bob would get another person as backup and Shirley would give him a sizable budget to pay for information from his informers and tasking his part-time operatives.

Janet was worried. "One of the factors in the equation that we have not explored is the helicopter. There was a helicopter in the vicinity the night of the murders. It probably was involved in smuggling. How can we get some knowledge of helicopters operating on the Canadian side of the border?"

"Good point!" Shirley chimed in. "Bob, what do you know?"

"Well, the Okanagan boasts a lot of helicopter companies. There are six flying schools training on helicopters, some the best in the world for mountain flying. The region is ideal for training due to the variety of the terrain and some of the instructors who are aces in mountain flying. There are ten helicopter companies based in the area. All have major maintenance bases here. Many supply craft all over Canada and other countries such as for fire fighting, helicopter skiing, surveys and oil field support. The main things, since 9/11, students are carefully screened – as are instructors and pilots, of course. I know a bit about this as I have a great friend who has one of the larger schools in the Okanagan. I guess we could talk with him, if you want."

"Great idea!" said Shirley. "Can we do it tomorrow?"

"Probably. Let me give him a call." Bob went outside on the balcony and placed a call on his cell phone. He returned a few moments later and announced, "All set, he'll see us for lunch, tomorrow."

"Where?" asked Janet.

"Oliver. We can easily be there by noon if we leave here by nine."

It was decided that, after the meeting in Oliver, Shirley and Janet would head home to work from their respective offices.

Shirley and Bob left Janet's room when the meeting broke up. About fifteen minutes later, Janet heard a soft knock on her door. She looked in the peephole, then opened the door and Bob quickly stepped in. They embraced with a long wet deep kiss. Both were very excited, panting heavily. Janet put a hand on Bob's crotch. He moaned and they kissed again. He placed a hand on one of Janet's breasts then in her crotch and she moaned. She squeezed. He squeezed as they kissed deeply again.

Bob was first to speak, very hoarsely, quietly, "I've been excited since I first saw you. Then, today on the boat, I couldn't keep my eyes off you. It's lust. I know it. But it's powerful!"

"Me too!" whispered Janet. "I need you right now. I haven't done anything for months. I just went through a nasty divorce. I'm probably not fit for socializing but I need you. Right now!"

They moved to the bed and helped each other undress. The first experience was too quick and rough but after a few minutes cuddling, they managed a sensuous encounter and another later. Bob returned to his room before sunrise.

Next day, in two cars, they made Oliver by noon. Bob followed Janet and Shirley, covering their back, always well behind a few other vehicles. Bob had arranged to meet his contact at a wine bistro on the main street in downtown Oliver. When they arrived, he was seated at a table for four on the patio. He recognized Bob and waved. Bob introduced Janet and Shirley to Rustem (Rus) Potter, owner of Potter Helicopters Ltd. Rus was in his mid-fifties, suntanned, with pleasant brown eyes, and a stocky frame. He was wearing blue shorts, brown leather sandals and a white polo shirt with his corporate logo on the left sleeve.

It was hot. The wall thermometer registered 104 degrees Fahrenheit in the shade. The patio was equipped with misting sprayers, which helped bring the temperature down.

After all were seated, Rus said, "Bob mentioned you wanted to learn a bit about helicopter operations in Canada and especially the Okanagan? Where should I begin?"

"Well, we're wondering how easily it would be to use a helicopter for cross-border smuggling," said Shirley.

"Ouch!" grimaced Rus. "Do you want to smuggle something?"

"No, no!" laughed Shirley. "We're tracking something that looks as if some cross-border smuggling was involved."

"Oh. Well, you won't find any of the legitimate companies involved. All are too busy this time of year. The ones with equipment remaining in the Okanagan have their machines tied up in exploration, heavy lifting for cell towers and transmission lines, highway work, firefighting and training. In winter, there's a lot of deployment to the ski hills or they're off to warmer climates for firefighting, or into equipment maintenance. For example, I'm considered one of the mid-sized outfits but I've got eighty helicopters and pilots all over the world. I run the alpine training from here. That's for advanced pilot training and I have students from Europe, Australia, New Zealand and some South American countries. I even have a contract to teach military pilots for Canada, Jamaica and Germany."

Janet said, "What about the pilots?"

"We all tend to keep our pilots busy. Good ones with mountain flying skills are valuable. After 9/11 we very carefully vet all applicants – mainly because they can wind up working in other countries for us. Mind you, we do have a lot to choose from, as there are many looking for work. Typically, good applicants are people with military training that we can bring up to advanced levels. We get a lot of applicants without sufficient experience that we either screen out immediately or, if they are really good, we'll help them upgrade, then have them fly as co-pilots on the machines that require two pilots. Mind you, if someone came to us with lots of experience, we would still have to test them and certify them before they were let loose with one of our machines."

"So, someone looking for work might be tempted to work for smugglers?" asked Janet.

"I guess so. There's lots of unemployment in the field. However, you have to be pretty good to continue to fly around here, as the conditions are tricky at times. But, getting a chopper may be a problem. All have to be certified airworthy, logs of usage and preventative maintenance have to be kept up to date and very careful track is kept by the authorities on the whereabouts of all aircraft and replacement parts. All parts have to be certified airworthy and there are good records kept on them."

"But Rus, is there a possibility that someone could obtain a chopper and keep knowledge of it away from the authorities?" asked Shirley.

"I guess it's possible in theory but where would they get the replacement parts to keep a chopper flying? They wouldn't be able to officially get certified parts."

"What about sneaking in some parts from another country?" asked Janet.

"The supply of officially approved parts is pretty tight," replied Rus. "It could be possible. Perhaps with false invoicing, I guess. Another angle would be to use military surplus parts. These are coded and can't be used in commercial aircraft but on some models the military version and the civilian versions have many parts that are interchangeable. It may be possible to access some military parts internationally, such as what was left over in Viet Nam when the Americans bailed out. But, if caught with military parts in your aircraft, you not only loose the certification of that aircraft, you lose your business registration."

"What happens to older helicopters? Are many sold off for spare parts?" asked Bob. "Could it be possible to rebuild one and fly it?"

"Yes. It is possible but you would not be certified and couldn't get replacement parts from regular suppliers. You could cannibalize one for the spare parts, but again no certification would be possible without approval of the source of the spare parts."

"What if you didn't care about certification?" asked Bob.

"You'd have a hard time flying in and out of airports and getting flight plans approved. And you could not legitimately sell the aircraft. But, if you want it just for smuggling, it's possible."

"So, we could try to track helicopter registrations and keep an eye on older ones or wrecks that could be rebuilt. And, we should try to find unemployed pilots who might be employed in smuggling," said Janet.

"Yes," said Rus. "You may also want to review flight plans registered with the government. Everyone legitimate has to file one, even when we do training. You may be able to spot someone frequently flying close to the border or across the border. We do have a mutual aid protocol with Washington, Idaho, Montana and some other states for firefighting, so some cross on firefighting and fire patrol assignments."

After thanking Rus and Bob, Janet and Shirley drove back to Bellingham. They followed Highway 97 to Highway 3 and followed it through Princeton, Manning Park, Hope, and Chilliwack, finally crossing the border at Huntington.

Chapter 13

David poked his head into his dad's office of the tribal council, and said, "Hi, Dad." Then he entered and shut the door. They were alone. "We're all set for tonight. There's still a good flow of water and no moon. Sunset is about nine-fifteen. The trucks will be there about nine-thirty. Johnny and Willie have alerted all the people on the reservation who may see the vehicles. Emma and Frank Wilson, who have the first house off the highway where the reserve begins, will be watching our backs. They could give us at least a ten-minute warning if we get raided from the landside. Johnny, Willie, Marcus and Charlie will be the inner sentries.

"We're monitoring the border patrol and sheriff's frequencies as well as RCMP and conservation officers. We're not getting too close to the border anyway. We'll let the water do the job. From our side, we'll look as if we're having a camp-out. We're even bringing hot dogs and marshmallows."

Joseph said, "If you're going to party, no drinking until after the job is done. Right? And no bonfires due to the fire hazard as that will attract attention."

"Yeah, Dad. Is the other side ready?"

"All set. The environmental research group has been camped out at the farm for the past week. I'll be leaving shortly. The committee protesting the proposed dam is meeting at the Oroville golf club at seven tonight. I'll put in an appearance there as well."

A moonless night had fallen. Lots of stars were showing in the clear sky well away from city lights. It was a warm night with the temperature beginning to fall below eighty-five degrees. Upstream, the men were wearing night vision goggles as the six of them offloaded blue plastic barrels from two large, white, ten-ton panel vans. They rolled the barrels down gangplanks from the truck bed to the river's edge. Each barrel, once it was rolled into the water, was checked over to ensure no bubbles and near negative buoyancy. The barrels were roped end to end in groups of ten, then pushed out into the river's flow where the five-knot current swept them downstream. One man was in each truck bed rolling the barrels to the gangplank where another man, standing on the ground, guided the barrels.

Another man beside the trucks checked off each barrel's number as it came down.

The job didn't take long, not more than twenty minutes. When completed, the gangplanks were stowed in their racks under the bed of each truck, the cargo doors closed, the drivers mounted up and the trucks departed. The four remaining men walked over to a Jeep, which had large offroad tires. David said, "Let me call Dad." He pulled out his cell phone, typed in a short text message and speed dialed. They then got into the jeep and headed over to Marcus's place, just a short distance away.

They would stand by until every barrel was accounted for at the arrival point. If a barrel or group of barrels were missing, they would don scuba gear and swim the river until they located it and moved it on. In that case, they would follow the barrel to the destination. The river wasn't wide, not more than 100 feet across. This night the water flow assured an average four-foot depth at the mainstream of the river. Experience had shown there was little chance of hang-ups.

Across the border, Joseph received the text message on his cell phone: "OK."

On the American side of the border, the river meanders through a marshland, known as the Chopaka Marsh, then gently empties into the narrow but long and shallow Similkameen Lake. Joseph, through the AFEI, the Environmental Fishery Enhancement Society, had purchased all the marsh and the north end of Similkameen Lake. The land covered both sides of the river and stretched a mile from the Canadian border to within three hundred feet of the old townsite of NightHawk, Washington.

On the other side of a small mountain, a road and an abandoned railway line ran beside the property but mainly out of sight of the river. This was the Chopaka Road, which linked the Chopaka-NightHawk border crossing port of entry with the Loomis-Oroville road at the remnants of the once booming mining and railway town of NightHawk. Population five. The Chopaka-NightHawk border crossing, just a few miles north of the NightHawk junction, was only open during the day from 9 a.m. to 5 p.m. and had little traffic.

Joseph and his crew were on the river's bank where the river made its first weaving bend near the start of the marsh. They were on a farm that had been purchased by the AFEI when they acquired the entire marshland. The little farmhouse now hosted a native couple in their sixties who served as custodians for the wetlands. Near the farmhouse, and just a hundred yards up from the river, was a large, well-maintained barn. Through his night vision goggles, Joseph was looking at the net that had been tightly stretched at a forty-five degree angle up across the river. It was designed to channel the barrels to their side of the river. Although the flow of water tended to create an eddy at Joseph's feet, where things gathered, the net would ensure nothing got past. From the time of the message, Joseph estimated it would be forty-five minutes before the first barrels arrived. He whispered to his men, "About forty-five minutes."

His crew was larger. He had a dozen men. Half were dressed in wet suits, all with night vision goggles. They were ready to wrestle the barrels out of the river, onto tractor towed hay wagons and into the barn where they would be transferred to a waiting truck.

The "catch," as Joseph liked to call it, went smoothly. When all barrels were retrieved and put in the barn, he sent a text message to David: "OK."

Inside the barn, using red lighting to help preserve their night vision and cut down on visibility to outsiders, the men were busy putting labels on the barrels describing the contents as "Pasteurized Fish Protein," then loading them onto a fifty-three foot trailer hooked up to a maroon-painted double rear axle Kenworth diesel tractor with a sleeper cab. The rig was completely within the barn and the barn doors were closed. Joseph reviewed the list of barrels, confirming that all were present, then turned to a man standing beside him, looking over his shoulder at the list. Joseph said, "Well, Ed, all accounted for. You've counted the barrels, done a random inspection of the contents and all the barrels have been weighed. If all's O.K. with you, it's time for the money transfer."

Ed pulled out his cell phone and speed dialed. After connection, he texted a series of numbers and after a few minutes, turned to Joseph and said, "Should be in your bank account in thirty seconds."

Joseph waited a minute then speed dialed, made a few keystrokes, waited, then confirmed: "It's there." He turned away from Ed and entered some more keystrokes to flip the money from the receiving bank in Belize to another account in Mauritius. After he received confirmation of transfer he closed and pocketed his phone, then turned to Ed and handed him some waybills "Here. Some waybills. Just in case you get stopped and for when you pass through the highway scales. They state your load originated on the coast at Aberdeen, Washington.

"The top is a waybill for a delivery of twenty barrels to a tree nursery just down the road, near Loomis. Once you get past Omak without problems, destroy that waybill. The next waybill shows a delivery for a nursery in Tri-Cities. Same deal, tear it up when you cross the Columbia River. The next and last one shows the load destined for St. Louis. Your load is well underweight, so you won't have any troubles at the scales. The last two rows of barrels, where you might get an inspector looking, are all the real liquid fish fertilizer. All other barrels are topped off with the same.

"I don't see any potential problems but don't use your engine brakes tonight when you come to the crossroad at NightHawk or down the hill into Oroville. That way, you're less likely to attract attention. Once you're on Highway 97, you're just another transport rig and you'll likely not attract any attention. Anyway, we'll be in front and back of you until you clear Omak. Just in case, you know. If you're ready to roll, let's check with my man monitoring the law enforcement frequencies and he'll check with the sentries."

"Thanks, Joseph," Ed said. I'll be on my way then. See you next month. You'll let me know what type of vehicle or vehicles to bring and the transfer point." They exchanged bear hugs. One of the men, who had been sitting in front of a laptop computer, gave a thumbs up signal. Ed mounted the cab and fired up the diesel while two men opened the front doors of the barn. Ed waved as he moved out. A small white panel van and a green Ford SUV followed. The SUV passed the truck and headed down the road. The panel van trailed behind the truck. Ed and his escorts would use night vision goggles until well down the road, then switch over to normal running lights.

Joseph turned to another man, Danny Wilson, who was the caretaker for the farm. "Danny, we'll keep some of the crew over a day or so. Bob and Arnold will pretend to do some land survey while JoJo and Stan will go paddling through the marsh doing their environmental assessment. If anybody asks, they have to have an environmental report ready by mid-October. I'll bed down with you tonight, then leave about nine. It'll give me a chance to talk with you all and we can do some more thinking how best to lobby against the dam they're proposing in the canyon."

"Great," Danny said. "We have breakfast at seven."

Chapter 14

The black Buick with four men in it turned south off Highway 3 onto the road leading through NightHawk Reservation Number Six. It proceeded along the road, weaving among low hills, passing a few scattered houses, eventually stopping in the graveled driveway of a dilapidated, two-room house. There was no lawn, just scattered sagebrush, dry dusty earth and rocks among a few old junked cars and rusting pieces of farm machinery. The shallow peaked roof was patched in many places with different color asphalt shingles and had one rain gutter hanging down at an angle.

Three men got out of the Buick. They were Asian. All were of similar stocky build. All had crew cuts. They were dressed in black suits, white shirts and black ties, black-laced shoes – an uncomfortable choice in the ninety-five degree heat. One had a scar on his right cheek running from right ear to upper lip. He motioned to one who then ran to the back of the house. He and his remaining partner drew their guns from shoulder holsters and went to the front door. They didn't knock. They kicked in the front door and rushed in with guns drawn. At the same time, the man in the back kicked in the rear door and entered. It took only a few seconds to move through the house and determine no one was home.

The driver, another Asian of similar build, brought in a can of kerosene and, starting with the mattress in the main bedroom, poured it around at the leader's direction then laid a trail of fluid out the front door. Once they exited, the leader lit a piece of crumpled newspaper and tossed it on the kerosene trail. They paused briefly to ensure the fire got a good hold – perhaps to admire their handiwork. They got back in the car which U-turned and proceeded quickly back along the reservation road the way they came.

As the car rounded a tight corner where the road was cut through the grade of a little hill, the driver slammed on his brakes, fishtailing the car to a halt. A tractor blocked the road. The car was hemmed in by the wall of the cut in the hill on both sides of the road. As the driver threw the car into reverse and began backing down the road, the front windshield of the Buick was shattered with a hole directly in front of the driver, whose body convulsed backward then slumped forward.

Those in the back seat didn't have time to comprehend that an arrow was sticking through the driver with three inches sticking out the back of his seat. Next, the windshield shattered on the passenger side and the man in the passenger seat slumped. He was dead with an arrow in his chest. The car, out of control, skewed backwards until it came to a halt with its rear wheels in the ditch and the rear bumper solid against the embankment.

The two in the back seat didn't realize their fate had only been delayed due to the black tinted windows. A voice shouted: "Throw out your guns then get out of the car! Get out now!" They complied, exiting with hands held high. Both jerked backward as they were shot with arrows through the chest.

David, Joseph and three others, each carrying archery weapons, ran up to the car, two men checking to ensure all were dead. One man turned off the engine. Joseph said, "David, Willie, load the bodies in the van and dispose of them. Dump them down the old number three mineshaft off the end of the road. It's plenty deep. They're not the first to get dumped there. You can toss in some lime to destroy the bodies later. Willie, you've got a key to the shaft entrance?" A nod from Willie. "Try to remove the arrows though. Move quickly as that fire will attract some attention.

"Johnny and Marcus, hook up the tractor to the car and put it in Johnny's barn – it's closest. You can take it to the chop shop and strip it for parts later but burn the front seat and smash and bury what's left of the front window out at the band's land fill ASAP – like today before dark. Once you're in the barn with the car, first priority is to deactivate the bug – you know where to find it. Until the car's away from the road, we'll keep the band's firefighters back down the road. Quickly now!"

Later, in the privacy of his Tribal Council office, Joseph and David debriefed. "That tracking system Donny got us from Little Spook sure worked well. We were alerted as soon as the car got out of Greater Vancouver. We had enough time from when they passed Manning Park, halfway to Princeton, to make up a reception committee. Once they passed Princeton, it was easy guessing that they were headed for Mona's house. That should teach Mr. Suk Kwan Lee a lesson but I doubt if he'll heed it. We'll have to put a permanent stop to him. I'll talk to Donny. He's got the right people for the job. No sense in us going down there; we might stick out a bit."

"O.K, Dad. I got ahold of Mona. She's both very thankful you warned her and got her out of the way but upset she lost her home.

She's not worried so much about the house as she is about her clothes, mementos, scrapbooks and family papers."

"Yeah, that's a bit rough," said Joseph. "You told her we'd replace the house, though. We can get a new modular home from Penticton pretty quick. Fully furnished. Give her the website address of the modular home company and tell her to pick something in a double or triple wide and what furnishing scheme she wants including appliances. That should perk her up a bit. If she chooses quickly, we can have her in her new home before freeze-up. In the meantime, ask her to stay where she is for a little while longer. Also, tell her we'll take her on a clothes shopping spree to the tune of two grand."

"Done. A little while longer means until the demise of one Mr. Suk Kwan Lee?"

"Right."

Two weeks later

Located on the East Side in an industrial area just beyond the fringe of one of Vancouver's downtown districts becoming trendy through urban renewal, the restaurant was one of the most popular ethnic Korean restaurants in town. It was on a side street half a block down from a busy artery. The street consisted of older one- and two-story warehouses nestled together, occasionally separated by parking lots. Directly across the street from the restaurant's large parking lot was a two-story warehouse with a storefront housing a marine supply store and a parking lot adjoining it.

At about twenty-five minutes after one in the morning the street was deserted and traffic on the main artery a block away was sparse. After a busy night in the restaurant, the receipts were tallied, staff had left and bank deposit made up. It had been a prosperous night. As was his custom, Suk Kwan Lee exited the front door of his restaurant with Liu Wan after Liu Wan had first checked the street for lurking strangers, then the parking lot to ensure their car, a black Buick, and driver were waiting, engine running.

Since the loss of his men on the Indian reservation, he was extra cautious, wearing a Kevlar bulletproof vest under his white shirt and red tie and blue suit jacket. Upon exiting the door, he made one step toward the curb and scanned the street, holding his gun hand on his pistol in its shoulder holster and holding the bank deposit bag with over $35,000 cash in his other hand. He waited while Liu Wan stooped, put a key in the lock at the base of the door to lock it.

Before Liu Wan turned the lock, Suk Kwan Lee was hurtled backward, smashing through the glass of the door and knocking Liu Wan into the doorjamb. Then Liu Wan heard the shot. It sounded distant, from a powerful rifle. He reacted by flattening himself on the sidewalk then crawling to the curb seeking a little shelter offered by a parked car. In the direction of the parking lot, another shot, a pistol shot, rang out which was immediately followed by machine gun fire, also in the parking lot. Then silence. Footsteps, sounding to Liu Wan like those of a heavy person wearing heavy leather boots, approached. A voice, a man's deep voice, said, "Liu Wan, you're dead if you touch your gun."

Still lying on his stomach, Liu Wan stretched his arms out over his head, gestured with his hands and said, "I'm not armed!"

The voice said, "We know. You've been spared to take a message to your bosses. Tell them not to mess with the Chief. Stay as you are for the count of sixty seconds. We have a rifle on you." The footsteps slowly receded. Liu Wan heard car doors close and the movement of three vehicles driving away. At the count of sixty, he cautiously got up and surveyed the damage. Suk Kwan Lee was lying in a bed of shattered glass mixed with a large pool of his own blood. He had been shot in the head with a high caliber bullet that tore the head apart like a smashed melon. Blood and brain tissue had sprayed across the upper doorway, on the doorframe and the wall.

Liu Wan then ran to the parking lot where he found their driver sprawled on the ground on the driver's side of the Buick. The driver's door was open. That side of the Buick was riddled with bullet holes. The driver was lying face down in a large pool of blood. His right arm was stretched out in front of him, his left arm by his side. His gun was on the ground just inches from the outstretched hand. Liu Wan checked the driver for a carotid pulse. Nothing. He then heard distant sirens. He evaluated the situation, ran back to Suk Kwan Lee's body, grabbed the bank deposit bag and ran.

The next day, Joseph was in his office when the phone rang. It was Donny Fortunato. He said one word: "Done," and then hung up, Joseph went to his computer and transferred another $50,000 from an account in Cyprus to one of Donny's accounts in a Bahamas bank. Donny called back and said, "Received. Thank you.

Chapter 15

The day after returning from the Okanagan, Janet had just arrived at her desk when the phone rang. It was Shirley. "I just got off the phone with Marie LeFrance of CSIS. It seems that Korean gang boss they were listening in on was killed last night in a gangland-style shooting. He was shot in the head by a high caliber rifle and his driver gunned down by what looks like the work of an Uzi machine pistol."

"Maybe that car of theirs that you tracked up toward Osoyoos last week had something to do with it?"

"Maybe. We had one of our people talk with the RCMP responsible for that area. Apparently there was a house fire on the NightHawk Number Six reservation about the time that car was in the vicinity. The woman that occupied the house wasn't home though."

"Interesting. Thanks for the "heads up" on this, I'll tell Fred and then call back."

Janet called Fred Mayfield over and filled him in. Fred said, "Number Six NightHawk reservation. Isn't that the one the Koreans traveled through that night the border patrol caught them? Didn't the tip that alerted them come from a woman there? Could the Koreans have found out she tipped the border patrol? Maybe they wanted to teach her a lesson? But their car disappeared immediately after. Maybe they met some resistance?"

"Good—no, great thinking, Sherlock Holmes! How about following that through and checking who the woman was, her house, etc.?"

"Will do. Wonder if we could get someone to do a flyover of the reservation. Maybe search for the car. A black newish Buick wouldn't be hard to spot if it was out in the open."

"That's a big "if,"said Janet. "Maybe Shirley can do something like that."

She called Shirley, mentioned Fred's thoughts and asked if Shirley's people had resources that could do a flyover. "We can have someone analyze the files of satellite passes for the time period when the black Buick was in the vicinity up to now," Shirley responded. "Probably also get a close-up of the place now on one of the next satellite passes. I'll get back to you. Oh, did you get the e-mail of the photos Bob took? I just sent them."

148

"Not yet, I haven't got into my computer yet. I'll get back to you if I haven't. If I have, I'll pass them on to our photo recognition people."

"I've passed them on to our photo people as well. Stay tuned. Bye."

She then e-mailed a request to Hector Skog, asking his assistance with experts to build a profile of the leadership and members of the Midlake Indian band and the other bands in the Okanagan and Similkameen valleys. She also asked if he could do the same with his contacts at the Canadian Embassy. Just after the e-mail was sent, her phone rang. It was Hector.

"Hi Janet, you must have had a good trip to the Okanagan. Mind filling me in?"

"I'm so sorry, Hector. You were next on my list, then a conference call at noon to all the players on the murder case. Yes, I think we made a little progress. This Midlake Indian band and/or some of the others may be housing smugglers. We got a tip on the Midlake band. Also, that inventor, Kenneth Davidson, had been selling the original single shot weapons before the Canadian Government bought him up, but we learned from a reliable source that he only sold to fellow Indians – or should I say, aboriginals in D.C. speak. We may have more information from the Kenneth Davidson track as we're trying to identify some of his hunting associates and our buddies in Bellingham are peeking into his computer files.

"There's also something surfacing with Koreans who were likely involved in smuggling the aliens across the border that night. We don't know if there is a connection yet. I'll fill you in more when we have the conference call with everyone at noon my time."

"You may also want your people to peek in to those computer files but I gather the source is a no-ask-no-tell?"

"Right. They can travel where we can't."

"Keep their leads out of the chain of evidence."

"Yes, sir. I'll get back to you on the conference call."

Next, Shirley called again. "We're starting to get a profile on the leader, or chief, of the Midlake band. His name is Joseph Branson. Age fifty-three. He's very high profile, on numerous committees both in the Okanagan and across Canada and the U.S. He's been very successful standing up for Indian rights and land claims. He's not from the Midlake band but married into it. You know, Indians have dual citizenship and can move freely across the border. Well, he was

----

born on a small reservation on the Olympic Peninsula in Washington State. He married the daughter of the chief of the Midlake band and was elected as chief when the old chief retired. He's very popular with the Midlake band. He keeps getting elected every four years with a large majority. He's been successful in expanding their lands, getting new housing and generally improving the welfare of a good portion of the band members. His latest publicity has been about bringing sockeye salmon runs back to the Okanagan and protecting the wetlands along the Similkameen River.

"We ran his name through all the American databases and found some interesting stuff. He spent eight years in the marines, much of it as a Navy SEAL. When he left the service – with an honorable discharge, I might add – he finished a B.A. degree in business management he had started while in the military. He's done some traveling abroad. That included a trip by motorcycle across Eurasia in 1999 from Vladivostok through Mongolia, through the "stans" etc. to Turkey as if following the ancient Silk Road.

"He travels a lot to Florida, often for a few months in winter where he has a house and boat on a canal in Marathon in the Florida Keys. Recently, he took his wife on a holiday to the Maldives – you know, just below Sri Lanka and India. It's the "in destination" right now if you're into sun and sand and pampering and have big bucks. He's also recently visited London, Turkey and Kyrgyzstan. He frequently crosses the border, mainly at the Oroville-Osoyoos crossing, usually on speaking engagements or meetings for the society that is working on salmon enhancement.

"He seems to be happily married, with three boys and one daughter. He's got one of the boys, David, involved actively with the affairs of the Midlake Band. The rest are in colleges. One's at Utah State, another's at Pepperdine U. in Malibu, California taking a business degree on an academic scholarship and the daughter is at Western Washington State University in Bellingham working on her M.B.A. David also has a good military record by the way, having served in the Canadian military for a term in their airborne regiment – which is a pretty elite commando-style regiment. He also attended university while in the military then finished off a business administration degree when he got out. Both the other boys are in ROTC at their U's. His wife is Hazel, age 47. They've been married for 28 years.

"She's well educated having attended a very expensive girl's school in Ontario, then got a Bachelor of Arts degree in social work at the University of British Columbia. She's also very active in affairs of the Midlake band and many of the activist native organizations. She's very popular with the members of the Midlake band and it's rumored she's a likely replacement for the chief whenever he steps down.

"Oh, hold on, we just pulled up the Chief's military records. His psych profile at the time identified him as remorseless, yet very social with good leadership qualities. He was on many covert operations, had a good sense of the welfare of his comrades and no remorse for killing in the line of duty. Interesting. Your profilers could have some fun with that."

"I think so," said Janet thoughtfully. "Can you put it into an e-mail and I will pass it along?"

"Sure. Done now. I've included a long list of the committees he's on and other things. I'll leave it to you to do the background checks in America for those we identified having spent some time here. You guys are good at that. Also, take a close look at his photo and then look at the photos we copied at Kenneth Davidson's house. He's in one holding an archery weapon."

"Bingo! A link! Thank you! The Chief warrants a closer look. How deep into the people of the reservation can your background checks go?"

"Well, we can identify the occupants by the census, registered births and deaths, drivers licenses, firearms licenses and such, registered voters, sometimes school records, and, of course the Department of Indian Affairs records. We can reference them to criminal records, credit records, and if there is anything newsy – such as wedding announcements or committee memberships etc. If something glaring pops up, we'll let you know and then get people on the ground to do current and past personal profiles – but discreetly, off the reservation."

"How about the other reservations in the area?"

"Well, we're on it but nothing glaring so far. Two of the chiefs are high profile as well but more so for their business acumen. They're great business visionaries and have done lots to make the bands very prosperous – everything from housing developments to wineries and resorts. They boast high employment and education levels. Midlake and NightHawk are not so progressive with considerable unemployment and lower education levels. There are some tie-ins between the NightHawk and Midlake bands as their lands adjoin in one area and they're sharing a tourism operation. Of course, all the bands are in that environmental enhancement project restoring salmon spawning grounds and protecting wetlands."

"What tourism operation?" asked Janet.

"You remember when we came home from Oliver on Highway 3 we went through Smelter Village which was the base for the Great Similkameen Mine tours? Well, that operation is quite successful from what we see. It's run by the Midlake and NightHawk bands. Chief Branson of the Midlake band was responsible for getting the funding and setting it up. He's still the CEO of it."

"Oh. Interesting. Could you get someone to take a closer look at it?"

"Sure. I'll ask Bob to take a peek. Also, we compared the other chiefs to the photos Bob took and they weren't in any. But the Deacon is. Also, the two guys that Bob identified as beating up that bartender do live on the reservation. They are both "imports" from other tribes, one from near Pasco Washington and the other from Oregon, who married into the tribe. Both have military backgrounds in the U.S. Marines. Both were Navy SEALs."

"Another connection? Connected to the Chief? Interesting."

"Well, as if that's not enough. They also have earned their colors."

"You're kidding, they're members of a biker gang?"

"Yep. Guess which one?"

"The Devil's Brew!"

"Of course. The Chief and his son, David are too. We're in process of verifying that."

After she hung up the phone, she filled in Fred on the conversation. He said, "Very interesting. We're getting a bit more on that alias Westley Miller. The face on the bogus driver's license has been matched to one Walter Ames of St. Louis, Missouri. He's got a long list of convictions for drug dealing, B&E and assault. He's been in and out of prison. He last served time five years ago and finished parole three years ago. No record since. No credit cards and no addresses in that name though. Our people are tracing ancestry and work history etc. Apparently, he's had truck driver training where he earned air brake and "B train" endorsements. He can drive the biggest rigs. We're searching commercial driver licenses for facial recognition but that will take some time. However, we're starting with Utah and Missouri."

"Good going! You know, I was thinking about that helicopter. I'm willing to bet it came from Canada but it could just as

----

easily have originated on our side of the border to do some smuggling. Maybe running cocaine into Canada. When I was up there with Shirley, we visited with the owner of a helicopter operation. Their FAA regulations are just as stringent as ours so it's real hard to keep a commercial craft flying unless there's certification on it. It's also hard to get parts without a paper trail. That leaves two things: either the helicopter is legitimate or someone is operating a craft privately without FAA certification and air traffic control and maybe without certified parts. We can get Shirley to do some investigating of helicopter operators close to the border on the Canadian side and we can do a careful analysis on this side. What do you think?"

Fred turned and looked out the window for a few moments, then said, "Yes, guess we should also research air traffic control for the area and try to correlate flight plans to the time of the event. But what if we have someone operating below the legitimate level? For example, how would they get spare parts? Maybe we should talk with parts suppliers and do some background checks on them? Perhaps we can talk with some helicopter mechanics and learn a bit about the underground parts market – if any."

"Good thinking Sherlock! You get on it from our side of the border and I'll talk it over with Shirley to see what they can do on the Canadian side. Do you have any connections with the FAA who may enlighten us? "

"I have a contact there. I'll give him a try."

The phone rang and Janet answered. "It's Hector. I just got a call from our friends in military intelligence. There's been another assassination with the archery weapon in Afghanistan – another tribal warlord who was loyal to us."

"Thanks for letting me know."

Janet called Shirley with the assassination news and filled her in on the idea of tracing helicopter movements and parts. Shirley said, "Glad you're on to it. I'll get back to you."

A few days later, Shirley called to say, "We've identified a small repair company in Mission, B.C. that hasn't been able to account too well for a few of their older helicopters. They're all the same model, Bell 212's. That's a very common chopper in both military and civilian use in many countries. Canada and the US military are phasing them out or have replaced them with new equipment but many other militaries still operate them. They've been around since

1968 and thousands have been produced. They have twin engines, a range of about 250 miles and are capable of carrying up to 5000 pounds. They're a real workhorse in use for everything from firefighting and oil field servicing, to logging, power line construction and mineral exploration.

"In the Mission workshop, two were being worked on about six months ago and the mechanics were cannibalizing a third for its parts to get the two operating. The owner of the shop claims he sold them to a couple of pilot/mechanics who wanted a hobby project to restore them in their spare time as they wanted to start their own charter business. They trucked them away and haven't been seen since. We've tracked the paper trail. They paid big bucks for them – one point seven five million dollars – but that was considered a bargain. Their payment was by electronic bank transfer from a numbered offshore account.

"The vendor wasn't upset or suspicious as he got his money with no problems. Up to the point of transfer, the FAA certification paperwork was kept up but we checked with the Canadian FAA and there's been nothing filed and no inspection for certification requests since. We're still checking other helicopter repair businesses and nosing around airfields looking for hobbyists restoring helicopters. We may turn up something else but this one looks interesting."

"That seems like a break," said Janet. "That vendor sounds a bit suspicious too. Will you be keeping an eye on him?"

"He and his employees are under surveillance."

"Now, where would they get spare parts?"

"That's a good question. The Bell 212 or its military version, the UH - 1N or "Twin Huey," is a very common chopper – like a Ford pickup. It's everywhere. Lots of spare parts and military surplus around. Legally, you can't put a military part in a civilian chopper but much is interchangeable. Maybe we could track some of the parts suppliers but there's also the idea of cannibalizing one to keep another flying. We have some of our resources asking around for spare parts. Maybe that will lead to something. Maybe something will pop on your side of the border."

"You've helped a lot. Maybe we should be concentrating on parts for the Bell 212 but also keep our eyes open for others."

A few days later, Fred came up to Janet's desk and announced, "We've got a break on that truck driver, Walter Ames.

Facial Recognition and handwriting have found a match to a commercial driver's license for a William Wilson, of Salt Lake City, Utah. I've got Salt Lake agents reviewing his background. Do you want surveillance?"

"Right on!"

Chapter 16

Joseph parked his car in the parking lot at Oak Dale Winery, situated on a rural hillside south of Kelowna, and walked to the bistro's patio. Donny and the bikers, through a legitimate business, owned the place. Donny was already seated at a corner table for two alongside a glassed-in railing that afforded a great view of the lake and some privacy as the patio jutted out over a two hundred foot cliff.

The restaurant was not very busy with only a few tables occupied by stragglers finishing a late lunch and sampling some of the dessert wines for which the winery was world famous. Donny saw him enter and waved. Joseph joined him. Two menus were already on the table and Donny had a glass of red wine half consumed. The bottle was on the table along with another glass. Donny poured a drink for Joseph and they clicked glasses and they said their old toast in unison: "To success!" The wine was an excellent eight-year-old vintage Cabernet Sauvignon bearing a unique label which Joseph remarked upon. "Cranky Boss? Where'd you think up that name?"

"Oh, our advertising agency is into funky names because the idea's caught on in the region. You know, like Blasted Church, Dirty Laundry, Red Dog and Blue Funk. This wine was named after one of our vineyard bosses who's always in a cranky mood."

"Oh, well. Whatever sells."

"So far this year, we've sold nine thousand bottles at fifty bucks a pop. It sells well. I've got enough in store for the next three years and the price will climb with each year added to the vintage. We've got newer vintages maturing."

A waiter hurried over to take orders, greeting Joseph with, "Hi Chief, great to see you again! Do you want some time with the menu or are you ready to order?"

"Hello Art, great to see you again too! A spinach quiche for me, plus a selection of your famous cheeses, please. I'll decide on dessert later. Donny, I presume you've ordered?"

"Same for me, please Art. And Art, make sure we're out of earshot and not disturbed."

"No problem, boss."

After the waiter left, Joseph said, "Thanks for helping with the Vancouver problem. Looks as if that's the end to it. His superior called and apologized profusely. Liu Wan has been promoted and wants to do business."

"Good. Good. The folk down South are happy with your last shipment. Everything went smoothly. They've even got a guy interested in that fish protein you packed on top of the bud for starting plants in a nursery."

"Glad to have satisfied customers. I'll get you some prices on the fish protein that you can pass along."

"I do have a complaint though. Seems you didn't tell me about the problem you had with the shipment before that one."

"Yeah, we had a little hiccup but everything was delivered, was it not?"

"It was delivered. However, you knocked open a hornet's nest by using an arrow. The powers that be have linked it to a terrorism threat and all hell is breaking loose."

"Oh shit!"

"Yeah, We had a great thing going. No one on this side cares too much about bud going south and they don't want to allocate resources to chase it, but terrorism – that's a far more serious threat and a lot of agencies from the two countries are getting involved. Some have turned a blind eye to the "status quo" in the past but won't and can't with a terrorism threat."

"So what do you suggest?"

"Stop playing with that fucking archery weapon, for one thing. It leaves too big a signature and has attracted attention. Also, use more caution when making shipments. Vary delivery patterns even more."

"OK. We're varying delivery patterns. You know, we must have at least thirty different ways of moving the goods and over fifty crossing points. We've got people inside border patrol so we know their plans and communication frequencies."

"Yeah, I know you're very creative. BUT when you've got this escalated to a terrorism threat, you don't just have Homeland Security involved. You've got others sniffing around over here. You've got to watch your back."

"Maybe I'll leave town for a while and let things cool down. I'll send David on a holiday too. He wants to go to the Maldives for some diving. We don't have any big shipments planned for a couple of months anyway. I've only got one shipment. That's tonight and it's small stuff – our meth going down and some guns coming back. After that, we can cool it for a while if you want."

"O.K., we can fill in with our Duluth, Skagway and Quebec transfer points if need be."

"I've been working on something that should interest you. Would you like another source of H?"

"IF, and that's a big IF. IF you can get it here, we can put it into our distribution system. We'd circulate it all across Canada, not a problem. That is, unless you've stepped on someone's toes to do it. I don't want to upset the status quo."

Joseph raised his right hand, palm out, looked Donny straight in the face and with a very sincere expression said, "Honest Injun, it's an entirely new and clean source!"

Donny rolled his eyes to the ceiling, began a belly laugh and said, "Oh shit. Honest Injun! Where did that come from? We would NOT want to swamp the market as that would drive prices – read "profits" my friend – down and probably attract the attention of our triad partners. The Chinese think they have an exclusive distribution system with us and will not be happy to learn we've got alternate sources. The triad can play very rough if they get mad. I don't want them getting upset. We can get away with it if we trickle it into the distribution system a little at a time."

"I'm good with that."

Joseph walked into the tribal center and placed a bottle of wine on David's desk. David carefully examined it and said, "Cranky Boss? Not bad!"

Joseph smiled and said, "It's a present for you from Donny."

"Was Donny cranky?"

"Let's say he wasn't too happy about us playing with archery weapons off the reservation. He's alarmed the arrows carry too much signature. Apparently the Feds have linked the arrow to a terrorism threat and are focusing some attention on it."

"He may have a point. Time to keep the arrows on the reservation?"

"Yeah. He also suggested we lie low for a while. I said we would after tonight. Do you really want to go to the Maldives?"

"Maldives? Vacation? Oh, yeah!"

David met Joseph at the mountain top entrance to the Great Similkameen Mine and they made their way through the rear access to Kenneth's workshop. When they entered, Kenneth looked up from a computer linked to a vertical boring mill. On the screen was a three dimension drawing of a part that was being cut automatically on the boring mill. He smiled, stood up and they exchanged bear hugs. Then, Kenneth described the activity in the room. He had four assistants, some at similar machines cutting parts out of blocks of carbon fiber, plastic and nylon, some assembling finished parts and testing the weapons. "We've done all the ceramic molding and now we are just finishing the machining of the last of the parts. Final stage is drilling and tapping the screw holes for the sights. We're doing real well. All the parts are within specified military tolerances. We've got a great crew here. As soon as we get the sights, we can start packaging."

Joseph said, "Good! We'll be bringing the sights across this evening. Can we be ready to go in two days?"

"Easy. If we get the sights tonight, we'll be finished assembly and packaging tomorrow."

"I've decided to move the factory. How soon can you pack everything for shipment and let me know the weight?"

"I guess another two or three days after shipment. When do I get my final payment, then?"

"We'll make the final transfer to your account the day the weapons are shipped out as agreed. I'll pay you another ten grand, cash in your pocket, to pack up. I'll bonus the boys working with you two grand each to help with the packing. When we set up again, you'll need your passport and a bathing suit."

Kenneth smiled. "Sounds good to me!"

Late afternoon that day, a helicopter bearing the logo and corporate name of *Red Mountain Fire Suppression Services Inc.* landed at the Omak, Washington airfield. Omak is not a big town and the airfield, OMK, not very active, save for daily courier flights, land survey flights, private pleasure and fire patrol aircraft. However, this day it was a hub of activity with fire-fighting aircraft using it as a base to fight a fire in the mountains on the nearby Indian reservation. Fire crews and their equipment were being flown to and from the fire lines by helicopter. Water bombers, two and four engine tanker aircraft, were landing and taking off at fifteen minute intervals using the airfield to refuel and reload with water and retardant mix for their next bombing runs.

The helicopter went unnoticed, as it had brought in a load of fire retardant, which had been rushed down from a firebase in Penticton, Canada as part of a mutual aid pact, to supplement a shortage caused by the wildfire. The quantity of fire retardant was not large but it would sustain the fire crews for a few hours until nightfall when a load that was being trucked in was due. No one took notice that some boxes, about a third of the load, were offloaded onto a pickup truck and driven away.

No customs officers were present at the airfield as the craft loaded up with a number of boxes that had been brought to it in a UPS truck. When asked, someone said they were loading supplies for the fighters on the fire line. It took off without incident and crossed the border on its prearranged flight path. Just across the border, the pilot received directions to conduct a fire patrol up the Similkameen River as far as Smelter Village then along the mountain ridge to Apex Mountain ridge and then back into Penticton. Apparently, someone had seen smoke in the area between the top of Great Similkameen Mine and Nickel Plate Lake. Just past Nickel Plate Lake, the pilot reported seeing smoke and that he was setting his craft down in a meadow to investigate.

The chopper landed in a clearing where a panel van and four men were waiting. The right side cargo bay door on the helicopter slid open and the co-pilot helped the men transfer the cargo to the waiting van. When the transfer was complete, the co-pilot shook hands with the ground crew, mounted up and the craft took off.

A few minutes later, the pilot was back on the air advising dispatch they were returning to Penticton base. He advised they had found an abandoned bonfire on one of the hiking trails and that he and his co-pilot had been successful in putting it out. Simple. Mission accomplished. The gun sights had arrived.

Next day, after a quick commute from Kelowna airport to YVR, Vancouver, Joseph caught the China Airways flight to Beijing, China where he connected to a flight to Bishkek, Kyrgyzstan. David was entrusted to get the goods to the charter aircraft in Kelowna.

The transfer of the cargo from the mine to Kelowna was uneventful. All the paperwork was ready and the Customs and Immigration office at Kelowna airport had been notified in advance

160

both of the arrival of the charter aircraft and the export cargo. The aircraft had landed at Kelowna the day before and the crew settled in at a local hotel to get some rest. The cargo was taken out of the mine after tourist hours in a rental van and it was only two hours later that it arrived beside the aircraft on the ramp in Kelowna.

David met Paul Gopal, the chief pilot of the flight crew, in the office of the ground services operator who handled visiting aircraft at the Kelowna airport. They then met the Customs and Immigrations officer at his office where David was cleared to accompany the cargo on the flight. The officer then accompanied them to the ramp to inspect the cargo. He verified the quantity and weight of boxes then signed off on the documents after they were loaded into the aircraft.

The aircraft had a crew of three. Pilot, co-pilot and pilot-mechanic. The chief pilot was Paul Gopal, brother of Rishi and co-owner. Paul wore a light blue turban, which complemented his light blue short-sleeved uniform shirt, and navy pants. Paul was forty years old, six feet tall, athletic, carrying one hundred ninety pounds and had a full black, curly beard with no gray hairs. His co-pilot, Umesh Jacobs, was younger at age thirty-five, short, muscular and clean-shaven with his black hair in a crew cut. The third pilot was Ramish Kakar, age thirty. David thought they looked pretty clean cut and professional in their tailored uniforms.

Paul introduced David and, after welcomes, Umesh began to walk around the aircraft making a pre-flight inspection. Ramish supervised the loading of the cargo and Paul and David entered the aircraft from the front door. Paul pointed out the washroom, the two first class easy chair seats and the two bunk beds just behind the cockpit and mentioned they had lots of food aboard – mainly frozen dinners to heat up in the microwave plus coffee and juices. As he entered the cockpit, he pointed out the jump seat that folded down from the door and that David could use to get a bird's eye view for takeoffs and landings.

The aircraft was a retrofitted Boeing 727, vintage 1975. It had been rebuilt for cargo service by Boeing in 2002 when it was equipped with more efficient and powerful engines, cargo doors, modern avionics and brakes added to the front wheels to permit landing on shorter runways.

"Paul, why three pilots?" David asked.

"We don't always take three pilots but, in this case, on a long trip, a third man helps spell off the others. As well, Ramish is a

161

mechanic and we thought that, because we were going to a couple of spots that were a bit remote, a mechanic might come in handy. He's very good at patching bullet holes – although we don't expect that on this run. Originally, the 727 was set up for three pilots, the third served as a flight engineer and sometimes, navigator. But the retrofit enables two-man operation – even one man in a pinch. Some of the older conversions kept the three-man configuration. So we use the seat for a spare pilot on long flights."

"We'll take a polar route, over the Arctic in a Great Circle, which is the shortest distance. We have airspace clearance across Alaska, Russia, Kazakhstan and Kyrgyzstan to Osh then on through China's Tibet, Bhutan, Bangladesh, India, and Sri Lanka. We'll land in Anchorage to refuel and refuel again in Osh. Although we have pretty good range and a light load, topping up in Anchorage is a good idea. Even though the new engines are over forty percent more efficient and more powerful than the originals, this is still a thirsty aircraft. We're looking at total flight time of over eleven hours to get to Osh.

"We will not be allowed to deplane in Anchorage, except to do the pre-flight check and check in with the meteorological people to update the weather charts. And, when we're on the ground in Osh, stay aboard or very close to the aircraft and wear one of our company coveralls that will identify you as flight crew. I gather we pick your dad up in Osh?"

"Yep, plus the next cargo."

The flight was cleared for takeoff at 11 p.m. It departed on time. David sat in the jump seat in the cockpit for the takeoff and enjoyed the thrill of a front view of the aircraft rolling, taking off and turning onto its heading for Anchorage. He was fascinated with the teamwork of the pilots and with the lights below. After a few minutes, he excused himself and left the cockpit for the comfort of one of the bunk beds. He managed to sleep through the refueling stop in Anchorage and logged a good eight hours sleep. After departing Anchorage, Paul climbed into the other bunk to catch some sleep, leaving the flying to Umesh and Ramish.

Chapter 17

It was early afternoon and hot. Bob was sweating, sitting in the left window seat on the last row of the restored school bus which was now painted light milky green and bore the logo and label: *Great Similkameen Mine Tours*. The bus was crowded with photo hungry tourists who, along with him, had paid their $45 for a tour of the mine.

The tour started in a large theatre room behind the ticket office in the "lower town" – Smelter Village - at the base of the mountain, with a historic video on the mine, its origins and evolution. Next, all endured a fifteen-minute orientation session on some of the features they would see and safety issues. Most poignant was the concern about vertigo when walking on the boardwalk suspended over the cliff face. Patrons were advised there was another, safer route into the mine that those with fear of heights could select once they arrived at the mine's town site at the four thousand nine hundred foot level of the mountain. They were told that, as safety was primary, they were to stay with the group. There would always be a lead guide and one following at the rear to prevent straggling. They were all given stick-on numbers and told there would be frequent head counts.

The bus had just come off Highway 3 and they began their climb on a narrow gravel road. The road ascended some three thousand four hundred vertical feet from the highway to the crest of the mountain, winding its way up the mountainside through a series of switchbacks. The grade was fairly steep in spots, Bob figured between ten and twelve percent, and the driver had to gear down many times. Bob figured a good part of the thrills for the tourists might be in the climb up and down the mountain in the retired school bus. A number of passengers were holding tight to the handholds and some were clutching each other.

The view of the valley below increased in magnificence with every switchback on the barren hillside until they entered the tree line near the top of the mountain. Many were taking photos from the open windows. The bus was kicking up a huge dust loud that was drifting behind them. He was beginning to think the ride down would be more risky, wondering how well the brakes were maintained and if the driver knew enough not to ride his brakes.

Eventually, they crested the hill and followed a wide, well maintained gravel road past a large abandoned open pit mine, heading west on a gentle upward slope until they entered the main gates to the Great Similkameen Mine. There the passengers disembarked and were given time for a bathroom break and visit to the snack bar and souvenir shop.

The group was reassembled in twenty minutes and the tour guide led them through the clapboard town that had once been home to the miners, pointing out buildings and their functions. They continued down to a landing at the top of the cliff face boardwalk where a walkway and stairs clinging to the cliff would take them down to the mine's entrance. At the mine entrance, cable car ore gondolas ran from the mine portal down to the smelters, perched on a hillside some two thousand nine hundred feet below.

The lead guide asked that people who did not want to walk the three hundred feet of boardwalk and stairs suspended on the cliff face with a two thousand nine hundred foot drop below to go with a uniformed guide who would take them into the mine from a safer route. Of the forty people in the tour group, fifteen chose the safer route. Bob elected for the cliff face route and was rewarded with a spectacular view of Smelter Village, over three thousand feet below. Few people ventured to the railing. Most tended to cling to the cable handhold on the rock face side of the boardwalk.

As they made their way downstairs and edged to the left around the rock face, the mine's entrance came into view. It was wide, designed to hold two ore cars on rails side by side but not more than eight feet high. As they entered the mine, the double track rails came together at a rail switch above a chute used to fill the gondolas and the tunnel narrowed to the width of one ore car. They followed the tunnel in for about two hundred feet, then entered a wide gallery where various old mining tools were assembled in a diorama and a man dressed as a miner, with helmet, oilskin rain gear and carbide headlamp awaited to demonstrate the tools.

The lead guide gave a talk and demonstrated each tool, showing the history of finding and extracting the ore. Most machines ran on air pressure from a hose attached to a steel pipe that ran down the center of the ceiling. As each machine was demonstrated, spectators had to hold their ears as the noise was deafening.

Eventually, the group moved on deeper and deeper into the mine. Bob noted the mine was well illuminated and ventilated as they proceeded between galleries and demonstrations and that well-marked emergency exits were prevalent along with a sophisticated and abundant closed circuit TV (CCTV) monitoring system. As the last stop on the underground tour, the guide took them down a shaft with many flights of stairs, then along a corridor to the generator room. In the lower corridor Bob noted a metal fireproof door bearing a sign: *Authorized Personnel Only* and a key pad lock. The generator room also had a significant metal fire door as entrance and another at the far end as an emergency exit. The lecture on the generators impressed Bob and he made a mental note to check how much of the electricity being generated was being sold back into the public electrical grid.

Taking lots of pictures, Bob fit in as just one of the tourists. After climbing upwards through a sloped tunnel that opened into a few galleries, they exited the mine through a portal that brought them to the upper boardwalk beside the souvenir shop and a refreshment stand among other buildings that served as museum dioramas. Bob continued to take pictures for the next half hour, while people visited the café, souvenir shop and exhibits before they were escorted back to the bus for the trip down. Again, he noted a high level of security equipment.

Considering his fear of the driver burning out the brakes, the trip down was more exciting than the trip up. Each hairpin turn had an emergency runaway track turning up hill where a vehicle, if it lost its brakes, could be slowed by gravity as it ran into a path of loose, deep gravel. The driver mentioned the "safety feature" of the runaway lanes and took glee in pointing out the recent tire tracks in some of them from busses with brake failures.

Once back in his motel room in Princeton, Bob reviewed his photos, concluding that unauthorized entry would be very difficult. "Time for Plan B," he thought as he downloaded and printed off color satellite photos of the area that Shirley had forwarded. He spent considerable time examining the satellite photos and frequently went back to his computer to use his company-supplied software to pull up closer details. He also had a set of drawings detailing the mine tunnels, which he pored over for a few hours. Toward midnight, Bob fell into bed and Plan B started to take shape. Time to do a little hunting.

Next day by late afternoon, Bob was in his Jeep on the public road running along the mountain ridge. He crossed into the Midlake reserve and proceeded a few miles until he found the side road he was seeking. It was nothing more than an abandoned track with deep ruts and large loose boulders from erosion carved over many years of neglect. Switching to four-wheel drive, he turned onto the road and slowly made his way for about a mile, where he parked in a sheltered area that could not be seen from the road or above.

Bob was dressed in camouflage pants and long sleeve camouflage shirt, well-worn and comfortable hiking boots and camouflage hunting cap. He also had a camouflage backpack with water, a warm black jacket, camouflage survival blanket, granola bars, LED flash light, night vision goggles and SLR camera with telephoto lens. Other than carrying a hunting knife in a belt sheath, he was unarmed.

Shouldering his backpack and turning on a hand-held GPS, he set out toward his destination, about a mile overland. It was fairly rough going for the first thousand yards as he followed a deer path until he crossed over a short hill but he soon linked up with an old, overgrown logging road and began to make good time. The road took him to a creek, which he followed upstream until it ended at a small earthen dam that was holding back a lake. The lake was about a half mile long and a quarter mile wide. Directly across the lake was a large log home with a dock holding a red canoe and, floating beside and tied to the short dock was a fourteen-foot aluminum boat with a small electric outboard motor.

Easing up the west side of the lake, Bob could discern a black Jeep parked in the carport beside a tan Nissan four-wheel pickup. A black quad was parked by the door facing the water. Facing the lake, at the rear of the house was a large patio with outdoor furniture and a large stainless steel gas-fired barbecue.

Bob found a vantage point where he could watch the carport, dock and patio. He nestled in at the roots of a large fir tree, making a hollow between roots and behind a fallen log and gathering some fallen tree needles to make a cushion and insulate himself from the damp ground. Comfortable. He could put his back on the tree and peek over the log for a good view.

After about an hour, Bob spotted a woman coming out onto the patio and starting the barbecue. He took some photos, managing to catch a great frontal facial shot, which would help for later identification. He noted she was native, maybe in her early thirties, with long black hair tied back in a ponytail and had a beautiful figure accentuated by very short white shorts and a short sleeve tan polo shirt.

He had his head down looking at the back of his camera playing back the digital images he had just taken of one of the most beautiful women he had seen recently when there was a loud "thunk" as an arrow imbedded itself in the tree just above his head. Instinctively, he ducked, hunched up trying to get deeper under the

166

----

log in front. A loud voice from about a hundred feet beside him said, "Don't move or you're dead!"

Chapter 18

Joseph's flight arrived early in the morning. Serge met Joseph upon arrival at Bishkek airport and drove him to his hotel to get some rest. He returned to pick Joseph up just before six p.m. for a meeting with Arnold at the office.

After greetings were exchanged and refreshments served, Arnold got down to business. "Joseph, everything's arranged at our end. Tomorrow morning, Serge will drive you down to Osh. He'll pick you up at the hotel at seven. That'll get you into Osh before four p.m. Stephen and his team are in Osh now. He's been paving the way.

"You may have read about some unrest between Uzbeks and Kyrgyz in Osh recently. Over a hundred twenty have been killed so far in Osh and Jalalabad in rioting and reprisals but the military has been called in and things are quiet now. The military has even asked the Russians to send in troops to help but they refused. The airport is well guarded by the military and it's quite a ways out of town. Martial law has been imposed there with a curfew from eight p.m. to five a.m. This will work in our favor, as it will keep everyone off the streets overnight.

"The airport remains open and there's quite a bit of night cargo traffic within the airport. Regular passenger flights tend to be during the daylight hours but there are some aircraft coming in from China and Russia to help move their nationals out due to the unrest and this may continue into the night. The military will bring the nationals to the airport in armored personnel carriers but there will be no regular passenger traffic at night after the curfew.

"As I understand it, you'll be transferring cargos between aircraft so there's no worry about getting vehicles on or off the airport grounds during curfew?"

"Correct."

"Refueling has been arranged. Customs and Immigration officers have been paid, as has the military guarding the airport. We've even arranged for a military escort for you and Serge when you get close to Osh. I'd send you down by scheduled aircraft but their flights in are a bit uncertain right now."

After a good meal in the Bar and Grill with Serge, Steven and Arnold, Serge dropped Joseph off at his hotel. Joseph had bowed out of offers to attend the symphony or do the bar circuit or the casino that Serge suggested. He just wanted a good night's sleep, as the next day would be long and busy. Serge understood and in fact said, "I'm glad you feel that way as I will need my sleep too. I'll see you in the morning."

When Joseph reached his floor, he checked in with Harma, the woman who was the floor boss. He called her his babushka – the Russian honorific for a grandmother – which she enjoyed and in return, she called him her son. She looked the part with her round peasant face, printed dress, grey hair tied in a bun, and ample figure on a sixty-something frame. She had a room directly in front of the elevators where she held court. There was a Dutch door, split in the middle with a board that served as a counter when the top portion of the door was open. From there, she controlled the floor, doling out keys to the guest rooms, vending pop, liquor and sweets from her fridge, handling laundry, ironing shirts and pressing pants, supervising the cleaning and bed making and basically acting as a concierge for anything the guest sought.

Joseph knocked on the counter, drawing Babushka's attention from the national game show on the TV. She got out of her easy chair and came to the counter. Smiling, she said, "Joseph, my son, are you turning in early?" She reached to a shelf beside the counter, out of sight, retrieved a package and placed it on the counter, then said, "Here is what you specified – a PM 9 mm, fifty rounds, two extra clips and a cleaning kit."

Joseph opened the box to discover a new Russian military Markarov 9.22 mm pistol with two extra clips and a box of Russian military ammunition. He carefully examined the gun and paraphernalia, breaking it down the gun to examine the innards, especially the floating firing pin. After a few moments, he said, "Excellent! How much do I owe you?"

"Well, when you asked, I estimated between two hundred fifty and four hundred dollars. As you can see, this is new and has never been fired. Three hundred fifty dollars."

Joseph pulled out his wallet and placed the cash on the counter. "Babushka, you did well. Thank you! I'm driving to Osh tomorrow and this may be needed."

"I know the problems there. It seems to be getting worse. Can I get you something else? Perhaps someone? I have a lovely young lady, one of my nieces, very blonde Russian and slim, from Astana available tonight." She moved aside and Joseph could see a beautiful younger woman sitting watching the TV.

Joseph took Harma's hands in his and slipped a twenty-dollar U.S. bill into her palms and held her for a few seconds. Their eyes met and he said, "My Babushka, nothing for me tonight. I must have a good night's sleep as I have a busy day tomorrow. Please, no disturbances. Don't let anyone phone me or knock on my door. Your niece is beautiful, but not tonight."

"Whatever you wish my son. Sleep well."

Next day, Serge picked up Joseph on time and they were soon out of the city heading west to Osh on an excellent four-lane highway, which Serge said had recently been upgraded through a World Bank loan. They passed through good, well-kept rolling farmland into sharp, rugged mountains which eventually brought them down into the very fertile Fergana Valley, a large valley where the countries of Kyrgyzstan, Uzbekistan and Tajikistan meet. About every twenty miles along the side of the highway, they encountered large bronze statutes ranging from deer to eagles to the occasional hero of the Soviet Union. Serge explained this was left over from the Soviet era when the art was contracted as a make-work and beautification project.

Serge pointed out another beautification and environmental project from that era which was the planting of elm trees along the roadside in the farmlands. They had grown huge and magnificent and lined the road endlessly. Joseph also noted to Serge the abundance of marijuana plants growing as weeds along the side of the road. They were not very potent but in his previous trip in 1999, had given him the inspiration to organize the hemp farm in Manitoba and develop a market for the cloth.

Midway, they stopped at a roadside café' frequented by truckers and had a hearty meal. Serge also ordered a takeout of bread, salamis, bottled water, fruit, cheeses and colas as he had been warned that not much was open in Osh due to the rioting and that the Osh airport had only a snack bar that was closed. They refueled, topping up their tank at a gas station just before beginning the descent into the Fergana Valley and the fifty-mile run into Osh.

Twenty miles out of Osh, they ran into their first military roadblock. Upon identifying themselves, they were given an escort consisting of a lead jeep with driver, lieutenant and two well-armed privates and a follow-up six-wheel truck bristling with a machine gun on a swivel mount on the roof of the passenger side of the cab. The gun was manned by a soldier and a contingent of seven well-armed

170

----

soldiers, a corporal and six privates, seated in the open back deck of the truck.

They passed through six more checkpoints but their trip to the airport was uneventful. The airport property was well guarded by the military. Soldiers with modern weapons were abundant. Check points and sand bagged sentry bunkers and dug in tanks with overlapping fields of fire seemed to be everywhere. The escort brought them to a cargo hanger where Steve was waiting. Serge and Steve made a point to personally thank all the soldiers with bear hugs and handshakes. Serge opened the trunk of the car and handed out a three-pound canned ham and a carton of cigarettes to each soldier and Steve discretely handed the officer an envelope. Happy, their escort bid them farewell and set out to return to their duty station.

Steve, Joseph and Serge drove over to the Customs and Immigration Office and, with the help of an envelope, a carton of cigarettes and three canned hams, cleared Joseph for exit from the country. The airport was quiet as the last scheduled passenger flights to Moscow and Bishkek had departed and the regular flight to and from Urumqi, China, which normally would arrive in the early evening, was cancelled.

Their next step was to clear the "in bond" cargo transfer with customs. Again, with the help of cigarettes, hams and an envelope to the officer in charge, the papers were quickly cleared. As none of their cargo was entering the country, simply being transferred (in bond) between aircraft for forwarding to international destinations, there would be no physical inspection of the cargo. When they were presenting their papers, the Chief Customs Officer said the first of five charters from Urumqi, China, which were coming in to evacuate Chinese nationals, was not due in until after midnight and there were only six cargo arrivals due before then. Their cargo charter was on time, due at seven p.m. and another, from Kandahar, was due at seven-ten p.m.

They then visited the aviation fuel supplier on the base and were assured their fuel had been prepaid and was waiting in the delivery truck at the parking apron for their aircraft's arrival. They returned to the cargo hangar near the apron that had been allocated to them for the transfer. There, Joseph was introduced to Steve's cargo transfer crew who were lounging around on forklifts, tractors, container elevators and cargo wagons. Steve took Joseph aside shortly after that and said, "I also have my own security guys posted around here. There are a couple of snipers plus two SWAT teams, one on either side of us, just in case. I've also got two guys babysitting the guy with the fuel truck. We also monitor all the airport, police and military frequencies and the officers of the surrounding military have been well paid. All we do now is wait."

At 6:56 p.m. their plane touched down and a lead jeep with a "FOLLOW ME" sign and flashing yellow lights escorted the aircraft to its parking spot. David was the first down the stairs from the aircraft to be met with a bear hug from his father who then introduced Steve, Serge and some of the cargo transfer team. When the pilots descended, Joseph bear-hugged Paul and David and introductions were made all round. Steve motioned to the fuel truck driver who brought his truck over and refueling got underway. Paul and Umesh went with Serge to file their flight plan and update their weather charts for the next leg of the journey while Ramish supervised the fueling.

At 7:03 p.m. a twin-engine cargo plane, an old Antonov AN-26 with Uzbekistan markings, touched down and was escorted over to the parking space beside the 727. Saqulain Hassan was the first down the stairs. He greeted Joseph warmly and was introduced to David and Steve. He asked Steve to convey his warmest greetings and gratitude to his father, whom he was confident had helped make the arrangements for a safe transfer.

They then discussed how best to make the transfer and settled on Saqulain, accompanied by Joseph, sample inspecting the weapons cargo on board the 727 and then, if the goods were satisfactory, Joseph would accompany Saqulain to his aircraft to sample inspect the opium. Once this proved satisfactory, both cargos would be offloaded simultaneously. Once both cargoes were on the ground, Saqulain would make a wire transfer through his satellite phone for the U.S. funds, another to the bank to release the gold to Joseph and Igor's account, then await confirmation on Joseph's portable computer. Joseph made a bank transfer to Arne's account and Steve confirmed receipt of it on his satellite phone a few moments later.

The procedure worked well. Saqulain was satisfied with his inspection of the weapons and Joseph confirmed the opium. Steve's cargo crew was quick to bring the cargoes out of the aircraft and place them on the ground between the planes. Saqulain made his financial transfers and, a few seconds later, they were confirmed on Joseph's computer. Both men smiled and shook hands and turned to Steve.

Joseph nodded to Steve and he gave his loaders a signal. The cargos changed aircraft.

Upon completion of loading, Joseph once again shook hands and exchanged bear hugs with Saqulain, saying, "Well, my friend, it is a pleasure doing business with you. I'm looking forward to the next order. In the meantime, may Allah be with you!"

"Joseph, it is always a great pleasure to see you," Saqulain responded. "Please tell Igor we shall meet again soon in the Maldives."

Joseph turned to Steve. "Stevie, thank you for everything! Please say thanks to your dad for me."

Joseph thanked Serge and the cargo crew and waved toward the roofs of some of the buildings, as if thanking the hidden response team members. After bear hugs with Serge and Steve, David and Joseph boarded the aircraft and Umesh retracted the stairs into their stairwell.

The 727 was first off the ground, climbing on its way to the Maldives. They left the Antonov refueling but Paul heard its pilot receiving clearance for takeoff about five minutes after the 727 had reached its assigned altitude.

Once they reached cruising altitude, David and Joseph set to work repackaging the cargo. David had brought along a quantity of five gallon plastic buckets and new tops labeled as a well-known brand of concrete waterproofing admixture. They also brought some full cans of the mixture and a cello wrap to secure the containers to cargo pallets. The opium bales were opened and the smaller inner packages were stuffed into the awaiting buckets. The buckets were topped off with a thin layer of the concrete admixture powder then sealed with self-locking lids.

Once rewrapped onto cargo pallets with cello wrap, Joseph felt it was unlikely the Customs inspector would open the cans and, if so inclined, it would probably be one or two of the cans on the top layer. He felt opening would be unlikely as each new top formed a seal on the can that would have to be broken to open. Each can had a label warning to avoid moisture in order to best preserve the contents. They felt they could argue opening for inspection would harm the product.

Once the transfer had been completed and the buckets secured to the pallets with the cello wrap, they were left with the problem of what to do with the rope and burlap, which had been the outer layer of packing for the opium. Paul and Umesh solved that by

----

a shallow landing approach which enabled Umesh to open the rear stairwell hatch after descending to ten thousand feet where he kicked out the garbage over open ocean about fifteen minutes before landing. When the stairway and door was secured, Umesh made his way back to the cockpit. As he passed the seated Joseph, who thanked him profusely, Umesh commented, "No problem – we often do it."

Chapter 19

<u>Seattle</u>

Janet was on the phone with Hector explaining, "We've made a little progress on the driver. His background doesn't check out. We're positive he's our Mr. Walter Aimes, alias the imposter Mr. Westley Miller."

"But you haven't made a positive, court-proof link to Westley Miller of the murder scene. Right?"

"Not yet. We'd like to increase surveillance. Under the guise of a terrorism threat, can you get us permission for wire taps and tracking bugs?"

"Consider it done. Paperwork should be in your hands in a couple of hours. Maybe you can catch them in the act of smuggling or transporting drugs that you can use as leverage to track back to the source of the murders. I'll make sure our Salt Lake City office allocates ample resources. Bye."

After talking with Hector, Janet took a call from Shirley, who said, "Bob was talking with his friend Rus Potter in Oliver. Seems there are rumors of a small helicopter parts supplier right on the border in Blaine, Washington, who's getting a reputation for supplying non-certified parts for helicopters. One of our guys took a look. It's located in a barn on a small acreage just east of Blaine. There's no signage and no office, just storage.

"There's an older family that owns and lives on the property. They rented the barn out about a year ago to a guy who pays his rent on time every month and claims he's running an e-mail business supplying the parts. He ships a lot by FedEx, DPL and UPS but also has customers meet him at the storage facility. They claim to have seen him exchanging parts for cash the odd time with customers. A good number of the cash customers have Canadian – British Columbia and Alberta – license plates.

"We've got the business card, name and phone number of the guy running the operation. I feel he needs a close look. I just e-mailed the info to you."

"We can get someone to try to buy from the guy. We'll get underway on a background check on him and the couple. If the couple who own the property come up clean, do you think they might co-operate with surveillance?"

"Yeah, the couple looks pretty clean but do your own check to be sure. They're on a fixed retirement income and seem anxious for a little extra money. You may be able to co-opt them. This is in your ballpark as the business is on the American side of the border but we have something special that might help a little later on. If we can get at the parts in the barn, we can equip all with some new high tech tracking devices. We may be able to put tracking devices on the vehicles of some of the cash customers too."

"Do I want to know this?"

"Not for the record, Janet. If we do it, we should bring in Homeland Security and their border patrol as we could track choppers crossing the border."

"Great idea if it leads to interceptions of smugglers entering America! But I think we involve Homeland Security only after things are in place, and then only at the higher levels. You never can tell, but they may have an informant or two in their ranks. I'm still concerned how the Koreans learned who informed on them and what may have been diversions. If we prove it works first, then we can get the higher ups in Homeland Security to lay a trap to try to track their mole or moles."

"A point well taken. Maybe you can get Hector to do something at a much higher level so that you can access the Predator Drone surveillance people in Moses Lake without the local ICE people knowing it. We can equip the drones with the technology easily enough. There's an electronic kit we could fit in aircraft and vehicles that would track the choppers in real time. We can lend a couple of units for the drones for a few months for a demo but ICE will have to buy their own if they want to keep it. I'll be pleased to set up a network of them along the border on the Canadian side and, of course, I'll get mobile kits to some of our people in the region."

"Sounds great! I'll talk to Hector and get moving on it."

"By the way, following up on your request to review satellite recon photos of that Indian Reserve Number 6, we got one photo of the Koreans' car parked at a small house – the house that later burned. There was no car visible on the next pass of the recon satellite but it did show the fire scene and firefighters and equipment in attendance. That was after the bug on the car stopped working. We checked the roads for fifty miles in the photos but no sign of the car. I also talked with Marie La France at CSIS. She said their listeners picked up an interesting conversation the day after the fire with one of the Korean bosses in a rage because four of his men never returned from the interior."

"Do you think they may have been eliminated?"

"Most likely."

"Any names mentioned?"

"Just one. No formal name. Just someone referred to as "the Chieftain" – or, that's how it translated out from the Korean they were speaking."

"Well, that's interesting. Think it may be that Chief Joseph Branson?"

"Let's flag him as a person warranting special interest."

"Already on it. Thanks. Bye"

A couple of hours later, Janet took a call. "Hi, it's Bob. I'm in Blaine. Are you free tonight?"

"Sure. Where and when?"

"Want to meet mid-way?"

"How about Mount Vernon, say seven p.m.? The casino hotel lobby?"

"Sounds great. See you then."

They met with a kiss and another, deeper French kiss. "I missed you!" Bob said.

"Me too. Last time I had any sex was with you. I need relief. NOW."

"Oh yeah! Me too! Let's get a room. Dinner can wait."

"You better believe it!"

As they walked toward the check-in desk, Janet whispered in Bob's ear, "I'm wet already!" Bob's hand was shaking when he signed in.

Once in the elevator, they held hands and managed a deep kiss before they reached their floor. They quickly found their room, opened the door with Bob entering first and switching on the lights. The room was spacious, well-appointed with a king-size bed. Janet closed the door after she entered and reached for the back of Bob's belt, pulling him around to face her, reaching for his crotch with her other hand where she found Bob was very solidly aroused. Bob wrapped his arms around her, squeezed tightly and gave her a long deep French kiss that ended with both panting and taking quick breaths.

Janet loosened Bob's pants and they let them drop to the floor where he shook them off his lower legs. Janet had a hand on his manhood while Bob undid her skirt and shook it to the floor. Quickly helping each other, they stripped. Moving backward, Janet pulled Bob to the bed, fell on it and pulled Bob on top of her. Bob had his hand on her crotch and, with the other, took Janet's hand off his penis, saying, "Foreplay for you comes first. I want three orgasms out of you before you touch my little friend again? O.K?"

"It's not little." After the second orgasm, Bob entered and pushed her to her third before he came for the first time.

After a quick clean-up in the bathroom, Bob and Janet were cuddled on the bed with Bob running his tongue over her breasts. Janet said, "I guess you were the one who found the helicopter parts supplier? "

"In a way. I followed up a bit on that hint Rus Potter gave us and found the company in Mission, B.C. that had sold some partly rebuilt Bell 212's. Then, nosing around a few companies repairing choppers led to the new parts supplier. Others took it from there."

"Are you keeping an eye on Chief Joseph Branson?"

"You can say that. There's every indication he controls the big league smuggling in his area. But proving it or catching him in the act on American soil is your game."

"I'm sure he's the one behind everything."

"Maybe. Enough shop talk. Let's get back to the important matters at hand." Bob put a hand on Janet's crotch and began massaging. She reciprocated. Soon she was wet and on her way to orgasms four, five and six.

They managed to take a dinner break about eleven p.m. then returned to their bedtime frolics. After a little sleep and a shower together they departed on their respective ways around five a.m.

Chapter 20

The flight to the Maldives was uneventful. All breathed a sigh of relief when they cleared Kyrgyz airspace and a second sigh of relief when they entered India's airspace after transiting Tibet, Nepal and Bangladesh. David and Joseph managed to get a few hours rest after repackaging the cargo. They arrived over their destination about ten in the morning in bright sunlight and were cleared for landing from the Northwest. The airport was on its own narrow island and Joseph could see a small freight boat, empty, about one hundred fifty feet long, tied up at one of the quays. Nearby at another quay was a one hundred and thirty foot charter boat.

Upon landing, the aircraft taxied to the end of the runway where there was sufficient apron to allow the pilot to turn it around. After making the U-turn, Paul brought the aircraft midway down the runway and off onto the parking apron. The airport was empty, save for a scorched old twin engine Beechcraft sitting in the field behind the fire hall that looked as if was used for fire drills. Following directions from the ground attendant, Paul brought the craft to a stop within a hundred yards of the cargo quay about one hundred yards south of a building that served as control tower, passenger waiting/transfer room and airport office. Paul, David and Joseph were first down the stairway and were escorted to the airport office by the ground attendant. A fuel truck pulled up to the aircraft and Umesh was tasked with supervising the refueling and checking the exterior of the aircraft. The cargo door was soon open with ground attendants offloading the cargo.

It took only ten minutes for the customs officer to approve the cargo papers as the customs duties and taxes had been prepaid by a customs broker resident in Male' and the customs officer had the confirmation documents on his desk. The cargo had been listed as concrete waterproofing admixture – a relatively high-value item that is added to concrete mixes to increase waterproofing and self-seal cracks. Joseph and David told the customs officer they wanted to enter the country to inspect the construction of their research lab and also to spend some time as tourists on a dive boat. They had reserved a scuba diving charter boat for three weeks. He took them across the room to the Immigration officer who stamped their passports with a tourist entry permit good for thirty days and welcomed them to the

179

----

country. He mentioned he had just been talking with the captain of the charter boat and wished them a great three weeks of diving.

The customs officer declined a physical inspection of the cargo commenting that he had seen enough of construction materials.

When David and Joseph emerged from the office, the cargo had been brought quayside to the cargo vessel, the *Mystic Moon.* A crewman was securing cargo hooks, dangling from the lifting cable of the ship's cargo crane, to the first pallet. In short order, all the cargo had been loaded aboard and secured to the ship's spacious cargo deck behind the wheelhouse.

As the cargo was being loaded, Joseph and David met the captain of the *Mystic Moon,* who introduced himself as Abdul Halim. He told them the trip to the island where the research lab was being built would take him about six hours and that the *Blue Northern II,* with Igor aboard, was there anchored offshore. He was aware that Joseph and David would be following him to the island on the dive charter boat, which was operated by his first wife's brother, Soli Kahleel.

David and Joseph walked back the short distance to the aircraft where they shook hands, exchanged bear hugs and thanked the pilots. Joseph said, "A great job, Paul. Thank you all."

Paul said, "No problem, Joseph. Anytime. Our refueling is done and we're off to Colombo to overnight. We have a cargo of high fashion garments for London waiting there. We'll be in Colombo in less than an hour and a half, so we'll have some time to relax and get a little sleep."

Joseph and David picked up their overnight bags, which Umesh had brought off the aircraft, and walked over to the charter dive boat, the *Manta Ray.* As they were approaching the boat's gangplank, a man on the stern deck waved to them and shouted, "David and Joseph! Welcome aboard!"

He came over to them, introducing himself as they shook hands. "I am Soli Kahleel, your Captain, and this is the *Manta Ray.* The vessel is two years old, fiberglass construction, and one hundred thirty feet long with big thirty-eight foot beam. She's powered by twin five hundred horsepower Cummings Turbo Diesels and has a cruising range of two thousand nautical miles. We have eight twin staterooms for guests, and one master suite, all above the water line.

"We have a crew of six, which includes one dive master, a photographer, engineer, cook, steward and deckhands. We are a full-function dive facility with undersea scooters, air compressors and nitrox for mixed gas diving, photography studio and even a recompression chamber. For your comfort, we have a hot tub and a sauna. We also have a variety of in-shore sailing and power craft. For diver comfort, we also trail a thirty-foot dive tender. We're equipped with all modern navigational and communications gear, including satellite phone and wi-fi."

"Well, Captain," Joseph replied, "it looks as if we'll be quite comfortable. First, as you know, we will accompany the *Mystic Moon* over to Minora Fushi Island where we're building the research lab. We'll have to spend some time looking over the construction and in discussions with our partner, then either come back here to pick up our wives who are expected in two days or have them flown out to the ship. After that, all we want is to be led through a great variety of good diving."

"Yes, I have met with Mr. Igor. He was kind enough to invite me for lunch and a tour of his lovely vessel, the *Blue Northern II*. He was here making arrangements but is now anchored off your island. Oh, I see the *Mystic Moon* is preparing to cast off. We'd best get underway as well. Mr. Igor has ordered me to stay close to it at all times. I'll have Sami, our dive-master, show you to your staterooms and then give you a tour of the vessel and our equipment. You have your choice of staterooms as you've chartered the whole ship."

Joseph and David were escorted to the Master Stateroom, a suite that was situated in the bow below the wheelhouse. It contained a living room/lounge with fifty-two inch flat screen TV and satellite reception of over three hundred channels, and three sofas, which also doubled as beds. They were led forward down a circular staircase on the right forward side of the lounge, which ended in a massive bedroom. The bed, king size, was centered where the two sides of the bow joined. It was raised about four feet off the deck to accommodate the curvature of the bow. Beneath and behind were polished mahogany cupboards.

Beside the circular stairs was a door, which led to the companionway of the next deck leading aft to the stern. This corridor had eight doors, four on each side leading to staterooms. Through the large window on the door at the far end of the companionway, one could see an outside deck and the ocean. In the master bedroom another door opened onto a spacious washroom with toilet, sink and a very large shower. It was pointed out that the shower stall was a steam shower – in case one needed to warm up after a hard day's diving or to work out a hangover.

Sami left Joseph's overnight case in the master bedroom and led them along the companionway. He stopped at the first stateroom door and said, "David, take your choice of stateroom. They are all similar but you may have a preference. Each has individual air conditioning so it doesn't matter if you are on the sunny side of the ship and each has its own ensuite with a shower We tend not to travel at night and we normally stay in the calmer waters inside the atoll so you needn't worry about which position, forward or aft in the ship, may give an uncomfortable ride."

David selected a rear stateroom with more windows.

The ship was underway by the time Joseph met David in the upper lounge. This was a spacious lounge behind the wheelhouse and above the master suite lounge. It also contained a fifty-two inch flat screen TV and assorted sofas. It had a wet bar along the wall (bulkhead) behind the wheelhouse. Its rear (aft) wall (bulkhead) was floor to ceiling glass with a sliding door in the middle leading to a large, one quarter covered, outside deck which held six lounging sun chairs, a round table with four chairs, and two hammocks suspended from the ceiling under the overhang.

A man, dressed in white slacks and tee shirt, entered the lounge and introduced himself as their steward. After they'd decided lunch would be a selection of sandwiches, the steward departing to organize it, and David went to the bar fridge, opened two beers and gave one to his dad. They clinked bottles and David said "Cheers," to which Joseph replied, "So far, so good. It's time to relax a bit. I talked to Igor. He'll meet us at the quay and show us the setup. He wants us over to the *Blue Northern II* for dinner after the cargo is offloaded and we've had time to look over the island. He's already got some technicians and other staff hired and he's pleased with the way the lab facilities and living quarters shaped up. Captain Kahlil says we're making pretty good time with the tide so we should be docking around four-thirty. It won't get dark 'till about six-thirty, so we have plenty of daylight to look around. After lunch, I'm going to try to catch some more sleep. You can keep an eye on the *Mystic Moon*."

Joseph awoke to the change in movement of the ship. The engines had slowed and the vessel was making a tight right turn. He dressed and went out on deck. He noticed the ship had rounded a breakwater and was preparing to come alongside a concrete quay opposite to the *Mystic Moon,* which had already tied up and its crew was preparing the deck crane to remove the cargo. Igor, standing casually with one foot on a bollard on the end of the quay, waved at him. "Joseph! Great to see you! Did everything go smoothly?"

"Hello my friend! Great to see you too! Yes, very smoothly. Paul and Rishi, Saqulain and Arne all send their best wishes. I gather things have gone well here?"

"Yes, the warehouse is ahead of schedule and the prefabricated buildings are in place. We have a few days of work left to finish off the accommodations and install and test the lab equipment, then we can send the work crew back to Bangladesh and get the labs running. Two lab technicians are here and the rest will arrive in two weeks after the rest of the catering, security and housekeeping crew who are due to arrive next week. I recruited most of them from Russia. I had no problems getting them working visas."

David joined Joseph at the ship's stern rail, then they jumped the few feet off the vessel onto the quay to shake hands and exchange bear hugs with Igor. Igor said, "Come, let me show you around."

As they walked the hundred-yard length of the quay toward shore, Igor waved his right arm, gesturing to the beach inside the quay and exclaiming, "Isn't this white sandy beach beautiful? This place could make a great resort! We've kept as many trees and bushes as possible so the island looks like a resort. There's good diving and snorkeling and good shelter on this side of the island. The workers should be content – if they like tropical climates, that is. We've even gone "green" with solar panels, a windmill, water distillation and sewage treatment but we have two diesel generators as well.

"We have excellent telecommunications, partly thanks to the Maldivian government's policy of covering all regions with cell phone service plus a satellite link. We're awaiting your hydroponics technician to set up the marijuana operation. We'll get him to set up a truck garden for vegetables as well. We'll even do a little fish farming under the guise of research. For those staying here, it may be isolated but it should be very pleasant."

'Under the guise of research'? David queried.

"Yes, officially, we are a marine research center searching for new insights toward cures for a variety of fish diseases and the potential of cultivating blue pearls in these waters. That covers a lot of ground. We will have two real researchers with the freedom to follow whatever directions they wish in their free time. In fact, we have two labs, one for the marine research and another, more isolated at the other side of the island, for processing the opium and meth.

"Regardless, all personnel will be working the processing lab or machine shop when needed. They have been carefully selected and will be well paid for, let's say, their discretion. Manufacture of the archery weapon and reconditioning of other weapons will be done in another building. It's nearly complete but the machines and tools have yet to arrive. When can we expect the machinery and equipment for the archery weapon?"

"It was packed up a week ago," replied David, "so it should be in a container on the Vancouver docks awaiting shipment now. Apparently, they transship in Colombo. I was told to expect at least eight weeks for delivery."

"O.K. Time for us to seek other orders for the archery weapon. I have the Syrian, South African and Brazilian armies interested."

"That's great! Igor, how are you handling accommodations? I see a lot of resort-like cottages," said Joseph.

"You're right, this is like a resort. But on a small scale. We plan on up to thirty-five cottages with four for visitors. There is a central dining room, a combination bar and activities center with pool table, shuffleboard and tennis court. There's even a golf driving range and putting green with artificial turf. There's dive equipment and compressor, snorkeling gear, surfboards and kayaks."

"How big is the island?"

"It's quite small, only a total of fifteen hectares above the waterline. But, for the Maldives, it's quite a common size. It's crescent shaped with this lovely beach on the lea side inside the crescent. And, as you can see, we added a breakwater and a quay. We had to ship in the rock from Sri Lanka along with the other building materials such as sand, cement, mortar, rebar, roofing and concrete blocks. The accommodations are clustered to one end. The office, recreation and cooking buildings are in the middle here, close to the quay, and the labs, machine shop, warehouse and hydroponics etc. are all toward the other end."

"Will you be accommodating both men and women?" asked David.

"Yes. There are some couples due to arrive but there will be a number of singles. One always worries about the social dynamics with lonely singles and jilted love affairs but the team leader has experience in contending with that in isolated Arctic conditions with long nights. That was a concern addressed in our recruiting process – we selected personnel who should be comfortable under these conditions. As well, some of the domestic staff have been selected for their ability and willingness to ensure comfort under direction. All also speak English and that is the mandated language of the operation, so there should be no language problems when your people are here."

"Ah, Ken will be happy here!" said David.

"Only if he's well supplied with Viagra!" said a laughing Joseph. "Mind you, he's pretty attached to Patsy, right now. I can see him wanting to bring her along."

"I don't know, Dad, he may be ready for a little variety."

"Igor, what about the meth production? When do you want it to start?"

"I've set up a distribution system across Eastern Africa and Nigeria. We'll fly the stuff to Zanzibar where we get our cash from major distributors. It will be their responsibility to move it on. Apparently, the guys controlling Zanzibar – the gatekeepers, let's say – do this all the time and have done so for centuries. They jumped at the opportunity for a quality source. Most of them are in the arms trade and known to me anyway. We are still awaiting some of the materials and lab equipment for that. I figure we should start production about three months from now. Is your man still willing to run the production?"

"O.K. You've moved quickly. Yes, as agreed, our man will handle production long enough to train your personnel and come back periodically for quality control and more training. He's looking forward to spending some time here. Are we still in agreement he'll be in and out every other month for the next eight months? I still need him for my own local production."

"Yes. When can we begin the hydroponics for the marijuana and the vegetables? The equipment you specified will arrive in about three weeks and we are just about finished the greenhouses for it."

"Well then, I'll have two men over here in three weeks. They'll bring the seeds. It'll take them two weeks or so to set up the marijuana grow op. We won't need grow lights as we have plenty of sunshine here and no point using precious electricity to force the plants to grow overnight. We can surround the marijuana pants with greenhouses for fruit and vegetable production. That will also be good camouflage."

"Have you decided how you want your share of the opium processed? I have good orders from the Sudan, Congo, Libya, Afghanistan and Somalia for morphine so I could easily get rid of it."

185

"Thank you Igor, but I'll take it as heroin as I've arranged distribution through my biker friends. That gives me a better profit margin."

"Then we will have to work out how best to get your goods to Canada or America."

"Yes, let's work that out."

Chapter 21

Janet took a call from Shirley. "I'm glad both our background checks turned out good on the couple living on the property where the helicopter parts are stored. How would you like to handle surveillance?"

"It's FBI jurisdiction. I've got a female undercover operative who could pose as a visiting relative. The owners are willing to rent us a bedroom on the ground floor with full view of the yard and storage shed so we can set up photo surveillance. I don't think we should try to co-opt the owner of the business. His background is a little cloudy. We suspect he's well connected in the criminal world. We'll bug his home and office, computers and all phones though. I've already gotten his phone records for the past year and have a team going over that. IRS has been helpful with his business tax records. Looks as if he does over seventy percent of his business with Canadians.

"I've got someone working with ICE and Canadian Customs cross-checking the sales made to Canadians. They're about one third through and guess what? Only about forty percent were presented to and cleared by Canadian Customs. Looks as if sixty percent may have been smuggled across or may have been smuggled out of North America. At least, that's with parts that are in the sales records.

"He's also doing a cash business. We're crosschecking this through FAA parts records as well but that's a little slower. We've checked his bank records and IRS filings. The bank records tally with his IRS filings, so he hasn't run afoul of the IRS – visibly anyway. He may not be recording all his sales and his reported income for what he claims to have sold seems to have a pretty high profit margin compared to similar helicopter parts suppliers. He may be laundering illegal sales by throwing the income into his legal sales."

"Why does that not surprise me? Yeah, the owner seems to be a risk. Good idea for the undercover operative. But we'd like to tag all the parts in the warehouse. You need a court order for that. Maybe better if you let us do it on the grounds that we are only interested in whatever's crossing the border?"

"No need. We've already got the court order. But you said you're going to supply the tracking devices. Is this similar to the tracking mechanisms that were used on the Koreans?"

"Partly. We can put that type on some spare parts but only where they wouldn't be noticed. They're good for following where the cargo goes. But they do have a limited life of up to six months due to the battery needs. We've also got something else, a so-called "passive chip" to use. It's like the RFID chips you see on the new credit cards only better. There's no battery so they're good forever."

"RFID?"

"That's short for Radio-Frequency-Identification. We call it a "passive chip" as it responds to a signal from a reading device. When the chip passes a reader, a signal is bounced from the reader to the chip and back to the reader. The credit card companies are now amassing data banks for "mining" information, such as developing profiles of customer's purchasing habits – even clothing sizes and brand preferences. The chips are great for showing who walks by a store display and we've improved on that. It's beginning to come in handy for us.

"However, when you use the chips the way we want to with the spare parts, you have to have sufficient readers scattered around to be worthwhile. Mind you, we have mobile readers that we can place in vehicles, aircraft and the like. Ours are pretty sensitive but you, or anybody can buy a simple version on eBay that can read from a short distance away. The only good thing about the cheap readers is that they get confused with multiple credit cards in the same wallet and they have such short range. The chips can be obscured by being wrapped in aluminum but our system is much more effective. We'll need time to get into the warehouse and plant them though. Even with a four-person crew, it may take a couple of nights, depending on the amount of inventory. And then, we'll have to go in and add chips when new inventory comes in."

"From what we've learned of the selling patterns, although he's advertising 24/7 parts availability, seldom does anyone pick up parts overnight after midnight. We've looked at the yard and may be able to get a bit of delay if we insist the owners keep the entrance gate to the yard shut. This could give a delay period for your crew to exit through the back way if someone shows up. We'll also place picket surveillance at the crossroads to give two to three minutes early warning. Plus, our telephone monitoring team will be able to advise when the owner receives an order and will be coming to the shed. That will likely be twenty minutes to half hour early warning."

"O.K. Let's do it. Let's start tonight. We may as well bug all his parts in stock and later get in and out to do new arrivals. But we should start with the parts for the Bell 212? And let's track his car too."

"Yeah. I'll call you back when I have set things up. Shouldn't be more than a couple of
hours."

Early that evening, the undercover operative, Sarah Jones, was introduced to Mr. and Mrs. Roth, the residents and owners of the farm property. Sarah moved into the farmhouse and set up in the spare bedroom that faced the storage shed. The Roths were sworn to secrecy. The yard gate was shut. Operatives gained entry to the shed from the back door and began tagging the inventory in the shed.

Next day, the business owner, Mr. Fred Weiss, arrived at the shed at ten a.m. Sarah had been forewarned from the phone surveillance detail that he was on his way out to get a tail rotor blade for a Bell 212 and the customer would be meeting him at the shed. When Fred arrived, he was introduced to Sarah by Ms. Roth as her niece from Baltimore, a marine biologist specializing in shellfish, who would be boarding with them while she completed a research project on the Puget Sound mudflats nearby around Blaine.

Fred Weiss, age forty-five, casually dressed and with an athlete's build, blue eyes and blond crew cut hair, was immediately awed with Sarah. She was wearing white short shorts and a pink and white halter top, and her pink-painted toenails nestled in open sandals. With her long blonde hair, Sarah appeared to be thirty but slipped into the conversation that she was thirty-six years old, had a Doctorate in Marine Biology from Scripps, was a full professor at Washington State University and had been divorced for four years. For Fred Weiss, it was love at first sight and he was eager to impress the lovely and inquisitive Sarah.

While waiting for the customer to arrive, the story he gave Sarah was that he had been a helicopter pilot in the Marines and had seen service in Iraq. He was still in the Marine Reserves and had one deployment to Afghanistan two years ago but his flying days were over due to an eye problem. He had started the helicopter parts business as he also had a mechanical background on helicopters from when he was growing up through working for his father, who owned a small fleet of helicopters in Texas. He had found a small niche in the parts business by having parts available 24/7. He had set up the business near the Canadian border of British Columbia as there was a good demand from smaller operators in the area on both sides of the border and he liked the geography.

After accepting a date for dinner, Sarah went back to her room when the customer arrived. She duly noted the make, model and license of the car and videotaped the driver exchanging cash with Fred and putting a part in the car. The car was from British Columbia. Sarah relayed the information by phone and e-mail. FBI alerted CSIS, Canada Border Services and ICE Border patrol. The vehicle crossed the border into Canada at the Aldergrove crossing and ended its journey at the Mission, B.C. airfield. The part had not been declared, according to Canada Customs. The tracking device worked splendidly. The surveillance system was in place and working well.

Three days later, Shirley received a call from Janet. "We've had time to take a close look at the inventory of parts in the shed. We estimate he has over three million dollars' worth of parts stored there. We've also observed some parts arriving and we later inspected and tagged them. An expert we contracted to look at the inventory records on Mr. Weiss's computers states that fully a quarter of the parts have military serial numbers – much higher if you only look at the Bell 212 parts. He's dealing in illegal parts. We're tracing the sources of those parts but so far, it looks as if all are coming from salvage and surplus dealers."

"Suspicions confirmed. I'm glad the tracking devices are working well. So far, half the parts that have been sold to Canadians have not been declared at Canada Customs. We have a small scale smuggling and illegal parts operation."

"Too small scale for us – especially when our objective is to catch terrorists and murderers. I'm having a little trouble with Homeland Security wanting to arrest the small-scale smugglers. They seem to need some positive publicity. I had to get D.C. involved to stifle it."

"My, my. The FBI used to be that way at times with communist cells and bank robbers."

"Before my time, I'm happy to say! Are the tracking bugs starting to show up in aircraft yet?"

"It's still early, but yes. So far, looks as if the aircraft are engaged well north of the border in routine stuff. One has been tracked to Vancouver Island where it's in use installing cell phone towers, another is at a firefighting operation in the middle of the province near Williams Lake and another on the Pacific Northwest coast logging in the Queen Charlotte Islands – you know, they call it

----

Haida Gwaii now. Nothing has been shipped into the Okanagan as yet. We've got equipment for the passive bugs set up along the border from Blaine, Washington to above Coeur d'Alene, Idaho but nothing's shown up crossing back into the U.S. We have to be patient. I'm sure this will lead to something."

"Speaking of tracking. Our people keeping tabs on the fake Mr. Westley Miller are still on the job. So far, he's been driving a big rig pretty steadily on a route between St. Louis and Yuma, Arizona. We'll keep up the surveillance though. He doesn't seem to be in contact with any criminal element. He's got a girlfriend he stays with in St. Louis but she's an elder care nurse and has no record or known criminal associates."

Chapter 22

Great Similkameen Lake

After the command, "Don't move! Or you're dead!" Bob froze, crouching down still holding onto his camera, which was pointed down and in the playback mode. He wedged the camera between his knees and slowly put his hands on top of his head interlocking his fingers. He then slowly turned his head in the direction of the voice. He saw a figure in complete head to toe camouflage, face covered by a camouflage hood with only eye and mouth holes, walking toward him, about two hundred feet way. He had what looked like a rifle, also in camouflage, which he carried with two hands with the muzzle pointing up to the left. "Right handed," thought Bob.

As the gunman came within ten feet of Bob, he started laughing, then pulled off his hat and stocking mask revealing his red hair and green eyes.

"Sheeit man!" Bob exclaimed. "What'd you do that for? You almost killed me! And I didn't bring a change of underwear!"

The gunman then doubled up laughing uncontrollably. "Bobby, you should have seen your face! Priceless! I wish someone had a camera on your face at the instance you heard the arrow hit!"

"Fine for you asshole! But you could have killed me!"

"Hey, you know I'm a good shot! Priceless man! Besides, I was a good foot and a half above your miserable head!"

"I didn't hear you sneaking around. Were you lying in ambush for me?"

"Yep. I saw you on the CCTV security monitors playing tourist and snooping around the mine yesterday. I figured it would take you until the next day before your little mind decided what to do next. Then, you'd probably look at the cabin on the lake toward evening. I didn't have too long to wait before you showed up. It was fun watching you play snoop. What do you think of my little playmate there?"

"Gorgeous man! Where did you come across her? "

"That's Patsy. She works for Joseph. He assigned her to be my housekeeper and to keep me happy. She's great man! Have I ever gone through the Viagra! She's even a great cook and a deadly bridge player! You've got to come up to the cabin and meet her. She's expecting you for dinner anyway. Besides, we need a fourth for bridge."

"I can't go up there like this. I need a shower and a change of underwear! What do you mean, 'a fourth for bridge'?"

"The lake's warm, go for a swim. I'll go over to the cabin and bring you a change of underwear – boxer shorts though – and a bar of soap and a towel."

"What do you mean, 'a fourth for bridge'?"

"Oh, when I figured you were coming to visit, I invited The Deacon to join us for dinner and bridge. He should be arriving shortly. We haven't had any outside company for all the weeks I've been up here. Only people we've seen have been the others working in the mine and Joseph and David. Joseph wouldn't let me have any contact with the outside world until my work was done. And now, I'm only to invite people he knows can keep their mouths shut and he approves of."

"Nothing like being certain I was coming."

"Yeah, well, I'm sorry you didn't know where I was but you should've had a hunch. I figured you'd check out the mine eventually. Besides The Deacon kept in contact. There was always an emergency extraction crew nearby and I have an emergency locator."

"Well, that's info The Deacon kept from me! Looks as if his loyalty is still to the Canadian spooks. We had you narrowed down to being on one of the local reserves, such as NightHawk Number 6 or up by Agar Lake or here. It took a bit of looking though.

"Yep. Oh, we don't discuss business in front of Patsy. O.K.? I'm still in deep cover. Besides, I'd like to hold on to her for a while. As far as she's to know, you guys are hunting buddies of me and Joseph. Besides, I cleared it with Joseph. He said it was cool to invite you up, now that I have finished the job and the equipment has moved out."

"O.K. We're hunting buddies. Which we are. What's for dinner?"

"Fresh elk steaks. I've also smoked some sausage. Delicious. I 'll give you some to take home."

"Elk? Out of season?"

"For you, white man. But I'm a registered Indian on an Indian reservation." He pointed at his weapon. "Besides, what did I invent this toy for?"

Ken went up to the cabin while Bob stripped, followed a path to the lake and went swimming. The water was warm and clear. Ken returned and threw him a bar of soap. Bob got out and toweled dry and dressed. As they were walking on the trail toward the cabin, they could hear a car approaching the house. "Looks as if The Deacon has arrived," said Ken. "Good timing."

They met Brian (The Deacon) in the driveway just as he was getting out of his car. "Ken figured you'd be out here," Brian said to Bob. "I'm sorry I couldn't tell you where he was but that was classified information above your pay grade."

"And he had the fun of scaring the shit out of me! You know how close he came to me with an arrow?"

The Deacon said, "You've been hunting with him long enough to know he's a good shot. You're probably more upset that he snuck up on you. What's the matter boy? You going deaf?"

"No. No. He was lying in ambush. Pretty sneaky. And how come you're withholding secrets from your American allies? You knew he was here all the time. And here I thought you were a double agent on both Canada and Uncle Sam payrolls."

"Need to know, boy. Need to know only. We couldn't have you acting funny around that lovely FBI agent could we? Too many secrets get lost in bed, you know. Remember, your role is tracking terrorist leads and chasing a cross-border smuggler/murderer. Besides, Ken can't be found yet. He's got to stay out of sight. Oh, by the way, thanks a whole lot for passing on that photo of me hunting with Ken when you shook down his house. Thank goodness, that didn't raise any suspicions with Janet. I notice you failed to include the photos with you in them."

"Well," said Bob, "with the photo, I thought if you had told them you were helping to sell the prototype version, it wouldn't be unusual to be together in a hunting photo. It helped verify that you knew him well."

"No harm done. Bob, you will report back to Shirley that you found nothing at the mine or at the cabin here. Ken, you may as well stay low for a little while longer, say a few more weeks at least. I gather that Shirley and Janet are making some headway with tracking the helicopter lead. So, Bob, you'll probably be diverted to work it some more. We've got to give them some hope and Joseph's bound to use his choppers for a cross-border run in the near future. That bastard needs a bit of a lesson for tangling with the border patrol. I gather from Donny that the Koreans have made peace with Joseph but have yet to use him for another border crossing. I think we'll play with that a bit. Maybe confuse the issue, yet enable the border patrol, Fibbies, DEA and Canadian agencies to earn some brownie points. We'll see."

Ken said, "Joseph and David are out of the country on holiday with their wives for a month or so. He said I can have the cabin and Patsy's services for the next few months, if I want. He's moving the weapon factory offshore and promised me a tropical vacation in a few months at the new location for production. We're moving into the fall hunting season and the hunting's good here. I'll hang out here for a little while. Besides, if I go home, I've got some lawsuits on the heat pumps to deal with and then there's my ex-wife and her lawyers who'll be hounding me."

"You going to work on making some more red-headed Indians?"

"Hey, at my age, you take it where you can! Joseph promised me a beautiful White Russian housekeeper when I go to the new offshore location. I think it's in the Maldives."

"Anyway," said Ken as they crossed the patio and moved toward the kitchen door of the cabin, "Come on in and meet Patsy. Drinks and dinner first, then you two can be bridge partners. With Patsy, I could beat Donny and Cindy."

The Deacon said, "You don't want to do that, boy. You know how that upsets Donny! Besides he's still pissed with you on the thermal heat pumps. You're going to have to make your peace with him on that soon. Let's meet the lovely Patsy! What's her religion? Do you think she's into metaphysics or astrology? What about native spiritualism?"

Chapter 23

8:07 a.m., in Studio A of the National Broadcasting Regional Center
in Kelowna, British Columbia, Canada

"Hello, my friends in radio land. This is National Radio –
Kelowna – serving the Okanagan, Shuswap, Similkameen and West
Kootenays. And… this is The Morning Talk Show. I am your host,
Tina Linkoff. Today, We'll follow up on a previous interview. I am
pleased to welcome back Chief Joseph Branson, Chief of the Midlake
Indian Band and former Grand Chief of the Federation of Okanagan,
Shuswap and Similkameen Tribal Aboriginal People. Chief Branson
has returned to update us on a very unique, and, may I say, effective,
conservation project. Chief, welcome again to The Morning Talk
Show."

"Thank you Tina, it's always a great pleasure to be here
again."

"Chief, today you are going to tell us all about the Aboriginal
Fisheries Enhancement Initiative – the AFEI – and the attempt to
return sockeye salmon to the Okanagan river system. I understand
you have some very pleasant news."

"Yes, Tina, as you and many listeners may recall, the AFEI
was founded five years ago as a joint initiative of the various
departments of fisheries, water management and aboriginal tribal
federations on both sides of the border. The objective we shared was
to bring natural runs of wild sockeye salmon back to the Okanagan.
As you know, even Okanagan Lake, before it was dammed, had
sockeye salmon making the journey to the Columbia River, out to sea
and returning in four to five year cycles to spawn. We still have the
trapped sockeye salmon in Lake Okanagan but, as they are
landlocked, they are called kokanee. They still spawn in four- to five-
year cycles but they do not grow as large as if they were ocean
raised."

"That's right. So what has been happening?"

"As I mentioned in my last visit, five years ago the AFEI
began a sockeye hatchery program releasing sockeye fingerlings into
the Okanagan River just below the last dam at Okanagan Falls. As
well, the streambed here in Canada was enhanced for over 20
kilometers to provide excellent spawning grounds for the returning
mature fish. Concurrently, tribes along the Okanagan River on the
U.S. side of the border also enhanced spawning grounds. Four years

----

ago, our first sockeye fingerlings were released to make their way down rivers to the open ocean."

"As you know, the fish have to migrate down and back following the Okanagan River to its confluence with the Columbia and then down the Columbia. It's a journey of over a thousand miles or sixteen hundred kilometers during which they have to pass through fish channels on over a dozen dams on the Columbia. It is indeed, an arduous journey – it's amazing."

"Truly amazing."

"Tina, we are now seeing the success of all this! Sockeye have returned to the Okanagan in abundance! This year, this month, thousands and thousands of spawners have returned to the point where the Department of Oceans and Fisheries has allowed us to harvest some for traditional celebration purposes. They recognize our historic food fishing rights. We have been allowed to net five thousand fish in Osoyoos Lake and the harvest is being shared with all the local bands in the Okanagan and Similkameen valleys. There will even be a short sport fishery for the next ten days with a quota of one fish per day per person."

"Wow! Marvelous!"

"Now, Tina, there's something I'd like to share with you and your listeners."

"And, that is?"

"This is something you can see for yourselves. The salmon have come upstream as far as Okanagan Falls lower irrigation dam but they can go no farther. There are lots of viewing spots along the river and it is truly a glorious sight to see the salmon spawning. This will go on for about another three to five weeks. It's nature at its best! If all goes well, we can look forward to a similar return in four to five years as the product of this run. The spawning channels are full."

"Chief, since you've been releasing baby sockeye into the river for each of the past four or five years, I guess we may expect similar success over the next few years?"

"Yes, Tina, we can hope for as bountiful runs as this year but we are at the mercy of nature and the potential for environmental pollution and some years will be better than others. This year, by all accounts, is exceptional."

"You've done well, Chief!"

"Not me, Tina. This has been the product of many, many helping hands on both sides of the border and a lot of faith that we can restore nature's balance.

"But we are very concerned that we are missing a golden opportunity. The waterway up from Vaseux Lake was man-made as an agriculture irrigation canal and a few small dams were built. The same for the canal and its dam connecting Okanagan Lake and Skaha Lake. The dams are no higher than fifteen feet each but they don't have fish ladders to let the sockeye pass. When the dams were built, nobody considered the fish. The run had been decimated long before the dams were built.

"But now, you should see the sockeye milling around at the lower Okanagan Falls dam. There are thousands wanting to go upstream! We have an opportunity to restock the upper lakes, Skaha and Okanagan Lake, above the dams but there are no fish ladders! We've got to change some attitudes in the Department of Fisheries and Oceans!

"As you know, our argument is that the sockeye once came to Okanagan Lake, as is evidenced by the fish – the kokanee – landlocked there. I feel we have the argument of "nature's heritage" on our side. We'll win eventually. But with your help, we can do this sooner rather than later. We need people to see the sockeye spawning and to see the ones milling around at the base of the dam. We need people to see the opportunity we are missing to restock Okanagan and Skaha lakes. We need people to share our concern, to be upset that these man-made dams have not been provided with fish ladders. They are not large dams, each is just fifteen feet high – but they are impeding the fish. We want people to join us to petition, to lobby, to browbeat, to cajole, to persuade the government bureaucrats and elected officials to get some action.

"Please folks, take your children to see the salmon run. Please show them one of the wonders of nature and show them part of their heritage and please remember, with many voices, we can make a change to improve their heritage."

"Thank you Chief."

"Of course, Tina. Thank you for having me."

"The Morning Talk Show will be back after the news."

The Chief shook hands with Tina and the producer, gave bear hugs all around and left.

Upon exiting the studio, Joseph was approached by a woman who introduced herself as Mabel Westham, a producer for CBC Television who said, "Chief, I heard you on Tina's show. Your appeal for fish ladders is very impressive! I think we have something visual

----

here for CBC television. I'm going to take a video crew down to Okanagan Falls this afternoon. Hopefully, we'll have some good footage for the early evening news. Would you mind joining us there for an interview? With luck, we may get picked up for the National news."

"You bet, Mabel. I'd love to! Your interest is most welcome! You're right on good visual material, the spawning salmon are wonderful to see. I'll be pleased to show you some good observation points and to be interviewed. What time shall we meet there?"

"I can get the crew there by noon, how about then?"

"Fine, I'll see you at the foot of the lower Okanagan Falls dam. I'll bring some of the local volunteers and the Mayor of Okanagan Falls – he's a great supporter. You may want to interview a few of them as well. There's a school bussing some primary kids out to see the run this early afternoon. You may want to put them into the story."

"Excellent, Chief. Excellent!"

The story made the early evening news for British Columbia and was picked up for the National at eleven p.m. and morning news across Canada, and on the internet.

Chapter 24

Nestled on a bluff in the northwest corner of Midlake Indian Reservation #1, about five miles from its nearest neighbor and fifteen miles from town, was an unusual piece of property. It was held by a band member who is the "locatee" or official possessor of the land. On the band's land registry, Richard William Charlie, a full-blooded Midlake Indian, inherited the land from his father, William Arron Charlie, in 1992. The land was fenced and totals seven hundred acres. It was not good land, mainly hillside with re-growth forest, but it included a hundred acres of valley bottom currently in pasture for some horses and a few steers.

The Charlie family had lived on the land for the past ninety years. The buildings – the old family home, a large barn, and a three-vehicle garage in good condition but needing a coat of paint – were set back on the property on a little knoll out of sight behind a bluff from a gravel public road that wound its way in and out of this corner of the reservation and ended at a popular fishing lake. If one were to stop on the road and look up, they would see a well-kept barbed wire and electrified fence. If they paid some more attention, they would see CCTV security monitors dotted along the fence line, nearly hidden in the trees. Many NO TRESSPASSING signs dotted the perimeter of the property and a locked gate blocked the driveway. Locals know it as a place to avoid.

The homestead served as a clubhouse of the Devil's Brew and William, "Wild Willie" Charlie was its caretaker/den master. He had been a "full color" member of the biker gang for twenty-five years. He was also a first cousin of Joseph's wife, Hazel.

Today, the clubhouse was the venue for a strategy session. Willie placed a plateful of sandwiches on a beat-up coffee table in the middle of the front room and filled a large cooler loaded with beer buried in ice at the front door. Company was expected. Soon Joseph and David arrived in an SUV, then two men, Fred West and Ralph Jones, arrived on big Harleys. They were followed a few minutes later by another two, Johnny and Marcus, on BMW motorcycles. They all exchanged handshakes and bear hugs and settled into the sandwiches and beer in the front room.

Fred West and Ralph Jones were "new" band members who had married local native women. They also had full aboriginal status identification papers and Canadian Social Security numbers that Joseph had arranged for them when they were recruited. Each had

200

petitioned for and received a hundred-acre land parcel from the reservation and their work for Joseph had enabled them to build fine homes. Their incomes were very good and, if asked, they would say they didn't have to work too hard.

Both were recruited by Joseph when they had left the U.S. military. Regrettably, each had only received general level, not honorable, discharges due to difficulties with their superiors. Both were known for their dislike of poor leadership but both had distinguished themselves under fire in the line of duty. For local cover, both were mountain flight instructors for *Red Mountain Helicopters*. Based in Penticton, the company was one of many helicopter flight schools in the Okanagan.

In addition to contracting its helicopters for fire-fighting, general construction and mineral exploration services, it enjoyed a strong and worldwide reputation as an advanced flight school specializing in difficult mountain terrain. Ralph and Fred were just two of fifty pilots working for Red Mountain. If one dug deeply into the obscured ownership of the company, one would discover Donny and Joseph represented the Devil's Brew as major owners through a network of numbered companies registered in tax havens such as Curacao, Nevis, Turks and Caicos and Palau.

Ralph had been a medivac helicopter pilot who had earned a reputation for daring to fly into "hot" war zones and in bad weather. He was a product of the 101st Air Cavalry, lean, six foot and a cranky age thirty-six. His narrow-set brown eyes, and his long black hair, cut in a mullet, accentuated his long narrow face and large hooked nose. In the military, he had earned the nickname, "Rotten Ralphie," for his profanity. When he was recruited by Joseph, he had over two thousand hours flying helicopters and had experienced, and survived, every imaginable condition from arctic cold and tropical forest to extreme desert and mountain conditions. He was also a qualified helicopter mechanic who loved to repair and restore aircraft.

Fred West had a similar background but had been with the Marine Corp. He was also a keen helicopter mechanic and had similar hours of flying in adverse conditions, including Kuwait and Iraq. Fred was short, stocky and balding, which resulted in a shaved head. He had brown eyes, a round flat face on a large head, and huge biceps from years of weight lifting.

After some small talk and their fill of sandwiches and beer, Joseph spoke up. "Well guys, let's get some planning done."

"As you know, the Californian voters narrowly turned down the bill to legalize marijuana. Many who voted NO felt legalization would bring in big corporations and squeeze out the small guys. They were probably right. Anyway, it means business as usual for now, except the Mexican drug lords are pushing in big time. Good thing our bud is better quality and in high demand. You know, the other day Donny was checking around and he got a line on how much bud from here, the Province of B.C. alone, is moving south. He figures production and sale is six billion a year but, of course, much of the revenue is sent to tax havens. He also figures close to eighty percent of production in the southern half of B.C. winds up in California. Now, we in the Okanagan have a good piece of that business, maybe thirty percent. That's including all producers associated with the bikers and larger independents."

"That's a lot of f-ing bud being grown and shipped," said Ralph. "We have to f-ing well stay creative to keep it crossing the f-ing border successfully. It's not just the increased f-ing surveillance by f-ing border patrol, DEA etc. but are there any signs of the f-ing Mexican drug lords planning to foul us up?"

"It's not just the Mexicans. We always have the Punjabis, Koreans and Vietnamese, even the White Russians who could get greedy. So far, our main worry seems to be the Mexicans. The Columbians are supplying most of the cocaine we bring in, so they're unlikely to be a problem. Right now, our distributors in America are concerned about Mexicans intercepting shipments but that's not our concern as we get paid as soon as we make a transfer across the border. It's their responsibility to deliver it after that. So far, we haven't seen the Mexican lords operating north of California. I hope it stays that way.

"In the meantime, folks, we have to move a lot of bud. We've got a neat opportunity to move a lot by chopper on day flights and we'll take full advantage of it. Donny's assembling forty-five tons and it looks like half that again for the next phase about four weeks later. We'll also bring in a few loads of cocaine and guns on our backhaul flights from the bud deliveries."

Fred and Ralph looked at each other with confused expressions. Fred spoke up. "At a ton, even a ton and a half a flight, that's a lot of flying. And we'll be doing this in daylight right under the noses of border patrol? How?"

"There's a mining exploration company, which we control, that's going to do some gold prospecting near the border just outside of Cathedral Provincial Park. The site's not accessible by road, so everything will be flown in. From the site, it's just a short hop through the mountains across the border. You can stay off the radar by flying up the Temple River canyon, which is the boundary for the west and north side of the park. There are creeks and streams also flowing into Washington at that point and there's great shelter due to narrow valleys between steep mountains that you can follow south and east. You come out in a canyon opening to a large valley along the Loomis River about ten miles south of the border. It has a logging access road into it from Loomis, Washington.

"Nearby, in the big valley, there's a reforestation operation contracted to one of our companies. Our partners can get a semi-trailer rig right up to the end of the road without raising any suspicion. They'll bring the cocaine in with the tree seedlings. They'll take out the bud then top off with apples from one of our tree fruit packinghouses in Omak. In the first phase, we'll have three trucks to take out the bud, one every other day. We may have to stockpile some of the bud we bring in by chopper until we have a load for a truck and just in case you get weather delays, but we'll be very remote. Besides, we'll have sentries out along the road to provide adequate warning and there are good exit trails and old fire access roads further into the mountains."

"We're into early fall now," commented Ralph, "so weather can be a f—ing problem. If we get an early f—ing snow, that would close down both mining and reforestation operations."

"Yeah, we want to get this whole thing done in a week. The other shipment run will be five weeks away when we'll be removing the mining exploration crew and equipment off the mountain just before winter sets in. That may be tricky weather-wise. To help shorten the flying distances, we can bring the bud in by truck to the Temple River. There's lots of empty Indian band land along it. In fact, there's an idle RV campground the government built for the tribe but the locatee didn't know how to operate it. That'll make a great staging area and afford some privacy. It's about seven miles to the border from there and another fifteen miles to the log landing deck at the road head from Loomis."

"I like it," said Willie. "We've got a lot of friends on that reserve who can earn a few bucks as lookouts. There's only one road in and it's not very busy at all. It leads up to the park but it won't be too busy this time of year – especially midweek."

"Fred and Ralph, we'll be using three choppers. One will be "official" chartered from *Red Mountain Helicopters* to relay cargo and personnel to the exploration camp. Johnny Olsen will be flying it. The other two will be our own from the reserve here and flown by you. They'll be the same coloring and numbering as the official aircraft."

Fred grinned. "Johnny Olsen's good. We've done this before. The "official" bird is required to have its identification transponder on high squawk so that border patrol can see where it is at all times. You want him to fly above the canyons as much as possible out in the open and visible to radar while we keep low to the ground going through the canyons undetected."

"Pretty much. He'll also shut off the locator when he lands for any period of time. Your choppers will be set up to duplicate his locator code so that you may turn yours on to occasionally run up and down the mountain on the Canadian side. You can expect him to take a lot of half hour breaks while you're in the air."

"O.K.," said Ralph. "The risk is on the American side but we can fly canyons all the way until the Loomis River valley widens out. Then what?"

"You don't have to go into the valley. The road terminates at an old log deck landing near the end of a canyon. You'll have lots of cover. The landing is flat and clear but surrounded by steep mountains. The spar tree they were using for the logging operation has been removed long ago so no obstacles. The reforestation camp is ten miles away on the Loomis River up another box canyon and that crew will be working the hillside much farther south, at least five miles away and up another canyon. They won't hear you and if they do, no problem."

"What about the mining exploration crew?" asked Willie. "Can they be trusted?"

"They'll be our people. David'll be up there serving as traffic control for the shipments. Donny is supplying the drill crew from his bikers in Kelowna and Vernon. We're taking up a couple of exploration drills for core sampling. The exploration company actually has a claim staked there and found some promising gold tracings. The boys will do some trenching and selective drilling. The bonus to all this will be the prospect of discovering significant gold to warrant more exploration next year. Anyway, doing some exploration so late in the season can be interpreted by some speculators as a sign the first showings may have been good. There's sure to be an upward play on the stock over the winter by speculators awaiting results of the drilling."

David said, "Dad, you mean you'll start some rumors and help run the price of the stock up?"

"Something like that."

"What's the name and price of the stock now and how can we get some?" asked Willie. "I always like a sure thing in a stock play."

"I can get you fifty thousand shares each at twenty cents. But, and this is a big BUT, you've got to promise not to sell until I give the word. If you sell early, you're just taking money from my bankroll that I put up to make an "orderly," quote and unquote, market for the stock. When making an orderly market, I'm likely to be on one side of the transaction buying and selling until we can build a feeding frenzy with the speculators. We have to wait until there is significant interest from outside buyers before unloading and I can assure you that will not be until the stock clears a dollar."

"How can you be so sure of that?" Fred asked.

"Many of the issued shares have been sold or optioned to banks in Europe. That leaves a smaller percentage loose in the market here and that can be manipulated better because the market is tight. The European banks have bought the stock on speculation. When it rises, they will sell to their own customers, but only after the stock passes a dollar a share. They have their own system of trading stocks so we never will see any back in our market."

Fred said, "So, if there's no gold, the hype of expectation for the late fall drilling results will be used to push the stock up past a dollar over the next few months and we can sell out when the speculators move in. What if the results are good?"

"Then sell enough to get your money back and a modest profit then hold the rest for the ride. We'll get some inside info from the exploration crew and first view of the assay results on the drill cores."

"Sounds good! I'm in," said Fred, as did all the others.

"O.K. guys, back to the business at hand. We've got to move forty-five tons of bud in less than a week. We start two days from now. Fred and Ralph, you'll be expected to have your choppers at the Temple RV grounds each day by seven a.m. where David, Johnny and Marcus and the exploration crew will be waiting with flatbed trailers loaded with both gear for the exploration site and a few tons of bud. Johnny and Marcus will handle security and logistics at the

----

staging site at the Temple R.V. Park. Markus, you and Johnny co-opt the residents of the reservation to be look-outs."

"What about parking the choppers overnight?" Fred asked. "Can we do it there at the RV grounds or do we have to fly back to home base?"

David said, "There's a large barn on the RV property where you can hide them. We'll have overnight security for them and the other equipment. The RV Park is pretty remote as well. It's the last housing on the road going up to Cathedral Lakes. The people who have the R.V. Park are being paid to keep quiet. In fact, they even get an all-expense- paid trip to Thailand for a couple of months."

"I guess we do the usual for security with a sentry along the road above and below the RV site, plus tie in the local residents for eyes and ears," said Marcus. "I guess six of us can handle the security and loading. Who will monitor the border patrol communications?"

"Willie gets that task. We also have our mole in the border patrol office."

Willie spoke up. "Should we also give the border patrol a diversion?"

"Not this time," said Joseph. "We don't want to give them a consistent pattern to analyze. We'll save a diversion for something else."

"I think we should sling the load in cargo nets below the chopper for quick release," Fred suggested. "If you preload the cargo trailers with the cargo already in nets, it'll save a lot of time and effort at the pick-up site. We need to allow for the altitude and weather problems so I think no more than a one-ton load. I presume we'll have a fuel stash at the exploration site, just in case we run a little short?"

"Good thinking on the pre-load. We can do the same for the cocaine coming north. A fuel stash is a good idea. We'll have some at the mining exploration site and at the Loomis River site. You can stash a couple of barrels at a site midway between the border and Loomis River site if you want. There should be a good spot somewhere. But you can scout that out on your first few runs."

"The run is short," said Fred. "We'll probably never need the stashed fuel but it's good insurance. The next run, closer to winter, may be more difficult. Besides, sounds like we'll be able to use the route again after the spring thaw."

Ralph spoke up. "We're pushing the f-ing maintenance on the choppers. We'll need some f-ing down time after this to do some scheduled f-ing maintenance. We're coming up to replacement time

----

on some f-ing parts. We can get it done within a f-ing week – enough time to get ready for the operation a five f-ing weeks or so from now."

"Good."

Joseph pulled a large topographical map from his briefcase and pinned it to a wall in the living room. They then set about plotting the route in detail.

The operation went smoothly, enabling the transfer of forty-three tons of bud in four days. Weather was not a problem except for some cross winds. The first two semi-trailers had delivered their cargos of seedlings to the reforestation operation and then drove further up the road to the landing site, unloaded the cocaine and guns and loaded up with bud. Once loaded with bud, they were escorted to the fruit packing plant in Omak and topped up with a cargo of apples. On the back hauls, the choppers brought two tons of cocaine and three tons of guns into Canada.

The only hitch, and a minor one, was the need to stash thirteen tons of bud while awaiting the arrival of the third truck. Four men guarded the stash for two days until the truck arrived. The final two tons of bud were brought in and exchanged for the last shipment of cocaine. The truck was loaded and escorted to the fruit packing plant in Omak where it took on apples. It then departed the packing plant at one in the afternoon following Highway 97 through Wenatchee, over the Blewett Pass through Ellensburg and Yakima following Highway 97 across the Columbia River to Biggs, Oregon.

The driver stopped for fuel in Biggs, Oregon on the Columbia River where the driver parked the rig and went into the fueling stop café for dinner. A waitress remembered him leaving the café and heading toward the parked trucks about nine p.m. The body of Walter Aimes, alias Westley Miller, was found in a large pool of his blood at 9:45 p.m.in a dark part of the parking lot behind a parked rig when the driver of that rig checked his tires. There was no sign of the truck and trailer Walter Aimes had driven.

Chapter 25

"What the hell is going on?" screamed Hector into the phone. "I thought you had this guy under surveillance?"

A very frazzled Janet responded, "We had surveillance teams on him but after the first two months and nothing seemed out of the ordinary, we eased back to only electronically monitoring the truck and trailer and his cell phone. There was nothing that seemed out of the ordinary until he picked up a load of trailer parts in Indiana destined for a trailer manufacturer in Yakima. We assigned a two-person team to watch him. Our people followed him to Yakima and then on to a forestry nursery in Leavenworth where he loaded up with seedlings and took them up to Loomis. They followed him into Loomis but aborted following when he got on a private logging road as it would have been obvious he had a tail.

"He was tracked electronically and the team marked time in Loomis. It looks as if he may have unloaded part of his load at one site, and then on for another ten miles further into the mountains where he stopped long enough to unload. The surveillance team picked him up again as he came through Loomis. It looked as if he had an escort as some other vehicles came out of the logging road at the same time. Our team fell back and caught up to him as he was loading apples in Omak. Relays of teams followed him to Biggs, where he was killed. It was dark, our team didn't see him get killed. They headed back to their car when he started walking to his rig from the restaurant. They waited for him to drive out of the parking lot, then resumed the tail."

"What happened to the truck and trailer?"

"It moved out of the parking lot and headed south up the hill along Highway 97. The truck then had a team of two drivers but our team didn't become aware of that until it stopped at a rest stop. Both look of Mexican descent. They had a car following them, which we became aware of when they stopped at a pullout about thirty miles from Biggs and changed license plates. Right now, they're just passing Red Bluffs, California. Both the car and the rig. The car following them may have brought the drivers to Biggs."

"Are you going to let the drivers take you to their destination?"

"Right. We've been co-coordinating with our California and Oregon offices, California and Oregon Highway Patrols, ATF and DEA. We may be able to bag some middle-level traffickers. It's a little complicated with the car following them but we have aerial surveillance helping."

"Good going on that. We could follow the distribution some more but I'd like to see the two drivers plus the one driving that car picked up for hijacking and murder. That takes priority this time. Do the Oregon police feel they have sufficient forensics and witnesses to pin the murder on the drivers?"

"We'll know more shortly, after the autopsy and forensics report and we meet the investigator in charge. Looks as if Aimes was stabbed to death. His identification was taken and that slowed down investigation a bit. It was only after the state police put his fingerprints into the national database that alarm bells started ringing. Our surveillance team only followed the truck."

"Ouch. I presume the surveillance team will get a little "how to do a better job" lecture?"

"Yes, but we must give them some credit for observing the license plate switch, picking up on the car following the rig and being discreet enough to not move in then."

"Janet, I'm bothered. Although this looks like a hijacking, apples have little value. Maybe the apples were a front for a load of marijuana or worse. If so, we've been sidetracked away from the smugglers crossing the border."

"That could well be the case, Hector. Anyway, we may put a little dent in a Mexican drug group if that truck has marijuana as well as apples. We'll know more when we see what is really in that trailer."

"I'll stay tuned, Janet. Good luck."

Early the next morning, Janet was on the phone to Hector. "The truck was followed to a warehouse in Bell, California. Our people ran a combined operation with California Highway Patrol, L.A. County Sheriffs, ATF, DEA and even the local Bell police force to surround the warehouse. With a little difficulty, they took down the truck driver and the car that was with it, arresting three suspects. One shot at the police, wounding a Sheriff's deputy in the leg, and was killed by return fire. They found a switchblade on one of the others. It has blood on the blade and is probably the murder weapon. The deputy's wound was a through and through flesh wound which missed major arteries. She'll be off work for a few months but is expected to fully recover.

"They sealed off the warehouse, preventing anyone from leaving and detaining anyone who came out. When they opened the truck, there were apples one pallet deep but you could smell the marijuana. Behind the apples, they found fifteen tons of marijuana. That discovery led to quickly obtaining a warrant to search the warehouse and the team found over ten tons of marijuana in a walk-in freezer along with six million in cash. They didn't wait for the warrant before entering as they had probable cause when they discovered the contents of the truck. They entered and detained all present, then waited for the warrant before conducting a thorough search."

"That sounds acceptable," said Hector.

"Anyway, all of the twenty-three people in the warehouse were arrested and charged. Plus the remaining two involved in the hijacking. We're bringing the hijackers to Portland, Oregon to be charged with murder and hijacking as the Oregon State police did the crime scene. We've turned over follow-up of the warehouse operation to our L.A. office. They can trace the ownership and things. Neither DEA, ATF nor our L.A. office was aware of any drug operation at the warehouse. So, they have a new thread to follow."

"Were all arrested of Mexican descent?"

"Yes. Most are known members of the Tijuana drug cartel. Half of them are illegal. I doubt if there's any connection to the Canadian smuggling operation except rivalry surfacing in hijacking a load."

"I bet you're right there. That leaves us empty on the Canadian smuggling/murder/terrorism case. Mr. Aimes could have loaded up the marijuana at the apple packing plant in Omak. If so, we don't know how it got across the border to Omak. The other consideration may be that the load was picked up in the mountains around Loomis."

"Maybe we can sweat something out of those we arrested – at least how they got on to hijacking the load of marijuana. That may give us a clue to the structure of distribution in America from the point where goods cross the border, but how do we learn more about the mastermind behind the cross-border smuggling? How do we trace the killer? My bet is the killer originated in Canada – unless it was the late Mr. Westley Aimes? But he has no real history of violence."

"Keep on it. Anyway, good show on taking down the hijackers. Looks as if there will be no problem getting convictions on the remaining hijackers."

"Thanks. We've got the attention of DEA now. They're working with us to set up surveillance on the fruit packing plant in Omak. As they supplied the apples, someone must be involved there.

It's interesting that it's owned by Chief Branson and a local individual. We're doing more research on it."

"Maybe that will lead somewhere. Bye for now."

A week later, Janet was talking to Shirley and Hector in a conference call. "We've got a little action with the helicopter parts distributor in Blaine, Washington that we penetrated. A couple of guys driving an SUV with B.C. plates picked up some parts and have been tracked to the Okanagan Midlake Indian reserve. Some of the parts were illegal military surplus. All the parts were for a Bell 212. In fact, there were some duplicate parts, which leads us to believe they may be for more than one helicopter. We have the location pinpointed."

"Great," said Shirley. "I'll alert our resources in the area for surveillance. Hector, I presume you'll alert the Canadians through the official channels at the Canadian Embassy in D.C.?"

"Yes. You can bring in your friends at CSIS and I'll advise their top brass. I gather you share some tracking with them. I'll also alert ICE, DEA etc. top levels. Janet, how do you want to play it with border patrol?"

"Thanks Hector. After that incident where the person who reported the Koreans crossing the border was found by the Koreans, Shirley and I are a little worried there may be a mole in the Oroville office. We've got one advantage though. Their drones are operated out of Moses Lake Air Base well away from Oroville. The drones have been equipped to track both the vehicle bugs and the passive chips but that is top secret classified so Oroville personnel are unaware of it. We've got a coalition of agencies involved in monitoring, including ICE but their involvement is out of Bellingham and way above the need to know level of Orville or any local border agents."

"So, how does the tracking work? I gather you must have that SUV bugged?"

"Yes, every vehicle that's been involved in picking up parts from that helicopter parts supplier in Blaine had a bug planted. That bug is good for six months before the battery fades. We're mapping destinations etc. but not many have been close to the border. This current lead is both within a short distance to the border and on an Indian Reservation."

"Interesting. So, there may be a connection between the Indian bands on both sides of the border?"

"We're still open-minded about that. The Midlake band in Canada has some members that are also in the local biker gang and that may be another avenue of linkages. We know the bikers are heavily involved in the drug scene there."

"What about these passive bugs your people put on the helicopter parts?"

"That's different. It's a new technology being adopted by the credit card people. When an external reader sends a signal, the chip responds with its identification. That way, its location can be pinpointed. It can even be followed if the chip is moving. All intelligence is beamed to a central control point at Moses Lake then on to us. If something shows up, we can vector the aircraft to where they should be able to pick it up with their FLEUR or visually. The powers that be seem keen to keep the tracking system top secret."

"I'm glad we're on a secure line. I'm anxious to learn how well this works. Good luck! Bye."

Chapter 26

David poked his head into his dad's office. "Hi Dad. I guess you heard about Westley Aimes?"

"Yeah. Did you also hear that the FBI had been trailing the truck and took down the hijackers when they arrived at their warehouse in Los Angeles?"

"No shit? Where did you hear that?"

"From Donny. Yeah, looks as if one of the Mexican cartels was sneaking up on the operation. Donny's saying our friends in California are going to teach the Mexicans a lesson and take out some the feds missed. In the meantime, his people need orders filled for Salt Lake City and parts east."

"Sounds reasonable. But, if the FBI had the truck under surveillance, do you think they followed it up to Loomis?"

"More than likely. That probably means they may have the tree nursery and the fruit packing plant under surveillance now. But, more than likely, they were following the Mexicans."

"So, we switch to another route for a while. We won't use the nursery or packing plant. Do you also want to continue with the Temple mining exploration camp route?"

"We may as well stick to that schedule but we'll have to use another way to move the bud from the Loomis River landing site. You and the crew can work up some ideas, then we'll discuss it with the crew in Omak. In the meantime, Donny wants some bud from that farm the Vietnamese have over near Beaverdell off Highway 33 to go to Salt Lake City. His customer will come to the border directly to pick it up. I was thinking of the crossing over near Midway, the one that takes us in behind Chesaw, Washington?"

"The one where you shot the border patrol guys?"

"No, that's probably still got the locals spooked. I was thinking a little farther east than that right into the head of Chesaw valley."

"That could work. There are three roads out of there so there are options for the customer how best to move the bud. Better not use a semi or even an RV though, as that could draw attention. Maybe a pickup or pickups with horse trailers would be good."

"Great idea. It's horse and cattle country. That wouldn't draw attention. I'll pass the suggestion on."

"How much bud is there to move?"

"Just a ton. It's the last crop of the season for that outfit, as they don't use grow lights. Ralph and Fred have one chopper overhaul finished. We can move it in a week when there's no moon. I guess we'll have to time it to run in and out just before dawn. That way, the customer, if he's using a horse trailer, won't raise any suspicions if they're on the road."

"O.K. It's just a short run, maybe twenty miles from the farm to the border then maybe four miles on the other side."

"But I don't want to get near that farm. Ralph was saying when you fly over, it's too obvious what they're doing there. They've got ten acres in plastic sheet greenhouses. It seems carved out of the forest with no other farms around for miles. If the RCMP flew over it, even those dumb asses would get suspicious. The Vietnamese have been telling the town folk they're growing ginseng but when the wind blows in their direction some are starting to wonder. There's no cause for us to alert the locals in Beaverdell by flying over them. Heck, the farm is almost in the town! We'll get Donny's people to bring the bud closer to the border for us to pick up."

"Do you want a diversion this time?"

"Yeah. It's still warm enough for some hikers on the Pacific Rim trail and Highway 20 is still open through the Cascades. Let's get Donny's people to set up some amateurs with a few kilos of bud crossing the border and taking the trail. That always draws down on border patrol resources as it's a long hike mostly off-road and at the extreme western end of the Oroville border patrol's district."

"That'll do it. Get them to shift most of their resources to the west so we can come in the east side. Cheap insurance."

"Are we bringing anything back on the return trip?"

"A hundred kilos of cocaine. We'll bring it right to the club house."

The night of the run was clear with no moon. At 03:00 hours, using night vision goggles, Ralph brought the chopper into a clearing outlined by solar powered garden lights. The lights dimly revealed a deserted campsite beside the Kettle River near Highway 33 about ten miles from the border. The river valley narrowed between mountains affording a run to the border in a radar shadow out of sight of air traffic controllers or border patrol land-based radar. It took only a few minutes for Donny's bikers to transfer the packages of bud to the chopper and it soon took off. In less than a half hour, it set down behind a pickup truck and horse trailer at the north end of Chesaw Valley on a gravel road about a mile from and out of sight of the nearest home. David was waiting with the driver and two men. Sentries were posted at the two main crossroads in the valley and one about a half mile down the gravel road. David had already inspected the cocaine shipment and it didn't take long for the driver to confirm the quality and quantity of the bud. The cargos were quickly exchanged and David and the driver made the money transfers to the offshore banks with their cell phones. David waved to the pilot signaling that the money had been exchanged and all was O.K. The chopper took off, headed home.

David turned to the driver, shook hands and exchanged bear hugs. "Hey Robbie, we've been monitoring the border patrol frequencies. It looks as if our diversion worked. Both their manned aircraft are way out west over the Pacific Rim Cascade trail as are most of their ground personnel. There's still the east side ground patrol but they're about twenty minutes away and heading west of here. So, it looks as if you're good to go. Good to see you have Washington plates on the vehicle. That won't raise any suspicion. You just look like any local boy moving a horse."

"Yeah, I'll change plates when I get to Idaho. Just the same, I think I'll head up that back road to the National Park at Lost Lake, then down the paved road and pick up Highway 20 east to Republic then over to Coulee Dam, then Spokane."

"Sounds good. It's close enough to sunrise that it looks as if you just got an early start on the day and farmers here get up early anyway. You'll blend in. We'll give you an escort for a few miles, then you're on your own. See you in a while."

After Robbie left, David climbed on his well-muffled and powerful dirt bike and set off on the gravel road to join up with one of the sentries a half mile down. They followed the road to the main east-west artery and headed west to the farm in NightHawk.

Chapter 27

Under clear but moonless skies the pilot of the border patrol's Aircon 405, the fixed-wing Cessna T182 – Turbo Skylane, equipped with FLIR, keyed the microphone to report her position at 02:00 hours. "Oroville Base, this is Patrol Aircon 405 East Zone One over."

"Patrol Aircon 405 West Zone Seven, go ahead. Over."

"Oroville Base, Patrol Aircon 405 West Zone Seven over Pacific Coast Trail southbound one mile in from border. S.Q. Out".

"Aircon 405 West Zone Seven. This is base. Copy S.Q. Out"

The pilot, Mary Vincent, turned to her co-pilot, Pete Rivers, and said through the intercom, "Aircon 17 should be over Winthrop about now, headed this way. They were to follow Highway 20 to Mazama after refueling in Winthrop, then take that side road northwest through the gap until they come up to the trail. That side road is a likely place for someone to park a car waiting for trekkers to come off the trail. If they don't spot anything, they're to follow the trail down to Highway 20. Anyway, if we spot something, they're close enough to come over and deploy a ground team."

"That's good. I guess we have to make a pass down the trail, then make a pass along the logging and water management access roads on both sides of Ross Lake. We could be at this for a few hours."

"Let's hope it doesn't come to that. Apparently, the tip we received specified the Pacific Rim trail and six people traveling at night. It's sort of a repeat of that one we had last May. Remember?"

"Yeah. It's unusual for someone to be trekking that trail at night. You'd expect them to rest overnight and travel by day."

"Strange. Maybe they want to duck the mounted patrol as those guys can only travel by day. They've been pretty effective in catching people."

"I guess so. There's another route. I guess they could also come down Ross Lake by canoe or kayak or such."

"My, you're creative tonight! Yes, we'll have enough fuel for a pass along it too."

"I think our bigger problem is spotting more than one set of trekkers. There could be a few sets along the trail."

"Not likely anyone will be traveling at night but we'll be able to spot the campers easily if they have campfires."

"We'll spot them. Then it'll be up to the horse patrols to go in at daylight and greet them or intercept them when they come off the trail and see who is only trekking and who's smuggling."

"Ah, here's something on the FLIR," said Pete. "Looks like a small campfire and two people. Maybe one person and a dog. The heat signature on one is quite large, as if it was a dog. The other is low signature except for a small part, as if it's a person in a sleeping bag."

"Only two people or one and a dog. Not our likely suspects. Make a note and we'll keep going."

A few minutes later, the pilots heard a radio transmission between base and Aircon 17: "Base this is Patrol Aircon 17 West Zone Seven South over."

"Patrol Aircon 17 West Zone Seven South this is base go ahead. Over."

"Base Aircon 17 at road end Payastan River and Pacific Rim Trail above Mazama. We have overflown a vehicle parked in the trail access parking lot. FLIR indicates cold engine and unoccupied. We are proceeding north on the trail. What is Aircon 405's status? Over."

"Aircon 17 this is base. Copy position and direction. Will dispatch ground patrol to the parking lot and position sentries along Highway 20. Aircon 405 current position ten miles north of you at fifteen thousand feet and proceeding south. Maintain your altitude eight thousand feet. Copy Aircon 405. Out."

"Aircon 405 base and Aircon 17. Copy."

Pete said, "I've got them on the radar. Hold it, we've got something on the FLIR. It's six people walking. They must have night vision assist as its pitch black down there."

Mary keyed the mike. "Aircon 17, this is Aircon 405. We have six bogies walking your way. Suggest you back off and plan intercept opportunity. We will maintain flight path and high altitude over flight. Over."

"Aircon 405 roger that. We are turning around and will land in the parking lot. Can you give us a possible ETA on the bogies? Over."

"Aircon 17 we have them about seven miles from the parking lot. Over."

"Aircon 17 this is Base. Ground support team with dogs ETA parking lot thirty minutes. Do you wish to call out the mounted patrol for sunrise? Over."

"Base, this is Aircon 17 copy. Affirmative. Call out the mounted patrol for sunrise at the parking lot. Out."

"Aircon 405 this is base. Proceed to Highway 20 and Ross Dam then patrol Ross Lake north and access roads. Over."

"Base this is Aircon 405. Copy Ross Lake North and access roads. Out."

"Well," Pete said, "the action may be back there but good thinking on Command's part to check the lake and access roads, just in case."

"You mean, in case it's a diversion or there are other operations moving during no moon. Anyway, we'll keep busy in this area for the next three hours or so."

"Hey, it's not as if we don't love to fly. Think of all the hours we're logging. Can I fly for a while?"

After another scan of the parked car, José Manuel, the pilot, landed chopper Aircon 17 in the empty center of the parking lot. As the engines and blades were winding down, he turned to Sergeant Jed Lee, his co-pilot. "Well Jed, you may be co-pilot in the air but you're Ground Commander when we're on the ground. Looks as if you get the honors of being On Scene Commander as you're the first here. You get to set up the intercept and play with guns."

As Jed opened his door and disconnected his communications cord to his helmet, he said, "Yeah. This should be fun. We'll set up an ambush on the trail just up from the path to the parking lot and wait. Sort of reminds me of deer season. I'll go in with night vision goggles and scout out a good area. They'll have night vision so we have to keep a low profile. Maybe best to get above them as few people think to look up. I'll let them pass me so that I can be blocker if they try to run back up the trail. We can stage the others here on each side of the path to the parking lot. You can do that. I'll take the AR15 with the night scope. Do you want the shotgun or the other AR15?"

José reached into the cockpit and retrieved his bulletproof vest which had also been serving as his seat cushion. Although against regulations, it was a custom of aircraft patrol personnel to sit on their bulletproof vests, reasoning that they would most likely be shot at from the ground. "The shotgun plus my Glock should do in case we need it before the others arrive. But I expect you'll want me in the air for the takedown. You want a portable megalight?"

Jed pulled out his own bulletproof vest from his seat and put it on. "Yeah. A million candlepower could come in handy. I guess I should take along some plastic handcuff ties. You better take some too. Let's keep our portables on Tack 5. Can you call base and have the ground support team switch to Tack 5 on their portables when they're five minutes ETA?"

"O.K. The bogies will take at least an hour, probably an hour and a half to cover the ground. I'll bet they're getting pretty tired and looking forward to getting off the trail and that should be to our advantage. We'll have a lot of people on the ground by then. When things get close, it would be better if the chopper was ready to come over you and illuminate the scene with the night sun."

"Right! You don't need a co-pilot for that but you may want to take along a couple of ground assault people just in case we need to block the trail farther up."

Jed left Jose on the road, proceeded through the parking lot past the car and along the path linking to the trail. Through the night vision goggles, Jed spotted a bluff just off the east side of the trail and found a spot along it where he could climb the face to the top, about fifty feet above the trail. Once on top, he settled behind a large fallen tree and found a spot where he could see as far as two hundred yards up the trail. The terrain was good for an ambush with a steep cliff face rising on the east side and sharp drop of about a hundred feet to the river below. He keyed his mike twice to alert Jose that he was settled in and all was quiet. It was returned with two clicks from Jose.

About twenty minutes later, Jed heard José in his ear bud receiver. "The ground team has arrived. Where do you want them?"

Jed keyed his mike and whispered, "I'm still worried about their night vision. Let's position a couple with a megalight in good cover beside the trail about 50 yards south of the entrance to the parking lot. We can keep others with a megalight near the trail entrance at the parking lot. The ones on the trail can ruin the bogies' night vision with their light, then we can take them down. If the bogies turn off toward the parking lot before those guys can light them up, the team at the trail entrance will have them and we can box them in."

"Affirmative. I ran the plates on the vehicle in the parking lot. It's a fifteen-year-old minivan owned by a Stan Meagres, age 26, of Bothell, Washington. He's had a few convictions for stolen property and drug dealing."

"Copy that."

About forty-five minutes later, Jed keyed his mike three times, signaling he had the bogies in sight. Five minutes later he keyed his mike twice, paused, then twice again, signaling they had all passed him. Forty seconds later, the ambush team lit up the trail with their megalight exposing the trekkers. When they did that, Jed also lit up the trail from his position behind the trekkers. "Hold it! Freeze!" he shouted. "Hands on your heads! Now!"

José began to start the chopper and two armed officers climbed aboard. The team waiting in the parking lot surged down the trail, which they lit with their megalight. In seconds the bogies had been divested of their backpacks, frisked, cuffed and were being led into the parking lot. All were athletic young men in their twenties. They were made to sit down on the ground.

Jed called José. "Aircon 17 stand down. All suspects in custody. Over."

"Copy that. Base, this is Aircon 17. Six suspects in custody. Out."

"Aircon 17, this is base. Copy six suspects in custody. Out."

José shut down the chopper and went over to look at the suspects. Some of the officers had instructed the suspects to put their backpacks on the ground and sit cross-legged behind them where each was photographed with their backpack. With a photographer snapping shots, the packs were opened and inventoried. The suspects had traveled light but it looked as if they were experienced trekkers as they were prepared for bad weather and each had arctic grade sleeping bags and ground rolls. Each packsack contained ten kilos (22 pounds) of marijuana.

Jed turned to José. "Well José, a good night's work. Even if it's only little guys we've caught."

"Yeah. My bet is these guys are just a bunch of independents trying to make a quick buck. Sixty kilos isn't that big a haul. You've got to give them some credit for the effort they went through. That's quite a hike. It must have taken them at least three days to get here."

Chapter 28

Janet woke to her cell phone ringing and bouncing around the nightstand. She rubbed her eyes while groping for the phone and trying to read the big red numbers on her bedside alarm. As she grabbed the phone she focused on the clock: 03:50. Flipping the phone open she said, "Yes?"

"Hi Janet. Good morning. Are you focusing yet? It's Richard on the ops desk."

"Oh, Richard. What's up?"

"The duty officer at Moses Lake drone surveillance called to say the border patrol drone has picked up a signal from one of your passive chips. They're tracking it and have been kind enough to relay their topographical tracking in real time to my computer. It's really neat! You can see the topographic detail, the mountains and valleys, rivers and roads on the map and the signal location of the chip. Without the chip signal though, it would be near impossible to make out the chopper or home in on the chopper's heat signature."

"Get in touch with Oroville Border Patrol and see if you can vector them to it. Maybe one of their aircraft can spot it with their FLEUR or radar and intercept."

"I did so but there's a problem. They have their aircraft at the extreme west end of their territory involved in capturing some trekkers carrying marijuana in along the Pacific Rim Cascade trail. That's why the drone is overhead covering their east sector. They have a ground patrol twenty minutes away, though. Hold it, the chopper's moving again heading north."

"Did you tell border patrol the source of your information?"

"No, as you had requested. I said we had a call from concerned citizen in Chesaw Valley who reported hearing a helicopter overhead. Moses Lake Control confirmed Oroville was not aware of or being supplied with info from the drone's tracking devices."

"Good – and quick thinking! No sense revealing our ace in the hole right now. The enemy may be scanning the border patrol frequencies."

"Yeah, or worse. I like your notion they may have a mole there. Anyway, Moses Lake control advises they have the chopper on the drone's radar and FLIR now and that they are relaying that to Border Patrol Oroville. It'll cross the border pretty quick, probably in two minutes."

"I know the drone can't pursue into Canada so that'll limit their ability to follow by radar. I wonder what range the passive tracking equipment has? Probably similar to the radar, I guess. We'll soon see. Can you ring up Shirley Bains at home for me and patch her into this conversation?"

"The C.I.A liaison? Hold on."

When Shirley came on the line Janet and Richard explained the situation. She responded, "I see the limitations on the equipment on the drone but I've got an idea. Leave it to me. I'll get back to you. Bye."

Richard said, "Moses Lake Control reports they've lost contact. The chopper went around the north side of Mount Baldy, which is about ten miles inside Canada, out of line of sight, flying low, hugging the ground."

Shirley was waiting impatiently for the phone to be answered. It was picked up on the sixth ring. "Bobby, it's Shirley. Time for you to get rolling."

"Shirley, Shirley. Give me at least a second to focus. It's just about four a.m.!"

"Good. You can tell the time! You're focusing. A border patrol drone out of Moses Lake picked up a passive transponder from a chopper. All they could do with the drone was observe. Looks as if the chopper dropped off a load in Chesaw Valley and headed back across the border. The drone lost contact when the chopper went around the north ridge of Mount Baldy."

"O.K. So, I'm in Kelowna. That's an hour and a half away. Nothing from our readers along the border showing on my computer. What do you want me to do?"

"Maybe we don't have enough readers positioned along the border. Why don't you head down toward Oliver with that new toy I gave you and see if you can pick up a response from a passive chip? Your new portable reader is supposed to be twenty times more sensitive than the stationary ones we have along the border. You're an hour and three quarters away from the last sighting and my bet is that it may be heading north a little more. Remember the bug they placed in the vehicle that picked up the helicopter parts?"

"Yeah, we know where the owner of the vehicle lives on the Midlake reservation and he was probably working on a helicopter there but we lost track of the helicopter when he flew it off his

---

property the other day. That was before your new improved toy arrived, I might add."

"Exactly. My bet is the chopper is not too far away, somewhere on one of the Midlake reservations. Why don't you take your new toy, explore around and see if you can get a signal?"

"Right now?"

"No, Get a couple of hours more sleep. No real hurry. You may want to charter a small plane and take your toy along when you over fly the reservations. Take Donna with you. She can give you a hand. Oh, and say hi to her for me, will you? Bye."

Bob hung up and crawled back into bed snuggling up to Donna who stirred and muttered, "Who was that?"

"Just Shirley. She says hi. Looks as if we're going to charter a plane and go sightseeing this morning."

By mid-day, Bob was on the phone to Shirley. "We located five signals when we flew over Midlake Reservation. They're in two different clusters. There's about 100 yards separation between them so likely separate choppers. I'm sending you the download from our software now. Looks as if five of the new parts are in use." Bob read off the numbers of each of the parts signals.

"That matches. They picked up five parts from the supplier in Blaine. Where are the choppers located?"

"On the back side of Midlake Number One reservation. Interesting, a Devils Brew clubhouse is nearby. The choppers are in the bush about 100 yards from a field. The closest public road is about a mile away but there's a gravel road from the clubhouse that runs parallel to the field. What do you want us to do now?"

"Send me the coordinates. I'll get a satellite photo. Not much we can do except set up more early warning posts somewhere between there and the border. Send Donna with that toy down to Oliver and set it up to monitor 24/7 and relay to your computer. You come down here today and pick up a few more toys to place along the border. Let's spot one in Midway and another in Keremeos, one in Hedley and another in Princeton for a few weeks and monitor them 24/7. Also, would be nice to put a monitor near the home landing site of the choppers, somehow."

"O.K. Can do. See you in a few hours. Bye."

Shirley picked up the phone and called her boss. "We will have the advanced land-based passive chip readers in place along the

223

Similkameen and southern Okanagan, and as far east as Midway. Local surveillance found the choppers at their base on the Midlake Reservation. At least, that's for public knowledge."

"I confirm. You may release that information to the FBI and the Regional CSIS counterparts and share results with them. Please ensure local border patrol is not aware of this. The field trial has gone well. Our black ops people monitored everything from one of the big bird satellites and pinpointed the chopper base. We have video of them lifting off, picking up the load on the Kettle River, the flight in to Chesaw and return to their base, but the others don't need to know that."

"Thank you."

Shirley then called Janet. "Hi, some good news for you. We've pinpointed the base location of the choppers. They're on the back side of one of the Midlake Indian reservations."

"Thanks. You and I figured as much from following the bug we placed on the vehicle that picked up the parts from the supplier in Blaine. Regrettably, nothing we can do about it for now. However, we had a break. Chief Patrol Agent Sanchez at Border Patrol in Oroville was on duty last night when the action was under way. Moses Lake Control was feeding him live monitoring from the drone except the passive chip information. The drone's FLIR caught the transfer of cargos in Chesaw. Looks as if they took back a load as well as delivered one."

"Guns or coke, likely?"

"Most likely. Anyway, while the drone's radar and our little toy were focusing on the chopper, Sanchez tracked the vehicle departing Chesaw. It's a pickup with a horse trailer. He commandeered the drone and set it to following the vehicle with the FLIR and radar. There were others at the drop site but they disbursed down side roads and over the fields on motocross bikes. He elected to concentrate on the truck and trailer."

"Good for him!"

"Unfortunately, none of his own resources were close enough to intercept but he called in the state police and local county sheriffs. They have the vehicle under loose surveillance. It's now into Idaho heading toward Boise and being tracked by a sheriff's chopper. We, that's us, ATF and the DEA, will intercept just outside of Boise and hopefully put a tracking device on the rig."

"Great! Are you planning to follow it to its destination?"

224

"Yes, if we can. It's always better to get more of those who are involved."

"Thanks, keep me posted. Bye."

A day later, Shirley took a call from Janet. "We followed the rig to a farm just outside Salt Lake City and in a combined operation with DEA, ATF and the local police we took the perpetrators down just as they were unloading a ton of marijuana. We took six into custody, got a search warrant and found some money, a large quantity of guns and cocaine in the farmhouse, plus a workshop in a barn where it looks as if they repackaged into street level quantities. It looks as if the bud was destined for Salt Lake City."

"What about the driver? Is he talkative?"

"No. He's a professional who's done a couple of three-year stretches for robbery. His name is Richard Bianca, plus he has a few aliases. He's very quiet. We know he's connected to a crime family out of St. Louis. He's lawyered up and seems quite willing to do the time. Same with the others, all have priors."

"O.K. Do you think that incident border patrol had on the west side of their region was connected as a diversion?"

"Very likely. We've interviewed all six of the suspects. All but one are new at the game. They seem to have been recruited for their athletic ability and outdoor skills and were in it for the adventure plus the bucks. The leader though, seems to have some connections. But he's talking. Seems he found it easy to score the bud. They picked it up in Princeton, in British Columbia, and were driven by the vendor to the trailhead in Manning Park on the Canadian side of the border. Apparently the vendor, a member of the local biker gang, the Devil's Brew, told them it was better to travel at night due to the mounted patrols which would come up the trail from the south. They set off during the day and camped a couple of nights. The last day they rested in the afternoon then hiked the last stretch in the dark using night vision goggles."

"Another connection to the Devil's Brew."

"Right. But we can't touch them as they don't cross the border."

"The St. Louis crime connection keeps popping up. Wasn't Westley Aimes connected to it as well?"

"Yes. We're exploring it."

Chapter 29

Joseph leaned out of his office and waved his arm and motioning David to join him. When David entered and closed the door, Joseph said, "We've got to get the mining exploration crew, their equipment and remaining core samples off the mountain. We've got a weather window for the next few days, then it looks as if we'll get hit with the first snowfall. Can you get the guys moving?"

"Sure, Dad. But do you still want to use the helicopter traffic to move some bud south?"

"Yeah. I spoke to Donny. His people have ten tons ready, and we have a ton of meth that can go down. Plus we can bring back a load of guns and a couple of tons of coke for Donny. Donny's ready to go today, so you can set things up to begin tomorrow. Use the same staging area at the Temple RV Park."

"O.K. We'll get underway at dawn. Ralph and Fred will be hard pressed with the near winter weather."

"Yeah. That may delay things. Good thing we have the fuel cached along their route, just in case."

"Good news from the exploration site. Some of the drill cores we brought down to be assayed look pretty good. One sample yielded eight ounces to the ton."

"Wow! That's major! Looks as if the stock is in for a good speculative run."

"Yeah, but keep it quiet. We need to see more results and get a profile on the extent of the vein."

The next morning at ten, Shirley picked up her phone on the third ring and noted it was Bob calling. "Shirley, we've got passive chips transponding near the reading station we set up in Keremeos. The activity is close by. We've been watching it for the past while and there's a pattern. Looks as if the choppers are following the Temple River up the mountains towards Cathedral Peaks before we lose track of them. They're operating out of the NightHawk Indian reservation that's along the Temple River. We can't get too close without being spotted. It's a lot of activity."

"Good. This could be interesting."

"In Keremeos, I managed to talk with a woman who lives on the reservation. She's a waitress at one of the local cafés whom I met when we went in for coffee. She said there was a mining exploration camp up near Cathedral Peaks and that she had been told they were flying the men and equipment out as they were shutting down for the winter. I checked around and found out that Red Mountain Helicopters has a charter to take the men and equipment down from the exploration site. That all seems legit but it doesn't explain why we're getting the passive chip signals. The signals are separate. That means two helicopters in use there that don't belong to Red Mountain Helicopters."

"Maybe they're flying under the cover of the legitimate helicopter?"

"An operation in broad daylight? Pretty brazen but it could work."

"Moses Lake Control has been using the drones only at night and border patrol tend to concentrate their manned aircraft to night-time hours too. Interesting. I'll relay this to Janet and see if she can get Moses Lake to scramble a drone for a high overhead look. In the meantime, keep snooping."

Shirley called Janet and relayed the conversation, to which Janet replied, "I'll get on to Moses Lake right away. I'll also get our people moving toward Loomis. I'll bet that's how Westley Aimes got his load. I'm looking at a topographical map of the area now. They're likely flying across the border into the Loomis River valley. Maybe we can intercept vehicles as they come out at Loomis. Damn, I wish I could inform Division Chief Sanchez at Border Patrol about the passive chips. As it is, we'll have to wait for the drone to observe the action and send the real-time video to Oroville Border Patrol."

"That, or you could report that your office received a tip-off."

"Of course! I'll start with that. On the basis of that, he can get his manned aircraft overhead."

At 10:30 a.m., Willie called David. "Tell Ralph and Fred to go to ground right now and hide their choppers. Our mole in Oroville Border Patrol says they got a tip and are putting up their Cessna and chopper to look over the exploration site."

"I'm on it! Will the mole let us know when it's all clear?"

"Yeah. Bye."

Janet picked up her phone again at 1 p.m. "Janet, Bob called to say there hasn't been a peep from the transponders in well over an hour. They're out of range."

Half an hour later, she called Shirley. "Hi, Shirley. Border Patrol Oroville sent up their chopper and fixed-wing aircraft and couldn't find anything. However, Moses Lake Control managed to get a drone cruising at high altitude overhead but they were only able to get it overhead about fifteen minutes ago. They're picking up the chips. They're not moving and must be grounded and there are faint heat signatures. We can't visually see them though. It's as if they're camouflaged. They're well south of the border. One's about five miles south in a steep canyon and the other is about ten miles south in a narrow gap at the head of the Loomis River valley. They'd be pretty hard to spot if you weren't looking for them. Let's not tell Oroville Border Patrol. I requested Moses Lake Control not to relay the drone's info to Oroville or even to inform them it was operating in their district."

"In other words, Oroville Border Patrol has a mole."

"Right. I think this proves it."

"Guess you should expose the mole. Isn't FBI supposed to be good at that?"

"Yeah, touché. We'll get on it. In the meantime, it may be nice to observe the smuggler's little operation. We'll involve DEA, Regional ICE and ATF and we may be able to follow them to their customers and build a bigger case. We'll avoid DEA local to Oroville as loose lips sink ships, they say. I'll work with a senior DEA level, probably out of Portland. I'll be working with ATF out of Utah and ICE out of Seattle."

"Ah yes, the ever patient and plodding FBI. Build a big case. Why not?"

"I've got three pairs of agents on their way to cover the roads out of Loomis. I've got FBI aircraft in Yakima and Tri Cities standing by to aid in tracking. In addition to picking up radio chatter which we hope the smugglers will be doing, I've requested Moses Lake to program the drone to target communications in Oroville – probably cell phone transmissions to Canada, maybe radio transmissions. We'll begin by telling Oroville Border Patrol the tip was a false alarm and see how long before the smuggling resumes. Anyway, the drone gives us first class seats for the smuggling and we should be able to identify the mole pretty quick."

"I like it! Go for it! Meanwhile, I've got a feed from Moses Lake and we'll watch the show here in real time too. Bye."

David answered the 2:30 p.m. call from Willie on the first ring. "Our mole says they were advised the tip was a false alarm. Besides the border patrol aircraft found nothing and they've gone back to base. You can resume."

"O.K."

At 2:31 p.m. sensors on the drone picked up a radio transmission and relayed it in real time via Moses Lake Control to FBI Regional Office Seattle where it came out of a speaker of one of the giant flat screen monitors showing video feed from the drone. Superimposed on the video, which showed the ground in a thirty-square-mile footprint, were the transponder and radio transmission "pins" – each showing the location of an aircraft part number or a radio transmission. Each radio transmission "pin" flashes when transmitting. The voice from the speaker said, "All clear." That was followed by two double clicks and then by two triple clicks, as if someone was pressing the talk key of a microphone. As the microphones were keyed, "pins" flashed showing their location.

"Look at that!" Fred exclaimed. "I guess that's showing us their sentry positions. They've got access very well covered three levels out from the drop point. No way we could get in there with a ground assault team charging in from Loomis."

Fifteen minutes later Janet, who had been observing the screen along with Fred Mayfield, pointed to a spot and said, "A heat signature's building over there. Looks as if one of them has cleared away the camouflage and is lifting off. Probably won't be long for the other one now."

Fred answered a phone on the desk in front and, after a moment, turned to Janet. "Our people in Oroville managed to monitor a cell phone call to Canada from the parking lot of the Oroville office of the border patrol. They didn't observe the phone in use but the person wasn't too smart – they used a phone for which they have a monthly billing plan. They've got that person under observation and are chasing down the cell phone records for the past year. Do you have any instructions for them?"

229

"They're to observe but not approach and begin a deep background check. Let's see who we're dealing with and who they're associating with."

Fred and Janet and a couple of agents were fascinated by what they were seeing on the screen. One agent pointed to the Northwest Loomis Valley sector of the screen and said, "That must be the end of the run. Looks as if this guy's dropping a load. That looks like a five-ton covered truck parked over here. Looks like three guys on the ground. Doesn't look as if the chopper is even landing – they must have the load suspended beneath it. Yep, you can see it now. Looks like they're hooking up another cargo to go north, see, one guy's got the cable end and is attaching it to that pile? Yeah, there it goes. That was quick."

"Yeah, a fifteen-second or less turn around," said Fred. "These guys are pros!" They watched as the chopper started to make its way up the canyon. "Now two of the ground crew have opened the cargo net and are lifting bales into the truck. The other guy must be in the cargo bay stacking them."

"That's their weak point," said Fred. "It'll be hard to intercept the chopper but we would have a better chance intercepting the guys on the ground loading the truck."

Fred pointed to a spot on the Canadian side. "This must be their loading/unloading site on the Canadian side. It's what, about one hundred yards in from the Temple River? There're a couple of flat-deck semis there. Looks as if one is partly loaded. What's this, over here?" He pointed to a vehicle partially obscured by trees.

"Looks like another truck," Janet said, "Maybe ten ton, like a rental moving van."

The second agent, Marion Walters, pointed to an aircraft identifier flashing between the two loading sites. "This has to be the Red Mountain Helicopters aircraft. It's squawking its transponder as required. Looks as if it is picking up a load in a cargo net. That must be the mining exploration site. Looks like eight, no, nine people on the ground."

Fred said, "Listen to the radio chatter. It just seems to be between the exploration site and the staging area below on the Temple River. The other choppers are keeping quiet. That's pretty professional."

They watched as the Red Mountain chopper flew its load down the mountain and deposited it on the deck of one of the flatbed trucks. Marion touched the screen and zoomed in on the chopper as

----

it then turned up the mountain and landed at the exploration campsite. She then zoomed out to the smaller scale, found another chopper and zoomed in on it.

"Oh, this is neat," she said. "The third chopper is going south but is taking a different route. Must be to avoid running into the guy flying north." They watched as it hovered at the drop site and the ground crew unhooked the cargo. It proceeded empty north to the exploration campsite and picked up a cargo. As it started to climb, it began to squawk the identifier of the Red Mountain chopper. "Now that's neat, this guy's helping out to bring a legitimate load down. He's flying quite high. I guess that's to allow his buddy to pass below him going up the mountain. Pretty sneaky."

"And illegal to broadcast a false identifier. Yes, these guys are good!" mumbled Janet as she turned to Fred. "We know the base of the choppers is on the Midlake Reservation. We have it pinpointed, but we can't reveal how we know that. We need to track their shipments and the movement of their ground crews."

"Yeah," said Marion. "Moses Lake Control showed us how to split the screens to track multiple targets but we do have some problems. We can only track six different targets at once. At its current altitude, the drone can track line of sight in about a fifty-mile radius. But there will come a point when we have to choose if we want to follow the guys in Canada or the ones in Washington moving southward, as the drone will have to be repositioned."

"Well, we can't officially enter Canadian airspace so those people will have to be the lesser priority. Major priority will have to be the cargo coming in and hopefully we can track some of the Loomis River ground crew if they split off from the cargo. Remember when our agents were on the ground following Westley Aimes? Didn't they say it looked as if the escort he had when he exited the Loomis River valley ended when he loaded up with apples in Omak?"

"Maybe Shirley's people can follow the Canadian cargo," suggested Fred. My bet is there are drugs and/or guns in the truck or both."

"I'll give her a call".

Early the next morning, Janet looked at her call display and picked up the phone on the third ring. "Good morning, Hector."

"Janet, I read the situation report you emailed overnight. You've been making great progress. I'm glad DEA is fully alongside and that ATF has joined in. Finding that mole in Oroville Border Patrol's office is great. What are you going to about that?"

"I'd thought we'd let it stay in place for a while to see if we can find more linkages and maybe use it to our advantage."

"Good. Good. Looks as if your CIA friends came through for you too."

"Yes, it was pretty easy to pick up on vehicles exiting the Temple NightHawk reservation. An operative followed a medium-sized truck, a rental moving van. It terminated at a house on the Midlake Reservation – premises that are renowned as a clubhouse for the Devil's Brew biker gang. The operative couldn't get onto the property but has flown over it and knows the layout. They're probably storing and sorting the cargo in the barn. The only other vehicles leaving the Temple reservation were the two flat-deck semis loaded with mining equipment and drill cores and they were followed to a storage lot of the mining company in Oliver. The operatives staked out the road by the clubhouse of the biker gang and noted a lot of traffic coming and going overnight and early morning. My bet is that the drugs, probably cocaine, were all distributed and nothing remains on site."

"No sense in alerting our Canadian authorities about that yet."

"Agreed."

"Do you have an update on the drone and the tracking of the targets in Washington State?"

"Yes, as you know, we followed the truck to Pasco, Washington in the Tri Cities near the Oregon-Washington border. DEA from their Portland office took over there. They managed to get a bug on it when the driver stopped to refuel. Right now, it's near Reno."

"Any luck monitoring communications at the delivery zone?"

"The drone is also targeting communications in the Loomis River Valley and that is very revealing. These guys seem to have sentries with cell phones and radios at the entrance of the valley from Loomis, another one midway and a couple just outside their delivery zone. Rushing them in the valley would be very difficult. We're also picking up three cell phones and a radio right in the delivery zone. We had a big bonus when they finished loading the first truck at the delivery zone. We monitored e-mail traffic and our people determined it was a money transfer. Looks as if the border smugglers get paid on delivery at the delivery zone. Anyway, we have some bank accounts to investigate. It looks as if cash went both ways though and that probably means they bought goods to go north too. In one transaction, cash went from an account in The Isle of Man to one in Belize then on to Antigua. The other transaction saw funds transferred from Mauritius to Turks and Caicos then to St. Kitts and Nevis."

"Interesting. It hints that someone of high rank is there to effect the money transfer or at least they want to verify the transfer. What next?"

"Moses Lake brought the drone home overnight to refuel. As the smugglers seem to only be operating in daylight, they didn't assign another to cover overnight. It's up again and has been in position over the scene from an hour before dawn. Looks as if the operation is continuing as the helicopters are back. So far, we've observed delivery of four loads to America and one to Canada."

"Have you got a handle on the magnitude of the operation?"

"I think so. We're estimating they're moving a ton of marijuana with each trip. We don't know for sure what they're shipping into Canada but it's likely guns and/or cocaine and that could easily be up to a ton per trip. So far, we've observed five loads going south and three going north but we came in late on the operation. The size of the money transfers indicates much more has transferred."

"That's still a fair bit of cargo."

"DEA agrees. They're putting a lot of resources onto this one. So is ATF."

"Good. You will too. I've authorized the increased budget you requested."

"Thank you! Yes. We want to track and identify the local crew that's receiving the cargo in Loomis River valley. When we're ready, we'll round them up and sweat them on the murders."

"What about the mole in the border patrol office in Oroville?"

"When we finish our background checks, we'll put that person to use. I think we can feed some misinformation and set up a trap."

"Good. Remember you once said there may be more than one mole?"

"Yep! Good point! We're still running with that assumption. We're looking deeply into the backgrounds of all the Oroville border patrol personnel. We feel there may also be a connection with the Koreans that is separate from this smuggling operation. So far, we've found two border patrol employees with unexplained purchasing habits beyond their salaries. One is a chronic gambler who loses heavily at the local casino. The other is a single mom with four kids who's not getting alimony or child support."

In the CIA's Bellingham office, Shirley picked up the phone on the second ring. "Hi Bob, that's quite a bit of good info you picked up."

"Thanks. We staked out the entrance road to the Devil's Brew clubhouse. We got a good vantage point from the bush across the street and pointed the new toy at the gate, then hooked it up to an iPod to send you what we got. The new toy works great. From one hundred yards, it easily read RFID chips on credit cards of people passing through the gate. If the credit cards are legit, we've got the names and addresses of all who passed by. Plus, of course, we have the license plates of all the vehicles. Plus, we have some facial photos of the drivers and passengers. That's great info, but what do we do with it?"

"Just remember, the "new toy" is top secret. It's saved us a lot of time and effort tracking those guys but we aren't going to reveal how we did it. Besides, they're in Canada and the drugs are being distributed in Canada – not our mandate to interfere. Our participation with the FBI is to concentrate on getting the killer or killers and the terrorist link, once they are identified, back across the border where they can be picked up."

"So, we've got to sort out who are the cross-border smugglers and which of them have been involved in the murders? I think we've got a pretty good handle on who's involved in the cross-border smuggling. We know it's Joseph and David behind it – but we've known that for a long time. You've got the RFID data of the participants on the Temple River side of the last operation and that matches with what the drone picked up. We've got the license numbers of all the vehicles coming and going to the clubhouse and on the Temple reserve plus, in most cases, we've got facial photos of all the drivers. Also, we've identified the pilots and you've got them under loose surveillance."

"Yeah, and Janet doesn't know that the drone's RFID reader also pulled out the credit card IDs from all the smugglers on the Loomis River site. That was only relayed to CIA channels. I'll have to figure out a way of getting that information to her from another direction – probably from a "known associates background check" on ones you have identified as players who have frequented the biker's den."

"That'll do. Our job is just to observe. Right?"

"Right. Janet's going to have to catch them red-handed smuggling into America and then make the terrorist connection. All we can do right now is try to give fair notice of a smuggling run."

Chapter 30

Janet and her team were assembled in the conference room down the hall from her office in Seattle. They had spent over two hours reviewing the smuggling methods and the profiles of the suspects. Fred had developed a diagram linking a pyramid of photos of the known players by perceived levels of importance and was explaining it. "Let's sum up: From what we can see, the top man is Chief Joseph Branson; immediately under him is his son, David."

The diagram was divided down the middle with one side labeled Canada and the other side America. Each side had a collage of photos and names identifying rank and likely roles. At the far end of the American side, two photos were isolated with dotted lines to Joseph Branson. These were the suspected moles in the border patrol office in Oroville.

"The headquarters of the smugglers is in Canada on the Midlake Indian Reservation as that's where the Bransons, the helicopter pilots, and a few of the senior "soldiers" reside and the helicopters are hidden. There are also a couple of "soldiers" residing on reservations along the Canada-USA border, most notably, the NightHawk Reservation, in Canada just a few miles west of Osoyoos and Oroville.

"In the U.S.A., there's a linkage to the Tonawa Indian reservation near the border as a few of the "soldiers" on the American side are natives and reside there. Also, there are some joint venture businesses on their property. There's also a linkage with the Tonawa reservation administration using their casino revenues to buy up ranches along the border opposite the Canadian NightHawk reservation. They have the right to declare the land as Indian reserve and they are doing so.

"It's interesting to note all the "soldiers," including the chief, have military combat backgrounds – that explains the good organization of the operations."

"Also explains the decoys, awareness of their opposition, and the variety of operations," Marion observed.

"We've also identified an interesting web of businesses owned by the Bransons – some through offshore numbered accounts and some charitable trusts. The businesses tend to be partnerships with local Indian tribes or individual natives on the American side of the border, such as a fruit packing plant, a public storage warehouse, a forestry tree planting business, a forestry tree nursery, land surveyors, etc. The list was e-mailed to you.

"On the Canadian side, many of their ventures are partnerships with the Devil's Brew biker gang but some are with other natives. They have interests in a helicopter charter company, that's Red Mountain Helicopters, a mineral exploration company, a hemp farm in Manitoba, a long haul trucking line, etc. Some of these are also owned by Devil's Brew members or by the Devil's Brew.

"The Chief is a significant public figure on both sides of the border. He's a very political activist involved in advancement of aboriginal welfare, restoration of fish habitats and even is involved in developing an old mine and mining town into a tourist attraction. He's been successful with land concessions from the Canadian government – getting them not only for his own reservation but also assisting other tribes to get concessions."

Marion raised her hand, caught Fred's attention and asked, "So this is the core of the cross-border smuggler operation? You've also provided background reading on the organized crime linkages. How solid are we now on that area? And, what overlap is there with Canadian organized crime?"

"Good questions," said Fred. "The Canadian one is the easiest to answer. There's a direct connection to the Devil's Brew biker gang. As you know, they're all across Canada and tightly affiliated with the major biker gangs in America. Some of the smugglers are full color members and as you likely read in the background notes, there's a Devil's Brew clubhouse on the Midlake reservation. We're quite sure they're using that clubhouse property to sort and distribute drugs and guns into Canada. We think the Devil's Brew has Asian connections for heroin as they're certainly distributing it across Canada.

The Okanagan is known as "biker territory." They've a significant presence, even in legitimate businesses, and getting them to Canadian justice is difficult as they're politically connected and may have co-opted some of the judiciary."

"As far as American organized crime," added Janet, "it looks as if these guys are tied into the St. Louis mafia syndicate, and Utah, Nevada and California biker gangs, at least for their marijuana distribution and as a source for cocaine transferring to Canada. DEA and ATF have been following the last shipments with great success as the distribution system is unveiled but they've only been able to identify up to mid-level players. However, the distribution pattern is

----

quite revealing. We had better luck following the money from the last cross-border transaction. There's a Columbian connection, which may be payment for cocaine. The other transaction was tracked back to a company held by a major biker gang in California."

Fred thought for a moment before responding. "In analyzing the smuggling patterns, there are some consistencies. Other than the brazen broad daylight situation a little while back, most of the crossings tend to be at night when there is little or no moon. We've seen some diversions, such as the Korean aliens crossing or the hikers transporting marijuana on the Pacific Rim Cascade trail. These keep the border patrol busy in another sector but we're not sure if that is a common pattern.

"We've found two moles in the Oroville border patrol base. One is definitely feeding information to these smugglers. Helicopters seem to be the major mode of transport for crossing the border and, so far, they are not aware that we can track them. The smugglers tend to hand off the cargos right at the landing site and money transfer is made electronically from that site. We can monitor and track that."

"They're creative in how the cargo is moved once it lands in America. So far we've seen a toy box recreational trailer, a horse trailer, five ton vans, and semi-trailer trucks." said Janet.

"Like a good military operation," continued Fred, "the landing zone is guarded with two or more lavers of sentries radiating out from the zone and able to give up to twenty-minute warning of intrusion. As well, the sentries seem to escort the load for a distance of up to thirty miles deeper into America. This makes an apprehension at the landing site difficult. The sentries could be hard to apprehend as they tend to have motocross motorbikes or ATVs and more than one escape route."

"But not impossible," Janet said. "Our main problem is probably how to ground the helicopter at the landing zone to prevent it from escaping back across the border. We can track the sentries from the drone."

"Providing they have at least one of the new chip credit cards in their pocket," said Marion.

"Yes, or a cell phone. But making a case in court for the sentries requires us to prove they were in on the action. We can't use the information from the drone in court. That's still top secret," said Fred.

"We'll just have to use a lot of troops and move quickly," Janet replied "We'll use helicopters of our own. We can always pick up those that get away at their homes or on the road and interrogate as if one of their people is talking. Maybe, some will cave in."

Fred said, "DEA and ATF have requested more time to reveal more of the distribution system and the key players and they would like to coordinate with us when we feel ready to pounce. They'd love to follow a few more shipments through the distribution system to identify the source and routing of the guns and cocaine going north."

"I like that but I'll have to check with D.C.," said Janet "Maybe we can track a few more crossings in order to build a bigger case and get a better picture of their smuggling routes."

"What about the moles?" asked Fred "I presume they stay in place and under observation until we pounce on an operation?"

"Yes. They can be useful for misinformation when we're ready to move."

"The next period of no moon is about two weeks away," said Marion. "We'll see if they get active then."

"Right, I've arranged with Moses Lake Control to give us twenty-four hour coverage with the drones for six days during the low/no moon period."

"You know," said Fred thoughtfully, "I've got a lot of respect for the way they did that operation into the Loomis Valley in broad daylight. If that mineral exploration at Cathedral Mountain resumes in the spring, I'd be willing to bet they'll repeat themselves with a daylight operation."

"No bet from me!" said Janet. "That operation was so smooth, I'd expect them to repeat it. Maybe we can get a jump on them? Marion, do some digging into that exploration company. Maybe you can find out if they're going to resume exploration up there and, if so, when?"

"I'm on it.

Chapter 31

Janet was on the phone to Hector. "We've been following the smuggling for the past three months. They tend to make one or two runs each period of no moon. The crossings differ each time but there is definitely a pattern. One or both choppers originate from the Midlake Reservation and tend to seek shelter from radar flying low either in the shadow of Mount Baldy or the mountains on the west side of Okanagan Lake.

"Sometimes, they move into the Similkameen in the east of the Okanagan and fly up valleys and canyons over the mountains into Washington. They're well away from normal air corridors. They stop to load up at campsites or farm fields near the border. They seem never to carry a load out of the Midlake Reservation but seem to carry cargos back in unless they have a lot to transport. They always cross the border by running low in canyons and tight valleys and always land in Washington State from five to fifteen miles below the border. They've never used the same route twice in three months.

"Their security at the drop zone is always the same with two or three layers of sentries giving them advance warning from overland approaches and the sentries are equipped with cross country motorbikes, snowmobiles in the winter, and they often disburse cross country when the cargo is transferred. They tend to have two or three people at the drop zone and it looks as if there is one in the chopper in addition to the pilot.

"Time of drop varies but it seems more common just before dawn. They often return to the Midlake Reservation at or shortly after daylight."

"What success have you had following the cargo to its American destination or destinations?"

"That's been very good. We've followed loads into California, Nevada, Utah and Missouri. We, that's FBI, ATF and DEA, have been able to observe the arrival and redistribution from the terminals and we've got profiles of all involved, right up to owners and managers of the enterprises housing the distribution terminals. ATF, DEA and we feel we can round up a lot of players and put them down with tight cases."

"O.K., when do you want to round them up?"

"The next border crossing will likely be in ten days or so. We can assemble our resources and be ready by then. We'll concentrate on the cross-border smuggling. I want to get the chopper or choppers and sentries but let the cargo on to its destination, if possible."

"That may be a bit tricky. What are you going to do about that or those moles in the Oroville border patrol office?"

"I was thinking of using them to create a couple of diversions which would get the border patrol to deploy their resources at two extremes of their patrol territory. That will narrow where the smugglers will come through if they learn of it."

"Then, you're going to try a trap without the local level of the Border Patrol?"

"Yes. We'd like to keep the moles in place and unaware for as long as possible. The regional level of border patrol has given clearance and briefed some upper level personnel who have been sworn to secrecy. They're providing some personnel and equipment, and they're very keen to see how the thing plays out."

"Are you going to inform the Canadians?"

"No, at least not at the local level right now due to the potential for moles. DC will keep the proper people in the Canadian Embassy up to date."

"O.K. fine, as long as the regional level of ICE is in the loop. Now, how do you plan to contain the smugglers? You've still got a pretty long stretch of border to respond to when they cross."

"You're right, even if we divert the majority of Orville Border Patrol personnel to their eastern and western extremes, we're talking maybe two hundred miles of border to cover. However, we can narrow it a bit to areas with roads, which is mainly east of Remel Mountain, probably west of Midway, so that brings us to a one hundred thirty-mile stretch of border.

"We're figuring to deploy three swat teams, each with two helicopters and four SUV's equally spaced out across the region. We're banking on our drone intelligence to follow the smuggler chopper from its base on Midlake Reservation to the point where they load up. Once we see where they're loading, we can narrow down the passes they'll likely take and we can then get our response teams moving where they can be vectored in by the drone to the landing site. We may be able to jump the landing site with our first choppers within one to five minutes of their landing which should catch them right in the act of transferring cargo. We'll be able to block off any escape roads. We'll rely on the drone info to identify the sentries and track anyone if they make a run for it."

"That's probably the best you can do given the geography," said Hector. However, you might be short of ground support as the SUV's can't move in as fast as the choppers."

"You have a good point. We'll have to rely on the good training of the SWAT teams in the choppers to try to catch the smugglers in the act of transfer on the ground. Ground back-up may be as much as twenty minutes away."

"You're tying up a lot of equipment and manpower here. If it wasn't for the fact we wanted the ones crossing the border for the terrorism connection, I'd be inclined to follow the transfer from the drone and nail the transporters when they got o their destination."

"I know, but we've got the destination distribution systems and key players well documented. It's time to move in on the cross border players."

"O.K. Go for it. And good luck! Let's hope we wind this up quickly. It's getting to be an expensive exercise."

Chapter 32

Larry Brown, customs broker and freight forwarder, was on the phone from Vancouver. "Marcus, your cargo has cleared the ship and customs and is sitting on the dock here. It should be on its way to you within the hour as soon as the boys have it secure on the trailer. They'll probably deliver it to you tomorrow morning. It looks pretty fancy – nice lines."

"Thanks. We start work at nine in this, the off-season. If you want, we can open the workshop an hour or two earlier to take delivery."

"How about seven?"

"Looking forward to it."

Marcus called Joseph. "The boat's arrived on the dock in Vancouver and cleared customs. It should be at the boat shop tomorrow morning."

"That's great! I'm looking forward to seeing it. That hull looked pretty fast when we saw versions of it in the Maldives. It was nice we had a choice of topsides, cabin designs, hardware and trim so you could fit it out to be attractive to buyers in the Okanagan. With the twin outboards you've ordered, it should go like stink."

"Trouble with boating on Lake Okanagan, you can never be the fastest – at least not for long. There's always someone who's going to trump you with a faster toy. At least this isn't one of those Miami-style offshore cigarette boats that gobble the fuel."

"Yeah, with the price of fuel today, that can be expensive. Billy Kakar says his cigarette boat burns as much as a grand an hour when he's running flat out. Mind you, he's pushing past ninety miles an hour. And he's a noisy bastard too! He likes the attention."

"That's too decadent for me! I'll be content with a forty-footer with a top end of fifty-five miles an hour and good fuel economy. I'm looking forward to taking orders once people see the sample."

"Anyway, we'll drop in to look at it in a couple of days. Give me a call after you've got into the hull and replaced some of the buoyancy material. You've got a set of blueprints, and you know what we need to replace."

"Right. I should have it out and on to the lab for "analysis" by noon. Bye."

Joseph leaned out of his office and called to David, who was in the general office working at a computer. "The boat arrives tomorrow. Have you got the spare set of blueprints for it that Igor sent?"

David stepped into Joseph's office and closed the door. "Yep, right here."

"Good. Let's review them and then I guess we should call Ross Emory and tell him to round up the lab boys as the heroin will be at the mine sometime tomorrow afternoon."

"Is he going to step down all of it at once?"

"Yeah, he may as well dilute all of it at once. We have the room to store it at the mine."

"Yep, like miles and miles of unused tunnels and stopes."

"My social calendar is free tomorrow afternoon, and so is yours. So tell Ross we'll drop by mid-afternoon."

"O.K."

Next day, David and Joseph arrived at the Great Similkameen mine entrance around 3 p.m. After entering and relocking the main door at the employee's entrance, they proceeded down the tunnel to the chamber that had been converted into the meth lab. They found Ross Emory working at a long stainless steel table along with five other people. An assembly line of sorts had been set up with bundles of heroin at one end of the table being opened and placed in a hopper of a laboratory revolving drum mixer. For each kilo bag opened, the step-down ingredients of powdered milk-sugar and quinine were being added in a ratio to a recipe prescribed by Ross. The ingredients were mixed for a few minutes in the tumble mixer to ensure thorough dispersion then dumped into the hopper of a packaging machine.

The cello bags came from a drum holding a large roll of cello tube. As the cello tube came off the roll, it was first stamped with a logo to identify the brand for creating a preference when sold to users on the street. It then entered the packaging machine which automatically filled the cello bags with one gram of the product. Filled and sealed bags came out the other end.

Next was a quality control station that weighed each bag, rejecting those over- or under-weight. Finally, there was a packing station where baggies were packed in cello bags of ten then into larger cello bags of ten tens and then into a one kilo package, which was sealed.

After saying hi to Ross and the workers, David and Joseph stood beside Ross and watched the assembly line for a few minutes.

Then Ross said, "I gather you want to store this stuff here and move only a little at a time?"

"Yeah, put it in the vault," said Joseph. "The logo we're using for it is from the Red Dragon Chinese Triad – the guys Donny's in partnership with. We'll only trickle this stuff into Donny's distribution system so the Triad doesn't become suspicious we're horning in. We're giving Donny a ten percent discount from the Triad price."

"You're using the same ingredients they do and to the same recipe to step the stuff down?" asked David.

"Yeah, no sweat. They add quinine to keep the taste a little bitter so that the lower levels think the stuff is purer than it is. They're maintaining a quality image – at least at this level – by using only milk-sugar. No telling what happens by the druggies stepping it down further down the chain – they use anything they can grab at times from baking powder to icing sugar and baking soda, maybe even borax. Yuck, I'm glad I don't use."

"Me too!" said David. "Better to be clean on top making the big bucks than down in the gutter waiting to die."

Joseph said, "I like to think we're not only making good money, we're also helping mankind weed out the weak."

"Good thought!" said Ross. "But meth is much more effective for that! Once hooked on meth, the lifespan of the addict is very short – two or three years."

"Yeah, but heroin can also do the job," said David.

"A lot of people would be upset if they heard our comments. But it wasn't that long ago, in the eighteen hundreds, that the American government paid bounty hunters to exterminate Indians. I had a great aunt who remembered hiding from the bounty hunters in Oregon. She always told me never to trust American politicians," said Joseph.

"Yeah. She was right. But we've learned to play on their greed," replied David.

"That was a pretty neat idea sealing the heroin into the boat's buoyancy chambers," Ross observed. "All you have to do is cut into the chambers and replace the heroin with buoyancy foam, then seal up the floor again."

"It worked well. At the factory, they injected foam into the chambers to cover up the packages of heroin so it was pretty well impossible to find – even with radar and dogs," said Joseph. "The boat builder was willing to co-operate. We were a little hard pressed to figure what we could export to Canada from the Maldives that could contain the heroin and not draw attention because they export very little. The company producing the fiberglass hulls has been a rare local success with not only a large domestic demand for their style of vessels but also a good export one. When we looked into it and found out they were already exporting to twenty countries, we saw an opportunity. Even considering we're importing from halfway around the world, the price/quality on the boats alone allows for profitable import. If they become as popular here, we'll do pretty well on the boats alone. We've got our native brothers in the boat business in Vancouver, Shuswap and the Kootenays interested from photos we sent. Once they test-drive the sample, we're expecting some orders. Plus, Marcus sees a good demand in the Okanagan."

"Spring and summer are a ways away right now," Ross noted. "I don't mind winter but hunting season is over and I'm getting bored with skiing and snowmobiling. When do you want to send me back to the Maldives so I can work on my wind surfing?"

Joseph said, "Getting bored, huh?"

"A little. Some variety would help."

"Well, you're in luck. Igor's got a huge order for meth and also some opium to process. You've produced enough meth to last us a couple of months of distribution here. You're just about finished packaging the heroin. We can spare you for a month. Want to leave the end of next week?"

Chapter 33

Joseph called David into his office. David entered and closed the door before Joseph spoke. "The guns arrived at the Omak warehouse. That's fairly good timing with only a few days to go to no moon."

"Dad, I spoke with Donny on his order for a ton of bud to go to Salt Lake City. Their people will be in Grand Coulee City tomorrow, standing by. I checked the weather forecast and it looks as if we'll have a day between storms tomorrow. Tomorrow night would be a good one for us."

"Yeah, lots of snow on the ground in the mountains and pretty cold. Tomorrow night, a Sunday night, there could be lots of snowmobilers out playing around up at the higher elevations."

"That could provide good cover for us. We can use snowmobiles for cross-country exit after delivery if need be or we could just blend back in with all the other snowmobilers enjoying a good time at one of the campgrounds. The boys from Salt Lake City came over in a four by four pick-up with a camper on back and towing a covered trailer with two snowmobiles. They'll blend in. Their trailer will be big enough to load the bud in a false floor and stow the snow mobiles on top."

"Good. They could set up at Sidley or Molson Lake at one of the campsites near Molson and blend in with the other tourists. If we bring the chopper in up the canyon following the old railroad line from Canada, we can land on the rail line or the end of the road for the exchange about half a mile up from Molson. It's not far for them to come from the campsite to the landing zone."

"That's less than a mile from the border. But what about the snow? It may be pretty deep there?"

"That could be to our advantage. It's plowed for the first half mile to the turnoff for the Bar H cattle ranch. That's a good place to land and for the RV to turn around. The ranch house is another half mile in from the road and behind a hill so they likely won't hear the activity. You go down and scout it out though. You may want to select a spot further along the rail bed closer to the border as you can always use the snowmobiles to pack the snow well enough for the chopper to land. You decide when you've scouted it out."

"What about our shipment of guns?"

"The boys can bring it down from Omak in the back of a couple of 4 x 4 pickups under their snowmobile deck. You can park them on the road and move the snowmobiles out for sentry duty. No one will take notice of the trucks because it'll look as if some folk, maybe a club, are out snowmobiling and they parked their trucks together. If you decide on a site up the trail, you can always move the goods by sleds behind the snowmobiles."

"Sounds good to me! I'll get things rolling. It's Ralph's turn to fly. I'll take Willie and we'll go through the border tomorrow morning and change vehicles at the farm. I'll call Danny to set us up with a pickup and camper and a couple of snowmobiles. We'll camp beside the boys from Utah and scout out the locals in Molson. That way, we should be accepted as just some guys out for a weekend of snowmobiling."

On the Saturday, David and Willie crossed the border at Chopaka - NightHawk with no problems. They showed both their aboriginal identity cards and their passports. Then they stopped in at the ranch to pick up some armament and to change vehicles. They had decided to use a truck and camper with Washington State license plates, which was waiting for them in the barn, along with two snowmobiles on a trailer.

Danny Wilson not only served as caretaker of the farm, he also kept a well-stocked armory storing and maintaining the weapons used by the Canadian-based crew who might need weapons when they deployed on the American side. The property had a small abandoned goldmine with a horizontal tunnel dug into the base of a mountain. It was a five-minute walk from the farmhouse. Danny had set up a workshop in the first gallery about a hundred feet into the mine. David and Willie looked at a wall full of various weapons and both opted for AK 47's, feeling the AK 47 was the most reliable assault rifle in winter conditions. Each took four additional clips for their weapon.

Although Danny maintained the weapons in perfect condition, it was always a habit when selecting a weapon to give it a careful inspection, perhaps even test firing it in the indoor range farther down the tunnel. Both spent half an hour test firing on the indoor range, then stripped and cleaned their weapons and reassembled them.

They stored the guns in a storage compartment at the rear of the camper. Danny gave them a guided tour of the camper, reviewing how to turn on the propane, light the stove and operate the toilet. Then they went over the snowmobiles, testing them for ease of starting, ensuring spare fuel and emergency kits, and testing the scabbards for ability to hold and quick draw the AK 47's. Lastly they checked the fluid levels of the truck.

They spent the night with Danny and his wife Muriel, enjoying her great dinner of rack of lamb and the long after-dinner discussion about plans and progress of the coalition formed to protest damming the Similkameen River. After a good night's sleep and a great breakfast of pancakes, eggs and homemade venison sausage, they left at nine Sunday morning.

MOLSON

The town of Molson, Washington, elevation 3780 feet, had earned its honor as a ghost town, having twice endured boom and bust. Molson, was about halfway between Oroville and Chesaw and within two miles of the Canadian border. It was founded in 1900 by The Molson Town Site Company due to a gold discovery which saw the town boom to a population of three hundred people being served by a newspaper, three general stores, lawyer, doctor, three saloons, dance hall, assay office, blacksmith and hotel. By 1901 the town was dead, down to thirteen people. Within that short year, the gold ran out and the miners and prospectors moved on.

In 1905, Molson was included on a new rail spur that ran northeast from Oroville into Canada to service a smelter and the town was reborn. Its rail station earned the honor of being the highest elevation rail station in the State of Washington. Again, the town began to prosper, serving the farmers, loggers and ranchers in the vicinity.

One J.H. McDonald laid claim to a homestead that included part of the town that the Molson Town Site Company sought to expand into, much of which had been squatted upon without legalities. McDonald won the land dispute and required everyone on his property to depart. Citizens then founded a new town of Molson half a mile away and closer to the rail line. The buildings remaining on the original tract of land developed by the land company were identified as "Central Molson." The dwellings on McDonald land faded away and the area nicknamed "Old Molson."

Today, little remains of the town. There is a red brick schoolhouse converted into a museum and café, a general store and gas station. The area is known for outdoor recreation drawing tourists to fish the local lakes, hike, camp and trail ride. Winter recreation includes ice fishing on the lakes, snowmobiling, and camping and cross-country snow shoeing and skiing.

David and Willie arrived at Molson before noon, went through the eye blink of the town and set up their campsite beside others in a government campsite on the shore of Molson Lake. Although there had been little snow on the ground in the Okanagan valley, the Molson area, with its high elevation, had close to four feet on the ground. Fortunately, it was not too cold with the temperature warming up to five degrees below freezing in the day and plunging to minus ten overnight. Plowed roads still had compact snow and ice surfaces that had been sanded. Where the road shoulders didn't drop off, snow banks, averaging six feet, formed walls beside the road.

The campsite had been well used. The road and vehicle pathways were plowed and much of the area compacted from snowmobile use. They selected a pull-through site that had recently been vacated and parked beside a picnic table and fire pit, on the righthand side. They had noticed a camper and covered utility trailer with Utah plates was set up six sites down but there was no one around. Willie said, "Looks as if the Utah boys are out reconnoitering."

"Yeah," said David. "Plenty of time to catch up with them later."

First, they dressed for the cold weather. After changing in the camper into long johns and snowmobile suits, and donning ski mask toques to wear under their helmets, they unloaded their snowmobiles, fairly new higher-end super-charged Bombardier Ski-Doos that had been modified for more speed and range and well muffled to run very quietly. They drove them the short distance into the Molson Museum, where the Molson Historical Society also ran a café renowned for home-baked pastries and fresh brewed coffee.

They stopped at the café for lunch and, over a leisurely meal of good old down-home cooking, met a few of the local folk and some other winter recreation enthusiasts. David initiated a friendly chat with the waitress, a cute thirty-something with a large wedding ring, happy to talk about Molson and its winter recreation. He asked if the locals ever got annoyed with the skiers and snowmobilers. "Well, not really," she replied, "but some do get pretty noisy at night. And we prefer people to stick to the approved trails rather than cross through someone's property. Most of the snowmobilers are very considerate. We do love the business they bring to our little ghost town. Mind you, it might be nice to bring in an anti-noise ordinance."

At the museum cashier's counter, they bought a locally produced map with the current trails recommended for the snowmobile riders and, with the willing advice of one of the local patrons, reviewed the map. They then returned to their snowmobiles and spent the afternoon reconnoitering. The snow had an average depth of four feet but the winds had created many drifts much deeper and, in turn, had laid bare some surfaces which were hard packed snow and ice. The main roads were plowed and there were many designated trails for snowmobiles branching off or parallel to the roads, mainly in the recreational area north of the town.

They found the road that ran northeast toward the border on a gentle downhill grade that had once been the rail bed for the Great Northern rail line that ran into Canada to Midway and on to the former gold rush smelter town of Greenwood. The smelter and gold were long gone but the rail bed remained. The tracks had been removed fifty years ago but little vegetation found a hold in the deep gravel of the rail bed.

The plowed road stopped at the last ranch before the border but a well-marked snowmobile trail, with fresh tracks, led north along the rail bed. The boys took the trail and followed it less than a mile until they came a NO TRESSPASSING sign alerting them they were approaching the border with Canada and crossing was forbidden. As they slowed their Ski-Doos they saw a mound built across the rail bed where a trench had been dug out across the bed and the earth piled on top to make passage difficult.

They stopped, dismounted and approached the mound for a closer look. The ditch and mound extended right across the path. The mound had acted as a shield that helped the winds fill in the ditch with a massive snowdrift but the top of the mound was icy, almost bare of snow.

Willie said, "I guess the border marker is buried somewhere in the snow. Johnny Mathias lives about three miles over the border from here. I talked to him the other day. He said he was hunting here last fall. He went up the rail bed on the Canadian side as far as this border point and found it pretty easy going in his quad. I'm sure it'll be even easier going for a snowmobile what with the depth of snow right now."

251

"Yeah, why do we need a chopper? If we get a run at it, we can clear that mound and ditch easily with a Ski-Doo right now the way the snow is."

"It gives us an exit route in case of emergency."

"It does that. There's a good spot for the chopper to set down about half a mile up the trail, just around the second hill. It's isolated enough so the sound won't carry too far. But I still like the original idea of landing right at the end of the plowed road. We can place a sentry up toward the ranch house to delay anyone in the very unlikely event they venture out of there. From the other direction, on the main road, if we need to, we can block off the road around the bend, let's say, with a snowmobile stuck or something. That should assure us time to get the transfer done. That way we won't have to use sleds and make two transfers from truck to sled then sled to chopper and reverse."

"Good thinking! People go to bed early here so I doubt if we'll see any traffic at all. If the chopper follows the rail bed they've got the mountain on both sides of the draw so they'll be below radar between the ridges of the mountains."

"Let's go back to the camper. The boys from Utah should be back by now. We can go over the terrain with them, then let's all go back to the restaurant for dinner."

"O.K. The meatloaf looked good."

"Speak for yourself. I'm looking forward to roast chicken and dumplings followed with fresh apple pie."

Back at the campsite, the boys from Utah—Wayne Simpson and Darryl Smithson—had arrived back at their camper and were standing outside beside a fire in the fire pit warming up with mugs of hot, steaming coffee. David and Willie introduced themselves and invited them back to their campsite where they built a fire in their fire pit, stood around drinking steaming coffee and discussing things. An hour later the four sentries arrived from Omak with two snowmobiles on the back deck of a pickup truck and parked in the campsite beside Willie and David.

They met in David and Willie's camper for a planning session. It was agreed that, during the transfer, two of the sentries would ride the skimobiles that the boys from Utah brought. They would leave two trucks in the campsite, which would serve as a rendezvous point for the sentries returning with the snowmobiles after the transfer. They would transfer the guns from the Omak

----

vehicle to the Utah vehicle at the campsite, thus no need to expose another vehicle at the delivery point.

If all went right, the Utah boys would return to the campsite to spend the night, load their snowmobiles and depart in the morning.

The Utah boys would lead in transferring the bud from the chopper to their vehicle. David and Willie would transfer the guns, which were in four cases, each weighing about eighty pounds, from the truck to the chopper, then help stow the bud in the trailer. As they wanted to keep the chopper's time on the ground to the minimum, the bud would arrive suspended on a quick-release sling under the chopper. The cases of guns would be loaded into the cargo bay of the chopper for the return run. They figured the chopper could be on the ground for less than a minute to pick up the guns after it dropped the sling of bud next to the Utah trailer. The marijuana would be packed in ten-kilo packages and they estimated, depending how close the chopper dropped its cargo net to the truck, it probably would take under seven minutes to stow the bud in the trailer, pack up the cargo net and depart.

After dinner, the Utah boys would reposition their vehicle at the end of the plowed road at the beginning of the northeast rail bed trail in an area plowed and designated for parking for snowmobilers. David and Willie and the Omak boys would keep their vehicle in the campsite and drive their Ski-Doos along the hard packed but plowed roads and parallel tracks to join them.

Around six o'clock, the boys got on their snowmobiles and drove to the restaurant. They had a leisurely meal with conversation roving from football to deer and moose hunting. They returned to the campers to snooze and wait. ETA on the chopper was planned for eleven p.m.

Eleven p.m.

Ralph had an uneventful flight. With the aid of night vision goggles, he brought the chopper empty from its hiding place on Midlake Reservation through a gap between mountain ridges north of Mount Baldy to the loading point at a remote government campsite three miles off Highway 33 and within ten miles of the border. There he picked up Joseph, and two of the boys hooked the chopper up to the cargo net filled with a hundred ten-kilo parcels of bud. As they took off, Joseph sent a text message to David: "Go," indicating they were eleven minutes out.

With high mountains close in on both sides, they followed the Kettle River well below the mountain ridges toward Rock Creek, then branched off into a tight canyon, flying low above the gentle grade of the rail bed up to the border. They set the cargo net of bud down directly behind the trailer of the Utah boys, then pulled the remote release and dropped the cable. The chopper then moved back toward the two snowmobiles where the cases of guns were lying on the ground about a hundred feet away and settled on the parking lot beside it. Wearing night vision goggles, David and Willie each pulled two crates of guns across the short expanse, then, together, hoisted each into the cargo bay of the chopper. Joseph positioned the crates in the cargo bay then signaled Ralph who wound up the blades as David and Willie scurried out of the way. The chopper was on its way back toward Canada forty-five seconds from its arrival.

Darryl, with a pen knife, made a quick sampling of three of the packages to verify the cargo, then he and David got into the truck's cab to make the money transfer as Willie and Wayne started loading the bud into the trailer. The electronic transfer went through quickly and was confirmed on David's iPad. Then David and Darryl joined the others to help load the cargo. With about twenty-five bales left to load, the call came in. It was Edgar, one of the farthest sentries who was positioned a mile away south on Mary Anne Creek Road at the crossroads before the entrance to Molson. "Choppers coming from the South! ETA 60 seconds! Move it! I say again: choppers coming. Move it! Move it! Move it."

The others also heard the transmission. David said, "Stop loading. Get moving. You've got three quarters of the load. Run for it!" They shut the cargo door of the trailer and Wayne and Darryl jumped in the truck and took off with Wayne driving.

David motioned to Willie and said, "Let's move out on the Ski-Doos in two directions as if we're running then double back when they begin to land. They won't be able to follow both and they'll probably go for the bud on the ground. We'll give Wayne and Daryl a little cover while they get underway, then bug out to the border!" He spoke into his walkie-talkie to the sentries: "You know the drill. Attack then fall back if necessary. Clear out after the truck passes. Help delay if you can."

Soon, the navigation lights of two choppers could be seen in the south. They were approaching fast with one a mile ahead of the other. In moments, the first chopper was above the transfer point. With a bit of a lead, the Ski-Doos split in two directions across soft snow. The chopper pilot focused on the remaining bales of marijuana sitting on the road in the cargo net. The pilot flicked on the night sun, brightly illuminating the scene, then came straight in and set down close to the transfer point and the remaining bales of marijuana.

Removing their night vision goggles and looking over their shoulders, Willie and David saw the chopper beginning to land and immediately reversed direction toward the chopper. In seconds they were well within range for their AK 47's. David and Willie halted, each covered a side of the chopper, one to the rear and the other near the nose of it. They grabbed their guns from their scabbards and each took cover beside their snowmobiles.

As the lead chopper flared down for landing and was still a few feet above the ground, a person jumped out of the open cargo doorway and, crouching low, ran clear of the prop wash. He saw Willie's snowmobile and opened fire with a machine gun spraying the scene in an attempt to keep Willie pinned down. As he started to fire, David put four shots into the gunner, who was outlined by the reflection of the bright light on the snow. Taking a hit that sent him flying sideways toward Willie, his gun jerked upward and his shots went wild. He landed on the ground and didn't move.

Willie popped up and began to put double shots low into the doorway of the chopper keeping those inside pinned down. Meanwhile, David pumped four shots into the Plexiglas window on the pilot's side of the cockpit. He must have made a hit on the pilot as the chopper, attempting to take off, lurched sideways then quickly dropped the remaining few feet to the ground and made a harsh landing on a person who had fallen from the doorway. The lights stayed on when the chopper crashed back to the ground, bathing the scene in reflected light and shadows.

David then moved his aim to the engines and put six shots in rapid succession where he thought it would do most damage. He then moved back to the cargo doorway and took over putting double shots low in the passenger compartment while Willie changed his magazine. When the craft came to a sudden halt on the ground, three people, dressed for combat in helmets, blue jumpsuits and automatic weapons, leaped out of the cargo/passenger door. One took a hit on the fly, fell to the ground and didn't move but the other two hugged the ground in prone position and began to return fire. David took one out with a three-shot burst to the head while Willie shot the other in an arm and leg.

With no other movement from within the chopper, David covered Willie while he mounted his skidoo and fired it up. Willie then covered David while he got his machine started. Holding their guns in one hand and steering with the other, they took off up the rail bed trail. Once around the first turn, they stopped and stowed their weapons, put on their night vision goggles then mittens on over their fingered gloves. Then they took off at maximum speed toward the border.

David was fifty yards in the lead and doing over fifty miles an hour when he hit the border barrier. With a massive spray of loose snow he was climbing the slope of the mound launching into a seventy-foot jump across the ditch "grabbing air." He made a perfect tail-down landing, slowed and looked back to see that Willie had also landed his machine well. Willie came alongside, gave a thumbs up and shouted, "Now that we're back in Canada, let's go visit Johnny Mathias! He's less than three miles away. I know the way."

The other chopper had elected to intercept the Utah boys' truck and trailer as it was departing the scene. It flew over Chris, the inner perimeter sentry, as the Utah truck and trailer were fast approaching that turn in the road. It was obvious to Chris that whoever was directing that chopper sought to block the road and capture the truck. When he had heard the alarm, Chris Marcus, an ex-army ranger and member of the Tonawa tribe, moved his snowmobile to put a little distance between him and the road, and took cover in a small copse of fir trees a hundred yards south and east.

The chopper passed right over him as it prepared to land about four hundred yards ahead. Chris then turned around to attack, motoring back toward the descending chopper. He maneuvered to keep on the rear and side of the chopper opposite the open cargo door. The chopper pilot had elected to switch on his night sun only at the last second as a tactic to both blind and stun the occupants of the truck. As the chopper illuminated the scene, it pulled diagonally across the front of the truck. Leaning out from the chopper's open cargo door, a combatant sprayed the ground around the approaching Utah boys with machine gun fire. Blinded by the chopper's Night Sun, the Utah boys played it safe and came to a quick halt.

The chopper pilot then began to land in front of the truck with the pilot making an effort to keep the side with the gunner in the open cargo door facing the truck. With the pilot's and door gunner's attention on the approaching truck, Chris was out of view behind and above them obscured by the snowbank lining the side of the road.

Bringing his snowmobile to a stop on top of the snow bank within two hundred feet of the chopper, Chris dismounted and tucked for cover beside his Ski-Doo, using the seat as a bench rest to carefully aim his gun. He held his fire until the chopper was in the last twenty feet of landing – when the pilot is usually committed to landing – then put a six shot burst into the pilot's side windshield. The chopper immediately lurched and tumbled sideways, crashing onto the road with the main blades hitting the road and snow bank and breaking off before the engines stalled.

Chris emptied his gun's clip into the passenger compartment and calmly waited, changing ammo clips, until he saw some people stumble and crawl out of the crashed chopper. The crash seemed to have stunned them as no one carried a rifle – they seemed more interested in just getting out of the wreck. He fired a few more shots to pin them down while the Utah boys safely maneuvered their vehicle past the chopper but there were no return shots. Keeping the crash survivors pinned downed with sporadic shots, he let the Utah boys get a lead of a half mile then emptied his clip into the fuel tank area of the chopper and took off on his Ski-Doo across open country toward the campsite. About fifteen seconds after his final burst of gunfire, leaking fuel found an ignition source and the craft exploded in a ball of flame.

Chapter 34

Janet and Fred had been called in to the operations room at FBI on Sunday night after the personnel monitoring the Moses Lake drone were alerted to the movement of one of the choppers off the Midlake Reservation. Janet arrived ten minutes before Fred and had managed to get a cup of coffee before joining a few others standing behind the console operator looking at the large LED screen which showed a topographical real time display. Janet recognized the border beacons and then focused on a "tag" moving south. She could barely discern the heat signature of a helicopter and the movement of its blades as it made its way toward the border. At her request, the console operator zoomed in on it and they watched as it hovered and landed. Fred arrived, greeted Janet and the others and joined the observers.

"I see three men," said Marion, one of the observers. "Oh, I see one of the sentries on the periphery, over there. See?"

Janet said, "If they stick with their routine, there'll be a few more sentries farther away. Does it look as if they're hooking up a cargo net to the chopper?"

"Yeah. Looks like a heavy load," said Fred. "But then, they've got what? Looks like about ten miles to the border."

Janet turned to an agent sitting on a chair at the next desk. "Victor, have you alerted the closest SWAT team?"

"As soon as we saw the chopper moving off the reservation, I started standby alert with all three teams. The choppers are warming up with their teams aboard and the ground teams are in their SUV's taking up their assigned positions on the main roads."

"Good. Good. Looks as if the closest choppers are the ones at the Lone Lake ranger station. Let's get them in the air ASAP."

"O.K. What about the others?"

"Not until we see which way this guy is heading when he takes off. My bet is the Chesaw area but we won't put all our eggs in one basket. These guys are pretty wily and know the area better than we do."

"Fred, you had the duty today, how did it go planting the tips with border patrol about smugglers?"

"We had a little help from Regional Office of ICE. They agreed to pass on one of the tips to Oroville as gleaned from a "reliable source." Coming from "on high" in their chain of command, I'm sure they'll take it seriously and will act accordingly. That will pull some of their resources to the far west. That tip went in this morning. The other tip we saved for this afternoon. We sent it in as a relay from the RCMP who had received a report of a busload of Asians acting suspiciously in Trail, B.C. and that someone who knew the language overheard a conversation that passengers would cross the border illegally tonight. So that should take some resources to the far eastern sector."

Marion spoke up. "Our electronic surveillance intercepted a cell phone conversation between one of the moles at Oroville Border Patrol and someone on the Midlake Reservation alerting them to the two intercept operations planned for tonight."

Janet said, "Good. This is sounding better. So, we've likely got the chopper crossing the border in what? An eighty mile stretch?"

"More like a hundred and twenty miles of possibility. But now that we see where he's picking up his load, that's more likely a thirty mile stretch, maybe fifty miles," said Fred.

"He's lifting off," said the console operator. "He'll follow the river toward the border for a few miles until it comes to a confluence. Then he's got a few choices of which canyons to run in order to stay below normal radar."

"Victor, get the two choppers from Lone Lake moving straight toward the border. Tell them not to go past the main road for now. That'll put them about eight miles below the border. I guess they're seven to ten minutes from it." She turned to the console operator. "Ruth, are you getting the positions of the Lone Lake choppers showing?"

"No. They're still out of range of the topographical view we're showing right now. Want me to zoom out till we see them?"

"O.K. Victor, call up the choppers we have at the Loomis campsite – what is it called?"

"Spectacle Lake."

"Yeah, call one of them in toward this area as back up. Do the same with one of the birds in Republic."

"Roger that."

They watched anxiously as the chopper with its contraband made its way toward the confluence. The pilot turned the craft southwest and entered a tight canyon.

"He's committed. He'll follow that canyon to the border. Looks as if he's following the old rail bed. That'll bring him out at Molson," said Marion.

"Victor, relay that to our teams and tell the choppers to move in," said Janet tersely. "Get their ETAs. Then, get the choppers remaining on the ground at Spectacle Lake and Republic in the air and headed this way to help cover the main roads. Also the same with their ground vehicles."

"SWAT Bird One estimates eleven minutes."

"SWAT Bird Two estimates twelve minutes"

"SWAT Bird Three, Spectacle Lake, estimates twenty-three minutes."

"SWAT Bird Four, Republic, estimates thirty-five minutes."

"Have Three and Four cover the main roads on their way in and then stay back six to ten miles unless needed."

"Roger that."

Fred pointed to the screen. "Their chopper's within a mile of the border. But look up there." He pointed higher on the screen. "There's some activity where the road from Molson ends at the rail bed. Looks like a pickup truck and trailer and what, one, nope two snowmobiles. That's probably his destination."

"O.K.," said Janet. "I count four people there. Let's see if we can spot the sentries."

"There's a heat signature about a half mile in on that road to the ranch house, see?"

"That's one," said Ruth. "Looks like another around the bend in the road leading toward town. See, there's a faint heat signature in that clump of trees just off the road on the left-hand side."

"Oh, yeah. That's probably the inner perimeter sentries accounted for. But what about the ones further out?" said Fred.

After a moment, with the observers looking at the screen, Marion said, "There's nothing obvious. There's too much recreational snowmobiling activity. Maybe they'll reveal themselves by radio transmissions."

They watched as the chopper came into the landing zone and dropped its netted cargo and cable right at the back of the trailer and then land about thirty yards away. They watched as two men, crouching down, dragged two boxes each to the open cargo door of the chopper. It seemed it was only a few seconds before the men scurried clear and the chopper took off, headed back the way it came toward the border.

"Damn, they're too fast for us!" Fred said. "The chopper's slipping away."

"Well, SWAT One is too far away to pursue them to the border. Victor, tell SWAT One to concentrate on the landing zone. We might be able to catch the ones loading and the vehicle."

Marion said, "We've got a cell phone transmission outbound for the scene. Looks like a wire transfer." A few seconds later, she said, "Here's an inbound received. Bet its confirmation. I'll get our people started tracing it."

About two minutes later, a radio transmission was intercepted and played on the control room speaker: "Choppers coming from the south! Move it! I say again: choppers coming. ETA 60 seconds! Move it! Move it! Move it."

"I see the source of that transmission. It's at the crossroads south of Molson. Now I can see a heat signature. Looks as if that sentry is moving out. Across country," said Ruth.

"Look at the landing zone. They've stopped loading the trailer. Two guys are jumping in the truck. Looks as if they'll try for a getaway," said Fred.

"Well, looks as if they'll be leaving some incriminating evidence on the ground. Also looks as if the other two guys are going to bug out on their snowmobiles. Victor, tell SWAT Two to incept the departing vehicle and trailer. Looks as if it can't turn off that road for quite a distance, so there's a chance to contain them."

"SWAT Two is now less than a minute behind SWAT One. They're both on the screen moving fast," reported Ruth.

They watched as SWAT One approached the landing zone. The two snowmobiles split into two different directions moving fast. "SWAT One should forget the snowmobilers for now," said Janet. "Looks as if they're bugging out. Priority one should be to seize the contraband. They'll know what to do." They watched as the pilot of SWAT One brought the chopper down for a landing and they saw the muzzle flashes as the agent in its open cargo doorway began firing. Ruth zoomed out with the camera revealing the two snowmobiles had circled back and the operators were attacking the helicopter.

They watched in horror as the door gunner jumped out and was shot, another fell out of the cargo door as the chopper crashed, and three men jumped to the ground, began firing and were shot down by the two smugglers. They watched as the two smugglers took off toward the border on their snowmobiles and there was no movement from the bodies on the ground or from the pilots.

Fred muttered, "Oh, shit, shit, shit." Then he crossed himself and put a hand to his forehead.

Ruth zoomed out until the escaping pickup and trailer were visible moving along the road. They could see SWAT Two cutting across the bend in the road right over a copse of trees radiating a heat signature and flaring to land on the road to intercept the fleeing vehicle. The camera was blinded momentarily as SWAT Two's pilot lit up the scene with its night sun and blinded the driver of the vehicle. After the camera adjusted, they could see the pickup coming to a halt and the chopper preparing to land. They could detect muzzle flashes of the chopper's door gunner spraying the road around the truck.

They saw the sentry emerge from the copse of trees and, instead of taking off, drove toward the chopper, keeping on the other side away from the open cargo door and the door gunner. They watched as he dismounted and fired into the cockpit and as the chopper almost instantly lurched out of control and crashed. They watched as he fired into the cargo bay and as some agents crawled and stumbled out of the wreck as the smugglers' vehicle maneuvered around the wreck and took off. They watched as the sentry kept the survivors pinned down until the truck and trailer were well out of range and as he mounted his snowmobile and took off across country while the chopper burned.

A stunned silence filled the room. How could this have happened?

Then Janet heard Victor on the radio ordering the next closest choppers, SWAT Three and SWAT Four, to move in.

She turned to him. "What's the status of our ground support? What's the ETA on the closest SUV?"

Victor replied, "Closest is fourteen minutes out of Molson, plus one to two minutes to get past Molson to the scene. Next is sixteen minutes and next is twenty-two minutes. Should I call State Police and Oroville Border Patrol to get some resources?"

"Yes, but we all know they're farther out. Alert them to the smuggler's vehicle. We need ambulances and paramedics. Bring them in too. Priority one is tell SWAT Three and Four they are to perform triage at both sites, Medevac the wounded and to secure the scene."

Fred said, "Closest capable hospital is Omak. That's over thirty-five miles flight or over sixty by land. I'll call them to be prepared for gunshot trauma."

"Molson has a volunteer fire department with some medical capabilities," said Marion. "Do you want to call them out?"

262

Janet said, "Yes, we must but they'll be at least seven to ten minutes to respond if we're lucky. Contact them."

"Ambulance service is handled by the town ambulance in Oroville. It's at least thirty minutes away plus the time to call in the crew."

"Do it. O.K., now, let's try to track and apprehend the smugglers' vehicle. Ruth, put a locator pin on it on the screen and vector in some resources to apprehend. Bring in the state and county police, even the border patrol for a radius of at least seventy-five miles. Let's bring that one down!"

"SWAT Five could be deployed to track the vehicle. They're twenty minutes away but could be vectored to intercept south of here."

"Do it. Tell them to coordinate radio frequencies with the local and state police and border patrol. Now, what's this?" Those not detailed to communicate with the other resources looked up at the screen to where Janet was pointing. A stream of over a dozen snowmobiles and vehicles were coming down the road and overland from Molson and many more could be seen coming through Molson toward the road.

Fred said, "Oh, Christ, lookie loos! Just what we don't need! The town folk have heard the shooting and see the flames and are coming out in droves to investigate. We're going to have a contaminated crime scene."

"Contaminated by well-intentioned people coming to the rescue," said Janet. "Maybe some can administer first aid and help avert victim hypothermia and shock. It's cold out there. We've got to get aid to our wounded quick."

"True, but we'll have a mess at the scene."

Janet said, "Victor, get us a high priority flight to Oroville. Fred and I will have to get there ASAP. Fred, call our coordinating partners at DEA, ATF and Regional ICE and tell them what's happening. I better call Hector in D.C."

Fifteen minutes later, Janet had just gotten off the phone after alerting Hector in Washington, D.C. when Marion poked her head into her office. "We're closing on the vehicle." Janet went to join the group gathering around the big screen and the console operator.

"These guys are pretty smart!" Ruth exclaimed. "Just past the crossroads, they pulled into a gravel pit and tucked in behind some cement trucks and waited. After our responding vehicles went by, they doubled back into Molson and then to the campsite on Molson Lake. They've abandoned the vehicle and jumped on a couple of snowmobiles with the outer sentries who also doubled back there and have taken off northwest onto Nine Mile Road. See it there? The road passes by Sidley Lake then parallels the border right close to it." All watched the top of the screen showing the road and the evading vehicles nearing the part of the road that came within mere yards of the border.

Marion said, "I hope that's pretty steep there by the border. I hope there isn't a path or open ground where they can run their machines across."

Fred said, "Looks as if they're off the road and are crossing pretty easily. Damn it! We've lost them!"

Janet's voice was weary. "Victor, as soon as you can, get some of our people over to the campsite to seize the truck and trailer. Then get on to the local RCMP in Osoyoos to advise of the incident and where the smugglers crossed into Canada."

"The first chopper load of wounded are on the way to Omak Hospital with two victims who are the most serious and two "walking wounded," reported Marion. "But I'm afraid we've overloaded Omak. They're asking to divert the next load to Wenatchee, that's another twenty minutes away at least but they've got a much larger hospital. We also have alternatives. We've alerted medics in smaller hospital-clinics in Tonasket and Republic."

"What's the count? How many wounded and how bad? How many have we lost?" asked Janet weakly.

"Looks like at least three dead at the landing zone and four wounded. Of those wounded, all are critical and have to be transported by air. At the other scene, we have three with broken bones and/or concussions, one with critical gunshot, two with major second- and third-degree burns and one dead. That critical gunshot victim will go to Wenatchee, also the burns."

Marion said, "Janet and Fred, your flight's arranged. They'll be waiting for you at Boeing Field in twenty minutes. A forensics team and coroner will meet you there."

"Thanks, Marion," Janet said, then turned to Fred. "Let's get going. Grab your warm clothes. It's going to be chilly there."

"In more ways than one."

Chapter 35

The FBI Challenger executive jet brought Janet and Fred, the coroner and a forensics teams to Oroville's Dorothy Scott Airport where the FBI assault group's Chopper Four was waiting. They quickly transferred to the chopper and were soon on the ground in Molson landing away from where the prop wash might contaminate the scene, on a stretch of the ranch's access road three hundred yards past the so-called landing zone where Chopper One had crashed at the scene of the first shoot-out.

On the way up from Seattle, the team members had changed into winter clothes consisting of heavily insulated snowsuits with parkas, wool toques, heavy socks, thermal mittens and snow boots. Still, Janet was unprepared for the piercing cold when she stepped down from the chopper. After she cleared the propellers, she stopped to quickly put on her snow mittens and pull her parka over her head. She took the time to look around and get her bearings, then joined the others walking toward the crime scene. It had been taped off and was well illuminated by portable lights hooked up to a small portable generator running quietly some distance away.

Her first glance at the scene took in three bodies covered with blankets, and the cargo net lying on the ground in front of the remains of the chopper. She saw a number of bloodstains in the snow at varying distances from the chopper's cargo door and assorted first aid residue such as bandage wrappers amid shell casings. Her eyes were drawn to the body in front of the cargo door. It had been covered with a blanket. She took in the wreckage of the chopper and noted it was very much as she had seen it from the drone's camera.

She turned to try to identify where the shooters had placed themselves and noted crime scene tape had been placed around churned up snow and tracks in two large clusters, one about a hundred yards to the front and right side of the chopper and the other about a hundred twenty yards to the rear and right side of the chopper. She assumed this was where the shooters had stopped their snowmobiles and established shooting positions. She found herself thinking, "These guys were pros with lots of nerve to feign a bug-out and return with a coordinated attack."

After looking at the scene, she noticed an agent waiving at her. He had been talking with another near the rear of the chopper wreckage. She walked over to meet him. He was wearing the

----

DEA/FBI issue snowsuit under a heavy parka with DEA emblazoned on the back and the top right breast. His nametag read "Moorcroft." He introduced himself as Special Agent Dan Moorcroft, the SWAT team leader from Chopper Three, the Designated On-Scene Commander.

"Welcome to the mess," he said somberly. We've got all the injured off to hospitals, just the bodies remain for the coroner. The bodies of the pilots are still inside the wreckage. Once the injured were moved off, we could shoo off the locals who had been giving first aid and secure the scene. It got pretty contaminated, I'm afraid. Some of the locals were on the scene before we were. At least we got some pretty good first aid assistance."

Janet said, "I've brought one forensics team from Seattle and a coroner. I understand Spokane is sending more forensics people."

"Yes, their chopper is on its way with an ETA of about half an hour. They've also sent a mobile command center and more forensics personnel by road and they should arrive in two hours."

Janet, looking once again at the empty cargo net, said, "What happened to the rest of the cargo?"

"If there was any, it disappeared before we could control the scene. Are you sure there was something?"

"I can guarantee you there was something like twenty to thirty ten-kilo bales of marijuana. We recorded the whole scene from a drone. You could see the individual bales."

"Ouch. I doubt if the locals will be very interested in returning the evidence."

"You're most likely right on that. From past experience, we know the locals are not too welcoming of the FBI and DEA. There's quite a frontier spirit up here and smuggling is a major employer. We've been recording the scene from the drone so we can probably track the ones who took the contraband but I wouldn't be surprised if it changes hands and gets disbursed among a lot of the locals. It could be very difficult to pursue."

"Interesting. The locals were sure helpful when it came to saving life and limb."

"Yeah, that's the American spirit. From Command Seattle, I asked you to send someone to the campground to find and secure the perpetrators' truck and trailer they apparently ditched. How did that go?"

"No problem with that. We found the truck and trailer and secured the scene. We opened the trailer and found a huge pile of ten

266

kilo bales of marijuana. I also sent a team up Nine Mile road to where the guys left the road on their snowmobiles. We've secured that scene as well. The ground at the border is pretty flat there. It looks as if they made a clean getaway."

"We'll have to get a forensics team to both scenes but tell them to concentrate on the truck and trailer. Speaking of which, let's look at the other chopper crash site."

"I notice you're feeling the cold already, I'll call over an SUV to take us to it."

"That'll be welcome!" Janet called Fred, who had been helping the coroner examine the bodies. He came over and she filled him in. She introduced him to Dan Moorcroft as they all walked toward an SUV that pulled up to the crime scene tape.

"No surprise that the bales of bud disappeared," remarked Fred wryly. "Some of the locals will be well supplied for a while. I guess we could later do a sting to get some of it back."

"It's not worth it unless a review of the video shows it was well organized," said Janet. "I wouldn't be surprised if half the town is involved and the other half will stonewall any enquiries. It's a small town. It'll be a very tight-lipped town as far as dealing with the feds."

The second crash site was similar except the chopper was a burnt-out heap of wreckage, still smoking. The snow banks on either side close to it had been melted and blackened from the fire and ice had glazed the road from the melted snow and the foam and water the firemen had used.

The chopper had been cordoned off with crime scene tape, as had the shooter's temporary redoubt, marked by depressions in the snow, snowmobile tracks and empty shell casings. Janet could easily see the angle of fire the shooter had used to take out the pilot and send the chopper crashing into the hard-packed road.

Dan said, "The pilot's body is still in the wreckage, probably burned to a crisp. Co-pilot managed to get out but took a shot in a leg. We'll have to wait for the wreckage to cool down."

Janet shivered. "May he rest in peace. Did you know him?"

"Her, actually. Her name is Lynda Carruthers. The other pilot is Susan Coyle. Yes, I know, uh, knew them both very well. We did a lot of training together."

"I'm sorry. This must be very hard for you losing so many team members."

Dan, trying to choke back his grief, swallowed, took a few deep breaths, then said, "Shall I take you to the truck and trailer site at the campground?"

"Sure."

Dan called over one of the men standing guard on the site and introduced him as his designated second in command. He left him in command of the two crash sites with instructions to send the next arriving forensics team to the campsite to handle the truck and trailer and to tell the forensics crew and coroner that had started at the other crash site that they were to handle both chopper crash sites.

When the FBI SUV in which they were riding drove past the museum, Janet and Fred noticed a fair-sized crowd of about twenty people milling about. Some turned toward the vehicle as it passed and Janet took note of more than a few one-finger salutes directed toward them.

"They seem not too enamored with the FBI presence," Fred remarked.

They shortly reached the campsites on the lake. The truck and trailer were cordoned off with crime scene tape and guarded by two agents who were taking turns standing guard outside and taking warming shelter in an SUV. The trailer doors had been closed. Fred noticed other campers in adjoining campsites and asked Dan, "Have the other campers been interviewed?"

"Yes. We've also run all the vehicle licenses and the names of all we have found to interview. We've found something interesting. The camper next to this one is a stolen rig. The plates don't match the rig. They were reported stolen a month ago and the VIN is for a vehicle stolen in Tri Cities about three months ago. There's no one home there. You'll see we've included it inside the crime scene tape.

"From our interviews, it looks as if three campers were involved, each with two men. Five campsites down, there was another camper with two men who met with the others but it moved out before the action started. Someone said they saw it parked at the crossroads at the entrance to Molson and it looked as if the guys were out on their snow mobiles on the trails around there."

"We'll have to check the drone's surveillance tape to see where they went," said Fred.

Janet took a call on her cell phone from Marion in Seattle. "Janet, this is heating up, the media have gotten wind of the shoot-out. In fact, there's a lot of video already on YouTube and other

Internet sites taken by the locals. We're inundated by the press and many of them are on the way to Molson. The first TV station to air it called it a shoot-out. They later altered it to an FBI foul-up of major proportion like Waco but with the smugglers winning. Oops, here I'm seeing it made the newspaper. The headline reads, WACO REVENGE: FBI LOSE BIG SHOOT-OUT IN MOLSON."

"Ouch!" said Janet "We'll have to call a press conference to lay out the facts. Draft up a script and run it past me, the boss and our lawyers before the conference. Minimize disclosure of the suspects etc. under the guise of "ongoing investigation" but play up the injuries to our people, family mourning and such. And play up how the local people of Molson came to the rescue – they can be credited for helping to save quite a few lives of the injured."

"O.K."

"I'll leave Fred in the field here at Molson and fly back for the press conference and de-briefing. There's going to be a Board of Inquiry on this one so we'll have to be prepared. As well, we've got to keep the momentum up on tracking the suspects and building the case."

As soon as she rang off, she caught another call, this one from her boss in Seattle, Special Agent Steve Wilson. Steve was in charge of the Seattle office. He was well apprised of the case and had always been supportive and encouraging of Janet's handling of it. He had given her free rein, as this operation was but one of many he had under his aegis. Steve said, "Hi Janet, looks as if we've got some problems with this one."

"Steve, that's an understatement. The only good thing going at the scene is we've secured almost a ton of marijuana and we have the electronic surveillance from the drone which can identify some of the players."

"Well, the press are having a field day right now. As this has been your operation, you and Fred get your asses back here pronto for a press conference. Then let's see where we go next. Hector called and said he's been ordered to call a Board of Inquiry and that team will be here tomorrow."

"The jet is still on the ground in Oroville awaiting orders. I'll leave this to the On Scene Commander and Fred and I should be back within two to three hours."

"O.K. See you then."

As Janet ended that call a border patrol vehicle pulled up behind their SUV. Roger Sanchez, looking very grim, got out of the passenger's side. He spotted Janet and called, "Agent Murphy! What the hell is going on here? Why weren't we informed of this operation?"

Janet muttered under her breath. "Oh shit. Not now, please."

Chapter 36

Brian (the Deacon) answered his cell phone. "Hi Brian, it's Ken. I'm due to leave town day after tomorrow. Can we get together before I go?"

"You gonna get some sun and sand?"

"Yep! All courtesy of the Chief."

That afternoon, they met at Brian's apartment in Kelowna. Seated around the kitchen table over coffee, Brian said, "So, the Chief's getting you to set up the factory for the archery weapon in the Maldives? That's where he moved all the equipment? Do you know where exactly?"

"It's an island in one of the northern atolls called Minora Fushi in Baa Atoll. It's a bit remote. I have to fly to Male' then catch a local flight to Hanimaadhoo airport, then it's a three- to four-hour boat ride or a half-hour seaplane flight to the island. Someone will pick me up at the Hanimaadhoo airport and get me to the island. Apparently, it's a tropical paradise with beautiful beaches and all sorts of resort amenities. The locals know it as a research station operated by an international company that's doing research on sea life, such as how to best cultivate pearls and also looking into local marine parasites.

"They've got things well set up with a marine research lab, hydroponics for fruits and veggies, solar and wind power, you name it. The accommodations are supposed to be great with everyone getting their own air-conditioned hut with satellite TV and full bathroom, a recreation hall and dining room. They've even got maid service. They've got all sorts of marine recreation from scuba diving to wind surfing and para-surfing."

"How'd you pick up all this knowledge?"

"Ross Emory's been over there a few times now. He goes for a month at a time then rotates back here for a month. He's helped them set up a meth lab, process some opium and got them started on the hydroponics operation. I've been sounding him out. He knows the Chief's sending me over soon."

"Are you planning on taking Patsy?"

"The Chief said no. He said I would be well looked after. Ross said the same. Apparently the catering staff has some very available and lovely Russian women."

"A little variety might help at your age!"

271

"Maybe."

"How long will you be there?"

"The Chief said up to six months this time. He's paying well. I'll have the same four guys on production as last time. We're flying over together."

"That means your equipment for the workshop and the materials have arrived there?"

"Yeah. It arrived a few days ago. Don't worry, everything's tagged with the passive tags and the software in the manufacturing machines has hidden "bombs" that destroy the software if someone attempts to operate it without me present. You can easily track it."

"Any idea how many weapons you're going to produce or who they'll be for?"

"Not really. The chief said they had two different orders, maybe a third. He mentioned producing some for inventory. I expect we could produce about two thousand. He asked me to specify materials for two thousand."

"Any idea how many people are on the island?"

"Ross said it varies but the last time he was there he counted thirty including the catering staff and security."

"Security?"

"Yeah, eight guys rotate guard duty. Apparently, they're pretty quiet and don't bother anyone but they do help out with the recreation, such as lifeguarding and lessons on the sports equipment. A couple are good bridge players – that's how Ross learned that they all are ex-spetsnaz commandos from the Russian army. They haven't got much to do but they monitor CCTV surveillance of the inside of the labs and other spots around the island. Oh, yeah, they've also got radar to keep an eye out for Somali pirates.

"There's a woman in charge of the island. She manages the catering, security, maintenance, and production personnel. Catering has four or six people cooking and four or five housekeeping. Maintenance has two who also double as gardeners and there are five involved – plus Ross when he's there – in the grow op and chemical lab. Plus, there's me and my crew when visiting. Some of the workers are couples, such as a couple of lab tech and cooking crew. Some of the security crew double as armorers maintaining weapons that are warehoused there – apparently the Chief's partner is a big guy in the weapons trade."

"So twenty-eight to thirty-five? Thereabouts?"

"According to Ross."

"So what's the layout like? I know you haven't been there, but what did Ross say?"

"Each gets their own cottage or hut but some are couples, so there's got to be more than twenty-five huts. There's a recreation building and a separate cookhouse. Plus, there's a small admin building, then the labs and warehouse."

"Labs? As in plural?"

"Yeah, one's for real marine research – there are even tanks outside for raising marine life. There's outdoor hydroponics for the bud and fruit and veggies with the bud under some camouflage. There's a separate building for the meth and other products – apparently, when they aren't producing meth, they're refining opium and who knows what else. There's another building that's a workshop – for the archery weapon, I guess. But Ross said he overheard one conversation mentioning weapons maintenance. Oh, yeah, he also mentioned a warehouse."

"O.K.," said Brian. He opened a briefcase and pulled out a small package and handed it to Ken. "Here are a few thousand microchips. That'll probably hold you for this visit. Also, here's a spare battery for your emergency identifier. No worry about it being out of range there as the signal bounces off the satellites in place for marine and air rescue. Can you build a unique telltale into the carbon fiber this time?"

"Thanks. Yeah, I'll add something to be a telltale."

"Will you be able to phone out or use Internet when you get there?"

"I gather they have satellite phone and Maldives has cell phone service but I've been told not to have any external voice communications. They say it's O.K. to use the Internet for banking and such but it will be monitored."

"Not even for a lonely lovesick guy to call his lovely Patsy?"

"Nope. The Chief has warned her I'll be out of touch." Ken reached into a pocket and brought out two micro cassettes and put them on the table. "Here are a couple of tapes of conversations I had with Ross and one of the other guys who've been over to "the resort." The tapes back up what I just told you. Maybe you'll glean a little more – just in case I missed something."

"Excellent! Now all that good work and the fact you're going on an enviable trip to a tropical paradise warrants a great dinner! I've made reservations at the Summer Vineyard, if that's O.K. by you?"

"Great choice! I love their rack of lamb. They've got a new merlot that will be good with it – nice and pricey but you've got a good expense account Right?"

Brian laughed. "Right!"

Maldives

Ken and his crew had an uneventful trip. They had flown from Kelowna to YVR then to London Heathrow (LHR) where they had to change airports to depart from Gatwick (LGW) for Male' (MLE). They flew economy class and overnighted at a modest hotel at Heathrow. All were excited as it was their first glimpse of England and they managed to find a genuine local pub for drinks and dinner. The flight to Male' was overnight and most managed to catch some sleep. They had to wait in Male' airport for three hours after clearing immigration, then took a two-hour flight to Hanimaadhoo (HAQ) where they were met by Jindra Recvik. Jindra was a tall dark solid man with a black brush cut and coal black eyes, somewhere in his mid-forties. He was dressed in designer blue jeans and white polo shirt, silvered sunglasses and foam beach thongs. He introduced himself as one of the security guards from the research station. When shaking hands with Jindra, Ken noticed he had large calloused hands and knuckles and huge wrists. Ken made a mental note: "Not someone to tangle with."

Jindra led them to the nearby quay onto a freight boat whose deck crew were loading some cargo onto the freight deck. He explained that the cargo was also bound for the research station and that they could find some sandwiches and soft drinks in the galley and a place to relax out of the sun as the trip would take about four hours.

Ken's crew consisted of Eddie Whitefeather, Rod Redfish, Sam Littlefort, and Ernie Wren. Eddie Whitefeather, age 26, was a first class machinist, and an expert on computer-driven tools. Rod Redfish, age 28, was a certified millwright who had shown a talent for gunsmithing. Sam Littlefort, age 21, was a ceramics specialist whom Ken had trained on carbon fiber technology. Ernie Wren, age 25, was also a certified machinist. All were members of the Midlake Band, residing on the reservation, and also members of the Devil's Brew.

Although tired from the trip, they were still excited by the new tropical world they had entered, of the hot blazing sun, high humidity, crystal clear ocean, lack of hills on the islands and white sandy beaches. Some managed to catnap. From time to time, some enjoyed the breeze from the ship underway by lining the forward deck rails and watching the flying fish come out of the crystal clear sapphire blue water to cross in front of the bow or leap the side wake. Occasionally, dolphins would swim with the ship, jumping in front of the bow across the ship's path.

As the ship came close to the sheltered bay and quay of Minora Fushi Island, Ernie Wren was the first to comment. "Wow, man, looks as if the stories Ross was spinning about the place are true! Look at the kayaks, sailing catamarans, sailboards and surfboards! And, look at the huts! Hey guys, we done come to de beach! Look at that white sand!"

Three people were waiting on the quay to meet the new arrivals. When the ship came alongside, a beautiful well-tanned blond woman waved at them. She was about five foot nine and one hundred twenty pounds, well proportioned, with short curly hair, and pink lipstick. She was wearing a long pleated mauve skirt complementing a white long-sleeved, open-neck blouse. Ken especially noted her great ankles and bare feet in leather sandals showing off bright pink toenails. Ken figured she was in her early- to mid- forties. She waved again and spoke with a slight Russian accent. "Gentlemen, gentlemen, welcome to our research station! We've been looking forward to your arrival."

Ken leaped off the ship as the first ropes were being secured, approached the woman and introduced himself and the boys. The woman introduced herself as Natalia Petrokoff, manager of the complex. She then introduced the people with her but, instead of listening, Ken found himself looking into Natalia's bright blue eyes, admiring her beauty. He was intoxicated by the slight fragrance of Lily of the Valley as he got close to her. She noticed his interest, took him by the arm, squeezed tightly, and started walking with him down the quay to the shore. She turned to Ivan, one of the men who had been standing with her, and told him to escort the others to their quarters and put Ken's luggage in the hut he was assigned.

"Darling," she said to Ken, "please excuse my formal dress but the crew on the boat are Muslim and I can't offend them by showing bare arms or legs. Let me show you around. As soon as your guys are settled in, we'll have an orientation session in the recreation building. I'm sure you'll love it here!" Ken was floating.

"I understand from Ross," she continued, "that you're a good bridge player. We'll see about that! I also understand you're a scuba diver. Diving's great here. Did you bring some of your own equipment? I'll have to check you out."

"Uh, yeah. I brought my dive computer, mask, fins and snorkel. Ross said you had all the rest."

"Right. You don't need a wet suit as the water's so warm – into the 30's Celsius – like soup. You'll never get chilled. I'd be delighted to take you out as your dive partner."

Ken was speechless as Natalia led him through a small square, pointing out the office, recreation building and cookhouse, then led him along a path dotted with bungalows. She said, "The huts are all along this path. Some are on the beach on the lea side – those we reserve for the VIPs and department heads. Yours is the first one on the beach here."

They stopped at the first hut on the beach. They entered and Ken surveyed the unit. It was all Ross had described and more. He said, "Ross forgot to mention the beach."

"Your luggage will be along soon. But let's walk back toward the office and I'll show you some more." She led him around the small island showing off the generator, the hydroponics operation, the chicken pen, the sewage treatment and desalination plants, solar panel array, windmills and the lab.

As they entered the machine shop, Natalia said, "This is your domain for now. We also use it for restoring weapons from time to time. You've got lots of machinery that's standard to the place but there's also the container of your equipment that arrived a few days ago that has yet to be opened – we thought we'd leave it for you and your guys. There's lots of electricity and venting in the building. I gather you use a kiln to form some of the parts from carbon fiber."

"Plus, I shipped over some plastic forming machinery and dies – the machines take a lot of electricity," Ken said. He noted the machinery was clustered to one end of the shop and that a 30 x 60 foot portion at the other end was empty except for some metal-topped tables. "I guess that empty space is for my stuff? We'll have to string some more wires for the machines. It'll do, but we'll need storage space for the finished weapons."

"That's another building. You can see it later." She looked at her watch then touched Ken on the forearm. "Everyone should be assembled in the recreation building for orientation and welcome now. Let's go over there." They took another path that led back to the

----

small square and the recreation building, situated across the square opposite to the office and kitty corner from the cookhouse.

They entered the building's main hall, which was well equipped with dart board, skittle, ping pong and pool tables, a chess set on its own table, sofas, four square tables and a stack of plastic chairs. At one end was a bar with ten metal-framed stools and some low-rise tables with plastic chairs. At the opposite end was mounted a 52-inch flat-screen TV and below it an entertainment center with CD player and stereo amplifier, with sofas, tables and chairs facing the TV.

About thirty people were milling about in various conversation groupings. Ken took note of some more beautiful women who seemed to vary in age from twenty to thirty something. Natalia called their attention and, when quiet, she introduced Ken and had him introduce his team, then went around the room introducing everyone by name and duties. Ken especially took note of Sanka Kergol, a raven-haired beauty with long black hair, seemingly jet black eyes and dark Mediterranean complexion who was introduced as a lab technician. The numbers of men and women seemed to be evenly matched but Ken noted what he thought were two gays and a lesbian couple.

Natalia then laid out the ground rules for working on the island. On workdays, breakfast was from six to seven. Work began at seven with a fifteen minute coffee/tea break at nine, then lunch served at eleven-thirty. Lunch was extended in order to allow for use of the beach etc. and work resumed at three – supposedly after the heat of the day, and ended at seven. Dinner was at seven-thirty. The workweek was six days a week with Sundays off. Sunday breakfast was informal continental, and make-it-yourself sandwiches were available for lunch. Sunday dinner was at seven-thirty. Rules on liquor were no personal liquor or drugs during the workweek except that wine and beer, limit two glasses per person, were available for dinner and pre-dinner from seven. Saturday night had an open bar from seven with hard drinks and bud sampling also available, snacks, music and dancing. The use of crack, cocaine, meth or heroin was forbidden.

Use of watercraft was open to everyone but they had to let security know what they were taking out and which way they were headed, as security would send out a rescue craft if they were gone too long. They were warned about the tidal currents, which could get up to four knots, and local wind conditions. Different people in security were identified for their ability to give lessons on the various watercraft, snorkeling and scuba diving. Scuba diving as a group boat trip was available every Sunday, and twosome dive buddy dives from the beach, with permission, over lunch hours.

Internet use was always monitored for security purposes and no one was to disclose their whereabouts. Cell and satellite phones were not to be used, except for emergencies and by permission and monitored only. It was noted there was electronic surveillance of all frequencies and that there was also radar surveillance in a fifty-mile radius.

The cooking staff was renowned for the variety and high quality of their meals and an abundance of fresh local seafood, chicken, fruits and veggies supplemented the imported food.

Natalia said there was a small canteen for personal toiletries and snack items beside the dispensary, located in the office, run by Sonja Recvik, Jindra's spouse, a registered nurse with combat experience, who served as their paramedic. Bar fridges in the cottages were stocked with pop, juices and water. Laundry was once a week and handled by the housekeeping people. Dress was casual.

Natalia stated that they were fortunate to arrive on a Saturday as the day off on Sunday would give them time for their body clocks to adjust from jet lag and to explore the recreational opportunities. "You may now wish to return to your huts," she said, "or explore a bit before the bar opens. Then we have dinner and you can relax. You're probably pretty tired and may want to go directly to bed, but there will be dance music in the bar after dinner. Tomorrow, you relax as well. Then, it's down to work on Monday!"

Over drinks and dinner, they got to socialize with the others. Ken, not sleepy, followed others from dinner back to the bar where Natalia was seated at a table with Sanka. She waved Ken over to join them and after greetings said, "I was just telling Sanka you're a scuba diver and we were planning on a couple of dives off the beach tomorrow. She's certified Advanced Open Water and also as a Dive Master and Instructor."

Ken noticed a degree of affection between the two women as Sanka put her hand on Natalia's forearm and smiled as she looked into Natalia's eyes. Then she turned and looked deep into Ken's eyes, saying, "Yes, would you mind if I joined you? I'd like to check you out."

"You mean a checkout dive to assess my level of diving skills?"

"That too." They all laughed.

During the course of the evening Ken learned more about Sanka and Natalia. Sanka was Bulgarian, from Varna, on the Black Sea. She was about thirty years old and never married. She held a degree in chemistry from a good university in Sofia and had accepted her present job for the money and the chance to live in a tropical paradise.

Natalia never hinted at her age but Ken deduced it just a little past forty after she described many of her experiences. She was from Kazakhstan, and her parents had been sent there as part of Stalin's program to mix up ethnicity in the satellite states of the great Soviet Union. Growing up during the Soviet era, she enjoyed the family's privileges as her father was a senior level bureaucrat and her mother was a doctor. When the Soviet Union collapsed, her parents were forced to migrate to Vladivostok due to local unrest directed at Russians by the native Kazakhs. She had received a scholarship to a good university in Leningrad where she studied economics. She then joined the Red Army, spent some time in Minsk and eventually left the service with the rank of Colonel. Igor met her at a Moscow nightclub and ended up recruiting her to manage the island operation. She was divorced from an army officer. She claimed to have one daughter, who was in graduate school in Moscow training to be a doctor.

Sunday, after grabbing some make-it-yourself breakfast with lots of coffee, Ken met the women at the equipment shed on the quay at the beach end. The shed was used to house the dive equipment and had an air compressor for filling tanks. Outside was a fresh water tank used to clean the dive gear and a clothesline strung between two poles, which was used to hang and dry the buoyancy vests and other dive gear. Ken noted the dive gear was all of the highest quality and in excellent condition. After they selected their gear, made up weight belts, checked their buoyancy compensator vests (BCs), tested their regulators and determined the pressure in their tanks, they put everything in a wheelbarrow with large double wheeled pneumatic tires that Ken pushed easily across the beach then along a path to a small cove with a secluded entry spot that Natalia had chosen.

They kitted up, checked each other's gear, then entered the water, putting on their fins when they were chest deep, then their masks and mouthpieces. Natalia had selected the entry spot because

----

the beach bottom sloped sharply and there were no waves to contend with. Their water entry was a few steps on sand until the water was chest high, then into a sloping rock and coral bottom. The water was clear and devoid of current.

After testing their regulators, Natalia signaled to go down. They let the air out of their BCs and quickly followed the bottom down into thirty feet of water. They paused to adjust the air in their BCs to achieve neutral buoyancy and tighten some straps, then, with Natalia in the lead, pulling a rope attached to a "Divers Down" red-flagged buoy floating on the surface, they moved along the reef, heading deeper. The red-flagged buoy contained a tracking transponder for security to know their whereabouts. Natalia said the tracking signal served as security in case of trouble, such as being swept out to sea by the tide.

With Sanka taking up the rear, they followed the reef deeper into eighty feet of water, leveled out and swam parallel to the reef. The reef had an abundance of marine life, some very colorful. Natalia pointed up and away from the reef and Ken could make out a large shape coming toward them. It soon came into clear view as a huge tortoise. Sanka grabbed Ken's left fin to get his attention and, when he turned, pointed away from the reef and below them. Ken followed her arm and finger and made out three large hammerhead sharks swimming away from them.

Farther on, they came up to fifty feet of water and Natalia guided them over an outcropping into a small valley. She reached down and grabbed onto a large rope that had been anchored into coral and strung the length of the valley, and she motioned Ken to do the same. She then made a fluttering motion with her hands indicating the presence of manta rays. She also motioned to wait, so Ken settled on the sand, holding on to the rope.

Sanka came up close behind him and reached her right hand around to gently squeeze his crotch, to which his member immediately responded. Natalia turned and saw Sanka, moved in closer and put her hand over Sanka's on Ken's crotch. Together they began rubbing. They were interrupted by a large shadow passing overhead. Sanka looked up and pointed at a large manta ray.

Their play stopped while they observed the spectacle in front of them. Ken, focusing on the ray, thought it must have been ten feet across. It was doing a lazy cartwheel no more than thirty feet in front of them. The ray had a flock of wrasse around it nibbling at what looked like fine sea grass growing on parts of its skin. After a few

----

minutes, the ray and its entourage lazily left. Sanka checked her air gauge, then Ken's. She noted Ken had consumed a lot of air and motioned to Ken and Natalia that it was time to go up and back. They retraced their path, ever slowly rising until they reached fifteen feet where they had a three-minute safety stop for decompression before slowly surfacing very close to their entrance spot.

Upon surfacing, Ken took out his mouthpiece and let out a bellow: "Ooh-wee! That was lovely! Thank you! Thank you! Both of you! Oh, my!"

"As you can see, we know how to make a dive enjoyable!" said Natalia.

Ken said, "Shall we change tanks and try again?"

Sanka said, "If you wish. But we should have a siesta first. We should get at least an hour's surface time before diving again to get rid of some of the built-up nitrogen bubbles in our blood. Of course, it will be nice to see what you are made of too."

Natalia said, "My place then. It's closest. I feel a threesome coming on."

The day passed very quickly for Ken. He discovered his two companions were bi-sexual and enjoyed each other's company as well as Ken's. They missed lunch as no one wanted to leave the bed. However, they did manage to get another dive in during the late afternoon – sans bathing suits in shallower water– and some interesting positions were attempted. Ken was grateful he had brought along a supply of Viagra but began to worry that it might soon run out. Natalia assured him the canteen had a supply.

The three stayed together for dinner but when it was over Natalia told Ken, "Tomorrow is a work day, my poor darling, and we've exhausted you. Tonight, you need to be by yourself for a good night's sleep. We can play hard on weekends but for workdays, we need our beauty sleep." After slight protest, Ken returned alone to his hut. Exhausted, he quickly fell asleep to pleasant dreams.

The first workday was hectic. Ken and his boys were tired from Sunday's strenuous activities. The boys, after meeting some of the young women of the housekeeping staff on Saturday night, had spent Sunday together learning the art of para-surfing where they rode surfboards and used parachutes to grab the wind. Ivan, one of the security guards was an expert and took great pleasure in training

----

them. The girls were already accomplished para-surfers and the boys were hard pressed to keep up.

Eddie was bragging that he managed to have his new friend, Tanya, spend the night with him. Sam smiled and said he was too tired Sunday night but his new friend, Rita, had kept him company Saturday night. Rod said he was just too tired to do anything but really enjoyed the company of Marie. Ernie talked at length about Annette and her skills as a masseuse.

Ken set a fast pace to get the equipment out of its shipping container and set up in the workshop. The most time-consuming part was getting the computers set up, running some additional power lines, testing the CAD-CAM machinery and double-checking the software. It took two days to set up the equipment and organize the materials. On the second day, Jindra took Ken to the warehouse where the raw materials were stored. He showed Ken around, indicating where finished weapons would be stored and his allocated spot for the raw materials. He helped him haul the first batch of materials to the workshop. The warehouse was three-quarters filled with cases of weapons. As they walked toward the far end, Jindra pointed out a wide ramp leading down to an underground basement. Ken could see a heavy metal door at the base of the ramp. He said, "That's off limits for you and your people. It's a munitions vault."

"Is much stored there?" asked Ken.

"Right now, about thirty tons of various ammo ranging from bullets to grenades, RPG's, mainly small stuff. Oh, yeah, some Semtex and some C-4. It's all climate controlled down there."

"Where do you store the volatile stuff for the meth lab?"

"It's in a separate underground vault under the meth lab. It's so volatile, someone in their wisdom decided it would be better separated from this warehouse.

"I'm sure they were right!"

Chapter 37

Chief Border Patrol Agent Roger Sanchez was livid. His blood pressure was up and had been so ever since he learned the FBI and ATF/DEA had an operation in his territory and had not informed him of it. He stood in the cold, looking at Janet and shaking in rage.

"Agent Murphy! What the hell is going on here? Why weren't we informed of this, this operation?"

Janet moved close, looked Sanchez squarely in the eyes and said, "Agent Sanchez, I owe you an explanation."

Agent Sanchez stared into her eyes. She could see the fury in his eyes when he spoke. "What is this, this fiasco? Is this another case of the FBI cowboys "going for the glory" and shutting others out? The least you could have done would have been to advise us you had an operation planned in our territory."

"I'm sorry, Agent Sanchez. I'll explain but it shall be for your ears only and in all confidentiality. I've been working with your superiors in Bellingham and Seattle and you may discuss it with them but you must keep secrecy with your own personnel – and your spouse. Do I have your assurance of confidentiality?"

Taken aback by the comment, Sanchez quietly said, "Of course. I may discuss this with my immediate superiors in Bellingham though?"

"Yes. We're short on time now but we can talk in the helicopter en route to Oroville. If you're in agreement, I suggest you leave your vehicle with your driver and join Fred and me."

Sanchez dismissed his car and driver and joined Fred, Dan and Janet in the SUV for the short drive back to Helicopter Four. During the drive, Janet and Fred discussed with Dan Moorcroft what remained to be done at the scenes. Once airborne, Janet, facing Sanchez, leaned forward to be closer to his head and began. "Agent Sanchez, we've been working on the case of the murder of your two agents. So far, it's led us to uncovering numerous drug rings and some successful arrests of mid-level operators across America and more is coming. We've also observed some cross-border drug smuggling in your district that seems related directly to one very professional gang. However, during the course of our investigations, we unearthed two moles in your department."

"Why wasn't I told of this? Who are they? How long has this been going on?"

"You weren't told because we didn't want to give any opportunity for the moles to learn they were under observation. And, we weren't sure if they had any accomplices in the department."

"How dare you! You mean I was under suspicion?"

"We cleared you but decided it was better to keep you out of the loop in order for you to behave naturally and avoid any potential for accidental information slips – such as you telling your wife and her acting differently towards certain people or even gossiping or you acting differently towards them at work."

"My wife?"

"Yes, it's a small town and you're part of a tight-knit community of law enforcement personnel. Information can spread quickly. We couldn't take the chance."

Taking a moment to contemplate, Sanchez said, "Are you inferring that one or both of the moles are well known to me and/or my wife both professionally and personally?"

"Yes."

"O.K., I see the point... And you left the moles in place? Why, because you had insufficient evidence for a case against them or because you wanted to use them?"

"We have good cases on each of them. No, our plan has been to use them. They've been most helpful."

"How? What have they been doing? Who are they?"

"One seems to have multiple contacts with organized crime. That one we have linked to your arrest of those twenty-two Korean aliens last year. As well, that one is linked to an aboriginal group. The other seems only to be linked to the same aboriginal group."

"Aboriginals?"

"Yes. Native Indians on both sides of the border."

"Oh. You mean like the NightHawk Band that has reservation land along the Canadian side of the border? On the American side, there's only the Tonawa tribe. They've got a lot of territory and have recently bought some land along the border."

"It seems some of the smugglers are from those bands but the leadership seems to be from the Midlake Band up in Canada."

"Surely their Chief, Chief Joseph Branson, isn't involved? He has a high profile on both sides of the border. I've met him and heard him speak about fish and wildlife conservation. He's very passionate about conservation. He's leading the fight against the proposed dam on the Similkameen. He's involved in that society that bought up the marshland on both sides of the river just west of the

NightHawk border crossing." He was lost in thought for a moment. "Oh, that backs on to tribal land on the other side of the border. Uh-oh."

"We're quite certain he's involved. That he's the ring leader."

"O.K."

"Now, as far as your moles are concerned, we wish to continue to use them. First, I suggest you retain your indignant attitude that we didn't include Orville Border Patrol. That will probably trickle back to the smugglers via your moles. If so, we may have a chance to use them to set up a better trap."

The helicopter began its descent to the Oroville airport.

Janet said, "We'll be landing in a moment. I'll have the helicopter fly you over to your office and drop you at the school grounds nearby or, if you wish, you can ride it back to Molson. There's going to be a Board of Inquiry on this. I'll ask for you to be invited to sit through it all so that you get the whole perspective. You'll probably be called to testify. That'll be an excuse to get you to Seattle where we can review the case and possibly plot a trap. I'll clear it with your superiors in Bellingham. Is that O.K. by you?"

"I don't think I have much choice. Anyway, it won't be hard to maintain an indignant attitude in front of my staff."

"Remember confidentiality please. Nothing even to your wife or in confessional."

"Confessional? You're serious! But who are these moles?"

"Right now, it's probably best to keep you ignorant of that. We'll go into it in Seattle."

The Board of Inquiry began a few days later. It was comprised of five senior FBI, ATF, DEA and ICE personnel brought in from Washington D.C. It lasted four days. Among others, Roger Sanchez, Shirley Bains and Hector Skog were called to testify. In one phase of the inquiry, co-ordination with the other agencies was thoroughly explored. During the inquiry, the entire case was laid out, beginning with the killing of the two border patrol agents and the discovery of the arrow from the archery weapon. The chairman of the inquiry recognized some information as classified only for private audience if he deemed it relevant. He stated as far as activities beyond America, he was more interested in information or the results of information rather than how it was obtained.

Janet and her people laid out the case as it developed step-by-step, noting the drug distribution networks unearthed, the arrests to date and pending. When they finally came to the trans-border smuggling they had observed leading to the ill-fated interception at Molson, it was revealed that the CIA had beefed up the technical capabilities of a drone operating out of Moses Lake and this was classified above the level of regional border patrol. In deference to a request from the CIA, the technology was not revealed, only that the helicopters and smugglers were tracked with the new technology.

At one point in the proceedings, the room was cleared of all but senior personnel who had sufficient security clearance, and a video from the drone over what had now been nicknamed "the Battle of Molson" was viewed, with Janet and Fred adding color. The video was played back many times in certain spots until all were satisfied. After the viewing, Janet was called upon to lay out the interception plan. She was grilled on it in great depth. After that, the court called on the SWAT team leaders to review the action.

At the end of four long days, Janet and Fred were mentally exhausted. Finally the members of the Board wound up the hearing and adjourned to deliberate. At ten o'clock the next day, the Board reconvened to present their verbal assessment. Only Fred, Janet, Steve Wilson, their immediate boss, and Hector Skog were present.

The Chairman of the Board of Inquiry, Andrew Jacobs, of ICE, called the meeting to order and said, "Our formal, written report and press release will come later but we feel it best to inform you first verbally of our findings.

"Firstly, you earn top marks for co-ordination with the other agencies. All inter-agency personnel have spoken highly of you and the good progress in the development of your case reflects inter-agency teamwork in sharing information and technologies and in allocating personnel and equipment in a timely and forthright manner.

"Secondly, if we only look at the drug seizures and personnel arrested, the drug distribution systems unearthed and under observation for pending action, you are to be commended. Again, your ability to demonstrate inter-agency teamwork is commendable.

"Thirdly, the intelligence you gathered, again, with good inter-agency teamwork, is excellent. However, therein lies a criticism. You developed good profiles on the cross-border smugglers. You discovered their organization was highly professional. In fact, you mentioned that most, if not all of the

----

individuals involved, have significant military combat experience. In fact, most served with elite forces? Am I correct?"

"Correct," said Janet.

"You underestimated your adversaries. You planned and executed the interception thinking, if anything, these people would cut and run, but instead they attacked. As well, you did not give sufficient thought to how to immobilize their helicopter or their sentries. Granted, you had very little time from when you saw what path their helicopter would take into our country and there was so much "clutter" of recreational snowmobilers that it would have been hard to distinguish the truck and personnel waiting or the landing site until the last minute. That is a flaw in your overall plan.

You had observed the smugglers in similar circumstances using cargo nets that allowed for a quick turnaround, but it does not look as if you took this into consideration. Our helicopter pilots weren't prepared for the feint of abandoning the scene the smugglers made and the accurate abundance of firepower the smugglers had at their disposal. Nor were our helicopters armored to offer them any protection. As well, due to the lag time for the ground support and other SWAT teams to arrive, you left the lead SWAT teams vulnerable. This may be excused by the need to cover so many miles of the border in anticipation of the crossing and, perhaps not to alert informers or the smugglers of your presence, but that is a fault in your plan. The fact that the smugglers were able to escape back across the border also shows a lack of planning and, perhaps, disorganization once the helicopters were shot up."

"We find the two following helicopter SWAT teams, teams Three and Four, and their pilots did act correctly by devoting their energies to helping the wounded and attempting to secure the crime scenes. It is regrettable that, in the confusion, the subjects' truck and trailer of contraband managed to elude you temporarily to allow the two suspects therein to escape across the border on snowmobiles with two of the sentries. There was neglect in not deploying ground vehicles along Nine Mile Road to anticipate use of it as a possible escape route. I understand those two men, whom I understand you have identified positively as Wayne Simpson and Darryl Smithson of Utah, have disappeared and, as far as you know, remain in Canada?"

"Correct."

"We conclude that you did not have sufficient experience in interceptions of this nature to warrant undertaking the interception. Mainly, you underestimated your adversaries."

"Yes, sir."

"You have perhaps exposed a shortfall in FBI and inter-agency training that needs to be addressed. That seems to be the need for more military-style training or military assistance in ambush and interception. Currently, we have the policy, especially along the U.S.-Canada border, not to use military assault aircraft to intercept and shoot down smugglers. And, we have to look at this incident as a simple smuggling operation and not a terrorist action. Thus, it is unlikely in the immediate future anyway, that military assault aircraft can be employed or co-opted."

"However, we do sympathize with your problem of how to intercept and stop an aircraft, such as a helicopter, especially when it seems their turnaround time is quick. If you are to attempt a similar interception, you need to minimize the potential paths the smugglers may take and you need to be better able to surround them and immobilize their aircraft."

"Janet and Fred, next month you will be relieved of your regular duty to attend a month-long training session at Quantico, Virginia, to determine better responses to future situations. In addition to FBI trainers, there will be military experts to train you on strategies and tactics. In effect, you will still be in pursuit of this group of smugglers but you need more training. You will take Agent Sanchez from Oroville Border Patrol and the SWAT team leaders with you.

"It's an inter-agency affair, so others will be selected from the ranks of DEA, ATF and others, to attend also. The State Department has called on the assistance of the Pentagon for this and there has been agreement to open military liaison. Which means, in effect, you will add a military advisor to your team."

"Now, I understand you have some funerals to attend and some wounded agents and officers to visit. Dismissed."

288

Chapter 38

Donny met David, Willie and Joseph in the clubhouse of the Devil's Brew on the Midlake Reservation. After grabbing a beer each from the bar fridge, settling down around the kitchen table and exchanging some small talk, Donny said, "Are Wayne and Darrel doing O.K?"

"Yeah," said Willie. "After they crossed the border they called me. I got Johnny Mathias to meet up with them and bring them to his ranch. Then we moved them to friends near Salmon Arm."

"O.K. Whenever they get homesick, I'll have some of the boys take them back East, maybe to Manitoba or Ontario and smuggle them back into America," said Donny.

"Right now, they seem to be enjoying the local hospitality," said David. "Willie and I dropped in on them the other day."

"You guys sure raised some shit at Molson. Your "Massacre at Molson" has had worldwide coverage. You sure made the Fibbies look like fools."

"Yeah," said Willie. "Some folk are calling it retribution for Waco."

"I hear the Fibbies couldn't hold onto the bud that was left on the ground at the drop site. The locals got away with all of it," said Donny.

Laughing, David said, "A lot of the town folk'll be happy with some high quality bud. Most of them are on our side anyway with no love lost for the Fibbies."

"Yeah, but the Fibbies got what was in the trailer. Give them credit for tracking that down so quickly," said Joseph.

"The Fibbies are downplaying what remained at the drop site, claiming only ten kilos disappeared. More like a few hundred," said Willie.

"Our customers are getting nervous," said Donny. "And that's bothering me! The Fibbies have been having too many successes recently. They've rolled up a few of our American distributors and have even followed some up toward the border in this region. I wouldn't attribute it to them just getting lucky, if you know what I mean. It's only this sector. The rest of our border crossings are going normally right across Canada."

"Well, we've always had a good inside track at the border patrol office. It wasn't their fault the Fibbies were gung ho to do it all themselves," said David. "I gather Border Patrol is not too happy the FBI didn't invite them. What a bunch of glory hounds."

"Yeah, but that goes way back to J. Edgar Hoover. It won't change," said Willie.

"Well, I've decided no more shipments crossing the border from the Okanagan for a while until things cool down. Capisci?" said Donny.

"Understood," agreed Joseph. "I see no problem laying off for a while, maybe till spring. We've got lots of ways we can move the goods to vary the delivery methods. But nothing wrong with cooling it for now."

Donny said, "The Devil's Brew has cross-border distribution set up right across Canada. You're just one of many. I'll route through others where the feds haven't been so active. As for here, I'd wait at least six months or so. After the "Massacre at Molson" the Fibbies will be out for blood. You can do what you like with your own stuff but nothing from the other producers goes across the border in this part of the country."

"I don't know. I can see laying off over the winter. But that daylight operation we had right under the noses of border patrol using the cover of supplying the exploration site? Come on, you've got to admit that one was highly effective. I think we should do it again late spring," said Joseph.

"I think it's too risky," replied Donny.

"We'll talk again, later," said Joseph

Chapter 39

Shirley called Janet and, after greetings, said, "You remember way back last fall you asked if we could keep tabs on that mining exploration company that was working in the Cathedral Peaks area along the border? Well, their head office is in Toronto and we sent someone in to see them. She was posing as a financial reporter. We also did a thorough background check of the directors and key staff."

"Yeah, yeah, you sent in a lengthy report on all that. There was a linkage to the Devil's Brew through large blocks of shares purchased by one of their corporate fronts but all the directors were clean. You got something new?"

"They came out with a press release. I've just sent it to you by e-mail. Seems some of the drill core samples proved very good for gold and silver and they're about to resume drilling in earnest. Their stock just took a jump. It's running close to three dollars. Looks as if there may have been insider leakage of that knowledge over the winter as the stock has climbed fairly steadily from around forty cents last October. It was trading around a dollar fifty last week. Interesting though, they've voluntarily suspended trading in the stock. Here, let me quote: "While awaiting further drilling." Unquote. They also mention that they have fifteen million in cash reserved for this year's exploration drilling program on that site."

"Did they say when drilling is expected to resume?"

"Yep, May 30."

"Don't ask how she came by this, but Marie LaFrance says that the exploration company has booked Red Mountain Helicopters from May 30 for a solid week of work to set up the site, then weekly supply flights through to mid-October where they're booked for a week to dismantle the camp for the winter."

"Good. Good. That gives us a couple of months to prepare."

Janet had assembled her team, composed of FBI agents and partners from the other agencies, in a conference room at FBI Seattle offices. The objective of the meeting was to plan out a trap for the smugglers using the Loomis River log landing. Prominent in the meeting was Roger Sanchez and one of his field operations supervisors, Ken O'Brien.

After she called the meeting to order and asked people around the table to introduce themselves by name, specialty and agency, Janet made it a point to explain the presence of Sanchez, O'Brien and an army colonel. "Before we get started with the planning exercise and your valuable contributions, it must be noted that border patrol agents Sanchez and O'Brien were not involved in our intercept at Molson so many months ago because we identified two moles in their office and we felt it best to keep everyone in Oroville Border Patrol ignorant rather than risk alerting the moles we were on to them. Since then, we have been able to work around the situation, retaining the moles. Only two people in the Oroville office are aware of the identities of the moles. They are with us now and have kept the information strictly confidential. We intend to use the moles for unwitting deception in this exercise.

"I'd also like to welcome Colonel Bruce Zyto from the Army Rangers based in Fort Lewis. He's here as an expert to work with us. We will also have access to the Rangers' training facilities to practice."

After some comments from around the room, planning began in earnest, beginning with an analysis of what went wrong at Molson and leading into a discussion of new tactics learned at the "advanced interception refresher" in Quantico. It was agreed their greatest problem would be incapacitating the chopper or choppers. They felt the element of surprise would be on their side this time, as they didn't have to cover so many potential routes and landing sites. If they could lie in wait, they would have a much better chance of success.

The sentries were a problem, as they had guarded the access roads for vehicles and gave as much thirty minutes' advance warning. It was decided the sentries would be taken out first by commando stealth land approach tactics and that each sentry merited a four-man tactical team. Colonel Zyto would take the tactical teams to Fort Lewis and military ranges in Washington State for practice and training on similar terrain.

Ways of accessing the Loomis landing site were reviewed and a hiking trail and two old fire access trails, mainly overgrown, were identified as of merit but could be accessed only by horseback or on foot. They could use a fire access road to get near the landing zone and it was decided to use horses to get within three miles, then proceed on foot. The tactical teams would be vectored in to the sentries by FBI Control, gleaning that information from the drone.

Horses and experienced riders would be provided by Oroville Border Patrol to guide and supplement the agents from the other services and the moles in the border patrol office would be led to think the mounted patrol was operating along the Cascade Pacific Rim Trail.

Another problem was the smuggler's landing zone in the Loomis canyon. It was out in the open in the middle of a barren "clear-cut" where the forest had been harvested. There was no cover for a mile down the valley and seven hundred yards up to the mouth of the canyon. On one side of the valley, a riparian way of trees had been left for fifty feet on either side of a stream but there was still three hundred yards of open ground to the landing site with no cover.

It was decided a six-person team, traveling at night, would hide in the riparian way to be aided by two six-person helicopter assault teams that would come up the valley after the sentries were taken out. The airborne assault teams would be flying in Hughes MH6 "Little Bird" helicopters which were configured to carry six SWAT agents riding on benches on the landing skids for quick exit and better field of fire when approaching a target. The element of surprise would be with them if the sentries were taken out.

The issue of immobilizing the helicopters was difficult. Although nets and cables had been used on the Mexican border, the approach had proven ineffectual. Current Rules of Engagement would not allow agents shooting first, unless engaged in an imminent terrorism threat. However, in case of air interception, in addition to radioed voice command to halt, warning shots could be fired across the path of the aircraft using tracers to be visible. At this point in the deliberation, Janet said, "We've managed to pry loose an attack helicopter, a BZ201 which Quantico developed and has been testing. It's armed with twin M34 - 7.22 millimeter Miniguns. It and the pilots will soon arrive at Fort Lewis where they'll practice on similar terrain."

It was felt it would be near impossible to get both of the smugglers' helicopters and all settled for one unless circumstances provided otherwise. Colonel Zyto recommended the attack helicopter be positioned between the border and the landing zone at Loomis so that it could come down on the smuggler chopper following it from the north toward the landing zone to block its exit avenue and pounce when the smugglers were making their drop. Agreed.

Joseph and Donny were having a serious discussion over lunch at the winery bistro. "I still think it's too early to start up," said Donny as he reached for a piece of calamari and dipped it in sauce.

"We've been quiet for over five months now. And our friend in Oroville Border Patrol says nothing's going on. It's business as usual. Apparently the FBI, DEA and ATF have gone on to other things – at least they're not making any arrests and haven't been seen in this area," said Joseph. "The Temple run is just too good to pass up! It's counter to the routine of the border patrol who put eighty percent of their resources into night operations. We operate in daylight under the cover of a legitimate operation. It's a great way to move a lot of cargo."

"Well, I still think they may be on to the packing house and tree nursery."

"O.K., so we won't use the packinghouse. We won't use the nursery. We can still put trucks into Loomis River valley with nursery trees from another source. We can use local trucks and we can transfer to our customers farther south, say at the ranch near Wenatchee, whatever."

"How much have you got ready to go?"

"Five tons of bud and a ton of meth to go down."

"I can round up another two tons. Maybe best to do it over a few days, that way, if we get an interception, we won't lose all at once. Plus, if all goes good the first day, we'll bring in some coke on the back haul the second or third day, maybe some guns too."

"That's a good idea, a little at a time over three to five days?"

"O.K."

Chapter 40

David had the airlift well organized. Just like the last times, they were using two choppers to fly under the legitimate Red Mountain Helicopters craft as it made its runs from the base in the failed RV park at the bottom of the mountain up the Temple River canyon to the mining claim near the peak, some six thousand feet higher in elevation. The run was not long, just sixteen miles, ending southeast of the RV park within a half mile of the 49th parallel, the border between Canada and the U.S.A.

The landing site for the mining claim was half way up a hillside in a cleft of the mountains that ran north and south into the U.S.A. The headwaters stream at the bottom of the cleft was the dividing line between a provincial park boundary and the mining claim situated on "Crown Land" provincial forest. By staying in the cleft below the ridges of the mountains, a chopper could slip across the border undetected by radar. Once across the border, there were three canyon routes to Loomis Valley and the drop zone, some twelve miles distant. The mining claim was isolated, completely out in the wilderness in rugged mountains that averaged eight thousand five hundred feet on their peaks. On the U.S.A side, the closest road ended at the drop zone, twelve miles distant.

Flying low in mountainous terrain was fraught with difficulties, fighting up and down drafts, sudden wind changes and gusts, weather shifts into fog, hail or sleet and with altitude making response sluggish and limiting the load. As pilots, Fred and Ralph had one thing going for them: they knew these mountains and their choppers' capabilities. Each had logged thousands of hours on the Bell 212 and, together, they did all of their own mechanics on the craft. When they got into the cockpit, they were at one with a very reliable machine that would do anything they asked of it.

At FBI Control Center in Seattle, Janet, Fred, Marion and Victor were getting a drone's-eye view of the operation. It had begun in the morning with the arrival at the Temple RV Park of the two bugged helicopters, six pickup trucks and a flat deck semi-trailer truck loaded with equipment. Soon another helicopter, this one "squawking" its official transponder identification, came in from the direction of Oliver and landed. Twenty minutes later, probably after a coffee break, the "official" helicopter loaded eight people and duffel bags, then took off toward the exploration site.

Marion said, "That's probably the crew for the exploration site going in first."

They watched as the chopper dropped off the men and their gear and returned to the RV park where the ground crew attached the helicopter's long line to a cargo net of equipment, lifted it off the trailer and headed up the mountain. They waited throughout the morning, watching various loads being ferried up to the exploration site. About one o'clock, a ten-ton van arrived at the RV park and they watched as bales of cargo, presumably marijuana, were taken out of the truck and placed in a cargo net.

One helicopter started up and, after warming up and hooking up to the sling's cable, took the load up the mountain, staying in the shelter of the canyons, across the border and to the Loomis River landing site where a similar ten-ton truck and two men were waiting. After dropping the load, the chopper landed and dropped someone off. The chopper returned the way it came. In the meantime, the second smuggling chopper was bringing a load and had just cleared the pass at the exploration site but selected a different path for the run down to the Loomis River landing zone.

They watched as the truck at the Loomis landing site departed with its two ton cargo. Victor said, "That may be all they're doing today?"

Janet said, "We'll know when the choppers return."

They watched as the choppers made it back to the RV park and were towed inside the big shed. "Looks as if that's it for today but there'll be more tomorrow or the next day maybe as they're keeping the choppers there overnight. In the meantime, let's follow those trucks, especially the one moving out of the Loomis River site. Our surveillance team is tracking it. The one on the Canadian side let's follow with the drone as far as we can. Shirley's people are also going to track it. Also, this gives us a pretty good idea where the sentries are placed."

Fred said, "O.K. I bet you're right. They'll probably run for at least one more day. The legitimate part of the operation is booked for a full week. Maybe they'll take advantage of all that time. When do we spring the trap?"

Janet said, "The more we wait, MAYBE the more we can track to its destination or destinations. It's a hard call. We've also got our assault teams standing by and they don't like being idle. Did anyone check the weather forecast?"

The decision was made to watch for another day. They watched next day as four loads were delivered. They noticed a pattern emerging, as the truck coming to the RV site was always a rented ten ton. However, different trucks went to the Loomis landing zone. One semi-trailer arrived for the first and second load but a ten-ton van came in for the third and fourth load.

The surveillance teams followed the trucks from Loomis River to a ranch in the hills on the east side of the Columbia River near Wenatchee, about a three-hour drive. They managed to stake out the ranch and observed other vehicles coming and going. Each was followed.

At the end of the day the smugglers' helicopters were bedded down and guarded in the shed on the RV park. Two of the Loomis River sentries departed, but two remained, one by the entrance to the logging road near the town of Loomis and one at a fork in the road about five miles up the logging road, where one fork led into another valley where a reforestation crew was camped. Janet said, "Looks as if two of the sentries are going to camp out. That may be a sign that the next day's going to be important. Let's spring the trap tomorrow. Victor, get on to the assault teams and Roger Sanchez and his people and tell them to move in for a morning assault tomorrow. We can give them the likely locations for the sentries but remind them we'll vector them in when we see where they are tomorrow. Did anyone check the weather forecast?"

Next day, in FBI Control Center in Seattle, Victor had been coordinating the assault teams from the early hours of the morning before Janet, Marion and Fred arrived at six-thirty. Janet walked in and handed Victor a cup of his favorite coffee that she had picked up at the kiosk across the street. He grinned and said, "Thanks, much appreciated. I need a caffeine jolt about now."

"Yeah, I figured as much. How are we doing?"

"All teams on the sentries are in place close to the positions we saw yesterday. No problem getting to the two sentries who camped out overnight but we'll have to wait for the others to show up before we can vector the teams in. In the meantime, our guys are hiding. As far as the landing site, our people made it to the riparian way and are hiding. We've got the two assault choppers and teams over at Spectacle Lake standing by and the attack chopper is sitting in an alpine meadow up by the border about a mile away from the smugglers' normal flight path."

"I guess we're set then. Let's see what unfolds."

They watched the RV site as the airlift for the exploration camp started up and the two bugged helicopters were readied. On the Loomis side, the other two sentries returned and assumed their former positions. With Victor's help, the assault teams assigned to the remaining sentries had no problem creeping up on them.

They watched as a semi-trailer truck following two people on cross-country motorbikes made its way to the Loomis landing site. Once they arrived, a radio transmission came from the site: "On deck. Check in if all clear." This was followed by four sets of double clicks and numbers from one to four from the sentries checking in. This was followed by a cell phone text message: "OK."

Janet said to Victor, "O.K., they've checked in and we've pinpointed them; you can tell the teams to take them out."

In the field, each team chose their own way to neutralize their target, depending on the circumstances. One was tazered in the neck, another tackled by two agents, another succumbed to a chokehold when an agent snuck up on him and the last was knocked on the head with a sap (not regulation), then tackled by another agent. None had a chance to give a warning.

They watched as the three men at the Loomis site opened the back doors of the trailer, spread out a cargo net and cable and proceeded to fill it with bales of something. Fred drew everyone's attention to the RV site where one of the smugglers' choppers was taking off with a load. Victor relayed this to the teams in the field and called in the assault helicopters. The attack chopper started up but stayed on the ground waiting until notified by Victor that the smuggler chopper was south of them.

Victor then told the assault team at the Loomis landing, "Chopper ETA eight minutes."

The Loomis landing zone (LZ) was a flat gravel lot at the end of the logging road from Loomis. It was surrounded for hundreds of yards by barren land of tree stumps and torn-up earth scattered with branches and rocks from the clear-cut logging that took place the year before; the area was now awaiting tree planting. On one side of the narrow valley was a riparian zone of tall trees and scrub brush, about three hundred yards distant, through which a creek roared, swollen by spring run-off.

Fred brought his chopper into the Loomis landing zone, gently setting his cargo sling of a ton of bud close to the rear of the waiting semi-trailer truck beside David and Mack, the driver. He then flicked the quick release lever that disconnected the cable from the chopper and, after it fell to the ground, David and Mack began to pull the cargo net away from the bales of bud. Fred then eased the chopper back across the landing to where Joe was waiting with the end of the cable for the next load. Fred settled his machine to within six feet of the ground long enough for Joe to run under and hook up the cable. He stayed hovering for the few seconds it took for Joe to hook on, duck out in front and give a thumbs up. He was beginning to lift off when all hell broke loose.

From a corner of his right eye, Fred saw a movement in the riparian zone and strained to look closer. He saw half a dozen armed SWAT troops in black fatigues and helmets running toward the landing. They had just cleared the bush and had fanned out. He toggled his helmet mike and shouted, "Bandits at the creek! Bandits at the creek!"

He continued to lift off, taking the strain on his cargo net and then accelerating upward and forward when he had the weight of the load. He bought the guys on the ground a few seconds by flying directly at the agents and dropping his load over them. Some scattered to avoid the falling cargo but others continued to advance at a run. Fred then brought his chopper back to the LZ and landed on the other side of the truck to afford a little cover from the approaching agents.

In the meantime, Mack had run from the back of the trailer to the cab of the truck and climbed into the cab. It looked as if he would try to make a run for it. As the chopper descended, Joe and David ran for the chopper and both dove head first into the open cargo bay. When Fred felt them add their lurching weight to the chopper, he pulled up and away from the running agents. Three agents stopped and aimed their weapons but thought better of shooting at the fleeing chopper heading down the valley toward other agents. They had strict orders not to fire unless fired upon.

The chopper flew down the valley for about ten seconds until Fred sighted two choppers about ten miles away coming up the valley toward them. He also saw a dust plume distant on the road and could make out three black SUVs coming fast. He turned right while climbing, almost shaving the boughs of some trees on a near vertical face of a mountain and doubled back up the canyon. He was too high for agents on the ground to shoot when he went back over the LZ where he noticed the agents had surrounded the truck's cab and were hauling Mack off his driver's seat onto the ground.

As the chopper gained a little forward stability after its turn, Joe and David managed, while hanging on to cargo webbing, to move forward toward the back of the pilot's seat where David picked up helmets with communication headsets from the net pocket on the back of Fred's seat. They put on the helmets. David was first to speak. "Shit, that was close. They must have been lying in wait."

Fred said, "Yeah, they must have taken the sentries first. They're coming in with choppers too."

"Can you outrun them?"

"They look like MH-6 Little Birds configured to carry assault troops. They're faster than us by fifteen to thirty knots but my bet is they'll just go to the LZ. Looks as if we're safe."

After a few more seconds flying up the canyon, Fred could make out a speck in the distance. It was growing. "She-it, I spoke too soon. Looks as if we've got a reception committee coming down on us from the north. Hold on!"

The two craft came toward each other at a combined speed of over two hundred seventy miles an hour. "I guess we're going to play chicken!" said Fred as he flew straight for the chopper. His opponent blinked first and dove below at the last second then came up and turned around to give chase. Fred said, "That's a BZ201 Police Special but they've rigged it with twin machine guns. Shit. It's faster than us. Shit. Shit. Shit."

While hanging on, Joe and David had hooked into safety straps hanging from the ceiling that would keep them in the cabin. Fred said, "I've got two AK 47s under the co-pilot's seat and six extra clips. If they start shooting, you've got to get them. Hold on!"

As the FBI chopper began to gain on them flying up their rear, Fred began evasive maneuvers just a few feet, it seemed, above the cascading creek. At one hundred twenty miles an hour, he was zigging and zagging around twists and turns in the river's canyon trying to keep outcrops of rocks and trees between them and the other chopper. He varied his pattern, sometimes jumping up and over an obstruction or left or right then diving down to creek level.

The FBI pilot got a clear shot and unleashed a tracer-filled burst in front of Fred as a warning shot. A signal to surrender.

"Shit. They want to play rough!" said Fred. "Shoot when I bring them up on the left hand side." He then pulled back and slowed his machine quickly, too quickly for the FBI pilot to react, and passed them on their left hand side. David braced himself beside the open cargo door on the right side and Joe, an ex-Navy SEAL, took position beside the open door on the left. He fired a short burst as the chopper passed by and another at the belly of it as the pilot pulled up and slowed down. The FBI pilot ducked his craft down and under, moving to the right side of their chopper. He then took a run at them and fired a burst before Joe put three holes in the windshield above the pilot and the FBI chopper lurched up and to the right.

As Joe paused to change the magazine, he noticed David lying on the floor in a pool of blood. "Dave's been hit!" he exclaimed.

Fred said, "Me too! I took one in the thigh! We've got one more chance, that's probably it! I'm going to get on top of them! Hold on. Left side again!"

Fred dove to the bottom of the canyon with the FBI pilot following and firing sporadic bursts but missing as Fred randomly changed direction and altitude. A short distance further up the creek bed the canyon tightened steep and narrow at a rockslide. Fred flew into the gap and immediately slowed, dove and turned left up a narrow box canyon that had been hidden. The other craft flew by, slow to respond, then slowed and began to turn around to go up the box canyon searching to again make contact.

Meanwhile, Fred had climbed straight up and was able to come down close on top of the FBI chopper to within one hundred feet from the right rear. This gave Joe easy opportunity to empty his gun into the single engine and upper fuselage of the BZ201. He must have hit a rotor blade as the chopper lurched out of control. Part of a blade flew away. The craft went down quickly, only a hundred feet or so, to crash into treetops.

As he leveled off heading up the canyon toward the mining camp, Fred said, "Those BZ201s are f—ing pigs to fly. Slow to respond and fatiguing to the pilot. I've flown them and hate 'em. We probably did the FBI a favor getting rid of that piece of junk for 'em."

"Dave's gone, man. Can you make it?"

"Shit! Think so. My leg's stiffening up a bit but I can still work the pedal. I've got a red light showing one engine's heating up but I can run on one if need be for up to thirty minutes. That's lots of time, especially with no real load on. But can you get into the first aid kit for some battle dressings and try to stop the blood?"

Joe did so and was able to get dressings on both sides of the wound. He then moved up into the co-pilot's seat and said, "We got about two minutes to go?"

Fred said, "We're pretty close." He keyed his mike and said, "Drill Base, Drill base, clear the deck, we've got a problem."

Fred brought the chopper in to a fast and bumpy landing at the exploration site. The ground crew and Joe helped get him out of the cockpit but the movement opened his wound again. They managed to staunch the bleeding with more dressings.

Ralph, with Joseph aboard, brought the other chopper in empty from the RV site, transferred David and Fred to it, then took off for the clinic at Midlake Reservation.

Chapter 41

Hector picked up his phone on the fourth ring. Janet said, "Hi Hector, you'll be pleased to learn our interception at Loomis River worked pretty well."

"Pretty well?"

"Yeah. We observed three shipments then moved in on the fourth. Caught them in the act. We seized a ton of marijuana and a ton of cocaine and we took down a truck driver and six sentries. Also, we've been following the first deliveries from a transshipment point in Wenatchee on the way to what looks like purchasers in California and Arizona. They used an assortment of vehicles to bring the goods to and from the landing zone to a transshipment point on a farm near Wenatchee. We staked it out and later arrested six people there. We also seized about two tons of weapons there that may have been intended to ship across the border."

"Good. Good. However, knowing you very well, I feel you're about to let the other shoe drop and tell me something went wrong. What is it?"

"Uh, yeah…Well, ah, we lost another helicopter…. But the pilots are O.K."

"What? You're gonna get a reputation for destroying expensive pieces of machinery! Nobody's going to want to assign any helicopters to you! How did that happen? But first, what about our agents and pilots? Is everyone O.K.?"

"None of our agents or pilots were shot. In fact, no shots were fired at the landing zone or when rounding up the sentries. We had one agent kicked by a horse that broke two ribs and another agent twisted an ankle crossing a stream. However, the pilots in the attack helicopter had a gun battle with the smuggler's helicopter when it fled the scene."

"Don't tell me, the smuggler pilot got the best of our pilots? Didn't we have pretty good armament? Wasn't that chopper equipped with twin machine guns and faster than theirs? Didn't you send the chopper and pilots down to Fort Lewis to practice interceptions? What did the smugglers have?"

"Looks as if the smugglers' helicopter had a more skillful pilot. There were two guys in the cargo bay shooting back with automatic weapons, probably AK 47s. Anyway, our helicopter sustained engine and blade damage that forced them down.

303

Fortunately, they had a fairly soft landing and managed to walk away."

"That's something."

"We picked up some cell phone transmissions between the mining exploration camp and the medical clinic at the Midlake Reservation alerting them to prepare to take some wounded. So, it looks as if our helicopter pilots scored some hits. I'll know more when they debrief. Right now, they're still sitting in the bush waiting for an airlift rescue.

"The smuggler's chopper made it across the border and landed at the exploration site. They called in another chopper and transferred some wounded. Our drone observed a chopper that took a bee line to the Midlake Reservation."

"Hmm, that could prove interesting. Did you get any of the leaders in the round up?"

"No. There were two guys at the Loomis LZ that dove into the smuggler's helicopter as it took off. I guess one may have been the guy in charge at the site. All those arrested though, were natives from the local area. They all have military combat service with elite branches and they've all lawyered up. I doubt if they will tell us anything. We did seize a laptop there and it will probably tell us something when our technicians go through it."

Roger Sanchez walked into the Oroville Border Patrol general office with two strangers, a man and a woman. He ushered them into his office, then he came out of his office and went up to Agent Doris MacKay, who was at her desk. She was typing a report on her computer. Doris was one of the few remaining heavy smokers in the office and was known for ducking out back every fifteen to twenty minutes to get a puff. Doris was a plump five foot ten two hundred sixty pound forty-three year old woman with black graying hair tied in a ponytail. She had been on the force for eighteen years, was twice divorced and living as a single parent with four children aged ten through sixteen. She served as the office administrator, scheduling and records officer for the detachment.

Sanchez said, "Doris, I've got a couple of people in my office I'd like you to meet. Can you join us?"

"Sure boss."

She got up and Sanchez let her lead him into his office then he closed the door. "Doris, this is Special Agent Martin and this is

Special Agent Wong. They're with the FBI." She nodded to each of them.

Agent Helen Martin said, "Doris MacKay, you are under arrest for espionage, aiding and abetting, smuggling and as an accessory to murder. You have the right to remain silent...."

Doris brought the back of a hand to her mouth and said, "No! No. Oh no! What do you mean?"

Agent Steve Wong came up behind her and proceeded to handcuff her while Helen Martin removed Doris's utility belt with gun, mace, handcuffs and radio. After Helen finished reciting Doris her rights, Roger Sanchez looked at Doris with a very sour look and said, "Doris, the FBI do not make a case lightly! I've seen the evidence they have on you and I've even heard some of your phone conversations alerting smugglers to our operations. I'm sorry, but you've lost all my respect."

Concurrently, Border Patrol Agent Scott Richmond, a fifteen-year veteran of the force, was pulling his patrol vehicle to the side of the road in response to a black SUV that pulled up behind him and turned on its blue and red flashing police lights. He was just into the start of his shift about four blocks away from Border Patrol Oroville office. He got out of his vehicle and was walking back toward them by the time the two FBI agents, along with Ken O'Brien got out of their vehicle. He said, "Hi fellas. What's up?"

Ken O'Brien introduced them and they showed their badges. Scott said, "You got something going down?"

Ken O'Brien said, "You could say that."

Special Agent Jim Smith said, "We're here for you. Scott Richmond, you are under arrest for espionage, aiding and abetting smuggling and as an accessory to murder. You have the right to remain silent...."

"What?" Special Agent Pedro Romo came up behind him and handcuffed him, then removed Scott's utility and weapons belt. Scott submitted saying, "Surely, you must be mistaken."

Ken O'Brien said, "Scott, they've been on to you for quite a while and have been very thorough in building their case. You've been leaking information of our operations and being paid for it. You're in big trouble."

"I don't know what you're talking about, said Scott, "but I guess I had better be quiet until I have my lawyer present."

Doris, with the advice of her lawyer, elected to "tell all" in return for a plea bargain. She readily named her contacts in Canada singling out David, Joseph and Willie but she claimed she knew nothing of anyone on the American side. She had been on retainer with them for the past five years. She had met Joseph through a mutual friend and had been recruited into one of the environmental movements Joseph had been promoting at the time. Things had started out small at a few hundred dollars each tip when she was asked, but it had settled into a regular retainer of one thousand a month.

Scott was a different story. He refused to talk until the agents laid out his financial records, a statement from two casinos where he had periodically gone into debt and transcripts of phone calls. The final stimulus was phone records and a taped conversation showing him talking to a Korean gang leader in Vancouver and a subsequent deposit originating in Vancouver of five thousand dollars into his bank account. He confessed to a gambling addiction that resulted in divorce and child support payments. Other mysterious deposits to his bank account and large cash expenditures were questioned and eventually led to other connections with organized crime and to the Midlake smugglers.

Janet's boss, Steve Wilson, was quick to call a press conference where the seized drugs were prominently displayed and executives from all the agencies were present to share the credit. In the press release that she read, Janet emphasized the interception was part of an ongoing multi-agency investigation where warrants in California and Arizona were being served as the press conference was taking place. She made sure to laud the great co-operation and teamwork provided by the DEA, ATF, ICE – border patrol and the local sheriffs and state police. She especially singled out Roger Sanchez and Ken O'Brien of Oroville Border Patrol for their "superb assistance and teamwork of their agents involved." She also tied the seizure into the "incident at Molson," linking the operation to the same "smuggling syndicate" and the arrest of perpetrators who had been present at both and that accessory to murder charges were pending for some. The photo opportunity of the large quantity of drugs ensured national TV coverage.

The press conference went well until the end when Steve Wilson asked for questions from the press. A reporter, Mary Jane

Veerdun, from the top Seattle TV station, asked, "Is it correct you lost another helicopter in this incident? Is it true it was shot down in a dogfight with the smugglers' helicopter? Why have you not informed us of that?"

This caused an uproar among the press. Steve Wilson managed to get everyone calmed down and then Janet came to the mike to explain, "Yes, we lost a helicopter but we are pleased to report the crew was not hurt. Our pilots attempted to intercept the smuggler's helicopter but it managed to flee into Canada."

As cell phones had been required to be turned off during the press conference, a few reporters ran out of the room frantically turning on their cell phones to call in the big news. First one out with it in press or on the air would have a full-blown attention-getting scoop. A few press reporters and all the camera crews and TV reporters remained and began pestering Janet with questions. Janet was forced to divulge that the FBI helicopter was an armed attack craft.

Mary Jane Veerdun, in front of her camera crew, with lights and camera running, asked, "Was your attack helicopter ordered to shoot down the smuggler's helicopter?"

"All personnel involved in the apprehension intercept were under orders not to shoot unless fired upon," replied Janet calmly.

Mary Jane would not let go. "Did that also apply to your assault chopper or were you gunning for the smugglers' aircraft?"

She had some inside information, thought Janet.

She paused for a heartbeat, then said, "The assault helicopter pilots were under orders to attempt to communicate first by radio and with other methods, such as hand or light signals, to order the smuggler helicopter to land. If that failed, they were authorized to fire tracers across their path – an international signal to surrender."

"And did they do that?"

"Yes."

"I see. Then they could shoot down the smuggler helicopter if they ignored it?"

"Yes."

"Then they opened fire – shoot to kill?"

"Apparently. We are still debriefing the pilots."

"And the smugglers shot back and shot down the FBI helicopter?"

"Yes, they shot back."

"I understand your aircraft was armed with twin machine guns and that your pilots had practiced with the military at Fort Lewis. What weapons did the smugglers have?"

"It looks as if they had assault rifles."

"So… your aircraft outgunned them – maybe was faster too – yet your helicopter was shot down and they got away?"

At that point Steve Wilson stepped in to end the press conference stating the gunfight and the crash were still under investigation and that more would be revealed once it was verified.

The press grabbed the downing of the chopper and played it up. The first newspaper headlined, "FBI Chopper Shot Down in Dogfight." The successful interception of the smuggling operation took a distant seat to the sensational sizzle of vividly playing up the dogfight.

The next day Steve Wilson met with Janet and said, "I've been on the phone a number of times to the powers that be in D.C. Regrettably the shooting down of our chopper has made huge international press coverage and the D.C. folk see it as an embarrassment. They've called for a thorough review of the incident."

Janet said, "Nuts! Here we go again! We've debriefed the pilots. But D.C. wants something more formal?"

"'Fraid so. They're rounding up a Board of Review panel from Headquarters and the other agencies. It will convene day after tomorrow."

The Board of Review moved along at a fast pace beginning with a review of the radio transmissions, a review of the statements given by the pilots during their debriefing in which they described, step by step, the interception and the subsequent crash. The "black box" of the helicopter was thoroughly reviewed. Mechanical airworthiness of the helicopter was reviewed and it was determined the craft was in excellent shape before the crash. The pilots were then called to testify to the accuracy of their statements, add other comments on reflection, and to answer questions arising.

Testimony by their instructors established that both pilot and co-pilot had extensive experience flying various types of helicopters and had been well drilled in interception practice at Fort Lewis. Both had some prior combat experience, the pilot having served in Iraq and the co-pilot in Afghanistan, but in transport aircraft, not assault craft.

When the pilot was on the stand, one of the Board of Review panel members, Gordon MacNeil, representing DEA asked, "Do you feel there is anything you could have or should have done differently? Or do you feel the smugglers just had a better pilot?"

The pilot, Agent John McCluskey, replied, "If you're trying to hang blame on me for pilot error, I take exception. The BZ201 should never have been used as an attack aircraft. It's a sluggish piece of shit."

That caused an uproar, shocking all including the official court reporter who continued typing but looked up at the pilot with an open mouth, as if saying "oh."

Gordon MacNeil jumped in. "Is that just your opinion or do you have something to substantiate it with?"

"Any pilot who has flown it will say the BZ201 is both fatiguing and slushy to respond compared to many others. It is not a nimble aircraft. It should never have been configured as an attack helicopter, at least as far as air-to-air combat is concerned. I am not alone in this opinion. I have documentation from an independent survey of border patrol pilots and others flying the craft for patrol and intercept who were unanimous in stating it is slushy, sluggish and fatiguing to fly. The border patrol had taken delivery of eleven such craft at the time of the survey and the independent survey was in response to pilot complaints. This is an open source document you'll find on the Internet. Here's a copy of the report for your record."

Hector Skog, representing FBI headquarters, was acting as chairman. He turned to Marvin Stout, the panel member representing ICE-Border Patrol, and asked, "Is this correct?"

Marvin replied, "Yes, very true. We wound up taking that type of aircraft off intercept service on the border."

The Board of Review wound up shortly after that. A confidential report was generated stating the FBI aircraft was outmaneuvered. It was recommended the BZ201 not be configured as an attack craft but was more suited to personnel transport.

A day after the report was handed down, Janet met Steve Wilson at the coffee machine in the office and Steve said, "Have you read the report on the dogfight?"

"Yes. Guess we're all clear. We didn't have any say in the choice of helicopters. They were assigned to us directly from D.C.

There's a rumor running around that we inherited that chopper from ICE."

"I wonder? It might be interesting to learn who had the brainwave to arm it with twin machine guns and make it an attack craft?"

"Not a pilot."

"No. I heard it was some engineer or mechanic who figured the guns and ammunition would be too heavy for our lighter choppers."

"Maybe. We'll never know. It'll be interesting what they come up with next. Can you see the border patrol equipped with missiles?"

Chapter 42

Ralph Jones brought his chopper in for a landing in the near empty parking lot of the Midlake Band's medical clinic. Two medical personnel in white smocks, a man, Doctor Jerry Rainbird, M.D, age fifty-five, and a woman, Nurse Mary Wildrose, R.N., age forty-five, were waiting with a gurney. Joseph had phoned ahead to alert them that Fred had taken a bullet in the thigh.

Joseph pulled open the left side cargo door while the chopper was touching down. Jerry and Mary sensed the urgency and, ducking low, pushed the gurney, which also had a plywood "spine board" and a large medical bag on top, to the open door. Joseph shouted to them, "We've got one unconscious with a thigh wound who's lost a lot of blood and one DOA."

Joseph made room as Jerry pushed him aside and clambered aboard. He saw the large bloodied battle dressing bandage on Fred's left thigh then looked sideways and noted the body covered with a blue tarp. He took a quick step toward the body and pulled the blue tarp off. He checked for carotid pulse and noted the large exit wound of the bullet in David's neck. Finding no pulse and noting there was no pulsing or oozing blood, he quickly pulled away to attend to Fred, looking at the bandage on both sides of the thigh and then quickly checking Fred from head to toe looking for other damage.

Joseph put the tarp back covering David's body as Jerry shouted above the noise of the engine beginning to wind down. "Sorry Chief, but I had to make sure."

Joseph said. "I understand. Let's take care of Freddie."

Mary pushed in the spine board and medical kit along the cabin floor then climbed aboard. Jerry said, "The dressing looks as if it's staunching the blood well but we've got to be careful in moving him. I'm going to get a saline drip going and give him some morphine. Then, we've got to carefully get him on the spine board, then on to the gurney. Chief, once we strap his legs together in order to use one as a splint for the other, I want you to slide the board under him while we gently roll him. Got it?"

Joseph nodded. Shortly, they had Fred on the gurney on his way into the clinic.

Joseph had recruited Jerry as medical officer for the band. An honor student on a military scholarship, Jerry had become a doctor and served with the U.S. Marines where Joseph had met him. When he retired, Joseph recruited him for the Midlake Band. He had no problem passing the medical exams for the Province of British Columbia and was enjoying his semi-retirement with a relatively small practice of a thousand souls.

He had met Mary when he arrived at the clinic as she had been in residence as the band's nursing officer/midwife for twenty years. She was divorced and Jerry fell in love. They were now man and wife. In collaboration with Joseph, they had seen to it that the clinic was well equipped as a surgery, which had proven itself time and again, enabling them to handle difficult births, broken limbs, cuts, stabbings and the occasional gunshot.

As they entered the surgery area of the clinic, Jerry said to Joseph, "Mary and I'll be busy here. You and Ralph can attend to David. Bottom cupboard, right side over there." He pointed. "You'll find a body bag. There's another gurney, just in the hall. Bring him in and leave him in the hall for now.

Joseph and Ralph did as they were told. Ralph found cleaning supplies and rags in another cupboard, then went out to clean up the cargo bay of the chopper. When he returned after putting the dirty rags in a garbage can, he said, "I guess I'd better get the f—ing chopper back to its f—ing roost cuz it may be attracting too much f—ing attention here." Joseph nodded and said, "Thanks Ralph. Much appreciated. Yeah, no sense going back to Temple River right now."

In a few minutes, Joseph could hear the chopper winding up and it was soon on its way at tree top level.

After about a half hour in surgery, Jerry came out to the clinic's small waiting room where Joseph was staring out the window. Jerry said, "Mary's making Fred comfortable. He'll be fine. He's still unconscious but that's because he's sedated. The wound was a through and through with a jacketed bullet so not any terrible ripping damage and it missed the major arteries and veins. Thank god it wasn't a mushroom hunting round. Looks as if you were playing war with the military."

"Close to it. We got jumped by feds at a drop site. Lucky Fred managed to control the chopper after he got shot and the bird took a hit. He just barely made it to the exploration site where we were able to tend to him. We transferred to Ralph's chopper to fly them here."

"We got some plasma into him, cauterized the wound and stitched him up. And we'll be with him for the next twenty-four hours at least to keep an eye on things. I didn't get a good look at the face, who's the DOA? "

Joseph, choking back tears, looked out the window again and said, "David. That's my son David."

Jerry came over and placed a hand on Joseph's shoulder. "Oh Joseph, I'm so sorry."

Joseph called Hazel. He didn't think it appropriate to tell her the sad news over the phone. He wanted to see her. Instead, he asked her to pick him up at the clinic. She arrived a few minutes later, took one look at his tear-stained face and feared the worst. She said, "It's David, isn't it? Is he dead?" He could only nod affirmative. She ran into his arms and they sobbed together.

After a few moments, he chokingly said, "We have lost a wonderful, wonderful son and a fine, fine warrior." He went back to crying. They hugged tighter.

With her head on Joseph's chest and hugging him, she sobbed, then pulled away in horror. "Norma, we've got to tell Norma and the children! The children have lost their father!"

"We'll do it together. Best if we go to the house. Also maybe pick up Norma's mom and grandma so they can stay with her. First, we need to talk with Jerry and Mary about arrangements."

Mary brought in cups of tea for them, expressed her condolences, hugged and comforted Hazel for a while. After a few moments, she turned to Joseph. "Fred's doing O.K. He's strong. He'll need some therapy later though. We'll keep him here for a few days. Is it O.K. now to call his wife?"

Joseph said, "The call should be mine to make. I'll do it right now." He went into the hall to make the call.

Hazel said to Mary, "I'm so sorry! I was so shocked to learn about David, I didn't realize someone else was involved. You say Fred's been hurt?"

"A gunshot to the thigh but he'll be all right."

Joseph entered the room. "Cora's on her way. She'll drop the kids off with her sister."

Jerry entered and Mary left, saying, "I'll check on Fred."

"We'd best wait here for Cora before we go to Norma," said Joseph. "I told Cora what happened but I think we should be here when she arrives."

Jerry said, "I know you're about to go and tell Norma but I don't think she should view the body as the face is quite disfigured. I can move him for now to our morgue locker but will you want burial later or what?"

Joseph met Hazel's eyes and thought for a few moments. "We don't want the police off the reservation involved so whatever we do will be on the reservation and quite soon. We don't want anyone viewing the body. For public consumption, we'll say he died in a fall off a cliff or off a horse. We can make up the story later. That would help explain the helicopter dropping into the clinic. For the sake of the tribe and the family, we'll need to have a funeral or celebration of life. Darling, what do you think?"

"He loved that trip he took to Asia. Remember him talking once over dinner that if he went, he'd want to be cremated – like the Hindus and the Buddhists?"

The funeral took place two days later. Tribal police blocked the roads into the reservation and admitted only listed guests, directing some to the Celebration of Life service and others, mainly bikers, to the cremation site. Press and the RCMP were not welcome.

The service was a commemoration to celebrate David's all too short life. It was held in the school gym, which doubled as the auditorium. Every seat was taken and many were standing for the short ceremony. No casket was present but a large framed head and shoulders portrait of David was on an easel centered on the stage in front of a number of chairs for immediate family and speakers and a podium. From the stage, The Grand Chief of the Okanagan Nation presided as the leader of the ceremony. After he called order, announcing the purpose of the gathering, he called for the three-step cleansing ritual. "In order to drive out bad spirits, for our prayers to be carried on to the creator, and bring in good spirits and good influences. First, we will cleanse with white sage."

A woman, the band's spiritual leader, finely dressed in beaded buckskin dress and moccasins, feathers in her black and gray braided hair and beads around neck, wrists and ankles, accompanied by three other women similarly dressed, started the ceremony by ritually lighting dried white sage contained in unglazed clay bowls. They passed among the crowd, pausing with the smoking bowls in front of every individual and, using a large feather, waving the smoke toward them. Typically, each recipient "smudged" by waving the smoke toward them with their hands and rubbing it over their hearts or faces.

After the women completed making their rounds of the audience, the Grand Chief held up his arms for attention and said,

"Now, we will call on the Spirit of Cedar to help our prayers be heard by our creator."

The women switched to another set of bowls, lit the dried cedar fronds in them and once again passed among the audience. In the audience, some chose to mumble prayers while others remained silent.

After the women again completed making their rounds of the audience, the Grand Chief held up his arms for attention and said, "We will now light the sweetgrass and pray together as the purifying smoke comes among us and rises to the Creator and spreads throughout the universe. For the benefit of those of us who share our spirituality with western religions, Pastor Brian West will lead us in the Twenty-third Psalm." The Deacon stepped up beside the Grand Chief and recited the Psalm, leading the audience through it as the women took the smoking pots through the audience

After the prayer, the Grand Chief called on Brian (The Deacon), to present the eulogy and on some family members to present stories. Brian did an excellent job, not only reminiscing about David's youth and his current happy experiences, such as his marriage to Norma, births of his children and hunting and fishing together, but also weaving in allusions to spiritual beliefs from Navajo, Hopi and Costa Rican tribes and of their spiritual roots in Aztecan beliefs and even their relationship to Tibetan Buddhism and the common "Nature Philosophy" spirituality shared with all native American tribes. He had all concluding that David's spirit had passed on to another life.

The commemoration concluded with all in the audience lining up to present condolences to the immediate family who had assembled in a reception line below the stage. From there, people went into the school's cafeteria where food and drink were served. When the last guest had offered condolences, the Grand Chief, the medicine women, some close male relatives, and a few male family friends, including Willie, Fred, Ralph, Donny and the Deacon, left in limousines, pick-ups, and cars in a procession to attend the cremation. Leading the procession were twenty members of the North American executive of the Devil's Brew riding large Harley Davidson motorbikes. Norma and her children, with her mother and father, Hazel and daughter, Veronica, stayed with the reception in the school.

The cremation was in a newly plowed field in a box canyon about two miles away from the school and half a mile from the Devil's Brew clubhouse. The provincial Forest Fire Protection

Service had been informed there would be a funeral pyre. As it was early into the official fire season and, realizing it was fruitless to object, permission had been granted. The funeral pyre was built partially into the ground. A trench, six feet wide, ten feet long and six feet deep, had been dug by a backhoe and the ground scraped down to bare earth for a radius of two hundred yards around the pit. At the bottom of the trench, two metal pipes were run parallel two feet apart the length of the trench. They had been perforated along the top and were connected to pipes in a shallow trench that had been backfilled to keep them cool. Underground, the metal pipes ran for twenty feet where they connected to hoses which ran to two large propane tanks that had been buried to keep cool with only their valves reachable a foot below ground level about two hundred feet from the pyre. Very dry firewood, some of it soaked in kerosene, was cross-laid six feet deep in the trench topped off with a one foot layer of wet cedar boughs upon which was laid the simple pine coffin containing David's body. The cedar boughs were intended to provide purification smoke at the start of the fire. Wood had been racked four feet deep surrounding the coffin and rising to three feet above the coffin.

A large white catering tent, and twenty porta potties had been placed three hundred yards away upwind from the pyre. Over five hundred bikers from the Devil's Brew and associated gangs were in attendance. As the procession of mourners from the formal service arrived, an honor guard of motorcycles joined them and approached the pyre. Beginning at a distance of one hundred yards, three lines of motorcycles and riders encircled the pyre facing it. There was an opening six bikes wide at one end of the encircling bikes for access to the pyre and for the cycles to exit through when the fire took hold.

The cyclists leading the procession entered the circle and took positions around the pyre. The Grand Chief, Joseph and his two remaining sons, Mike and Martin, emerged from the lead vehicle, a black Hummer, which had stopped at the entrance to the circle. Slowly, greeting some of the nearby attendees and accepting condolences, the small entourage made its way to the end of the funeral pyre.

When all were in attendance at the site, the sage, cedar and sweetgrass smudging ceremony was repeated, with the medicine women walking among the audience. At a signal from the Grand Chief, the medicine women began uttering a low chant and the Grand Chief handed Joseph a wooden torch. He turned and presented the

----

pitch coated end of the torch to Mike and Martin, who had each been given lighted candles by one of the medicine women. Together, Mike and Martin lit the torch. Holding the lighted torch high and turning full circle, Joseph shouted, "This man was a fine warrior! He died in battle as a warrior! He died with honor!" As he thrust the torch into the center of the pyre lighting the cedar boughs, a cheer went up from the crowd. He then stood back holding Mike and Martin tightly with an arm on each shoulder and backing away as the fire took hold. Behind them, the cyclists, starting from the inner circle out, began to move through the opening and cross the field to park around the catering tent. As the fire took hold, the propane was turned on to accelerate the fire.

The caterers laid on a plentiful and exotic buffet. Six bars were set up, each dispensing draft beer, assorted local wines, soft drinks, and hard liquor. Sugar bowls of bud and coke were on the bars and on the side tables in the tent.

The Grand Chief, Joseph, Mike and Martin and the Deacon mingled with the crowd for a half hour then departed to return to the other reception.

A few hours later, with the onset of darkness, only fire coals four feet deep remained in the pit. The group had disbursed, many to the clubhouse to continue drinking, leaving two less than sober braves to tend the fire, then recover the propane cylinders and fill in the trench and when things had cooled down.

That night, Joseph and Hazel were in their front room with Veronica, Mike and Martin. Veronica, the oldest at age 26, was a younger version of her mother. Mike, the older of the two boys, age 24, most resembled his father. Martin was the youngest, at 22, was tall and athletic like his brother. Mike said, "Mom and Dad, Veronica, Marty and I have been thinking. Should one or all of us quit college to help here with the family business?"

Hazel spoke up first, "How nice of you to think of it! But no, your dad and I talked about this the other night and we're both in agreement that we value you all getting an excellent education first and perhaps some worldly experience too. Then, later, depending on what you feel, we will always welcome you into the family business. On the other hand, if you choose not to, that's fine with us too. You'll always have our support and love."

317

Joseph said, "A good education, for aboriginals like us, is a rare commodity. So very few from our tribe have managed to go to university or enter a profession. We're working hard to change that. We're fortunate to have many of our young people now in colleges and universities and to have improved the retention rate of kids in school but much more has to be done. You're all bright and talented. We need you well educated.

"As I have said before, we have an obligation to help our people and an obligation to our ancestors who suffered so much from the coming of the white man destroying our ancient way of life and massacring our people. We must copy some of the white man's ways to outsmart them and take back some of what belongs to us – and that begins with a good education and experience in their "system." If you want to be a warrior, learn the ways of war of your enemy and use that against them. Not only in combat. The same goes for business and politics as both are different branches of war. We can easily justify supplying drugs and weapons to weaken the white man and for them to kill each other and we must support the welfare of our own people to prevent them from falling victim to drugs, alcohol and the depravation the white man has brought to them."

Hazel said, "We have lots of money to afford you good educations. Even if we were to stop all business today, we are wealthy and, as you have seen, we have been using some of our wealth for the betterment of our people."

"And same for political power and profile. You have been able to accomplish a lot, such as increasing the size of the reservation," said Veronica.

"And nurturing our wildlife, such as returning the sockeye," said Martin.

"And improving schooling," said Mike. "O.K. we go back to college. We love you, Mom and Dad."

Three days later, Joseph met Donny for lunch in the bistro at the Oak Dale winery. As usual, Donny had picked a quiet time and ensured their table was secluded. After being served their food, Donny, while pouring a wine he had selected, said, "I know you're hurting pretty bad right now but we need to talk. And I apologize in advance if I offend you in our discussion. We're long-time friends and brothers of the Devil's Brew and we will always be so."

"But?"

"You've sure fucked up our distribution system in this region."

"You're blaming me for the shootout?"

"Shootouts. Plural"

"Why? We got jumped by the FBI. That's all. They were following the supply lines stateside to the source."

"Nope! I got it from a very reliable individual that this is all a legacy from you using that f-ing archery weapon on those two border patrol officers a while ago."

"What? I stopped using it as I promised you!"

"You're associated with a terrorist threat somehow linked to that weapon. Anyway, it resulted in the Americans spending big time and money for the FBI, DEA, ATF and even ICE working together to track you down and in the process, they took down a lot of people in the drug distribution system on their side of the border. Add to that your successful shootout at Molson, which very much embarrassed the Fibbies – not that they didn't deserve it – and you have a lot of their resources dedicated to catching you. You're hot, man! H.O.T.! Get it?"

"I know that! I didn't need you to spell it out for me. It started with the archery weapon?"

"My sources say you and most of the others crossing the border on the smuggling have been identified by the FBI and warrants are out to apprehend at border crossings if and when you cross into America. Soon they'll be approaching the Canadian government for your extradition. They've started picking up your soldiers on the American side. You've got to lay low. Effectively, you're out of the smuggling business for now. They're concentrating on this sector – your back yard."

"What about extradition? Are they going to try that?"

"Not for a while. Apparently, they have some legalities they have to hurdle first. By the way, they arrested your two moles at Oroville border patrol and they've been talking."

Joseph was quiet for a while and Donny let him stew while finishing his glass of wine and pouring himself another. Then Joseph said, "Well, I guess I'm entitled to some bereavement leave – at least that's a good excuse to leave town for a friendlier climate."

"Where to? You can't go to your villa in the Florida Keys and staying in Canada may not be a good idea as Canada would have to honor a call for extradition if the Americans decide to go that route."

"I have a place in mind. A friend asked Hazel and me to spend some time on his yacht in the Maldives. Then, again, I promised to take Hazel along the Great Silk Road someday to meet some friends of mine. I guess we may want some new identity documents to take along, just in case."

Joseph turned the supervision of the meth lab and grow-op at the mine over to Willie who felt he should lay low in the mine or the backside of the reservation. They agreed that no cross-border smuggling would take place in their area for a while. In the interim, production from the mine would be channeled through Donny's Canadian network and, if he wished, Donny could move stuff across the border at other places across Canada where the Devil's Brew operated.

Joseph's "soldiers" on both sides of the border received large bonuses and were told it would have to tide them over for at least a year. All traces of contraband, including hard and soft records, were removed from the Omak warehouse, fruit packing plant and the Nursery to thwart the FBI if and when they served search warrants. The entrance to the weapons cache at the ranch at NightHawk was temporarily sealed by backfilling the entrance with rock.

Two days later, after turning all the Band's affairs over to his assistant and band manager, Gloria Muntz, Joseph and Hazel flew to Vancouver and caught a flight to Hong Kong where they spent a week playing tourist. Then they caught a flight to Bangkok, and settled for a month at a beachfront condo in Jomtien Beach, South of Bangkok on the Gulf of Siam. It was owned by an Indian chief from northern B.C. who offered it to them. After a relaxing month, they flew to the Maldives, with a stop in Mauritius to do some banking.

Chapter 43

Janet caught the call from Hector on the second ring. "Hi Janet. You're to join me in a séance tomorrow afternoon with the various agencies you met before on that weapon. Can you make it?"

"The usual time? I'll meet you at your office. Something new at their end?"

"Looks like it. See you tomorrow."

The next day, having made it to D.C on a red-eye flight, Janet met Hector in his office and, after greetings and with coffee in hand, she settled into an easy chair across the coffee table from Hector. "I hope we'll learn something positive," she said. "I'm getting pretty frustrated by the intractability of the Canadians not allowing "hot pursuit" into their territory across the border and their lack of co-operation concerning the Chief and his smuggling ring. They're stonewalling the request for extradition papers."

"Yeah, I can see why you're frustrated. You almost had him. Good try though. You redeemed yourself after Molson."

"But some, probably the key ones, still got away!"

Hector looked at his watch and said, "Oops, we're running close to the wire. We'd better get going – you know what parking's like at the Pentagon!"

The meeting was assigned to a conference room in one of the inner blocks on the floor housing the procurement offices. Janet recognized the same faces from last time: Sandford Crosley of CIA Langley; Caroline Weston of State Department; Ruth Dempsey of Homeland Security DC; Roger Pearson and Martin LeRoy of the Canadian Embassy DC; General Keith Baker of military intelligence and his aide, Captain Adam Chavez. There was a new recording secretary who was introduced as Chief Petty Officer Mary O'Hara. Janet was surprised to see Shirley Bains and her boss Richard Adair from CIA Bellingham also present.

General Baker called the meeting to order. "Ladies and gentlemen, let's get started. I shall be the chair for this meeting as we last met under my chairmanship. Our Canadian friends, Messers Pearson and LeRoy have something they wish to share with us. Who wants to lead off?" Martin Le Roy slightly raised his right hand as a gesture that he would lead. "O.K. Mr. LeRoy, please begin."

"Ladies and gentlemen, thank you for meeting with us again on such short notice. We are pleased to advise that our search for Kenneth Davidson, the inventor of the archery weapon, has borne fruit. We have located him, co-opted him, and have him under surveillance. Our intelligence people have learned that the factory has been moved out of British Columbia, where it had been situated on the Midlake Reservation – which ties in with your smugglers, Janet, and may explain why such a weapon was used in a smuggling operation. The equipment from the factory has been sent to a remote island in the Maldives and will soon be set up by Mr. Davidson. Now, are there any questions?"

After many people congratulated the Canadians for their success in finding and co-opting the inventor, Janet commented, "So, there's no evidence left in Canada? Is someone culpable left in Canada? How can we get at the new factory?"

Caroline Weston spoke up. "Janet, you and Shirley and your people have worked hard on this and made good progress. But I can see some frustration, perhaps reasoning that all may have been in vain because you didn't get to the source of the weapons. Not so. Look at how many drug distribution systems and drug seizures you and your multi-agency partnership have taken down during this! It's been excellent work. You'll be prosecuting at least three hundred people. Now though, your role in this is over as far as the archery weapons source is concerned. It's out of your jurisdiction – out of your hands. This is now a matter for the State Department, the Pentagon and NATO."

Janet said, "Thank you for those kind words. When looking at your main priority to locate the weapons factory, I see your point. However, there are still the cross border murders to deal with."

Roger Pearson stepped in. "Janet, you're right and we have some information that might assuage you there. It looks as if the Chief's son, David Branson, was the leader of the smuggling operation. Shirley, you have analyzed voice prints of various transmissions during the operations observed, and identified the son's voice doing the leading? And you've shared this information with Janet and her people? "

"That's right," Shirley replied.

"You never had the Chief's voice on the transmissions?"

"Yes, we did. We have him mainly giving or receiving short text messages. But we also have him 'in the open,' so to speak, right after the conflict at Loomis River. He called the medical center on the Midlake reserve to notify them they were bringing in wounded."

"You have identified the other voices and between you on the Canadian side and Janet in America, they are under surveillance?"

322

"Yes."

"As they have yet to be caught in Canada by the Canadian authorities, the best that can be done is pick them up if and/or when they legally enter America?"

Janet said, "That's what we've done. There is the possibility of extradition for those who were involved on U.S. soil and are now in Canada. However, all but two are natives and have dual citizenship. Extradition of natives – well, it's messy. And, I hesitate to say, Canadian authorities seem to be less than co-operative right now."

Martin Leroy said, "Yes, messy and difficult. It opens a hornet's nest concerning aboriginal rights and freedoms. But you can apprehend them if they enter America."

"On top of that," commented Shirley, "the surveillance techniques are classified and we may have been beyond the law in some instances. It could be hard to make a case without disclosure of how information was obtained."

"Point taken," said Hector. "We know who they are. We've observed them in action. Only thing we can do is either catch them in action again and get them dead to rights. Or, we can interrogate them when they enter America and see if anyone confesses – and that's unlikely. At least we have some electronic advantages – which we can't use in court. We could help the Canadians make a case but that will be very slow."

"Now that the moles have been taken out of Oroville border patrol, I don't see the FBI continuing in the lead on the smuggling operations. It really belongs back under the jurisdiction of Homeland Security and the IBET, sorry, the Integrated Border Enforcement Team," said Caroline Weston.

"Yes, thank you," said Ruth Dempsey. "Our regional people have always been included in the loop with Janet and her people – we've always had good cooperation. But, you're right, time to get back to normal operations and this is within the aegis of the IBET."

Janet was forced to say, "No problem."

"Janet, there's one thing that might please you," said Martin. "David, the Chief's son, is dead. He was apparently killed in a hiking accident on the reservation by falling off a cliff – which occurred the day of the shoot-out at Loomis River. The local authorities were not allowed to see the body and the Chief had it cremated in a funeral pyre on the reservation. We have it from a very reliable source that David died from gunshot wounds sustained at the Loomis River ambush."

Hector broke the silence on the way back to the airport. "Well Janet," he said, "looks as if you'll get some positive comments for your personnel file from the Secretary of State. But you're terribly quiet. What're you thinking?"

"I'm thinking I've just been blindsided and taken out of the game."

"You have. But it was nicely done. Besides, you've got lots of work ahead of you shepherding the many arrest cases to trial from all the smuggling operations. You'll be busy."

"Still, I'd like to have nailed the Chief!"

Chapter 44

Bob LeMay and Donna Cleveland had been hiking with Anne Cagney and Rick Simms for an hour since eight a.m. when they had parked their vehicle at a parking lot near an entrance to the Trans Canada Trail. Anne and Rick had been brought in from Vancouver for the event. They had followed the trail for about two miles then branched off overland following a southeasterly trail across a sparsely treed hillside and down into the lush meadow of a shallow valley. They had avoided the gravel road they knew was at the far end of the valley and concentrated on crossing the meadow into the woods on the other side. Closer to the woods, they could see the underbrush was clear, mainly grass trying to grow despite the shade canopy of the pine trees and the oily, pungent dead pine needles smothering the ground around the trees.

All stopped as Bob looked at the GPS. It was on his left wrist and looked not much bigger than a scuba diver's watch. Donna said, "We must be pretty close now."

Bob said, "Yeah, I think so. The signal's pretty strong directly ahead and another one over there." He pointed with his right hand to a spot about one hundred yards away. "Let's look at the closest one first." They started walking into the woods directly ahead. The trees were thinly spaced, easy to walk among. A few yards in, they came under camouflage netting and upon a helicopter.

"Bingo!" said Donna. "Let's take a closer look."

"We'd better wear gloves and be careful. We don't want to add any fingerprints or destroy any telltale evidence." All took out latex disposable gloves from their pockets and put them on.

Bob and Anne started at the tail end and Donna and Rick started at the front. Donna called out, "Bob, looks like a couple of bullet holes in the front windshield."

Bob said, "Yeah, here's one that went into one of the engines. There's an oil leak. Looks as if they took a lot of unfriendly fire. I don't see any name or registration numbers."

Donna had worked her way around to the pilot's door, had it open and was looking in. "There's some dried blood here. Some on the seat part way up and on the base of it, some on the floor on the left side – looks as if the pilot must have been hit."

Bob had made his way around to the cargo door, slid it open and looked inside. "Empty of cargo, there're a few shell casings – someone must have been shooting from back here." Bob moved a few paces back from the helicopter. "It's a Bell 212." He took off his backpack, a small hiker's bag for day hikes, retrieved a camera, and took photos from all angles. Anne held the pilot's door open for him and he took some flash shots of the blood she pointed out to him, and also of the cargo bay and the spent cartridges. He took a spent shell, put it in a cello bag and put it and the camera in his backpack.

Donna took a plastic baggie out of one of her pockets, opened it and sprinkled its powdery white contents into the recess of a tie-down cleat in the floor just beside the door. Anne then closed the cargo door and said, "All right, on to the next one."

They followed the GPS, walking easily through the woods, to the next chopper. Similarly, it was a few yards into the trees and sheltered with a camouflage net. Rick remarked, "They must use the meadow for landings and takeoffs, but how do they move the choppers to their hiding places?"

"Probably have a self-loading trailer," Donna answered, "or one of those flatbed tow trucks that pull the car right up a ramp to the flatbed. I don't see it, though. Lots of tire tracks. Wonder if that means they have other choppers? Maybe just a lot of manpower."

Again, they carefully looked the chopper over outside, then opened the doors and looked in. "No markings again," Bob noted. "This one looks pristine. No bullet holes, no blood or spent cartridges." Donna opened another baggie of white powder and spread it under a seat, then Rick closed the door.

"Yeah. Well, let's get going. Anne and Rick are in for a long day. We'll continue our path in a loop that'll bring us back to the Trans Canada Trail only about a mile from where we left it, so it won't be too bad a hike back to the cars. Besides, it's downhill."

Rick said, "We should make it to the police station by noon."

"That should be fun! We'll have to wait around there for them to get organized," said Anne.

"Yeah," said Bob. "But at least you can come back here by car on the gravel road. In the meantime, Donna and I will be back in Kelowna visiting Donny to establish an alibi."

Bob and Donna said their good byes when the foursome returned to where they parked their cars. Anne and Rick drove off toward Midvale on the back road running along the border of the reservation while Donna and Bob headed east, then north to Kelowna. At twelve fifteen, less than fifteen minutes later, Anne and Rick entered the small farm town of Midvale, population nine thousand. The police station was easy to find and they pulled up and parked in front in Visitors Parking, then went in the front door. A woman was seated at a small, cluttered desk placed behind a chest level front counter. She got up as they entered and came to the counter. Rick noted her nameplate on the desk: Lynda Evers, civilian clerk. "Hi," she said. "How can I help you?"

Anne and Rick went into their act, playing the roles of an excited couple who had been hiking in the woods and had made a huge discovery. Rick said, "We belong to the Alpine Rovers hiking club in Vancouver and were doing a day hike along your Trans Canada Trail. We got off the trail to photograph some eagles and we found a helicopter in the bush. It's got bullet holes in it!"

"And it looks like blood on the pilot's seat!" said Anne.

Lynda said, "Hold it! This is too much for me! Let me call in the sergeant – she's just at home on lunch." She picked up a phone and dialed. It was answered on the third ring. Bob and Donna could overhear as Lynda said, "Sergeant Morrisson, I've got two hikers here who claim to have discovered a shot-up helicopter." Lynda hung up and turned to Rick and Anne. "She'll be right here. She just lives a couple of blocks away."

Five minutes later a police car drove into the lot and parked around back. A woman in RCMP police uniform, with insignia showing the rank of sergeant, entered through the back door. She was a stocky brunette with medium length hair, a round face and large hands. She asked Lynda, "Are these the people you called about?" Lynda nodded yes.

She turned to Rick and Anne and said, "I'm Mavis Morrison, the commanding officer for this detachment. I understand you've discovered a helicopter wreck while hiking?"

Rick and Anne introduced themselves as Steve Duncan and Belinda Reeces. Sergeant Morrison and Lynda began to take notes, carefully getting Steve and Belinda's full names, addresses and phone numbers and looking at their driver licenses for identification. Then Sergeant Morrison said, "I'm sorry for the preliminary details. Now, let's hear about your discovery."

Rick began their story, with Anne jumping in from time to time to embellish a point. "As we mentioned to Ms Evers, we're from Vancouver on vacation. We belong to the Alpine Rovers Hiking Club in Vancouver and we were on a day hike along part of your Trans Canada Trail. Here, let me get my map out of my backpack and I'll show you where we entered the trail and where we went."

Rick unfolded the map and Anne pointed to the spot where the road came close to the trail. "That's where we parked the car, at the parking lot beside the trail alongside the road. We followed the trail this way." Anne ran her finger along the map. "Then we decided to branch off where there's easy hiking up a hillside and into a shallow valley. We saw an eagle going to its nest up that way and thought we could photograph some." She continued tracing her finger across the map. "We came down into this shallow valley with a beautiful meadow and we saw some more eagles on the other side, so we went across. When we got to the other side, we figured we'd just cut through the woods and catch up to the trail again, here. See?"

Rick said, "But, as we started through the woods – they're not at all dense there – we came across a helicopter. It's under some camouflage netting. So we took a close look at it."

"But we didn't touch nothing!" said Anne.

"It has no markings," said Rick, "which is unusual, I guess. It's got a bullet hole in one engine, the one on the left side and there's oil on the ground below it."

"And, and there are two bullet holes in the windshield on the driver's side! And, there looks like dried blood on the driver's seat and floor!"

Sergeant Morrison said, "Did you touch anything? Are you sure?"

Both said, "Nope."

Rick said, "We watch so many crime shows on TV like CSI that we know not to touch a crime scene. We backed off. I took a couple of photos. Here, I'll show you! Then we hightailed it out of there to here."

Rick fumbled with his backpack and produced the camera. Starting with a couple of photos of a nesting eagle, he was careful to show only exterior photos of the chopper including close-ups of the bullet holes. Sergeant Morrison excused herself to make some phone calls, went into her office and closed the door. She emerged ten minutes later, approached Rick and Anne and said, "I've been on to my superiors at regional headquarters. They have a team on the way and should be here within the hour. My jurisdiction is only for the town of Midvale. I have also called out the tribal police from the Midlake Reservation as the helicopter is on their reservation. Their officer will be here within the hour as well and will escort the team. I expect you'll accompany the officers to show them the exact location

----

of your discovery? You won't have to hike all the way in as we can get vehicles to the meadow by that gravel road."

"Yes, we will. We'd be pleased to," said Anne.

"Are you sure you can find the spot again?"

Rick said, "Oh, yeah. No problem. We always carry a GPS with us while hiking. We recorded the coordinates." He brought out his GPS, fiddled with it and showed it to the sergeant. "Here, see?"

"Good, I also tried to contact the Chief of the Midlake Tribal Council, Chief Joseph Branson. It's protocol to ask permission for the police to attend to a matter on their reservation. He and his family are out of the country and can't be reached. But I talked with the person in charge, she's the band manager, a Ms. Muntz. She looked up the coordinates on the tribal landholding map and says yes, it is on tribal land but what they designate as "open range" not allocated to a specific locatee. I explained that we have seen photographs taken by a couple of hikers that vividly shows a shot-up helicopter. She has no objection to us investigating. Thus, as far as she is concerned, as the one left in charge, we are invited in and no search warrant necessary. Now, we have to await the arrival of the investigators. There's a good café just up the street if you want to take a short lunch break."

Rick and Anne elected to get some lunch. When they were settled in the café and their orders taken, Anne said, "So far everything is as predicted. I'm not surprised the band manager gave the O.K. to enter tribal lands."

"Yeah. She had to. Otherwise it might look as if she had something to hide. Or she might be completely unaware of the smuggling activities."

"Here's a cute thought: if we lead them in from the gravel road alongside the woods, maybe they'll be able to spot the other chopper first."

"Good thinking! We can lead them right to it first. Let's see how it plays out."

After a forty-five minute lunch they went back to the police station and met with the members of the investigation team: an RCMP corporal and two constables and the tribal police officer. Rick and Anne repeated their story, reviewed their topographical map and showed the photos and the GPS positioning. The lead RCMP officer was a Corporal Dennis Tremblay, who had a French Canadian accent. Corporal Tremblay turned to the tribal police officer, who had introduced himself as Joseph Charlie. "So, Officer Charlie, you have also spoken with the band manager who has given permission to enter tribal land to investigate. You can take us there by that gravel road, eh?"

"No problem. We'll follow the main road west out of town past the old stampede grounds and pick up the gravel road on the other side. It shouldn't take more than fifteen or twenty minutes."

"Great! Great. That'll give us plenty of time to do forensics before dark if this is the real thing. I've got a forensics team on the way but we'll go in first. Eh? Best we get on our way then. We'll follow you. Eh?"

After a short drive of fifteen minutes, they parked their vehicles on the gravel road beside the meadow and proceeded on foot. It looked to Anne that the group was going to miss the first chopper so she said, "I think it's this way," as she plunged into the woods. Shortly, they found the chopper under its canopy of camouflage netting. All were excited. Then Anne exclaimed, "This isn't the chopper! The one we found had bullet holes in it!"

Out came cameras and the chopper was photographed in detail.

Corporal Tremblay said, "Mon Dieu! Another chopper! Sacre' Bleu!"

Joseph Charlie rolled his eyes and muttered, "Oh, shit!"

Corporal Tremblay said, "O.K., a generous discovery. Now, where is the other one?"

"It's a little farther on," said Rick. "Follow me."

Corporal Tremblay detailed an officer to stand guard on the first chopper and circle the perimeter with crime scene tape. He reported his findings by secure radio to RCMP Regional Command and told them to speed up the forensics team. The rest followed Rick and Anne farther down the meadow until they encountered the next chopper under its camouflage canopy.

"Ah, so this is the one you photographed, eh?" said Corporal Tremblay.

"Yes, this is the one!" said Rick. "This one has bullet holes."

Corporal Tremblay also fenced the second chopper off with crime scene tape and reported the discovery to RCMP Regional Command. He was told the forensics team was only ten minutes away. He dispatched the second officer back to the road to guide the new arrivals. As they awaited the arrival of the forensics team, Corporal Tremblay made a careful examination of the second

330

chopper and took some photos, then took out a notebook and began making notes.

Upon arrival, the forensics people split their team between the two choppers and began their examinations. Corporal Tremblay then called Regional Command for more personnel to help secure the scene and assist with forensics and for a flat-deck truck with crane to remove the choppers. He was told to expect the arrival of a police helicopter in about an hour with a sergeant and an inspector from Kamloops, about one hundred fifty miles distant, as they had been dispatched to aid in the investigation.

Corporal Tremblay turned to Rick and Anne and said, "Thank you very much for reporting this! Helicopters are often used for smuggling and this may be the case here. You are right that someone may have been hurt in this aircraft, if what we see is really blood, but blood often goes along with bullet holes, so this may be the real thing, eh? I'd like you to keep this confidential and, until we have completed our investigations, we must be able to reach you. I have your addresses and cell phone numbers and email and I understand you will be going on to Osoyoos for a few nights? Eh? After my officers get your statements, what happens next at this site is many hours of tedious investigation so there is no sense or need for you to hang around here. You may depart then, eh? We will follow up with you to review your statements later. And you may be called upon to testify in court. And thank you again!"

"What's going to happen to the helicopters?" asked Anne.

"I am sure we will find evidence of their use in smuggling – probably some traces of cocaine and/or marijuana. If so, we can confiscate the aircraft under our *Proceeds of Crime* law. They're worth over two million apiece, I think."

Eventually, after giving their statements and being interviewed and thanked by the inspector and sergeant, Rick and Anne took their leave and headed to Osoyoos. They had booked accommodations under their aliases at a desert resort, which boasted a five-star hotel with a first class bistro, its own winery and a good eighteen-hole golf course. The company was footing the bill and Shirley had told them to pretend to be recreational tourists for a week, hiking on various trails in the area and sampling the wineries, to help establish their cover story.

In the car, Anne was on her cell phone passing the story of the discovery on to the news reporters at the two local TV news stations, the three radio stations and the local daily newspapers. She transferred one photo of the shot-up helicopter from the camera to her iPhone and sent it to the TV station that was the highest bidder at three thousand dollars for the exclusive photo.

About half an hour out of Midvale, they passed two TV station mobile units and Rick remarked, "Bet they're on the way to the scene. Good that you provided each station with a map of the location and the best access roads. I doubt if they'll ask permission to go onto the reservation – they'll just do it or make a big fuss on TV about it if they get stopped."

As expected, the story received local, national and international coverage.

A few days later, the RCMP released a statement that they had seized the helicopters, valued at over four million dollars, as "proceeds of crime," as both contained traces of marijuana and that one, the one that had been shot up, also contained traces of cocaine. It was surmised the helicopters had been involved in a cross-border smuggling operation and the shot-up one may have been used in a recent incident in Washington State where FBI, Border Patrol, DEA and ATF were involved in a shootout with smugglers. The RCMP public relations person was pleased to announce they had put a dint into cross-border smuggling in the Okanagan region.

Two days later, the Deacon, Bob and Donna were enjoying a leisurely dinner at one of Kelowna's trendy bistros when Donny came up to the table saying, "Hi guys. I suggest you try the calamari!"

Brian (the Deacon) said, "Donny, try this merlot! We've got an extra glass." And Donny pulled up a chair and joined them, motioned to a waiter and ordered a plate of calamari for all.

The Deacon said, "You seem happy enough tonight! I guess those weren't your choppers that the RCMP stumbled on the other day?"

"Assholes, they sure did a number on the Chief! Not that he didn't deserve it, though. He's been getting a little too cocky lately. This may teach him a lesson. He's out of pocket a couple of choppers – chump change. But he did lose a few good men. He certainly stirred up a hornet's nest and it'll take a while for things to get back to normal."

"Where is the Chief?" asked Donna.

"Last I heard, he's taking a vacation in the Maldives. He said he and Hazel needed some time away to get over losing David."

The Deacon said, "Let's assume the boy has gone on to a better life. Joseph and David were very close. It'll take a while for the Chief to get over it – if ever."

"Donny, it's surprising the RCMP found the choppers," said Brian.

"Well, if I hadn't been having dinner with Bob and Donna here when the police discovered the choppers, I'd really suspect you had a little to do with it."

Bob, holding his left hand to his heart and in mock horror said, "Donny, I'm shocked that you would think that!"

"Well my friend," said Donny with a stern face while looking Bob squarely in the eyes, "If I was really upset, you wouldn't be here."

The Deacon said, "Donny, we've had a good relationship scratching each other's back from time to time. You didn't want those helicopters. Somebody's done you a favor."

"Why?"

"Let's just say: in future, don't buy any spare parts from a certain helicopter parts company in Blaine, Washington. The parts may be full of bugs."

"I see." He paused and was lost in thought for a moment then said, "O.K., I get the point. So I owe you one. Let me order another bottle of wine. They've got a great Small Lot Malbec I've been itching to try."

Chapter 45

<u>Maldives</u>

It was Sunday night and Ken was thoroughly drained. The weekend had been arduous. He, Natalia and Sanka had been together since Friday evening – even though he had to work a full day Saturday. On Sunday, they had enjoyed a day of scuba diving and parasailing between their sexual romps. Friday and Saturday nights had been exhausting with little sleep for Ken, as both women had demanded his attention into the wee hours of the mornings. Both had expected him to be responsive with an almost constant erection yet expecting him to come when he brought one or the other or both to orgasm. Sanka had developed a habit of wanting the attention of both Natalia and Ken before she could achieve a deep orgasm.

Part of Ken's problem was of his own doing. He had been hitting the Viagra hard. About a month ago, he had switched to a stronger tablet which had helped a lot yet his partners seemed to demand more and more of him. Friday night he needed just one of the more powerful tablets to keep him charged but Saturday, he had taken one at noon and another in the evening which kept him charged through most of the night. Sunday they went scuba diving. The first dive was deep to one hundred thirty feet, which was the deepest Ken had ever been. For the between scuba dive intervals, he had taken another two Viagra and washed them down with a high caffeine energy drink. He had long ago run out of semen and his groin ached. He could fake coming – just as long as he could keep an erection, the girls were happy.

That evening, after dinner, Ken said goodnight to the girls after walking them to Natalia's hut. He said he was exhausted, had a headache behind one eye and a groin ache and just wanted to get a good night's sleep before work the next day. The girls kissed him good night then entered Natalia's hut and Ken wearily set off for his hut.

Once there, he collapsed on his bed without even taking the time to undress, and fell asleep almost instantly.

The sub had arrived at its assigned position and had been lurking at three hundred feet for the past four hours. They were twelve miles offshore, technically in international waters. In an hour, nightfall would allow them to come in closer to shore. The captain's orders for the mission had specified the sub come up to fifty feet half a mile from the open ocean side of the island where the SEAL team would transfer underwater to their mini-subs for the assault.

The SEAL team had practiced their assault for a week then boarded the mother sub at Diego Garcia, a secretive American military island not far away in the Indian Ocean. After a week of drills assaulting a mock-up of the island and its buildings, the team felt fully prepared.

The sub was specially equipped as a mother ship for the SEAL team. It was a large converted ICBM carrier where the huge cargo bay for the missiles had been reconfigured to house the SEALs and their equipment. Behind the sub's sail, into the deck had been built a large hatch with hydraulically operated clamshell doors for a large wet chamber that that housed mini-submarines and surface assault craft. When the chamber was flooded, the mini-subs were accessible from within the mother sub by an airlock escape hatch. The remainder of the former missile silo area comprised bunks, equipment storage, machine shop, compressor and storage bottles for compressed air, helium, nitrogen and other gases used in diving and underwater repairs, recompression chamber, sick bay and a separate galley for the SEALs. There were accommodations for fifty SEALs.

On this voyage, the sub was traveling light with only one SEAL SDV Platoon, which consisted of eleven SEALs, a medical dive technician and four maintenance technicians. SDV was short for Swimmer Delivery Vehicle. The mini-subs were SDV MK VIII MOD 1 vehicles. They were an updated version of an SDV that had been in service with the SEALS since the mid-seventies. The SDVs were "wet" subs where the passengers and pilots were transported in a "fully flooded" compartment sitting on benches in the water in their dive gear breathing either from their own scuba gear or from regulators hooked up to the subs compressed air cylinders. Breathing from their own individual breathing apparatus, they would emerge from the parent sub through an airlock to the flooded hanger and the SDVs mini-subs while the parent sub hovered underwater at fifty feet. The mini-subs were basically stealthy ferries to move the divers more quickly to their destination and conserve energy.

Powered by lithium-ion batteries, each SDV carried four passengers, a pilot and a co-pilot. In some operations, the passengers would emerge to do their assigned tasks while the pilots kept the SDV hovering nearby. Sometimes the SDV could be "parked" on the bottom of a bay or harbor and the two pilots freed to join the others

----

or to do other assigned tasks. The SDVs were difficult to drive and the pilots took extensive training. Many who began the training were scrubbed out as the course progressed.

On this mission, conditions, both concerning the targeted personnel and the topography, were ideal for tasking the pilots for part of the land assault. They would come ashore after the security guards had been taken out and assist in the search and destroy mission. Two SDVs would be deployed while a third would be retained in the hanger pod as a spare. The raid would not be against heavily entrenched soldiers. Intelligence determined there were eight security personnel, of whom only three were on duty overnight.

The full combat contingent of eleven SEALs of the platoon would participate in the raid. That meant one mini-sub would carry six and the other five. As it was a night attack, the mother sub could lurk offshore at periscope depth enabling the electronic wizards aboard to link with an unmanned drone orbiting over the island. During the assault, the drone would relay real-time video of the island from its camera and from the helmet cameras of some of the SEALs to the sub's control room and the SEALs' wardroom.

The water was very warm and clear. This helped reduce air consumption and stress. The men were comfortable in their gear. Each wore a multi-pocketed jumpsuit, pockets bulging with equipment, over a thin wet suit. After carefully checking and triple checking their dive gear, entering the air lock, flooding it and boarding and untethering their SDVs was uneventful. The SDVs soon cleared the hanger and were on their way.

The teams planned to conduct a pincher assault by approaching two sides of the island at once. One team would land on the lea side while the other had a slightly more difficult landing, running with the tide down on to the seaward side of the island. The SDV pilots were to bring their teams in close where the swim to shore would be less than two hundred feet. Once they dropped their teams, the pilots would take their SDVs around to the beach and quay that served as the harbor, positioning at the two ends of the beach underwater at twenty to thirty feet where they would await a signal that the security personnel had been taken out. At the signal, they would bring their SDV in shallower, closer to the quay, ballasting the SUV to stay on the bottom, and then swim ashore to assist their teams. They would bring satchels of explosives ashore to be used later to destroy the factory, labs and warehouse.

Deployment went as planned. SDV Alpha, comprised of three swimmers and two SDV pilots, had the longer run to get around the island to the lea side but the mother sub had positioned up-current, enabling the pilots of both SDVs to use the current to their advantage. The three Alpha swimmers left their SDV and headed toward shore on time at 01:03. Similarly, the swimmers from SDV Bravo headed toward shore at 01:04. Both teams had closed on the shore within a few minutes.

Each swimmer carried an archery weapon, not only for the silence it afforded but because it could also be used underwater. The second swimmer towed an equipment satchel. The lead swimmer of the first pair from SDV Bravo, designated Bravo One, found a cleft in the rock and coral shoreline which allowed some shelter from the waves and current where he and his teammate were easily able to get out of the water, stealthily climb the few feet to the breakwater and take off their dive gear, which they stowed between some rocks just above the tide line.

The other two members of their team, designated as Bravo Two, landed as planned one hundred yards farther down. They and the Alpha One threesome managed to easily get out of the water, cross the sand undetected to reach the high water line and similarly stow their dive equipment. From the satchels of gear they brought with them, they extracted helmets with radio headsets, TV cameras and night vision goggles. Using the night vision goggles, they moved forward to a well-traveled path running parallel to the beach.

The pairs split left and right in opposite directions paralleling the path. They moved quickly and silently from cover to cover offered by trees, shrubs and buildings. On the sheltered side, Team Alpha, only three men, made a similar approach with each man emerging from the water about fifty yards apart and, with fins off, cautiously but quickly running to the vegetation marking the shore line There, they removed the rest of their dive gear, checked their weapons, donned their night vision goggles, then found the path running parallel to the shore and, keeping off the path, followed it while keeping good separation.

Bravo Two was the first to spot their quarry. One of the sentries was walking along the path toward them. He fell backward silently as an arrow pierced his chest. Crouching low, one of the SEALs silently came forward to ensure he was dead, took his assault rifle with night scope, then pulled him off into the bushes. The lead man keyed the mike on his radio twice to say one sentry down.

Bravo One's arrow went through the chest of the second sentry who was enjoying a quick smoke while sitting on the edge of the quay in front of the scuba shack. After checking to ensure the sentry was dead and taking his weapon, the lead man of that pair keyed his mike twice to signal they had taken out another sentry.

The three men of Alpha One closed in on the office. It was their initial objective to take out the security person monitoring the CCTV and radar. With one guarding their rear, two approached the entrance door. Flipping off his night vision goggles, a SEAL eased up to the window and peered into the lighted general office. His partner, beside the door, had also slipped off his night vision goggles.

On a signal, he tried the door handle and found it unlocked. He swung it open silently while the other slipped in. The two moved silently across the general office toward the security room where they could see a man sitting at a desk facing a number of CCTV screens. In the center of the wall was a large flat screen with a radar display set for a fifty mile radius. The man's back was to the door but they could see he was reading a pocket book. On a hand signal from the leader, pointing with his right hand mimicking a pistol, the second SEAL brought up a pistol and shot the security guard in the back near his neck. Almost instantly, the guard keeled over, slumping onto the desk.

There had been almost no noise from the air pistol when it fired a tranquilizing dart. A classified weapon, the magazine of the dart pistol held twenty darts and a CO_2 cartridge built into the magazine, which provided the firepower. Effective range and accuracy was short at thirty feet but the weapon had proven highly efficient at close range, partly due to the speed at which the tranquilizing cocktail worked. Each dart held enough venom to knock out a two hundred pound person for five to six hours. Multiple hits with darts were deadly. Two darts in succession would kill.

After disabling the weapons they found in a wall locker in the security room, the two SEALs exited the office joining their waiting partner. The leader keyed his mike twice to say they had taken out a sentry and followed that with four keys to signal they had cleared the security center.

In the meantime, Bravo teams One and Two were completing their first objective of circling the island ensuring all sentries on duty were taken out. When they met up, their leader uploaded a signal to the overhead drone that was relayed to the two SDVs and their waiting crew now in position underwater at the harbor entrance. On receiving the signal that it was safe to come ashore, the pilots brought their subs to rest on the bottom of the harbor near the quay and began to unload the satchels of explosives and their shore equipment.

Bravo One and Two were then to join in working on their second objective: to first find the quarters of the remaining security personnel and the manager, and immobilize them. During training, they had formed the opinion the guards would most likely be billeted in the huts closest to the office and would probably keep some weapons in their huts. They joined up with Alpha One for a sweep of the cottages. Two men split off right and left to go behind the cottages to catch anyone if they tried to escape. One man stayed hidden beside the path watching the other cottages while a pair on each side silently entered the cottages.

Upon entering a cottage, one SEAL held a gun on the sleeping figure in the bed as well as keeping an eye on the bathroom. The cottages were spartan and small, just one room with a bathroom on the back wall, with nowhere to hide except the bathroom or under the bed. After dialing reduced CO_2 power on the tranquilizer gun, the other SEAL would quickly go to the foot of the bed, rip off any covers and shoot a dart into the body, usually putting a dart in the abdomen. If a weapon was found in the room, it was disabled. With the guards they immobilized, they usually found a pistol and an assault rifle. They left the task of identification for later after all were immobilized. As a team exited a house they would signal to the leader how many had been immobilized.

In the third cottage, they were lucky as they immobilized two men asleep in bed together – both security guards. If their intelligence was correct, that left only one remaining guard – whom they found in the fourth cottage in bed with a woman. Storming the fifth through twenty-third cottages was routine and went quickly with the SEALs performing their assault like journeymen. In a large number of the cottages, couples were found nestled in bed and immobilized. A number of cottages were empty, which the SEALs assumed was the result of the "coupling" they had encountered and a few did not look lived in.

As they approached cottages near the shore, Team Alpha One entered a cottage where one SEAL immobilized a beautiful black-haired woman who was on her back naked in bed. Perhaps he and his partner were slightly distracted by her beauty but they failed to notice the woman in the bathroom. She shot the SEAL by the bed in the leg before his partner put an arrow through her heart. At such close range, the arrow went right through the body and out the back wall of the cottage.

Mark White, the SEAL who had been in the shadows guarding the path, ran up to the door of the cottage where the shot had come from. With his back beside the open door and his weapon in a ready position, he said, "Clear?"

From inside, a voice said, "Yeah, f---ing clear. Stu took a shot in the leg. It's not bad though. I'm getting a bandage on it. A woman surprised us but she won't be doing that again."

After a moment, Stu, the wounded SEAL, managed to hobble out of the cottage and sit on the front steps where he was detailed to cover their rear while the rest finished clearing the cottages. Mark traded weapons with Stu and replaced Stu on immobilization duty.

The gunshot surprised all the SEALs. But it was only one shot and the sound of the surf hitting the shore was fairly noisy in background. The shot may have awoken some or all of the people yet to be immobilized but the leader did a quick tally: two to go – at least according to the latest intelligence they had.

The next cottage hadn't been occupied. It was like a hotel room awaiting the next guest. The next, and last cottages were occupied and the entrance team quickly darted the persons in the beds and double-checked the bathrooms. When they exited, they met up with the raid leader for a quick huddle while two men stood guard. Lieutenant Jay (J.J.) Jones, the raid's leader, said, "O.K. Looks as if we've got them all, but we can never be sure. Everyone, watch your backs. Bravo One and Two, you know what you have to do: get identities, laptops, software etc. from the cottages and take care of the factory workers once you ID them. You've got Alpha Two with you outside covering your six. I'll take Stu back with me to toss the office, rec room and cookhouse then see how Alpha and Bravo pilots are doing with the warehouse, labs and factory. Call me if you need me."

With Stu's arm over his shoulder and hanging on to Stu's equipment belt, J.J. helped Stu back toward the office and sat him down in a position in the bushes where he could have a good field of fire towards the little square and its approaches, yet be in concealment. He then entered the office and began to toss it looking for software disks, external drives and computers. Using a screwdriver he had brought along, he took the hard drives out of the computers and stowed them in a watertight bag along with software CDs and external memory drives he found. When he was finished

----

with the office and adjoining rooms, he went on to the recreation center, then on to the cookhouse.

Meanwhile, teams Bravo One and Two were re-entering each cottage. While one searched for identity papers, cell phones and computer drives, the other positioned the victim or victims, stepped back and focused his helmet cam on the face. The upload was relayed to Control Center where facial recognition software scanned the image. If a face was recognized, there would be a response. In the meantime, if the other SEAL found identification in the cottage, it was verbally relayed to Control Center.

There were five hits. The SEAL team had been briefed to seek out the five involved in manufacturing the archery weapon. Although each team recognized the people, they sought confirmation. And sanction. Almost in succession, Eddie Whitefeather, Rod Redfish, Sam Littlefort and Arnie Wren were identified. For each, the facial recognition software or passport confirmed their identity, then a senior officer in Control Center would say, "Confirmed. Target sanctioned." The SEAL with the dart pistol would put two more darts into the individual and then move on to the next. In the process, they collected the spent darts.

When they came upon Ken Davidson, he was in shorts and a tee shirt on the bed lying in a fetal position facing the wall. A tranquilizer dart was sticking in his back at his left shoulder blade. In attempting to reposition him for a facial photograph, they found rigor mortis had set in. As they took the facial photo, one SEAL spoke. "Control, we'll be giving you a full scan of the body here as well as the head photo. This looks like Davidson, at least he's the only redheaded guy we've come across. We've found a passport for him. He's dead. He's in rigor mortis. There's no sign of wounds on the body except for the dart we shot. He wouldn't be in rigor yet if he succumbed to the tranquilizer."

A voice from control center said, "Agreed. Fully body scan. Bring him out with you for autopsy."

"Roger that."

The SDV pilots had come ashore and were in the process of checking out the labs, warehouse and machine shop. One pair entered the machine shop. They were tasked to retrieve hard drives and software then destroy all machinery. One man in each pair had a helmet camera streaming video full time to Control Center.

The second pair first reconnoitered a lab that turned out to be the marine research lab, then went on to the next building, which they discovered to be the meth lab. They also found the underground storage for the meth chemicals. They set charges to destroy the lab and storage vault, then went on to the warehouse. Randomly opening cartons and cases, they identified wooden cases of guns, and cartons of medical equipment and clothing.

They soon found the ramp leading to the basement and a locked door. With a small charge of plastic explosive, they blew the lock off the door and entered to find rows of munitions ranging from bullets to RPGs and Semtex. They set charges in the stacks of munitions where they felt they would have the greatest impact then left to retrieve their dive equipment and rendezvous with the others at the quay.

The Lieutenant's voice came over the radio: "Time to assemble and head out. Time to get your gear." The teams reassembled at the quay after they had collected their dive gear. They had spent almost three hours on the island. Stu's teammate had retrieved his dive equipment for him and he had no problem gearing up. The pilots of the SDVs were first to get back in their dive gear and they swam out to their vehicles. Once aboard, they brought their vehicles to the surface and alongside the quay where the waterproof bags of equipment and seized items were loaded.

The body of Ken Davidson was stowed in the SDV that had brought only five men to the island. When the rest of the assault force members, in their dive gear, climbed aboard the vehicles, the SDVs eased away from the quay and proceeded semi-submerged, running on the surface a half mile offshore where they dove to fifty feet to link up with their waiting mother sub. They were soon tucked into the wet hanger where the clamshell doors closed above them. When the hanger doors closed, lights went on in the wet hanger and the men, in groups after securing their subs, took their turn entering the air lock. The last group brought in the body of Ken Davidson and the waterproof satchels.

While the SEALs were in the locker room changing out of their dive gear, a voice came over the announcement speaker. "Now hear this, now hear this, Acoustics operators expect land-based detonations in ten minutes." About ten minutes later, the metallic sound of an explosion could be heard throughout the sub's hull. One of the SEALs said, "That was a big one! Must have been the ammo dump."

Another SEAL said, "Yeah, too bad we didn't get to see it in real time. Anyway, it's nice to be warm and dry and heading back to base. It'll be fun to see the replay from the drone. It'll be ready for us in the galley as soon as we dry off and get our gear properly stowed. Mission accomplished."

The body of Ken Davidson was put in a body bag and placed in the sub's walk-in refrigerator.

Chapter 46

Once again, Janet and Hector were summoned to a meeting at the Pentagon. As before, they met in a conference room in one of the inner blocks on the floor housing the procurement offices. Hector and Janet recognized the same faces from last time: Sandford Crosley of CIA Langley; Caroline Weston of State Department; Ruth Dempsey of Homeland Security DC; Roger Pearson and Martin LeRoy of the Canadian Embassy DC; General Keith Baker of military intelligence and his aide, Captain Adam Chavez. A new recording secretary was introduced as Chief Petty Officer Steve Richards.

After self-help coffee and buns and hellos, General Baker took the lead. "Ladies and gentlemen, Ms. Weston called this meeting and has requested me to chair it. Pentagon, State Department and CIA officials have concurred that, as a thank you for your hard work on the archery weapons leak, you may see that your labor was brought to fruition. This is highly classified so I must remind you this is to be kept classified. Do I have your concurrence for the record?"

He went around the room asking each; all agreed. At a nod from General Baker, Chief Petty Officer Richards keyed a laptop computer and a map of the Maldives appeared on the big screen on the wall at the far end of the conference table. "Now then, we determined the weapons factory was moved to the Maldives. It was located in one of the northern atolls. The island is called Minora Fushi in Baa Atoll." Using a laser pointer, the general circled the atoll and pointed to Minora Fushi. "The island's very remote on the northwestern outer edge of the atoll about thirty miles away from a few sparsely populated islands. The closest cluster of population, about three thousand people, is in the center islands of the atoll, about fifty miles away where there is a regional airport and a small commercial seaport."

The map was zoomed in to the atoll and then into Minora Fushi. "Minora Fushi is not large. About six hectares in total with a maximum elevation of four feet. It was recently leased from the Maldivian government by a non-profit organization, ostensibly for the purpose of establishing a marine research station. The benefactor behind the project is one Igor Romanoff, a notorious arms dealer with strong linkage to the Russian mafia and, possibly with the Russian Federation."

The screen changed to a photo of Igor Romanoff. "He is considered, currently, one of the world's larger private arms dealers.

We have observed him having dealings with the Taliban and Al Qaida." A photo of Igor shaking hands with four men in Afghan costume appeared. He has also been linked to Chief Joseph Branson – in fact, they have been observed together recently in the Maldives." The screen showed a photo of the Chief, Hazel and Igor leaning on the rail of a yacht.

"The State Department determined that the existence of the factory was prejudicial to the best interests of America and its allies. In close collaboration with Canada, the CIA and the Pentagon were assigned to terminate the operation. A joint operation was mounted and successfully concluded."

Janet asked, "Excuse me General but are you saying the factory has been destroyed?"

"Indeed. A covert assault by Navy SEALS destroyed the factory. But before I open the floor to questions, we have a video of the operation taken by an observation drone that will walk you through the assault. The video includes relays from helmet cams that some of the SEALs wore. The SEALs made a covert underwater approach. The video picks up from their arrival ashore." He turned to Chief Petty Officer Richards and asked him to bring the video up on the screen.

Janet was fascinated with the assault, watching as the sentries were neutralized and some of the team entered the office to neutralize the remaining security person, then as some worked their way through the huts and others entered and cleared the cookhouse, recreation center, labs and the other buildings. During lulls in voice transmissions from the combat radios, General Baker added commentary.

"The attack began at zero one hundred hours on Sunday night. Obviously the security people were priority targets. The other inhabitants, whom we determined would be twenty-seven, were mainly to be sedated with tranquilizer darts to incapacitate them for five to six hours. However, some were sanctioned. There were two sentries on patrol and they were silently eliminated. The security officer in the office monitoring the CCTV was sedated before raising an alarm. Most of the personnel on the island were sound asleep."

They listened to a transmission and watched a video from a helmet cam showing an unconscious man in bed. "Lead One, Bravo Two: Control, we'll be giving you a full scan of the body here as well as the head photo. This looks like Davidson, at least he's the only redheaded guy we've come across. He's dead. He's in rigor mortis. There's no sign of wounds on the body except for the dart we shot. He wouldn't be in rigor yet if he succumbed to the tranquilizer."

"Bravo Two, Lead One: Agreed. Full body scan. Bring him out with you for autopsy."

General Baker said, "The team was tasked to bring out the inventor, Kenneth Davidson, alive. Regrettably, when the SEALs found him, he was dead with no obvious wounds. They recovered his body."

Janet asked, "Did he have people working with him? I can't see him building all those weapons alone."

Martin LeRoy said, "You're quite right. He took four men with him from the Midlake Reservation."

General Baker said, "Yes, these men were identified and eliminated."

The general pointed to the screen where two SEALs could be seen entering the largest building and they watched the video from a helmet cam as the SEALs searched the building. "That turned out to be a warehouse storing arms and munitions." The video returned to an overhead shot from the drone showing the layout of the island. "To the left of it is what turned out to be the machine shop and factory for the archery weapon. A good distance past that, say a hundred yards is what turned out to be a meth lab." They watched as other pairs of SEALs entered the other buildings and sent helmet cam feeds.

They watched as two SEALs entered the machine shop and supplied a helmet cam video as they searched the interior. "The team was tasked to collect all computers or computer hard drives and other storage devices from the offices and the dwellings of the personnel," narrated the general. "That has proven valuable concerning some activities of Mr. Romanoff. We feel we also retrieved all software relating to the archery weapon. They also recovered identity papers of all personnel. Most of the personnel were from the former Soviet states."

Caroline Weston said, "Things go quiet on the video for a while from here. The team had lots of time to reconnoiter. They spent over three hours on the island. General, could Chief Petty Officer Richards please fast forward?"

The general directed Chief Petty Officer Richards to do so and they settled on the next start point where the SEALs extracted. Janet watched as some members of the team, with waterproof bags,

----

presumably filled with computers, hard drives and such climbed aboard one of two small submarines that had come alongside the quay. She took note of two SEALs carrying a body bag that was placed aboard the second sub. The subs then departed the small sheltered bay, nearly submerged, making a very low profile.

General Baker said, "The Swimmer Delivery Vehicles met up with the mother sub about half a mile out in the channel. We'll have to fast-forward again. If you please Chief Petty Officer."

"Aye sir."

The monitor pulled back and presented a view of the whole island. Janet noted the clock in the bottom right side of the screen had advanced one hour. Everybody watched as a fireball erupted from the machine shop." General Baker said, "Every piece of equipment in the machine shop was destroyed by linked individual charges."

A few minutes later, the meth lab blew with a huge explosion dwarfing the one at the machine shop. "The team discovered a storage vault for the meth chemicals," General Baker explained. "They're highly volatile as the explosion can attest."

Two minutes later, another explosion with a huge fireball, by far the biggest of all, obliterated the warehouse. General Baker said, "The team managed to access an ammunition vault in the basement of the warehouse. It held enough explosives to destroy most of the island." They watched as the shockwave from the explosion tore through the office, cook house and recreation center, flattening them. "As most of the dwelling huts were on the other side of the island, some were spared, so some of the tranquilized personnel survived."

Janet asked, "And our troops? How did they fare? Did all survive?"

"There was only one injury. A woman, apparently the manager of the project, managed to shoot one of our people. He sustained a leg wound but he was able to finish the mission."

"And the woman?"

"Terminated with prejudice by the SEAL's partner."

Janet asked, "What has the Maldivian government said about this raid?"

Carolyn Weston spoke up. "They were brought into the loop just a few hours before the raid, by being alerted to the possibility of a drug lab. Drugs are very much frowned upon by their society, so it was an opportunity to lend a friendly hand, so to speak. And that was how they took it. The explosions were heard and seen by some inhabitants of the islands thirty miles away and the Maldivian navy sent a vessel over to investigate the next day. Their official conclusion is that a meth lab blew up. They treated and arrested the survivors, collected the scattered weapons from the warehouse explosion and destroyed what was left of the marijuana crop. Mr. Romanoff has interceded and the Maldivian government has settled upon deporting the survivors."

Sandford Crossley said, "We made sure the press in Male' got a story they could verify that drugs from the island were being distributed in Male'. This resulted in significant political uproar that is still going on."

Janet said, "I'm sorry, but I have to ask: Was Chief Branson on the island and, if so, did he survive?"

Martin LeRoy spoke up. "No Janet, he wasn't there. Our intelligence sources were watching him and his wife in Zanzibar where they were guests on Igor Romanoff's yacht. Mr. Romanoff was also aboard the yacht."

"Darn."

"Ken Davidson was found dead when the SEALs arrived," said Roger Pearson. His body was taken to Diego Garcia for autopsy that revealed he had a massive heart attack. He had expired earlier that night, probably around ten o'clock. The toxicology scan revealed an extremely high level of Viagra in his system. It's likely he succumbed to an overdose of Viagra."

"Viagra?" said Hector incredulously. "I didn't know that was possible."

Sandford Crossley said, "Oh yes, quite common. For example, a leader in Nigeria succumbed to it a few years ago while entertaining three young ladies. Mind you, someone had switched his pills for extra strength ones."

Janet said, "Secretary Weston, General, Mr. Crosley, Monsieur Le Roy and Mr. Pearson, I thank you very much for your consideration in showing us the outcome of this investigation. I, for one, welcome the closure this brings. However, I still feel Chief Branson is an integral part of the whole affair and he's still at large. I'm missing the full sense of closure due to that."

Carolyn Weston said, "Thank you Janet. We've greatly appreciated your earnest participation and the successes you've had under the constraints you've encountered. I agree, the matter of Chief Branson is still up in the air but for now, it's eclipsed by the fact that we have successfully tracked and destroyed the weapons factory."

Epilogue

01:23 hours GMT Kandahar, Afghanistan

It was an ideal night for Abdul Khan, the Taliban squad leader. There was a quarter moon on a cold but snowless night, He and his two comrades, brothers Hanif and Chukkar Mohammed, had just left the safe house, a farmhouse on the northern outskirts of Kabul and were walking into town.

Their target was the newly appointed mayor of Kabul. He would be killed just two weeks into his term as a lesson to the townspeople not to support the reformers and infidels. Abdul carried the new archery weapon they had trained on the previous week. He was the better shot with it and it would be his honor to kill the mayor. Hanif and Chukkar would support him with their standard issue AK 47's and grenades, if necessary. It was their plan to lie in wait in the second floor of a ruined building across and down the street from the mayor's home.

The mayor had to descend a flight of fifteen steps from the doorway of his home and, although there was a wall surrounding a courtyard and driveway leading up to the house, their perch gave them a line of sight to the door, the steps and the waiting car.

They had an easy exit to a back lane and down it a few steps into the back entrance of a house on the next street, the home of a faithful member, where they would hide in a secret cellar until the turmoil they created died down. Things looked good. Abdul felt they had planned it well.

Predator Drone Control Base, Nevada

Airman Mark Stevens kept his eyes on the array of monitors in front of him as he toggled his headset microphone and raised his hand overhead. "Colonel Smith, sir, I've got a lock on a passive chip in my sector that is moving."

Colonel Steve Smith walked up behind the sitting Airman Stevens and looked at the monitors, following Mark's finger pointing to a transponder overlaid on an infrared video currently showing a square block of road, houses and vehicles. "Verify the identity of the chip?"

"Yes, sir. It's one of the archery weapons and it has moved from its storage position. There are three people walking with it down the street. It looks as if they are heading into Kabul."

The Big Bird satellite over Afghanistan and Pakistan was programmed to track the chips in the archery weapons. Since arrival, the movement of each of the weapons had been tracked as they were distributed across the country and the local fighters trained in their use. The satellite surveillance revealed the weapons had been disbursed to diverse sectors of Afghanistan, a dozen locations in the northeast tribal region of Pakistan and to a house outside a military base in Abbottabad, Pakistan. Storage areas and training sites of multiple weapons were identified and a decision had been made to leave them in place until used in offensive situations. It was reasoned better to follow weapons as they were deployed from the arsenals and the training areas, as it would help intelligence gathering. At or near likely point of use, such as an ambush on coalition troops or targeting a friendly warlord, they would be taken out if resources were available.

It was not only the drones that were equipped with the monitoring system. All combat aircraft and ground troops communications vans had been equipped. As well, combat officers on patrol or covert operations had wristwatch style monitors capable of identifying and locating a chip as much as six miles away.

"The street looks deserted except for the three men with the weapon. O.K. We have open orders to shoot if it is moving or in an ambush position and at night but we're to seek minimum possibility of noncombatant casualties."

"This one is in the clear, sir. There are two others with guns right beside the sniper. They must be combatants."

"Get a bead on it and take it out. We may be able to get the other two guys along with the sniper."

"Yes, sir." Colonel Smith watched as Airman Stevens manipulated the console control for the drone, first drawing a bead on the target with a laser then releasing a rocket. They watched the video in real time as the rocket followed the laser beam to its target. After the explosion, they counted three men sprawled on the ground in pieces.

"Chalk another one up for the good guys! That's eight this week that the drones have taken out."